MILLION DOLLAR MEN

BOOK 2 IN THE MJ FERNANDEZ SERIES

MILLION DOLLAR MEN

BOOK 2 IN THE MJ FERNANDEZ SERIES

JOE SALERNO

Printed in the United States of America

Published by Igniting Souls
PO Box 43, Powell, OH 43065
IgnitingSouls.com

LCCN: 2025909221
Paperback ISBN: 978-1-965419-09-0
Hardcover ISBN: 978-1-965419-10-6
e-book ISBN: 978-1-965419-11-3

Available in paperback, hardcover, and e-book.

Any Internet addresses (websites, blogs, etc.) and telephone numbers printed in this book are offered as a resource. They are not intended in any way to be or imply an endorsement by Igniting Souls and affiliated companies, nor do Igniting Souls and its affiliated companies vouch for the content of these sites and numbers for the life of this book.

This is a work of fiction. Any resemblance to actual persons, living or dead, or actual events is purely coincidental. Names, characters, places, and incidents are either the product of the author's imagination or are used fictitiously.

Dedication

To my family:

Publishing a novel was a dream turned reality with *The Decision*, but to expand the series with *Million Dollar Men* goes beyond my wildest imagination. My amazing wife, Missy, continues to encourage and support me as I navigate my literary adventures. Words cannot express how much I love and appreciate you. I am the luckiest man on the planet.

And to my daughters Erin and Paige, and grandsons Christopher and Bryson, I hope this demonstrates the importance of pursuing what brings you happiness. Believe in yourselves, as I believe in you, and you will accomplish great things. LYTM

To the readers:

Million Dollar Men is dedicated to each of you. Your deep affection for the hard-charging, underdog-defending MJ Fernandez inspires me to sit at the keyboard. Thank you for your gracious feedback and unwavering support. Let's continue to experience MJ's relentless pursuit of the truth together, while never forgetting what she says about coincidence.

1

2:38 a.m. The stench of death permeates the crisp, early morning air as neighbors stand on the sidewalk in bed clothes ranging from a T-shirt and sweats to Mrs. Rothschild's signature grey and blue checked flannel robe. People are rubbing the sleep from their eyes while shielding them from the red and blue flashing lights that have invaded the neighborhood like ants at a picnic. The heat radiating from the triple-decker house can be felt by everyone watching, despite being outside the 150-foot perimeter established by the fire department.

The noise created by the firefighting efforts is deafening. The roar of the fire is compounded by the sizzling sound of water striking the burning wood. Rafters and joists crack as their weakened state responds to the weight of the second and third floors. Multiple firefighters are shouting instructions through bullhorns. The police are yelling at bystanders to remain behind the barricade. Dogs are barking at the strangers on the street. It is controlled chaos.

Most are shocked by the smell of the fire. It is not the sweet, inviting smell of the fire pits a few of them use in their backyards during the summer to make s'mores for the kids.

The thick, acrid odor created by the flames' consumption of everything it touches will hang in the air long after the fire is extinguished and remain in the noses of all in attendance for the rest of their lives.

Agnes Rothschild, the neighborhood matriarch, looks around with growing concern as she walks through the crowd, comforting others and mentally checking off the names on her list as she does so. She completes the silent roll call and begins weeping as she watches firefighters struggle to keep the flames, which are racing violently through the old wooden structure, from jumping to the adjacent homes.

Dylan, Lily, and the kids are not standing with them. She has counted three times. Mrs. Rothschild reaches for the shoulder of the young woman standing next to her to steady herself. Sobs wrack her eighty-six-year-old body as the reality of the tragedy she is witnessing and smelling hits her with the force of a hurricane.

2

ngela Bergman's cell phone buzzes quietly on her nightstand. She rolls over slowly, careful not to disturb her husband. Her phone never rings at this hour with good news. There has been a fire, possibly one that ended someone's life. If so, her job will be to give the family an explanation as to what caused the deadly blaze—the question of "why" falls to others.

She gently swings her legs to the side of the bed, rubs the sleep from her eyes with the palms of her hands, and grabs her husband's maroon terrycloth bathrobe as she stands. She peeks back over her shoulder as a floorboard creaks despite her tip-toeing.

Angela answers in a hushed tone as a creaking hinge on the bathroom door reminds her to add another item to her husband's honey-do list. "Bergman," she says.

"Sorry to wake you, Angela."

"It is nice of you to say, but…"

"We have fatalities. A man, a woman, and two small children."

Her head drops, and she closes her eyes as she repeats a silent prayer she has had to say far too many times. Although a twenty-three-year veteran, gut-wrenching despair returns. She has three kids of her own, and visions of a recurring nightmare of losing them to fire race through her thoughts. "Where?"

"187 President Street. They are still knocking down hot spots. On-site command does not believe this was an accident."

"You know the drill. No one gets in until I say so."

Angela hangs up, deciding to forgo a shower. She will need to scrub away the smell of the fire when she gets home anyway. She heads to the garage and grabs one of the fire scene outfits she keeps on a shelf above the stand-alone washer and dryer, which are used only for those clothes. She refuses to mix her family's laundry with clothes that retain the smell of smoke and death in every fiber.

After dressing, she snatches a bright green Yeti from the cupboard and fills it with hot, black coffee. She moves quickly to take an inventory of her trunk, confirming the presence of the equipment she will need.

As Angela arrives on the scene, she notices an older woman wearing a flannel robe standing just outside the yellow tape. The observer is alone and motionless, staring at the rubble. Perhaps she is a family member? The thought drapes a heavy cloak of sadness on Angela's shoulders as she maneuvers her vehicle around the various news trucks that have positioned themselves for a dramatic background shot as they relay the tragedy to the world.

Angela is sitting on the back bumper of her car, putting on her boots, as a man approaches. She looks up knowingly. "Morning, Chief."

"Morning, Bergman. You have your hands full. My guys think there are multiple ignition points, and they suspect accelerants. I have already contacted the State, and the dogs are on their way."

"Thanks." Angela is not a fan of small talk.

Between the Tyvek suit, goggles, respirator, and boots, every inch of Angela is protected as she grabs her kit and heads to the far corner of the scene. She will work methodically, using a grid approach to complete the first of multiple passes. Small flags will be placed in the spots she finds of interest. Photos, more flags, and eventually, evidence collection will come during subsequent passes.

First, she will let the scene speak to her… It always does.

3
___

I t is 6 a.m., and Brian McMillan slams his left hand blindly onto his cellphone in an effort to stop the annoying buzzing. He notices the stubble as his right hand slides down his unshaven face. His bare feet find the cold and uninviting bedroom floor as he accepts the need to keep this job. His probation officer has made that abundantly clear.

He is close to the finish line and reminds himself daily of his commitment to never spend another night lying in a 6' x 9' concrete box staring at iron bars or using a stainless steel toilet in front of another man ever again.

Brian works for MAS Roofing, a female-owned company dedicated to giving convicted felons the opportunity to learn a trade and providing a way out of the revolving door that many find themselves in. While not the best job when Mother Nature refuses to cooperate, it is honest work.

He started as a "gopher," but quickly learned that those who pay attention to detail and are willing to repeatedly carry heavy bundles of shingles up and down ladders without complaint are given the chance to do more. Although Brian would be described as having a medium build, he was deceptively strong, which allowed him to seize the opportunity. A few months later, he got a small raise and started lugging heavy objects less and swinging a hammer more.

After taking a shower, he points the remote at the television before putting on a pair of tar-stained blue jeans, a shirt with the company logo over the front left pocket, and a well-worn pair of Timberlands. The lead story is a live shot from the scene of a fire in Brockton that claimed the lives of a family of four, prompting a painful memory from his youth.

Brian and a handful of friends decided to have a party in the hayloft of a long-abandoned barn his buddy Johnny found at the end of a narrow path, deep in the woods. His friend, Alex, was in charge of music, Sally was responsible for the beer, and Brian brought the lighting. Laughter filled the rickety structure until Jenny accidentally knocked over one of the lit candles while she and Henry were dancing. The flame caught a few remnants of hay, and the place went up like a tinderbox.

They had barely gotten down from the loft when they heard the scream of sirens racing toward them. Smoke billowed from every crack and crevice by the time they reached their cars. For a moment, one they did not have, they stood awestruck, coughing and taking in large gulps of air as they watched flames shoot thirty feet into the star-filled night sky. By the time they had turned their cars around and begun racing back toward the main road, the first fire truck had already made the turn onto the overgrown dirt road leading to and from the barn.

Despite not having been there in years, the property owner was furious, relentless in his pursuit of having charges filed. As the one who brought the candles and matches, Brian took the brunt of the charges, including trespassing and arson.

Brian shakes off the thought and heads for the door. He cannot be late.

4

T he three-way call, using numbers exchanged via different anonymous Gmail accounts, crackles as the lines
connect.

While the others cannot see him, the assassin puffs out
his pride-filled chest. He nailed it. This job is the gateway
to enhancing his fledgling reputation as a solo operator and
boosting his new bank account in the Caymans. That's where
the "best" keep their money.

He takes a strong, but congenial tone. "The initial phase
of this operation is complete, but payment has yet to be
received."

A stern, powerful voice responds without hesitation.
"You get paid for filling the *exact* order, not a derivation."

He understands that remaining calm no matter the situation is critical for his long-term success, but these guys
are doing the one thing they shouldn't: fuck with his money.
He responds after a slow, deep breath. "The *exact* order was
filled. Collateral damage couldn't be avoided."

A third, venom-filled voice explodes into the silence.
"You are a fucking idiot! Collateral damage draws unwanted
attention, particularly when kids are involved."

The sound of rocks being broken swirls in his head as
the assassin grinds his teeth. Spittle flies across the room as
he begins to unravel. "I expect payment before the close of
business today. Collection efforts for failure to pay will not
be pleasurable... for you."

The powerful voice returns. "We will discuss this and let
you know."

Their nonchalance pushes him over the edge as his pacing becomes infuriated stomping. "LET ME KNOW?! Who do you think you are fuckin' with?"

The words reverberate around the small room as he feels the tattoo on his neck begin to redden. The heat of fury races toward the top of his head as he realizes silence is the only answer he is going to get.

The burner phone strikes the wall with enough force that a large fragment is left embedded in the sheetrock as the remnants clatter across the floor.

A haunting grin spreads across the assassin's face as he silently begs them not to pay.

5

Reggie Jacobs' tires squeal in anger as he swings his car onto President Street; no flashing lights or siren. Without confirmation, there is no reason for him to be there. He was out late, and the schnapps he added to his coffee this morning isn't working its intended magic. To make matters worse, he has to deal with "her" again.

Reggie's arthritic right hand grabs the compostable four-cup drink carrier holding two large Dunkin' coffees from the passenger seat, while his left foot kicks open the driver's door of a vehicle that has seen better days. He shakes his cleanly shaved head, wondering yet again why the most senior detective in the squad isn't assigned the newest vehicle. It is another thing making him question whether the department values his years of service. It may finally be time to turn in his papers and move to Tennessee, where he can spend his days fishing, playing golf, and drinking bourbon.

"Bergman!" Reggie yells and holds a "virgin" cup of coffee up high so she can see it. Offering an olive branch is better than getting another suspension for screaming at some overly sensitive female co-worker.

Angela finishes walking a section of the grid and heads to the perimeter. She removes her respirator and unzips her Tyvek suit to her waist. "Jacobs."

"Morning, Bergman. Thought you might need a cup." The sweetness in Reggie's voice is giving him a toothache.

Angela eagerly reaches out her arm, like she drained her always-present Yeti hours ago. "Thanks. You the lead?"

"If it's arson."

"Still have some work to do, but I've located six different ignition points as well as signs of accelerant. I will deny saying this until everything is confirmed, but this appears to be arson. I'd bet my pension on it." She closes her eyes, probably needing a moment for the caffeine to enter her bloodstream.

The annoyance in Reggie's voice is unmistakable. "Shit. What do we know about the vics?"

"I only know them as victims. The kids were in their beds. The male adult was found in the hallway between bedrooms, presumably trying to get to the kids. The female adult was sprawled on the floor near the door in what I presume to be the master bedroom. The Medical Examiner just took the remains to the morgue for autopsy." Angela takes another sip of coffee. "By the way, I have not found any evidence of smoke detectors. You should check with the landlord."

Reggie cannot hide his resentment. No woman tells him what to do… period. He feels the top of his head turn beet red as the schnapps in his coffee takes hold, and his disingenuous kindness falls to the background.

He grits his teeth before responding. "Landlord is my first stop."

"Thanks again for the coffee." Angela briefly holds up the cup to say "cheers" as she smirks, then repositions her respirator and heads back toward the grid she has established within the debris.

Reggie lumbers back to his patrol car, disgusted with himself for letting the bitch get under his skin. He should have brought her decaf. Tennessee is looking better and better. Maybe he can land something to supplement his pension that doesn't require heavy lifting, long hours, or dealing with know-it-all women.

6

Agnes Rothschild has seen families come and go as the neighborhood has experienced its cyclical transformations. She refused to leave after her husband passed, and treats everyone who has lived on President Street as a member of her extended family. Most refer to her as Savta, the Hebrew word for grandmother.

She has been glued to the same spot for hours, having been positioned there by firefighters as they modified the size of the cordoned area once the presence of bodies was confirmed. Every part of her aches, but it is nothing compared to the pain she has endured in her life, as the crudely tattooed green numbers on her left forearm will attest.

Agnes imagined the conversation between the woman shrouded in the white bodysuit and the bald man she presumed to be a member of the police department. She knew he wasn't happy based on his body language as he stomped back toward his vehicle. She watched him change direction upon seeing her standing there, alone.

Nothing about their forthcoming exchange excites Agnes.

"Excuse me, ma'am. Detective Jacobs with the Brockton Police Department. May I ask you a few questions?"

Her arms remain locked across her body, holding her bathrobe closed and creating a protective barrier between her and the meaningless death that occurred on the other side of the yellow tape.

Her eyes never leave the rubble. "How may I help you, Detective?"

"May I have your name? Do you live near here?"

"My name is Agnes Rothschild. I have lived on President Street for more than fifty years."

"Ms. Rothschild, did you…."

Her body remains stationary, but her head turns slowly toward Reggie. "Excuse me, Detective, it's *Mrs.* Rothschild, or Agnes." She will never dishonor her husband of sixty-two years.

"Sorry. Mrs. Rothschild, did you see the fire last evening?"

She adopts a cautious tone. "Yes." The police have never been friends to the residents of this part of the city.

"Did you see anyone who did not look like they belonged? Someone out of place?"

"Not that I noticed. I was busy looking around to see who from the neighborhood was outside… and who wasn't." Her head droops as she finishes her thought.

"Was anyone missing?"

This time, she turns her whole body, the impact of hours of immobility forcing her to recoil while she swallows her wincing. Daggers shoot from her bloodshot eyes as Agnes looks deep into Reggie's soul, while her chastising finger silently stabs at the destruction.

Reggie looks up from his notes. "Oh… Yes… Sorry. What can you tell me about them?"

Agnes' stare returns to her primary objective, unable to hide a painful gasp. "A lovely family. Dylan and Lily were not married, but had been together for years. They saw no reason to do so. I tried to convince them otherwise, but I guess that is irrelevant now. They are… I mean… were caring parents. The children were smart, fun-loving kids. Ages eight and eleven."

Tears again slide down Agnes' cheeks. She wipes them with the damp sleeve of her bathrobe as Reggie fumbles in his pockets, looking for something to hand her.

Her gaze falls as she sniffles and fights to regain control of her emotions. "Dylan worked construction. Plumbing mostly. He fixed my toilet a couple of weeks ago. He would not take any money, not even for the parts. Lily worked at the prison during the day. She was some kind of secretary. She also picked up shifts as a bartender at Jazzies, a bar around the corner."

"I know this is a hard question, but can you think of anyone who would want to hurt…" Reggie glances at his notes. "…Dylan, Lily, or the kids?"

Agnes's head snaps up. "Do you think they were murdered?"

This time, Reggie softens his tone. "I am trying to understand what happened and why. I am exploring all possibilities."

Sadness migrates toward rage. "They were caring, benevolent people. Why would anyone want to hurt them?"

Reggie finishes jotting down his notes and pulls out a business card. "I am sorry for your loss, Mrs. Rothschild. If you think of anything else, please give me a call."

Agnes blindly stuffs the card into a bathrobe pocket as her focus returns to the oversight of the woman wearing white.

She must protect those who can no longer fight for themselves.

7

Reggie's mind leaps to three questions as his feet shuffle back to his unmarked patrol car. *Why this house? Why these people? Why now?*

Knowing many arsonists stick around to watch, he was hoping the old woman would point to a stranger meandering around the neighborhood while the fire burned. Revenge, excitement, and occasionally, sexual gratification are the biggest draws. Whatever the reason, the exhilaration comes from watching the devastating, yet graceful dance of the yellow and orange flames.

Reggie returns to the station, swinging through the kitchen area, grabbing a cup of black coffee that looks and smells like it was brewed last week. He heads to the darkest spot in the building, the "bullpen," where the detectives sit.

He throws his wrinkled, blue polyester sports coat over the back of his chair and plops into it as he sheds his tie. He takes a sip of the scalding sludge and enters Dylan's name into the police database.

It doesn't come as a surprise to learn Dylan has a record. All petty crimes that occurred when he was in his late teens and early twenties. Dylan is also listed as a known associate of two lower-echelon members of the Dead Presidents, a gang started years ago by a few guys who lived on President Street in Brockton.

However, Dylan appears to have found his way out of that life, keeping his nose clean for the past twelve years. On paper, Dylan seems to be like every other guy, just trying to scratch out a living to provide for his family.

When he enters Lily's name, he confirms what Mrs. Rothschild shared. She is an employee of the Department of Corrections. She worked as the administrative assistant to Samuel Johansson, the prison warden, at MCI – Cedar Junction, more commonly referred to as Walpole, due to its location.

Reggie's heard the stories about Johansson, a career Correctional Officer who worked his way up. He has been shanked twice but refuses to walk away from the job. He is a hard ass and reportedly a fan of the "carrot and stick" approach. Rumor has it that he uses a lot of sticks and not many carrots.

Reggie smiles at the prospect of speaking directly to Johansson, someone who shares his personal view of criminals and how those animals should be treated. While expecting little of value to come from the call, he dials the phone as his mind ticks off a list of Walpole's current residents who are there as a direct result of his talents.

"Good morning, Warden Johansson. Thanks for taking my call."

"It is not a good morning, Detective. Lily was a terrific person."

Reggie unknowingly sits up straighter in response to the rebuke. "Yes, that's why I'm calling. I am hoping you can tell me something about Lily that will help with the investigation."

"I can offer very little, but I will do my best. She started working here about three years ago. She was a solid admin. Everyone liked her. She had an infectious smile, something you don't often find in a place like this."

Reggie draws a crude picture of a burning house on a small notepad while going through the motions. "Did Lily ever come into contact with the inmates?"

"Never as part of her job. As you know, the administrative offices are segregated from the cell blocks. She may have visited an inmate at some point, but I would need to review the visitor logs to know for sure. But, no, never as part of the job."

"What were her primary duties, exactly?"

Johansson releases a frustrated sigh. "She kept my calendar, handled the mail, did the filing, answered the phone… things any administrative assistant would do. I'm happy to send a copy of her personnel file should you believe that to be helpful."

Reggie ignores the warden's unspoken message. "That would be great, thank you. Was she going to lose her job when Cedar Junction suspends operations?"

Walpole's record of inmate-on-inmate attacks was higher than state and national averages, which is why it is one of the prisons the Commonwealth is planning to shutter over the next couple of years.

"In all likelihood. Like most DOC employees, she would have been offered something within the system, but I do not believe her personal situation would have supported a change."

"Why do you say that?"

"The geography may have been difficult for her to overcome. She was not married, but had a couple of kids. She had pictures on her desk, but that is all I know about her personal life. Sorry, I cannot be of more help, Detective."

Reggie accepts the warden's message this time. "Thanks for your time, Warden. I will look for that file."

"Goodbye, Detective."

Reggie returns the phone to its cradle and shakes his head from side to side. The feeling in his gut is getting worse. Something has been gnawing at him since he met with Bergman. But then again, it could be the cup of sludge he has been drinking.

8

Angela exchanges solemn nods with the bathrobe-clad elderly woman who has only left her post twice throughout the day. Despite the lack of hard evidence, she knew the woman's eyes had captured and catalogued everything Angela had done.

After sharing a deep emotion with only their eyes, the matronly woman turns and shuffles from the scene, occasionally lifting her sleeve to her face.

Angela leans against the bumper of her car for the last time today. She tilts her head back and shakes out her long brown hair. The smell instantly confirms it has been sequestered in the hood of a sweaty, white polyethylene suit for more than nine hours.

As she suspected, the accelerant detection canines hit on the six different locations Angela marked as likely points of origin. After ensuring proper chain of custody, she sent samples from each spot for analysis. All that remains is to tell that idiot Jacobs and write up the final report.

The hair on the back of Angela's neck stands up at the thought of Jacobs. His "good ole boy," misogynistic attitude has no place in today's world. She has had to fight it her entire career, but he is one of the worst. The last time they worked together, he explained her sole purpose was to do what he, as the lead detective, commanded. *That should be simple enough.* She told him to fuck off and did what needed to be done. He did not like it, and she did not care.

"Jacobs"

"It's Angela Bergman."

Reggie offers no pleasantries. "Got a definitive answer for me?"

"My report will outline the evidence, but it was arson. Burn patterns confirm six different ignition points. Photos and measurements will show the fire burned circles, each with a two-foot radius, deep into the wood at these locations, which is abnormal behavior for fire, as you likely know. The lab has the samples, so we should know the exact nature of the accelerants by the end of the day tomorrow."

"Any additional insight you can offer now?"

Angela takes another deep breath. "My guess is this was not their first time. This fire burned hot and fast. Even with smoke detectors, it would have been next to impossible for this family to get out. What I cannot tell is whether you are looking for one or multiple firebugs."

"So someone wanted this building to become a pile of ashes, and maybe the family, too."

"I saw you with the older woman. Did she give you anything?"

"No. She has a neighborly connection to the victims, and it looks like she has become their champion, which should be fun. I have an appointment with the landlord first thing tomorrow."

"My full report will be ready within the next forty-eight hours, presuming nothing else pops in the interim." Angela smiles to herself. "Oh, and do not forget to ask about the smoke detectors."

Angela hears Jacobs swearing as the call disconnects. She has done her job and says another silent prayer for the souls of those lost, asking a higher power to ensure Jacobs does his with the same commitment and diligence.

9

Brian's employer has secured the exclusive contract for the roofing and gutter work of twenty-five "McMansions" being built in a new development in Weymouth. The extravagant homes are nothing like anything he has lived in, nor ever will. Houses with more bathrooms than bedrooms, and there are a lot of bedrooms. He chalks it up to people having too much money and not knowing what else to do with it.

This morning, Brian is standing with the project manager in what will eventually be a three-car garage, reviewing the home's blueprints spread atop a piece of plywood set on two sawhorses to create a makeshift table. Their debate on approach is just beginning when a plumbing company truck skids into the driveway. The driver, someone Brian met while he was a guest of the Commonwealth, jumps out and sprints toward them.

A loud, weird excitement is blurted out. "You guys hear?"

Brian doesn't bother looking up. "We ain't got time for this right now, Jeremy."

Undeterred, Jeremy Carter stands at the threshold of the soon-to-be garage with his shirt untucked and his boots untied. "It's fuckin' crazy, man. Dylan's house caught fire last night. Him and his whole family is dead. I just worked with the guy the other day. Ain't that some crazy shit?"

Brian looks up from the blueprints, recalling the morning news, and subconsciously moves his aching jaw back and forth with his left hand. He knew, well, sort of knew, the guy who died. Dylan was part of a crew that worked for the development's plumbing contractor, and their paths crossed now and again. Their last interaction was not one of Brian's finest moments; an argument that went completely off the rails over where Dylan should park his company truck.

Dylan wanted it close to the house so he did not have to walk "a mile" every time he needed something. Brian told him to move his piece of shit van so the roofers didn't have to worry about dropping something on it.

The screaming that ensued was vile and filled with degrading comments about each other's mothers. At one point, Brian asked Dylan if he "kissed his kids with that mouth," which cranked the heat beyond its boiling point.

Dylan began sprinting toward the structure as Brian jumped onto the ladder with his gloved hands, positioned the insteps of his feet on the outside of the rails, sliding down as if coming down a fireman's pole.

Knowing his probation period was almost complete, Brian could not afford a fight, but he was not going to take any shit either. Within seconds, they were in each other's faces.

Then, it went from bad to worse.

With the speed of a mongoose, Dylan threw a jab with his left, following it with a monstrous roundhouse right. Both swings hit their mark, staggering Brian backward, woozy and confused. Brian somehow kept his wits about him and never raised a hand, not even to block the punches. Dylan was about to continue the pummeling when Jeremy jumped between them.

Fortunately, there were no supervisors on site. After regaining his balance, Brian spat out a tooth and a mouthful of blood, then continued to swing at Dylan with the only option available: his words. Dylan told him to "fuck off" and casually strolled to his van, moving it to the end of the driveway, out of harm's way as Brian had originally requested.

Death always brings odd feelings, but this one feels creepier for a reason Brian cannot identify.

10

Thirty-year-old investigative reporter, MJ Fernandez, is the talk of the town. She wishes her fifteen minutes of fame would fade, if not disappear entirely. As one of the latest winners of a Pulitzer Prize, she spends most of her week declining a ridiculous number of job offers, speaking engagements, and requests for interviews from around the globe. She could write her own ticket but refuses to walk away from Eric Spagnola, the pain in the ass editor who stood behind her when she uncovered an unimaginable story, which catapulted her into the treacherous worlds of pharmaceutical research and organized crime.

She is loath to admit it, but she thrived on the danger. There was a certain energy coursing through her veins during that harrowing period—something she had never felt before and secretly hopes she will experience again. She is quick to concede, however, that the cavalier attitude she displayed toward her own safety required major adjustment.

An acquaintance introduced her to the former Navy SEAL-turned-personal trainer that MJ now works with multiple times per week. In addition to improving her situational awareness, she is aggressively pursuing black belts in Brazilian Jiu-Jitsu and Taekwondo, and is quickly moving up the ranks in both, further boosting her already extraordinary level of fearlessness.

MJ's investigative mantra is simple: Truth above all else. While this seems simple enough, her approach is not always as pure as one might think. MJ tip-toes along the tightrope of legality, occasionally stepping into the darkness, but solely for the greater good, and never for personal gain.

After today's training session, MJ lets the steam of the shower work its magic as she twists her head from left to right, her cervical vertebrae cracking in relief. As the hot water begins to run out, MJ decides she will do something she has not done in a while: grace the office with her celebrity.

This is the longest she has ever sat idle. True to her long-standing approach, she has declined each of Spagnola's recent suggestions for her next story. The real concern for her, however, is the fear that maturity is taking its toll, as evidenced by the politeness she displayed while telling him to pound sand.

MJ prefers to pick her own assignments. She understands that not every story will be a Pulitzer candidate, but they cannot be run-of-the-mill either, particularly now. She continues to make this statement to Spagnola, the man who nominated her to the Pulitzer Prize Board.

Sixty minutes later, MJ strolls into the newsroom like she owns the place, which is nothing new. She acknowledges a few people as she heads to her desk and finds a pile of pink message slips carefully placed where her laptop is supposed to sit. Most are from other reporters—vultures picking at the bones of her story, searching for scraps they can spin into gold.

Spagnola finds his way to her desk before she can complete her cleaning regimen by pushing the pink pieces of paper into the rusted and dented trash can below her desk. He smiles and invites her to join him in his office. The last time they played this game, he threatened to end her career because of her office antics. She is not concerned today.

He closes the door to his fish-bowl-like office and adopts a familiar tone. "Nice to see you, MJ. It has been a while."

"I have been holed up, contemplating the meaning of life." Ever the smart-ass.

"Have those efforts borne fruit?"

A conspiratorial smile appears. "I am sad to report they have not, but I am committed to spending as long as it takes."

Spagnola peers over the top of his reading glasses. "I am sure you are, but you have exhausted the leeway the Propentus exposé garnered. Time for you to get back to work, and I have just the thing."

MJ knew this day was coming. On the positive side, she is bored, though she will never say that aloud. "I will not like it, but I am happy to listen."

"There was a fatal fire in Brockton. My sources tell me it was arson…"

MJ had seen a headline. "Stop," she demands and starts to stand. "I am not investigating a fire, even an arson that killed someone. That is not what I do, and you know it."

"It is not your usual storyline… that is true. But you need to get back in the saddle. Now."

Taking one step toward the door, MJ says, "I know I have to come up with something. I am working on it, but I am not sifting through the ashes of a burnt-out triple-decker in search of spiritual enlightenment."

MJ knows she is pressing her luck, but does it anyway. Allowing her smile to deliver her final answer, she opens the door and walks briskly back to her desk. She grabs her laptop bag and ignores everyone standing between her and the elevator. She should have known better.

She grumbles to herself as she boards the elevator, "A fire… he must be out of his goddamn mind!"

11

Reggie sits at his desk, casually hiding the empty Jameson nip that fortified this morning's coffee, and mulls over Angela's "not their first time" comment.

During his almost thirty years on the force, he has seen depravity even the most talented fiction writer couldn't dream up. Nonetheless, here he sits reviewing the statewide database, stunned by the number of convicted arsonists currently residing within the country's seventh smallest state. Not all of them are murderers, but they are all driven by the flicker of the flame.

Reggie sorts the one hundred and seventy-three records into different categories. His first slice eliminates those incarcerated on the night of the President Street fire, which only shaves twenty-six names from the list. The remaining list is segmented by geography, so he focuses his initial efforts on those currently residing inside the Interstate 495 belt.

His eyebrows lift as he notices one individual directly linked to President Street. Reggie reviews the record of the twenty-nine-year-old, unmarried male who was released from Walpole eleven months ago for a non-arson-related charge, piquing Reggie's interest in this particular individual. *A typical repeat offender*, he thought cynically

The most recent conviction happened when Brian McMillan was at a bar in Whitman and noticed a guy pushing a woman around. He stepped in. The abuser ended up in the hospital, and Brian's chivalry earned him an aggravated assault charge… and another stint in prison.

Reggie closes his eyes, picturing the conversation between McMillan and his public defender. The one where the attorney, whom Reggie knows is lazy and quick to blame his workload for any failure, convinces McMillan to plead guilty under the guise that the judge would take mercy given the facts.

He didn't, sentencing McMillan to eighteen months.

The record reflects that McMillan was a model prisoner. With the Commonwealth's pursuit of lower incarceration rates, he was released after only serving nine and a half months. He then began a one-year probationary period. Reggie notes that McMillan's probation file is pristine, including passing every drug test and starting a job at MAS Roofing a week after being released.

Reggie turns his attention to the details that brought McMillan's name to the surface. While a resident of President Street, McMillan earned himself a sealed juvenile record for trespass and arson. He chuckles to himself as he reads the name of the arresting officer.

After a quick call and the promise of beers and a Sox game, Reggie learns the fire was an accident. However, the property owner called anyone and everyone, screaming for the heavy-handed conviction of the person who brought the candles.

After expanding the geographic circle in his next pass, Reggie spends the remainder of the morning narrowing the initial list to eleven fire-lovers. While none seem likely, he has learned you always do the work. Failure to do so allows criminals to get away with murder… literally. He cannot let that happen again.

After a lunch of stale peanut butter crackers, Reggie spends the afternoon battling traffic along Route 24 and Interstates 93 and 495 to lay eyes on each of the eleven convicted arsonists. All but the last provided an alibi and the name of at least one person who could easily verify their story.

When Reggie interviewed Brian McMillan, Brian explained that he worked until 8 p.m., when darkness made standing on a steeply pitched roof too dangerous. On the way home, he grabbed something from Burger King for dinner. Brian rummaged through the trash to pull out a time-stamped receipt, which read "8:22 p.m." as proof of his innocence. After attending an AA meeting at the First Evangelical Church in Brockton, McMillan said he arrived home around 10:30 and went straight to bed because he needed to get up early the next day.

Reggie begins mentally outlining his approach to confirm the alibis of each flame-loving felon, but has already ruled out ten of the eleven. Reggie interprets the gnawing in his gut to mean there is something "off" about McMillan and his carefully crafted story, which catapults him to the top of the suspect list.

Sitting in his prowler, drinking cold coffee leftover from this morning, Reggie scrolls through his phone. He stabs a meaty index finger on the email icon and finds Angela Bergman's draft report.

Two of the ignition spots used kerosene as an accelerant; the remaining four contained formalin. A quick Google search reveals that formalin is highly flammable and is used in a myriad of ways, including the preservation of tissue samples in research labs, taxidermy, and, of course, the embalming of bodies.

Reggie erases his mind's whiteboard and replaces it with a plan to contact funeral homes in the area to identify missing embalming fluid, but he quickly realizes the task is much larger. He also needs to contact hospitals and research facilities, of which the greater Boston area, including the biotech-rich area of Cambridge, has plenty.

A quick sip from a flask he pulls from his sports coat pocket props up Reggie's bad attitude. Another drink, and he decides to return to the dark confines of the bullpen to spend additional time allowing a computer screen to strain his eyesight.

His optimistic objective of cross-checking his list of arsonists against their favorite accelerant fails miserably. Worse still, his continued research on the subject reveals that anyone can buy formalin from Amazon, causing him to flip his computer mouse across his cubicle.

With the last of his optimism crushed, Reggie rubs his temples. He needs to think.

He is snatching his jacket from his chair when a yellow Post-it on his cubicle wall, near the final resting spot of the tossed mouse, catches his eye: *McMillan fought with Janssen.*

He does not recognize the handwriting, and he has not mentioned McMillan to anyone. How would someone know to bring this to his attention? A brief, inquisitive look around the empty space provides no answers.

Reggie adds this new piece of information to the thoughts bouncing inside his head and feels the excitement of the hunt cautiously return. If true, there are a series of new questions.

Why did McMillan omit this? What was the fight about? Who started it? Was it bad enough for McMillan to then kill Janssen and his entire family?

With a renewed spring in his step, Reggie heads to where he does his best thinking: any barstool with a decent cheeseburger and a few cold beers.

12

Reggie's annoyance was obvious as he responded to the homeowner's request to meet him at the burned-out dwelling at 9 a.m. instead of 8. Donnie had explained in their brief phone call that he already had an appointment with the insurance adjuster to walk the site at 10 and hoped to make a single trip to what was left of his rental property.

After flashing his badge to scare off the public adjusters attempting to shove their business cards into Donnie's hand, Reggie returns from the curb to reclaim the power position.

Donnie steps forward, his hands shoved deeply into his front pockets. "I am sorry this happened, Detective. They were nice people."

Reggie sets the tone, but is perplexed by the body language. "Mr. Montgomery…"

"Call me Donnie."

"Okay, Donnie, what can you tell me about this property and your tenants?"

"I bought this place a few years ago, as an investment. I own three different rental properties on the South Shore. Do you know what caused the fire?"

When Reggie answers with another question, Donnie realizes the detective isn't open to answering his questions. "Do you use a management company?"

"I am pretty handy, and I live in Abington. No need to waste money on that," Donnie replies with a dismissive shrug.

Reggie holds Donnie's gaze. "Who holds the mortgage?"

Donnie's eyes drop to the soot-stained sidewalk. He starts squirming and drives his hands deeper, if that is possible.

"TD Bank. Um… I am current on the payments. Honest. I was behind for a little while, but I am all caught up as of a couple of months ago. You can check."

Reggie continues to apply pressure. "I will. Does TD Bank hold the mortgages on your other properties?"

"Yeah. But like I said, I am current on everything now. Any idea what caused the fire?" Donnie presses again.

The detective scribbles something on his notepad. "Okay, what about the tenants?"

"They paid on time. My favorite type of tenants." Donnie laughs at his own joke.

Reggie lunges into Donnie's personal space. "This is no laughing matter, Donnie. Four people died in a building you own and maintain."

Donnie recoils, like a puppy who was just whacked on the nose with a newspaper for peeing on the carpet. "Um… I am sorry. I use humor when I am nervous."

Reggie glowers at Donnie without blinking. "Why are you nervous, Donnie?"

Donnie's right eye twitches. "No reason. Just this whole thing. Can you tell me what caused the fire?"

Reggie turns the screws a little tighter. "What do *you* think caused the fire, Donnie?"

Donnie's pitch goes up half an octave. "I got no idea. Why would I?"

Reggie seems to take joy in the discomfort of others, quickly erasing the space Donnie reclaimed. "I'm just wondering if you have any thoughts on the topic."

"Nope." Donnie bounces from one foot to the other, avoiding the questions as if dodging bullets.

"Okay, Donnie. We will come back to that. You said you maintain the house yourself. Have you done any electrical repairs lately?"

Donnie's nervousness wanes. "No, no electrical repairs on this place. Ever."

Reggie smirks and drops the hammer. "The arson investigator found no evidence of smoke detectors, Donnie. No melted plastic, nothing. Why is that?"

Donnie's shoulders stiffen, and his hands return to the bottom of his pockets as nervousness morphs into abject fear. "Maybe they got all burned up?"

"I expected you to say that, Donnie. That's why I have asked the arson investigator to test for the presence of polymers in the areas where you would be required to have a smoke detector. The results will tell us if they were present, as required by code. And, whether you are lying to a police officer."

Donnie's eyes stare at the cracks in the sidewalk as he struggles to maintain the awkward silence, his feet continuing their dance of avoidance.

After thirty painful seconds, Reggie continues the interrogation. "Back to the tenants."

No jokes this time. "Nice couple with two kids. They lived here for two years. Never a problem. That is all I know. I swear."

"Okay, Donnie. Have you pissed anyone off lately? Maybe someone who wants to torch your buildings to teach you a lesson?"

"Nobody I can think of, Officer."

Reggie takes another domineering step forward. "It is Detective."

Donnie instinctively retreats. "Sorry… Detective."

"I'm coming to see you again, once I speak to TD Bank about the mortgages and the arson investigator about the smoke detectors." Reggie hands Donnie a business card. "Call me if you would like to tell me anything before that."

Reggie walks to his illegally parked car, removes the police placard from the windshield, and drives away, leaving Donnie feeling unsettled.

• • •

Reggie's next stop today is Flush-It-All Plumbing, Dylan Janssen's employer. In addition to gathering general background on Dylan, the goal is to unearth details relative to the fight with Brian McMillan.

Upon arriving at the business address he found online, Reggie downs the last of a spiked coffee and heads for a weathered, red steel door marked "Office."

Pushing inside, he finds a teenage girl with a small chain hanging between the matching studs in her nose and left ear. She is startled by the unexpected visit, her cellphone falling onto the desk with a thud.

Reggie looks around the 12' x 12' room that holds only a gunmetal grey desk from the 1950s, with a phone and laptop sitting atop it. "I am Detective Jacobs. Is the owner here?"

The teenager sits up straight and blindly slides her hand around the top of the desk, searching for her dropped security blanket. "No, sir. He's at a job site."

"I am investigating the death of Dylan Janssen and need to speak to him. Which jobsite?"

"I'm not sure I can say. Let me check."

Smart girl. Reggie watches as she spins the squeaky desk chair around, holds her hand over the phone, and whispers, as if it is going to make a difference in the tiny space. After a couple of minutes of silent nodding, she ends the call.

"He's at the new subdivision in Union Point." She says nothing more, returning her attention to the captivating content displayed on the little screen in her hand.

<h1 style="text-align:center">13</h1>

Reggie makes good time heading across Route 27, winding his way toward the recently widened Route 18, then turning into Union Point. He spots a Flush-It-All Plumbing truck and pulls into the dirt driveway of a framed-out home that reminds him of a skeleton.

"Excuse me, I'm looking for the owner of Flush-It-All Plumbing."

A hulk of a man steps out, barely fitting between the first-floor wall studs. He extends a symbol of a lifetime of manual labor. "Peter Youngblood. I presume you are the detective who scared the shit out of my daughter?"

Reggie shakes the giant's hand but ignores the comment, wondering how someone of Youngblood's size fits beneath kitchen sinks.

"Detective Reggie Jacobs, Brockton Police Department. I'm investigating the fire that killed Dylan Janssen and his family."

Sympathy does not appear to be Peter's strength. "I have a lot to do, Detective, and now I'm down a guy. What can I do for you?"

"What can you tell me about Dylan Janssen?"

"In what sense?"

"In any sense. As a person, as an employee, etc."

"Dylan was one of my best guys. Really good at his job, and he worked his ass off. To be honest, it'll probably take two guys to replace the amount of work he did. He was never a problem."

Reggie appreciates his directness. "What can you tell me about a fight he got into with one of the roofers?"

Peter unleashes a heavy sigh. "As I understand it, Dylan wanted to park the truck next to the house, and one of the roofers told him to move it. Words were exchanged, and there was some pushing and shoving. They worked it out."

"So you did not witness it firsthand?"

"No, I have projects all over the South Shore going right now."

"Are there any witnesses? Anyone you can point me to?"

"I will ask, but a lot of these guys are… Let's just say they've had bad experiences with law enforcement."

One of the workers overhears the conversation and hollers out to the driveway. "I SAW IT!"

Reggie steps toward the skeleton, immediately ignoring Peter. "And your name?"

The lanky man easily weaves his way through the home's ribcage. "Jeremy Carter."

"You saw the fight, Mr. Carter?"

"Yeah, Dylan was fightin' with Brian McMillan. I know Brian from prison. They was fightin' about where Dylan should park. Dylan had a ton of shit he needed to lug in, so he wanted to be close to the house. Brian told him he couldn't 'cuz something could come off the roof and hit the truck."

"Seems reasonable."

"They was calling each other 'motherfuckers,' talking shit about each other's family. It got real nasty."

"Nasty?"

"Yeah. Brian pushed Dylan's buttons, asking if he 'kissed his kids with that mouth.' That sent Dylan over the edge. He shouted something 'bout keeping his kids out of it or he'd kick Brian's ass. Brian yelled something like 'give it your best fuckin' shot' and slid down the ladder real fast."

"And?"

"They kept yelling. Then Dylan hit Brian in the face a couple times before I broke it up."

"Did Brian throw any punches?"

Jeremy gets more animated as the story continues. "Nah, he didn't get no chance. Dylan was bigger, and he was all over Brian."

"What happened after you broke it up?"

"Brian was spitting a lot of blood and a tooth, I think. Then he said something about Dylan 'gettin' his.' Dylan told him to 'fuck off' and walked away. They ignored each other after that."

"Anyone else see this?"

"Nope. Just me, but it was loud. You'd have to be fuckin' deaf not to hear it."

Peter steps between Jeremy and Reggie, apparently having heard enough. "Is that all, Detective? As I mentioned, I have a lot of jobs and fewer guys."

"I'm good for now. Jeremy, I will need you to come to the station to give a formal statement. Here is my card. Call me and I'll set everything up so you don't miss a lot of work. Thank you for your assistance, Mr. Youngblood."

Reggie spins and kicks a rock down the driveway as he returns to his car—time to ask Brian McMillan about a missing tooth.

14

Brian notices a wretched smell on his drive to the jobsite today. A thorough search of the back seat reveals a handful of greasy fast-food bags on the floor. A couple had science experiments inside. He rolls down his windows as he parks and, with his nose held, tosses the offending bags into the trash. Fortunately, it is not supposed to rain today.

A few hours into his day, Brian is working on the ridge cap of a new home when he notices the detective who cornered him the other day walking up the crushed stone driveway of a different home under construction, five sites away. Fear washes over him as he watches Jeremy bound from the shadows of the home's framing.

He knows from his time in prison that Jeremy is a people-pleasing weasel, desperate to cover his own skinny ass. To make his life easier while in prison, Jeremy decided it was safer to heel to the demands of the shot-callers from the Dead Presidents than risk being on his own.

The vivid memory of Jeremy creating a distraction so another inmate could be shanked winds its way into Brian's thoughts. He notices a slight tremor in the hand holding his roofer's hammer as he relives the horrifying experience.

The klaxon sang as he and his lunch flopped onto the floor. Correctional officers ran everywhere, swinging their batons and screaming at inmates to get down. Brian lay face down, his heart slamming against the grey and white checkered tile, his arms and legs splayed out to the side, like he did the one time he went skydiving.

Every new "fish" quickly learns of Warden Johansson's reputation. Simply put, you don't fuck with Johansson. On this particular day, Johansson responded to the alarm himself.

The vision of Johansson, dressed in a suit and tie, racing to the prisoner who had been stabbed, while hollering for medical assistance, replays over and over in Brian's mind.

Johansson squatted, carefully avoiding the pooling blood, and whispered something into the injured inmate's ear. The pall of terror overtook the inmate's face as Johansson's knee pressed deeply into his lower back; an unforgettable image. Within seconds, the medical team took control, and the kid was never seen again.

Brian re-buries the unnerving memory.

He is once again witnessing Jeremy's penchant for ass-kissing play out in real time. It must be about the fight with Dylan, and Jeremy's role as hero. The fight should not have happened, but if Jeremy sticks to the truth, there should not be any problems.

Brian's only mistake was coming off the roof, and that is not a crime.

15

Agnes Rothschild stands at the door ten minutes early, a shawl draped across her shoulders over her nicest dress. She adjusts the hat bobby-pinned to her grey hair, steadies herself, and rings the bell.

"Good morning, Mr. Mendoza."

Benjamin Mendoza, the owner of Mendoza's Funeral Home, has been a stalwart in the neighborhood for years. He smiles softly. "Savta, I have told you, please call me Ben, or Benjamin if you prefer. Please come in. How may I help you?"

Agnes shuffles softly, following Ben to his office. She fiddles with a well-used tissue as she sits ramrod straight in the small chair beside the loveseat, facing Ben. She steels her resolve and takes a deep breath. "Benjamin, I am here to talk about Dylan, Lily, and their kids. I am their only family, so I must take care of the things that must be taken care of…" A single tear seeps from the corner of her left eye. "… and I need your help."

Because of his business, Ben has comforted many in their darkest moments, and Agnes knows today will be no different from most of this man's days. He quickly moves to remove her burden, adopting the soothing voice he has likely mastered in his unique position over the years. "Savta, I am happy to help in any way I can."

"Thank you, Benjamin. It should not be much. A short service and… four urns." Despite feeling the stress release from her shoulders, the knot in her stomach remains, as her religious beliefs battle with the concept of cremation.

"Of course, Savta," Ben says compassionately. "Do you know if the coroner has released the bodies?"

Agnes slouches in the chair, a new burden sliding into the newly created vacancy. "They will not talk to me. I am not next of kin."

Ben leans forward and places a gentle hand on Agnes' knee. "Do not worry, I will let them know we have been hired. I will take care of everything."

"Thank you, Benjamin. You are truly a blessing to this neighborhood."

· · ·

After escorting Agnes to the sidewalk and saying good-bye, Ben stands outside, pondering the business he has built on the back of a relentless commitment to his community and relationship-building. While the generosity he offered does little to help his bottom line, Ben has found that the depth of his compassion, spread by word of mouth, is more cost-effective than any other form of advertising. Besides, it is what any caring member of this tight-knit community would do.

Ben is a member of the Chamber of Commerce and of every lodge within a twenty-five-mile radius. His philanthropic efforts have earned him seats on the boards of local non-profits and charities. Every politician, police officer, EMT, and fireman knows Ben Mendoza's virtues. To the chagrin of his competitors, he is the only funeral home they recommend and promote.

For someone unable to finish medical school, Ben has made a good life for himself. However, at sixty-two years old, retirement is on the horizon, and he has no perpetuation plan for the business that has been his reason for being for more than thirty years. He tried selling the business locally a couple of years ago.

After that failed miserably, he contacted the national conglomerates that buy out retiring funeral home directors. While he is able to demonstrate that Mendoza's is profitable most years, he quickly learned that no one is interested in purchasing a funeral home located in Brockton, Massachusetts. The demographics and average income of its residents erase the interest of those companies whose sole focus is the profit margin of each funeral.

The harsh reality that Mendoza's will close upon his retirement caused the unexpected need to infuse his retirement account with a different revenue stream.

After months of cajoling and a few envelopes holding one-hundred-dollar bills, Mendoza's became the only funeral home contracted to handle the deaths of prisoners occurring at the facilities within his assigned sector of the Commonwealth. While he is not selling high-end caskets or urns, his margin on each quietly handled indigent death is five times what he makes on a traditional funeral.

A few months after winning the contract, he bumped into a prison warden at a local charity event. After one too many Manhattans, Ben inappropriately toasted the prospect of more people dying in prison. The warden's response was bewildering, but the seeds of an unexpected friendship were sown.

Ben smiles at the fond memory as he trudges back inside, heavy-heartedly concerned about the cost of today's kindness.

16

Reggie pulls from the curb and uses his patrol car as a sounding board. "McMillan has a prior arson conviction, a penchant for violence, no solid alibi, and a witness says he threatened Dylan. Everything points to guilt, but they aren't enough to convince the prosecutor to file charges. Goddammit!"

His daydreaming shifts to the gurgle in his stomach and a rare steak at Stockholder's. As he drives down Shea Memorial Drive toward Route 18, Reggie catches sight of someone on the roof of another home under construction. He pulls into the home's crushed stone driveway.

The screech of the closing driver's door barely ends before Brian climbs down the ladder and begins walking toward Reggie across what will eventually be a sod-covered, irrigated lawn.

"Detective."

Reggie's arrogance is palpable. "I've been looking for you, McMillan. I got more questions."

Brian smiles. "And, what might those be?"

"Let's start with the easy one. Why didn't you tell me you were in a fight with Dylan Janssen?"

Brian doesn't flinch. "Didn't think it mattered. I don't know what that jackass Jeremy told you, but I didn't throw a punch. Took a couple, and lost a tooth, but I never raised a hand."

Reggie relishes any opportunity to be condescending. "That jackass, as you call him, told me exactly what happened, including how he saved you from a real ass-kicking." The aggressive tone returns. "He also said you threatened Dylan."

Brian's posture tenses as he pauses to choose his words cautiously. "Threatened him, how?"

Reggie's smugness matches his volume. "Did you, or did you not, tell Dylan he'd 'get his'?"

"We said lots of nasty shit to each other."

Reggie shifts and brings his right hand up to rest on the grip of his handgun. "You did not answer my question. Care to try again?"

Brian's carefulness becomes defiance. "I don't recall saying nothin' like that."

Reggie takes three steps toward Brian, who steps backward stride for stride to maintain the gap between them.

"That's bullshit and you know it." Reggie snickers. "Whatever. Play it your way, shithead. Violating your ass back to Walpole will bring me great joy. You can hang out with the other morons stupid enough to challenge me."

Reggie chuckles to himself as the gravel crunches beneath his feet with each stride toward his car. An invisible wall of stench attacks his sense of smell, forcing him to spin back around.

"This yours, McMillan?"

Brian answers the obvious. "Yes."

"It fuckin' stinks!"

"I had a bunch of greasy fast food bags on the floor in the back."

"I've smelled dead bodies that weren't this bad. That's not rotten fast food." Reggie walks close to the car, inhaling deeply through his nose while peering into the open windows. Reggie retreats and quickly pinches his nose with his left thumb and index finger.

Reggie restarts his trip toward his car as he emits a cartoonish voice. "I promise you, our next conversation will not be pleasant, McMillan."

• • •

After a foul-smelling ten-minute drive, Reggie bellies up to the bar at Stockholders, having complete faith in the medicinal benefits of draft beer. After two pints and thirty minutes, he realizes he can smell the heat coming from the chicken wings delivered to the guy who slid down a seat when Reggie grabbed the barstool next to him.

Moments later, the smell of steak refocuses him on the pangs that brought him here. Large gulps from a half-full pint glass help the steak and accompanying fully loaded baked potato address his hunger while concurrently serving as therapy for his mental exhaustion.

The tidbits of information on the whiteboard in Reggie's head point to only one conclusion: McMillan is the guy. The homeowner's guilty mannerisms are an afterthought, although it is possible he hired McMillan to set the home ablaze.

Reggie sips the beer he ordered for dessert and smiles at the blonde sitting on the other side of the bar. Ten minutes later, as the shame of being shot down replaces his exhaustion, he flops his debit card on the bar.

With his preferred plan for the remainder of the evening erased by the stuck-up blonde, Reggie returns to the station to write up today's events. He passes a fellow officer walking in the opposite direction as he heads for the bullpen.

Reggie smiles. "How's it hanging, O'Leary?"

"A little to the left these days."

Reggie laughs and yells over his shoulder. "Beers soon?"

"Absolutely! You're buying!"

Reggie arrives at his desk, immediately spying another note in the same spot as the last. This one is in different handwriting and is on a different colored Post-it. Searching for the unknown messenger, he spins around a little too quickly. He steadies himself with one hand on the desk and another on his chair, as his glassy-eyed quest comes up empty.

He re-reads the Post-it four times before the meaning bleeds through the haze of dessert: *McMillan's car holds the key.*

His anger skyrockets because he did not connect the dots, overshadowing his concerns about the unknown author of the notes stuck to his cubicle wall. Reggie grabs his cell-phone and calls the last person he wants to speak to.

"Bergman, it is Reggie Jacobs."

Annoyance screams through the phone line. "What do you want, Jacobs? My shift ended hours ago."

"What does formalin, or formaldehyde, smell like?"

Bergman's tone flips on a dime. "Wait. What? Did you find some?"

Reggie throws a pen across the empty room. She makes everything so goddamn difficult! "Can you just tell me, or do I need to call someone else?"

"Jesus, calm down. It's hard to explain, but most descriptions talk about it being a strong, suffocating odor. Some compare it to the smell of burnt matches that have been dropped into a jar of vinegar. Others say it smells like wicked strong pickles. Maybe you can swing by a funeral home and ask them to let you take a whiff?"

Grinning from ear to ear, Reggie ends the call without warning, then slams a drunken fist on his desk. "Got you, you little fucker!"

Next, he scrolls to find the number of a special contact. A number he can only call once.

17

Fortunately for them, they made the first payment. But he is not fucking around this time. "The last phase is complete…"

An angry voice interrupts. "The faces of two children remain plastered all over the news."

The second voice, the one that reminds him of the drill sergeant from *Full Metal Jacket*, continues where the first left off. "Your failure to execute the mission without collateral damage, which was easy enough to do, is alarming; a fact to be shared with others seeking a reference."

The assassin throws his hands into the air and then screams at the phone he holds in front of his face. "I fulfilled the fucking contract. Period. Final payment is due… NOW." Restraint be damned.

The angry voice rages, "When we are done with you—"

The drill sergeant regains control. "Enough. Suffice it to say, this operation failed to meet the defined parameters for engagement."

The killer struggles, but swallows his anger and visualizes tearing these two assholes apart with his bare hands. The strength gained from his hours in the gym makes it a delightful possibility. "I delivered, and this is the last time I am going to say this: Final. Payment. Is. Due. And I expect the money to be deposited within the next two hours." This time, he disconnects the call, leaving his employers to experience the deafening sound of silence. Fuck them!

• • •

The shouting is uncontrolled as the two men remain on the call. "This is unfucking acceptable…"

The drill sergeant returns with a vengeance. "Stop! We *must* maintain operational control. He is correct relative to his delivering on the assignment. His failure to demonstrate self-discipline and his apparent disregard for the innocent are matters to be communicated to the appropriate people."

He will not be dissuaded. "You're goddamn right they are! I am making the call the moment we hang up!"

18

After a restless night, Reggie cringes at the sunshine creeping between the slats of the bedroom's window shades and throws off the blankets while cursing his lack of sleep. He takes a swig from the half-empty bottle of Jameson on his bedside table to settle himself as he moves to cash in one of the many chits he has acquired during his career. He sits up, leans against the headboard, and wipes the remnants of sleep from his eyes as the call is answered.

"It's too fucking early for this, Jacobs."

"What… No 'Hello,' your Honor? I need a warrant for a residence and a car."

The judge sighs cautiously. "What do you have?"

As is often the case, Reggie leaves out any detail that might sink his plan, including his secret messenger. "I have a suspect in the fatal Brockton fire of the other night. He has a prior arson conviction; has no one who can vouch for his whereabouts the night of the fire; he was in a physical altercation with the deceased male, who witnesses state he also threatened; and I believe his vehicle smells like one of the accelerants confirmed to have been used."

"You want me to issue a warrant based upon your nose? Are you out of your fucking mind?"

The urgency in Reggie's voice increases. "I need to get into the suspect's home and car before he cleans everything up."

"Bring the warrant to my office for review, but listen and listen very fucking carefully. The rationale needs to be tight. I'm not going to sign a warrant based upon your olfactory capabilities. Understand?"

"Thank you, your Honor."

• • •

Demonstrating a level of resourcefulness and ballsiness missing in most people, Reggie stands before the judge ninety minutes later wearing a crumpled suit, which is two sizes too small, and a loosened tie around his neck.

"Thank you for seeing me, Your Honor."

The judge removes his reading glasses with his left hand and angrily flings them toward the side of his desk. "Cut the shit. I told you to tighten this up, Jacobs. What the fuck is this?"

Reggie steps closer to the mahogany desk, which is strewn with briefs and pleadings. "I know there are a few small gaps, but…"

The judge leans back in the well-worn leather chair. "Small gaps? I would hate to see big gaps!"

Reggie plows forward. "I left out the piece about the odor as you directed. Even without that, there is enough to show probable cause. You have the prior arson conviction, an established history of extreme physical violence, the fight he had with the deceased, which was followed by a threat of future violence just days before the fire, and lastly, no alibi. This passes the smell test. No pun intended."

The judge's exasperation envelops the room. "Jacobs, confirmation of the prior arson conviction arises from a sealed juvenile record you have not formally secured." The judge types a name into his laptop. "As to the prior convictions, this guy was last in prison because he was purportedly protecting a woman in a bar. The warrant mentions his being at an AA meeting until 10:30 the night of the fire, but no alibi after that. I find no specific link between him and the fire. A blind man could drive a Mack truck through the holes in this!"

"Your Honor, the multiple aggravated assault convictions prove violence is not new to him. He was in an altercation with the deceased male a few days prior to the fire, and was overheard saying 'he'd get his.'" Reggie conveniently leaves out that Brian took the beating without any attempt to defend himself.

The judge leans forward, placing his forearms on his desk. "Listen to me. This warrant is razor fucking thin. If I sign this, it is *very* likely it gets kicked, which means anything you find would be ruled as 'fruit of the poisonous tree,' and you will be letting a killer go free… Again."

Ouch… that still stings. "This case involves two deceased adults and two dead children. The prosecutor is on board if you sign the warrant." He crosses his fingers behind his back before making this final statement.

"I don't see it, Jacobs."

A blackness in Reggie's eyes glares across the desk. "Did you *see* your daughter's DUI disappear?"

The judge's face reddens with revulsion as he leans back into his leather chair. "Ah… Now I understand. You're calling in your chit? Sorry, not on this one. I will look like an asshole signing this fabrication."

No turning back now. "Your daughter driving the wrong way on 128 *was not* a fabrication, and I handled that *for you.* No fuss, no muss."

Reggie abused the judge's willingness to do anything to protect his only child to add another chit to the pile he's ruthlessly collected over the years.

The self-disgust on the judge's face as he is likely recounting handing his marker to Reggie all those years ago is obvious. After twenty seconds of painful silence, the intensity in the judge's unblinking eyes falls to the desktop as he growls through pursed lips.

"If it will get you out of my office, and put the chit back in my pocket where it fucking belongs, I will sign this goddamn thing, but only for the car, which your nose says is the key." The judge retrieves his glasses and grabs a pen. He crosses out any reference to the home, then throws the executed warrant across his desk. "Now get the fuck out!"

A smirk spreads across Reggie's face as he retrieves the paperwork from the floor, and a condescending tone springs forth. "Thanks, Your Honor."

A minute later, Reggie slams the flat of his hand on the inside wall of the courthouse elevator. The judge gave him half a loaf for a whole marker. Shit! Getting the judge's daughter out of the DUI took a lot of effort and finesse.

● ● ●

After taking care of things at the station, Reggie navigates the afternoon traffic like the infamous tortoise, taking comfort in knowing who eventually won that race. After a fifty-five-minute drive that should have taken twenty-five, Reggie parks his patrol car in front of an unfinished home and watches McMillan climb down from the roof once again.

19

A tow truck arrives two minutes later as Reggie smugly thrusts the warrant into Brian's hands. "Told you our next conversation would suck. This is a warrant to search your car. The flatbed is here to transport it for processing. Now give me the keys."

Brian goes from being dumbstruck to irate in a nanosecond. A quick glance explains they are looking for evidence connected to the fire that killed Dylan Janssen and his family.

A ridiculous assertion, but he has learned a few life lessons when dealing with law enforcement, most of them the hard way. First, keep your mouth shut. Second, they are going to do whatever they want, and lastly, hitting a police officer is never a good idea.

"I was just about to quit for the day. How am I supposed to get home now?"

"Not my fuckin' problem. Here is a receipt for your car. I will take a bunch of photos and videotape it being loaded onto the flatbed. I don't need you making up shit about us damaging it."

The flatbed operator attempts to rub the odor from his nose after attaching a rusted chain to the front of the vehicle's frame. He holds his T-shirt over his nose and mouth as he reaches through the open driver's window to put the car into neutral. He returns to his truck and begins manipulating levers on the edge of the truck's bed. With the squeaking of steel and clanking of chains, Brian's car is eventually secured to the flatbed.

Brian is clenching and unclenching his fists rhythmically, somehow keeping his arms glued to his sides, but he cannot hold his tongue. "This is fuckin' bullshit and you know it."

The shit-eating grin on Reggie's face exposes a small gap in his front teeth. "See you soon, McMillan. Promise." Reggie gives the tow truck operator a thumbs-up and arrogantly struts back to the curb.

Brian's thoughts race as he watches the vehicles move down the street. The weight of the potential consequences shatters him. He has no idea what he is going to say to his boss, but that doesn't matter. This is going to stick to him like bark to a tree, no matter the outcome. His hopes of successfully completing his probationary period and starting anew have been destroyed.

He digs deep for a positive, finding only one. He was not thrown into the back of Jacobs' car and returned to Walpole. Not yet, anyway. His rage quickly devours the positivity. Brian spins and launches his hammer at the unfinished house, watching it sail cleanly between the studs. He could not do that again if he threw it a hundred more times.

Brian marches into the skeleton structure and retrieves the hammer as a familiar craving engulfs him. Fortunately, his cellphone is in his tool belt, not the car.

He silently recites the Serenity Prayer as he opens the Uber app and requests a ride to the church near his home. Next, he calls the only friendly person in his life and asks himself a simple question: *Why is being innocent so damn hard?*

20

The meeting and his sponsor, who dropped everything to meet him there, helped Brian's anger ebb. He did not share tonight, but some of the weight created by the afternoon's events sloughed from his shoulders, for which he was entirely grateful for his meager support system. Sobriety is his for another day.

The smell of pizza sauce and garlic wafts from the small triangle-shaped box in Brian's hand as he exits Mario's Pizzeria. But before he is three feet down the sidewalk, flashing blue lights blind him—three patrol cars come to a skidding halt against the curb in front of him. Six police officers jump from the vehicles and holler at Brian, using their doors as a shield.

Bystanders use their cellphones to videotape the excitement as subconscious habits kick in and Brian drops to the sidewalk face down, the memory of the prison klaxon ricocheting inside his head.

Reggie is wearing a bulletproof vest with the word *POLICE* emblazoned in reflective yellow. He holds his service weapon in front of him as he races toward a prone Brian. Within seconds, he drives a knee into Brian's back, pinning Brian to the ground as he over-tightens handcuffs on his wrists.

Pain and anger cloud Brian's thoughts. It barely registers as Reggie tells him he is being arrested for arson and the murders of Dylan Janssen, Lily Whitaker, and their two children.

Another officer joins Reggie, and they drag Brian to his feet, recite the Miranda Rights, and perp-walk him toward one of the patrol cars, leaving a slice of steaming pizza on the sidewalk… cheese and pepperoni side down.

Brian knows better, but the gravity of the situation drives him to break rule number one. "Jacobs, I told you I had nothing to do with this."

Reggie pokes the angry bear. "Are you waiving your right to remain silent, McMillan?"

Another officer spins Brian so that his back is facing the car and pushes his head down, guiding him into the back seat.

Brian blurts the only thing that comes to mind. "Fuck you, Jacobs."

21

Single, thirty-nine-year-old Walter Erickson, a certified genius, successfully leads the criminal defense arm of Silverman Erickson. Despite his average build, which some might refer to as a "dad bod," Walt successfully leverages his intellect, charm, and quick wit in both the courtroom and his personal life.

After braving upstate New York winters for their three years at the Syracuse University College of Law and withstanding the enormous pressure of being new associates at large firms in Boston, Walt and his best friend, Jonathan Silverman, rolled the dice, betting on themselves.

In a relatively short period of time, and with the help of some national publicity, they have successfully grown their practice to a point where they can gladly give back to the community.

Walt has qualified as an SJC Pro Bono High Honor Roll Attorney, providing in excess of one hundred hours of pro bono legal services annually. Judges across the Commonwealth appreciate Walt's intelligence and bombastic trial antics when his well-known pragmatism fails. This makes him their first call when they have an unrepresented suspect accused of a significant crime. Arson and murder meet that criteria.

His newest client, Brian McMillan, waddles into the small conference room situated off the courtroom, looking like he is still getting familiar with the restrained ability that comes from double-shackled ankles. Walt wastes no time, starting the moment the door latch clicks shut.

"Good morning, Brian. My name is Walt Erickson. I am a partner at Silverman Erickson, and I have been assigned by the Court to represent you in this matter."

"It ain't no good morning."

Most of those Walt represents stare at the floor. Not Brian.

"Fair enough. I should have asked. Is it okay if I call you Brian?" Walt places the first brick of trust.

"Whatever."

"Feel free to call me Walt. I have taken a quick look at your jacket and know you are familiar with the legal process. As you may know, in murder cases, there is a requirement calling for a mandatory 'not guilty' plea. I will ask for bail, but you should expect it to be rejected by the Court given the severity of the charges."

Walt clears his throat and continues his spiel. "Today's proceeding should be relatively quick. You will then be processed and taken back to MCI – Cedar Junction instead of being held at the Plymouth County Correctional Facility. The prosecution will argue the alleged actions violate the terms of your parole."

Brian looks up in horror. "Bullshit! I ain't violated nothing."

"I will come by later this afternoon to learn more about you, share the information I receive from the prosecution, answer any questions you have, and then we will begin to formulate our plan of action. How does that sound?"

Brian bristles, likely at the prospect of being forcibly returned to the one place he undoubtedly wanted to leave behind forever. "Sounds like bullshit! I ain't done nothing. I ain't no saint, but I ain't got nothing to do with this. I'm sure you heard this a million times, but I'm innocent."

He's right. It is the most common phrase Walt has heard from his clients, but he can count on one hand the number of times it was actually true.

Walt smiles gently as he watches the weight of what is happening crash down on Brian. "Hang in there. We will talk again later today, after I have had a chance to review everything."

22

On the afternoon drive to Walpole, Walt leverages his photographic memory to consider the information the prosecution shared at the arraignment. The thin file of evidence provided to him suggests that the case against his client was put together quickly, which Walt always finds suspicious.

Court-appointed attorneys, like Brian's last attorney, are notorious for being overworked and rarely spending time actually trying cases. Brian trusted his last public defender and paid the price. Walt's first step must be to demonstrate that it will be different this time. He cannot just say the words; his actions must convey that he is an attorney who is committed to his client.

After clearing security at the prison, Walt is led to a room he has been to many times before. Brian's body language tells Walt that it is the first time his client has been handcuffed to a thick metal ring attached to a steel table bolted to the floor. Brian's hands are folded, as if he is praying. The heavy sense of doom is overshadowed by the stale smell of those who have sat there before him.

"How are you holding up, Brian?"

Brian stares at his hands this time. "I shouldn't be here."

"I understand. Why don't we start with you telling me about yourself?"

Brian lifts his head, surprised. "Why?"

"I would like to know whatever you are willing to share. Let's start at the beginning. Where were you born?"

"Brockton Hospital."

"Where did you grow up? Always a Brockton kid?"

"Nah, different places, but all on the South Shore."

"Any family still local?"

"I got a sister in Arkansas, but she don't speak to me no more. My parents died in a car wreck a few years ago."

"I'm sorry to hear that. What about education?"

"Graduated high school… barely. Was learning the roofing business until all this shit." Brian's handcuffs clank against the steel table as he instinctively lifts his hands to motion around the room.

Walt lays another brick before wading into the deep end. "Good for you. Hard to find good tradespeople these days. What can you tell me about your arson conviction?"

Brian falls into a calm rhythm. "It was an accident. Me and some friends went to party in an old barn. A candle got kicked over, and the place went up. The owner was batshit crazy and demanded the person who brought the candles be charged with arson." Brian tilts his head and grimaces. "That was me."

"So you did not purposely set the barn on fire?"

Brian glares at Walt. "Why would I? We were seventeen-year-old kids looking for a place to party. It went bad is all."

Now, onto questions to which Walt already knows the answer. "Okay. What about your aggravated assault convictions?"

"First one was all me. I was in a bar and a guy bumped me, spilling my beer. I wheeled on him and hit him in the face with a beer bottle. No excuse."

Walt is impressed with Brian's personal accountability. "The second?"

Brian remains on the path of candor. "There was a drunk guy pushing this girl around in a bar. She was takin' it at first, but got fed up. She shoved back, and the guy backhanded her, knocking her into a table and splitting her lip. I couldn't watch no more so I jumped in. Next thing I know, he is on the floor unconscious and bleeding, and I am sitting in a chair with my hands cuffed behind my back, watching the girl tell the cops I stuck my nose into her business. They ran my name, and that was that. Spent nine months of an eighteen-month bit here in Walpole… because I had a shitty PD."

Walt does not point out the real reason or react to the attorney comment. "Do you drink anymore?"

"Got sober in prison. Been sober for eighteen months. I go to meetings and work the program." A darkness accompanies the rapid change in Brian's tone. "Was walking home from a meeting when that dickhead Jacobs arrested me."

Walt makes a mental note of the difference in Brian's demeanor. "Okay, what can you tell me about Dylan Janssen?"

"He was a plumber on the Union Point project. We were on the same site sometimes. One time, we got into an argument about where he should park his truck. We were screaming at each other, then he sucker-punched me. I never threw a punch. I don't know nothing else about him."

Walt pokes him to get a reaction. "Except that he's dead, right?"

Brian's remorseful tone gives Walt pause. "Oh… yeah… He's dead. His whole family is dead."

"Did you threaten Dylan?"

"I didn't threaten him. I said 'he'd get his' as I was spitting out my bloody tooth."

Walt is not going to split hairs today. "Okay, let's talk about your car."

Brian scrunches his face, perplexed. "That asshole Jacobs took my car. I had to take Uber to the AA meeting. And I still got no idea what the hell my car's got to do with anything."

"What did Detective Jacobs tell you?"

"Nothing. Handed me the warrant, said he was takin' my car to be processed, and he would see me again. The asshole was laughing about it."

"Where were you the night Dylan and his family were killed?"

Brian is exasperated. "Like I told Jacobs, I was working on a roof 'til it got dark. I stopped at BK for dinner and then headed to the AA meeting at the Episcopal Church. I was home by 10:30 and went straight to bed. I even dug the BK receipt out of the trash and showed it to him."

Walt takes note of the receipt. "Anyone that can vouch for you?"

"Maybe the server at BK, and Calvin, the facilitator at AA, but that's probably it." Walt sees that Brian is pissed, but remains open and credible when answering questions.

"Okay, Brian. Let me take you through what the prosecutor shared with me. We will talk through each point in detail, but I am going to start with the high-level basis for your arrest. You may have heard the phrase 'means, motive, and opportunity.' The prosecution uses these as high-level guardrails in determining whether or not to formally file charges. Let's get the last two out of the way. In short, they are using the fight you had with Dylan, including your threat, as your motive. Dylan beat you, and you wanted revenge. As for opportunity, no one can vouch for you from 10:30 p.m. until 7:30 the next morning. That is plenty of time to set the fire, ditch your clothes, and still get to work on time."

Brian cannot sit still. "Sure, I yelled, but I didn't fight back. I never even lifted my hands. I just took the punches. There is nothing I can do about being alone. I am close to having all my shit behind me. Why would I fuck that up?"

Walt remains factual. "Their argument will be that while you did not fight back at that moment, you were embarrassed and decided to take revenge. To give Dylan his, as it were, and his family got caught in the middle."

Brian sits back, pulling the handcuff chain taut against the metal ring, causing the cuffs to bite into the thin skin on his wrists. A single droplet of blood hits the silver table that is scratched and gouged by years of angst. "That's bullshit."

"I get it. I am telling you what they will say. Not what I believe. As for being alone. We are all alone at times. I am not concerned with that aspect. Now we get to the means."

23

MJ feels a buzzing on her left ass cheek while escorting Snoopy to his favorite dog park, where he leaves a deposit a couple of times per day. She used to take this stroll on autopilot, but never again.

Pulling her phone from the back pocket of her jeans, MJ learns someone has been arrested in the arson/murder case Spagnola wanted her to cover. She stops short upon learning the name of the attorney representing the suspect.

Walt Erickson is the one who first suggested an ingenious but treacherous solution to the problem she and others faced during her Propentus investigation. The group successfully navigated the life-and-death situation, and a lifelong friendship was born. As MJ restarts her journey, she smiles and asks Siri to give Walt a call.

Holding her phone to her ear, MJ waits two rings before Walt picks up.

"Hey! Surprised you still talk to us common folk. Wish I could have seen the look on the faces of the fine folks at Columbia when you snagged your Pulitzer wearing Chuck Taylors and sporting pink streaks in your hair. Tell me you did not wear sweats."

MJ is glad he cannot see her blush. "Fuck you!"

Walt's laughter reverberates through the receiver. "That is the MJ we all know and love! This is not your one free phone call, is it?"

She refuses to let him best her in any verbal exchange. "You would be the last guy I would call if it were."

"Fair enough. What's up?"

"Nothing really. Just learned you are representing Brian McMillan, thought I would call to say hi."

Walt freezes. "Hold on. Are you calling as a friend, or as a crafty and dogged investigative reporter?"

"Calm down, big guy. I saw your name and thought I would call since it has been a while. No hidden agenda. Promise."

"I should have known. A respectable reporter who is looking for a comment does not start a conversation by telling someone to fuck off."

"Jonathan is right, you can be a real asshole."

The grin that must've appeared on Walt's face comes through in his words. "True. What's it like to be famous?"

"Lots of job offers, a few speaking engagements, but now my editor says I have to return to my real job. Starting my search for the next big story."

"You'll find one."

MJ gets playful. "Aww… You still care."

"Of course I do. Ready for that date?"

MJ loves the banter… to a point. "Christ, Erickson, let it go, would you?"

Walt chuckles. "Never. Listen, I have to run. We should get together for a drink. I will bring Jonathan and Emily as chaperones."

"Sounds great! Tell them I said hello. Take care, Erickson."

MJ ends the call and plays her part in the process, using a small plastic bag to collect Snoopy's latest gift while wondering why Walt got so intense when she mentioned the fire.

24

Brian is ashamed. The one place he vowed never to return has once again become his home. Although it has only been thirty-four hours, the prospect of this being his final residence demolishes his spirit.

He spent last evening scowling at the rusted bottom springs of a top bunk, wondering whether it will hold his snoring cellmate's weight, almost hoping it doesn't. In his dire search for a silver lining to this nightmare, he decides that not being assigned to an overworked public defender could be a positive.

It is almost time for the lights to come on, representing the official start of another day in his slow march toward death. Brian's eyes are closed, and a tear slides down his cheek. He knows that being seen crying in prison will lead to an entirely new set of problems, and the moniker that would follow would create unwanted attention. He wipes it away without being obvious and rubs his sore wrist, replaying the discussion with Walt, still struggling to wrap his head around it all.

When they discussed the "means," Walt told him accelerants were found in his car and explained the smell Brian noticed was the combination of two flammable liquids found in or on his car. Walt mentioned kerosene, which Brian quickly explained was something everyone comes into contact with, given the use of portable kerosene space heaters on job sites when it was cold.

Brian pulled harder on the handcuffs, allowing more droplets of blood to fall onto the table when Walt showed him a photo of a work glove sitting in the trunk of his car.

Further still, the police lab matched the chemical makeup of the formalin on the glove to what was used to start the deadly fire.

After gathering himself, Brian identified the glove as one he had lost at a job site within the past couple of weeks, and he vehemently denied placing it in the trunk of his car.

Brian had no idea what formalin was, and after Walt's quick science lesson, the two men searched for possible explanations, but neither could identify any conceivable reason for Brian to come into contact with the hazardous compound.

Brian recounted noticing an odd smell the day after the fire and believing the cause was a bunch of greasy food wrappers, one of which held a half-eaten cheeseburger and another a handful of fuzzy green fries. He still could not shake Walt's distressed expression at the end of their discussion.

Knowing he never put his work gloves into the trunk of his car, a logical question raced through his mind. Walt noticed the inquisitive look on his face and encouraged him to share his thoughts, but Brian remained committed to following the first rule of being a suspect… even if this new attorney seemed to be on his side.

25

Brian is drawn from his depressing thoughts by the loud clanging generated by a baton being dragged back and forth across the steel bars of his cell.

"Let's go, McMillan. Someone wants to see you."

As his cellmate continues to snore unfazed, Brian swings his legs around and sits up with a confused look. He takes his time putting his feet into his slides and standing up, making sure not to ram his forehead into the rail of the top bunk. One scar is enough.

"Who is it?"

A set of handcuffs is swinging around the guard's index finger. "You know the drill, face the wall and walk backwards toward me… slowly."

Brian does as instructed and stares at his distorted reflection in the stainless steel toilet and sink combination at the other end of his tiny home.

The guard leads Brian through a series of dingy hallways, where he finds himself in the same small concrete square where he met with his attorney. His handcuffs are switched to the set strung through the table's metal ring. He notices the blood from his last visit has been cleaned up. After five minutes of solitude, the door scrapes along the floor as it is shoved open by a monster of a man.

"Can't say I am surprised to see you, McMillan."

Brian has a history with this visitor. "Warden."

Warden Samuel Johansson drops his 6'4" frame into the chair opposite Brian. His silver hair is buzzed high and tight, as it has been since his days as a teenage Marine. His precisely tailored suit, matching paisley tie and pocket square, and freshly shined loafers make him look like he belongs on Wall Street, not in a prison meeting room.

"You are not going to be a problem this time."

"No, sir."

Johansson leans forward and whispers, intensity radiating from his steely, grey eyes. "It is a statement, not a question. I would hate to see you get injured in the yard again."

"Understood, sir."

Johansson stands, towering over Brian and wearing a menacing smile. "Welcome back."

26

The drive back to his office flew by. Walt spent the entire trip wrestling to balance the information he had been given by the prosecution and the innocence displayed by his client.

Since reading the damning information from the D.A.'s office, Walt's sole focus has been searching for a rational explanation for the reappearance of a lost glove, as well as the presence of kerosene and formalin in and around the car of a recovering alcoholic who climbs roofs ten to twelve hours a day.

Walt's career has been singularly focused on ensuring the prosecution does their job regardless of his client's innocence or guilt. On paper, it looks like they did, albeit very quickly.

Pushing through his office door and settling in the chair behind his mahogany desk, Walt's thoughts shift without warning, dredging up the surprise call from MJ. He has had a crush on her since the moment she walked into the firm's conference room all those months ago. It has been the topic of many a joke, but the butterflies that take up residency in his stomach each time her name is mentioned suggest it is much more.

His partner and best friend, Jonathan Silverman, knocks on his door casing, then leans against it, watching Walt sitting quietly at his desk with his eyes closed. "Ahem. Am I interrupting your meditation?"

Walt sits up, returning his feet to the floor. "Very funny. It's this new case."

"From the look on your face, I do not need to ask how it is going."

"Prosecution has a solid case from what I can see, but my client is very credible in his pleas of innocence."

"That is nothing new."

Walt's thoughts morph into the sight of Brian gasping at the photo of the formalin-soaked glove sitting in the trunk of his car.

"No, but there is something about this kid that is kicking my acid reflux into high gear. He is open and honest about his past and has taken major steps to get his shit together. He was genuinely surprised to learn what the prosecution found in his car. Either that, or this guy should be in Hollywood collecting golden statuettes."

"What does your gut tell you?" A question the two of them have asked each other for years.

"The jury is still out. But if you pressed me for an answer right now, I would say this guy might actually be innocent. However, I do not know how, given the evidence forwarded by the D.A."

"Wow! A solid maybe. I cannot remember the last time you used the word 'innocent' when referring to a client." Jonathan chuckles lightly.

Walt flips Jonathan the bird. "Yeah, yeah… By the way, your favorite Pulitzer Prize winner called to say hello. I promised drinks with you and Emily as chaperones."

"Sounds great!" A quick wink is followed by a hastier spin to return to his own office. "I will let you set it up, since you have your own agenda."

27

The choir is singing "Ave Maria" as a small group of people awaits the priest's entrance procession. The hard wooden pews echo with the sound of periodic crying and work to defeat the attempted whispering throughout the church.

The priest begins to walk toward the altar, following two neighborhood kids who serve as the altar servers for this Mass. As he blesses the urns before climbing the final steps to the altar, Agnes Rothschild's gentle weeping gives way to a deeply felt sobbing.

Reggie Jacobs slips in at the last minute and sits in the back row on the aisle. He does this for every murder victim, but it is not for religious reasons. He is staring at the back of approximately thirty-five heads, making it all but impossible for him to identify their owner, with one exception. Mrs. Rothschild is sitting ramrod straight in the front pew.

The Mass reaches the point where the priest asks if anyone would like to share a story or say something about Dylan, Lily, or their children. The silence, as heads systematically look left and right, is deafening. After a painful twenty seconds, Mrs. Rothschild rises.

Agnes is dressed in black. The small netted veil on her hat struggles to hide her bloodshot eyes. She attempts to rub the creases from her dress, then lifts the veil shielding her face. A heavy sigh escapes as she steadies herself with one hand, grasping the pew in front of her.

"Most of you refer to me as Savta, but Dylan, Lily, and the kids always referred to me as Mrs. Rothschild despite me telling them a million times not to. One day, I asked why. They said that while calling me Savta was not a bad thing, they had a deep desire to teach their children the meaning of respect, and drove the message home with this small gesture. Besides, you know how stubborn Dylan was."

A needed moment of levity echoes throughout the church.

"This tragic event has stolen the lives of four young, loving people. People who would do anything for a neighbor in need, including sending their son to carry an old lady's groceries whenever they saw me shuffling home from the market. Dylan and Lily were tremendous parents, doing whatever it took to support their children's interests, whether attending dance recitals or sitting in the freezing rain to watch a soccer match. Their love for each other and their children was obvious and unyielding."

Agnes wipes a tear from her eye and brings her brief eulogy to a close: "We will hold these souls in our hearts, as members of the President Street family, for the rest of our lives. They will not be forgotten." She bows her head toward the urns, pulls the veil back over her face, and gracefully sits back down.

The service concludes, and Reggie conscientiously observes each attendee as they exit the church. Some gently place a finger into the holy water and cross themselves. Others chat quietly as they meander out, their obligatory attendance complete.

Agnes shuffles toward the exit, following a person who catches Reggie's eye. The ill-fitting sports coat reveals someone who spends a lot of time at the gym, and likely enjoys the benefits of steroids. The man is walking with his head down, wiping stray tears from his eyes as he somberly steps toward the exit.

Reggie scoffs loud enough for the mourner to hear. "Fuckin' crybaby!"

Agnes' head snaps up as she hears Reggie's remark. The piercing glare from behind the veil sends a clear message, one that Reggie understands but ignores.

Reggie stands to leave once the attendees have departed, angered by the fact that he has yet again wasted an hour of his life.

28

Walt is worried, unsure how to interpret the agita that kept him awake most of last evening. Fearing his gut has misled him, or worse, that he missed something, he races to the office and re-reads the entirety of what the prosecution has provided, a step his memory skills make completely unnecessary.

The prior arson charge, which caused Brian's name to pop up in the first place, is not overly concerning. Yes, it will give the prosecution an opportunity to flaunt the drama of an arson conviction, but the truth is, it was an accident, something with which most can relate upon reflection of their own teenage years. He makes a note to ask his paralegal to locate the other five people in the barn that night.

There is a witness to the fight with Dylan who confirms Brian never threw a punch. This cuts both ways. On the defense side, Brian has learned from his past mistakes and refused to engage in anything more than verbal sparring. Or as the prosecution will argue, he was embarrassed by the beating and took steps to rectify the injustice. Two prior aggravated assault convictions likely tip the scales toward a jury believing the latter, although Walt will not concede the point.

Brian being alone from 10:30 p.m. until he is seen on the job site at 7:30 a.m. is a red herring. Walt has successfully handled this issue a number of times in the past. He will ask every prosecution witness where they were on the night of the fire. Statistically speaking, at least one will have spent the weekday evening alone. Issue neutralized.

The glove is the one thing he cannot reconcile. The prosecution secured a search warrant for Brian's home on the strength of the findings in his vehicle. A team of forensic investigators was breaking down the door to his apartment as Brian was kissing the sidewalk outside Mario's.

While they found no traces of formalin or kerosene in the home, nor on any of his clothes or boots, they found the glove's purported match discarded on the floor in the back of Brian's closet. The police report states, "…the suspect attempted to hide the remaining glove…," a speculation Walt is convinced he can keep out at trial. But he makes a note to better understand Brian's intention behind keeping a lone glove.

Walt paces around the coffee table in his office, the information tumbling in his head, when his secretary buzzes. "Prosecutor's office on line three, Walt."

Walt stops on a dime, mystified, and sprints around to the other side of his desk. A pile of papers scatters across the floor as he searches his desk for a pen and a legal pad. "Erickson."

"Walt, Ginny Giancomo."

Walt knows Virginia "Ginny" Giancomo, who honed her verbal and physical fighting skills growing up in East Boston. She joined the prosecutor's office to bring her personal view of justice to life, immediately after graduating Magna Cum Laude from Boston College Law. She has had plenty of opportunities to go into the private sector and reap the financial benefits of her experience, but her devout sense of right and wrong will not be abandoned.

"Hey, Ginny. What can I do for you today?"

The two spent the past six weeks engaged in a fierce battle that left them both exhausted and scarred. Walt came out the victor this time, but he never gloats. He has been on the losing side before, and it is no fun, particularly when neither you nor anyone else expected such an outcome.

"Calling on the *McMillan* case. We have sent over everything except a handful of lab results that we're still waiting for. I will send those as soon as they come in."

"Thanks." Walt stares at a photo of a quad sculling on the Charles River hanging on the other side of his office, pondering the real purpose of the call.

"Half expected you to call inquiring about a plea agreement after reading the package."

Walt's eyebrows rise as Ginny throws a line into the water. She does nothing by accident. "I was just reviewing everything for a second time, and candidly, I do not see a reason to broach the subject with my client."

"Nice try. We both know you only need to read it once. The case is rock solid, Walt. Your guy had means, motive, and opportunity. Three strikes and you're out."

Walt remains cordial, but the reality of her statement generates warning bells. "Suffice it to say, we do not see it the same way."

Ginny reels in the empty fishing line. "Fair enough. See you in the ring, Walt."

Walt shudders at the thought. He has no interest in becoming her next victim in court, nor of her third-degree black belt in judo.

Walt sits back as the bells in his head are quickly replaced by a voice repeating a simple question: *Why would she bring up the topic of a plea on such a "rock-solid" case?*

29

Brian is convinced the room shrinks between visits. The windowless, grey concrete walls serve as a clear reminder to all exactly where they are. He shuffles in with his orange jumpsuit unbuttoned. The white T-shirt he was given upon arrival is already working hard to match the color of the concrete.

After the now-familiar handcuff protocol, Walt watches the officer leave before speaking. "Good morning, Brian. Sleep any better?"

Brian does not want to admit it, but it is like riding a bike. "I had a dream about the glove in my trunk with the index finger and thumb pointing at me like a gun. Not hard to figure out what that fuckin' means."

"I am sure the dream has any number of meanings. And sleep is a good thing. We need you rested and sharp as we prepare your defense."

Brian slides down the front of the seat, pushing his feet forward under the table as far as the metal ring on the table will allow, resignation dripping from every word. "Whatever."

Walt flips over a sheet of paper on a fresh legal pad. "Okay. We will recap at the start of each meeting to make sure you understand where we are and what is going on. I have reviewed every word of the material forwarded by the D.A.'s office. Twice. You and I have already discussed their anticipated means, motive, and opportunity approaches." He takes a deep breath before proceeding. "I received a call from the prosecutor late yesterday. She mentioned an expectation of my reaching out to discuss a plea agreement. I told her I did not see a need. That said, I have an ethical obligation to make you aware of the conversation."

Confusion bursts through the fog that has taken up permanent residence in Brian's mind. Did the prosecutor really want to talk about a plea? Or is this court-appointed flunky floating the topic to see how he reacts? In the end, it does not matter as Brian's belligerence blasts through.

"That is the right fuckin' answer. I am innocent."

Walt leans forward slightly, lowering his voice. "I am concerned about the gloves, Brian. You allege you lost one, which magically reappears in your trunk, soaked in the same formalin used to set a fire that killed a family of four. The other was tossed on the floor in the back of your closet." Walt takes a calming breath. "Why did you keep the one you did not lose?"

Brian looks down at the table as the redness of shame replaces the pallor on his face. "Money is tight, man. I only got two pairs. I kept going back to search for the one I lost. Now I only got one pair, but I guess that don't fuckin' matter, now."

"We need positivity, Brian."

Brian's emotional rollercoaster bottoms out as the ride continues. "Hard to be positive when the deck is stacked against you."

Walt pivots. "I need to learn everything I can about your gloves. I need to track their every movement. From when you bought them to the day you lost one. For example, did you store them in the same place every night? Where did you place them when you were on a jobsite? Things like that. The gloves are the key at the moment."

Brian shrugs. "I bought them at Home Depot in Rockland. We were doing a job out there."

"How long ago?"

"When I first started working for MAS, about ten months ago. I had to borrow money from a buddy for gloves, a hammer, a tool belt, and boots. I was just out of prison and broke. Paid him back with my first paycheck."

Walt smiles at the pride in Brian's voice. "Okay. Where did you keep them?"

"They could be anywhere on a jobsite. I used 'em when I was handling shingles or lumber. Other than that, I would drop 'em off the roof, or leave 'em somewhere on the site when I wasn't using 'em. But, I always rounded 'em up at the end of the day." Brian can tell Walt's not thrilled with that answer, but he cannot change the truth.

"What about at night?"

"Usually in my house with my tool belt."

Walt keeps scribbling. "Can you remember the day you lost them?"

"We was putting up sheathing. That is the plywood on a roof. We got done with that, and I remember dropping 'em between the rafters of the section we planned to do next. When I got down, one of 'em was gone."

"How long between the drop and getting down?"

"An hour or so. We had to add ice shield to the sheathing we just put down."

A puzzled look appears on Walt's face. "You keep saying 'we.' Who else was there?"

"Kevin Underwood. Another ex-con. He is a decent shit, not a scumbag like Jeremy."

Walt ignores the commentary and captures the new name in his notes. "Anyone else on the jobsite that day?"

"Plumbers, electricians. Guys like that."

"Their names?"

Something clicks for Brian. "Look, if you think somebody is gonna own up to grabbing my glove, or saying they saw who took it, you are wasting your time. Snitches get fuckin' stitches."

Walt acknowledges the familiar phrase. "I got it, but I am still going to ask."

Belligerence returns with a vengeance. "Fine, waste your time. This whole thing is fuckin' bullshit anyway."

"For this to be true, we would have to show someone got hold of your glove, used it for the fire, and then planted it in your trunk."

Brian sits up hastily as his attorney arrives at his own, unspoken conclusion. He places his elbows on the table. The steel ring forces his hands to hang like a praying mantis. Raised eyebrows accompany a silent smirk.

Walt leans back, reacting to Brian's implication. "Is that what you are telling me now, Brian? You are being framed?"

Brian doesn't blink. "You said it, not me."

Walt's head starts swinging back and forth like his mother is trying to feed him Brussels sprouts. "Listen, Brian, I'm a bottom-line guy. You know that bullshit never flies, unless you can unequivocally prove it, which is all but impossible."

Brian remains steadfast, refusing to break eye contact. "I told you, I did not do this, so something fuckin' happened."

"What you're suggesting cannot be proven. But, as the client, it is your call..."

Brian sits back, pleased. "Good, I'm innocent, and it is your job to prove it."

Walt chooses not to correct Brian's misunderstanding of the role he plays. "You did not let me finish. I will do what you want, but I am also obligated to give it to you straight, and right now, the facts are not on our side. You are facing life without the possibility of parole. You are a young guy, so I am wondering if you should reconsider the concept of a plea agreement; it gives you a chance of leaving this place alive."

Anger is the next stop on today's wheel of emotion. "If you ain't on my fuckin' side, I'm going to ask the judge for a new attorney!"

"That is certainly your choice, but if you do that, you will get a PD that is buried in work and does not give a shit about you. I am very good at what I do, and I do give a shit." Walt takes another calming breath. "Listen, just think about it while I chase down a few people, and see what I can learn about your glove?"

Brian remains confrontational. "You better hold up your end."

"Count on it."

Brian watches as a red-faced Walt tries not to slam his legal pads and pens deep into his leather briefcase. He needs to know where his attorney stands, and is inwardly pleased that Walt doubled down.

His entire future rests on those three little words.

30

Ginny snarls before Reggie clears the door casing. "Tell me you looked at someone else."

Reggie raises his arms to defend himself. "Whoa there, hello to you, too. I looked at the landlord. He was behind on the mortgage for two months, but according to TD Bank, he is current on all properties and has been for the past four."

"Anyone else?"

"There was no need. I found a guy with a prior arson conviction, a history of violence, who had a fight with the deceased a few days prior, and no alibi for the night in question. Oh, and he lived on President Street as a kid. That was plenty in my book, so I took it to a judge."

"*Without* discussing it with me!" The vein on Ginny's neck is visibly pulsating as she restrains herself from throwing her "World's Greatest Mom" coffee mug across her office.

A cocky, unshaven Reggie unbuttons his poorly fitting sports coat and flops into a chair. "Relax, counselor. You have plenty for probable cause, and the odor piece isn't even mentioned in the warrant, but it is a bonus. The smell of his car was open and obvious. And let me remind you, I got a judge to sign the warrant. You're solid."

Ginny is ready to leap across the desk to squeeze the nonchalance from Reggie's throat.

"I can hear Erickson already. 'Your honor, Detective Jacobs secured a search warrant by circumventing the process to obtain my client's juvenile record, describing a wretched smell, and twisting a judge's arm. Is that how our justice system is supposed to work?'" Ginny walks from behind her desk and peers down at the disheveled detective, her voice a scratchy whisper. "Listen, you pompous ass, I do not know what you did to get the judge to sign off, but if this warrant gets kicked, everything goes with it, including the glove and lab results. A murderer walks, and that's on you… again."

Reggie smirks as he stands to leave. "I did *my* job, counselor. It is *your* job to make sure it doesn't get kicked."

Ginny closes her eyes, visualizing Jacobs in her dojo, gasping for air as she slams his fat ass to the mat. "Get the fuck out… And you are to do *nothing* on this case without my approval. Understood?"

Ginny's resentment takes control as she watches Reggie arrogantly stroll out of her office. Her plan of getting plenty of media face time during a trial that ends with an arsonist who killed four people, including two young children, going to prison for the rest of his life could go sideways.

She had hoped it would be an amazing entry point for her aspiring political career, but the arrogant bastard who just left her office has put that objective in jeopardy.

31

Lunch is a salad, complete with brown lettuce leaves, one ring of raw onion, and one small tomato… no dressing. The entrée is a slice of cold cheese pizza, which reminds Brian of Mario's, but even that memory cannot overcome the reality of what is sitting on the cracked, red plastic tray he is carrying.

Brian meanders to an unoccupied table, needing space to think about his meeting with Walt. Finding peace in the chaos is never easy.

Every attorney who has represented Brian in the past has told him that innocence has nothing to do with the law. The question is whether or not his attorney can successfully create reasonable doubt.

His problem… How to create doubt about a fuckin' glove someone put into the trunk of his car. He knows Walt is right about the "I was framed" defense. If they cannot solve for the glove, he is going to be eating brown salad and shitty cold pizza on Wednesdays for the rest of his life.

Deep in thought, Brian breaks the cardinal rule. He is not paying attention to his surroundings. A guard walking between the tables positions his baton to push Brian's meal off the table. The maneuver is completed quickly and discreetly, accompanied by a whispered message: "The warden says hello."

Brian's face is as red as his meal tray as he instinctively stands to defend his tasteless lunch. His fellow inmates loudly urge him to get retribution. He knows any action on his part will trigger a number of responses, most of which result in bruises, broken bones, or something much worse. He swallows hard and calmly sits back down as the message he just received brings forth a familiar nausea.

Brian learned a valuable lesson during his last stay at this particular establishment. He had noticed a difference in the timing of and reaction to certain inmate attacks. Most were handled without a sense of urgency, while others were handled quickly and efficiently, as if the officers and medical team knew it was coming.

The injured inmates involved in the instantly handled attacks never returned, while the other victims often did. Brian started asking around to see if other inmates also noticed the trend. The few who entertained his questions refused to discuss it, and everyone else ran from the conversation like a gazelle being chased by a lion.

Brian remembers the day like it was yesterday. The sun was reflecting off the razor wire atop the twenty-foot concrete walls. Four inmates swarmed him as he was enjoying his brief time outside the confines of his personal concrete box. The barrage of punches and kicks coming from every direction forced him into the fetal position on the ground. That day, the guards failed to display the urgency Brian knew they possessed.

It took six sutures to close the cut above his right eye. The cracked ribs took time. The other bruises that covered his body eventually turned yellow and faded.

During his first follow-up examination, instead of gently checking his broken ribs, the doctor pressed on them with all of his weight and whispered. "The warden says hello, and that you should stop asking questions."

With his release date quickly approaching, Brian eagerly embraced the suggestion, imitating a Buddhist monk during the remainder of his stay.

The phrase is a trigger for Brian. While less physically impactful this time, Brian's mental stability wavers as the words do their damage.

32

M J throws another blueberry coffee pod into the Keurig and her jacket into its familiar spot on the floor. She cannot shake Walt's reaction when she mentioned the fire, deciding to glance at the articles written so far. She shoves aside a half-empty pizza box, placing her coffee-filled Yeti in the newly vacated spot on the coffee table. She retrieves her laptop from the industrial safe in her bedroom closet and sits cross-legged on the couch.

After digesting the limited information available online, MJ concludes there is nothing special about the fire. Certainly a tragedy, but the police identified and arrested a suspect quickly. Now, the legal process will ensue at the glacial pace for which it is known.

She Googles Brian McMillan's name, finding more than expected. After bypassing the articles about the fire, she consumes the articles about Brian's prior convictions. Sure, two aggravated assault charges seem to indicate he is quick to anger, but respect is the first word that comes to mind as she learns of Brian's willingness to do what too few are: stepping in to defend a woman being abused. The bar was reportedly full, but Brian was the only one who cared enough to confront the abuser, who apparently left the bar with a concussion, some cuts and bruises, and a clean record.

Anger washes over MJ. The system is clearly broken. How did the abuser go uncharged while Brian is sentenced to eighteen months in prison for protecting a stranger?

She will never understand the mindset of a woman who moves to protect the person abusing them. Over the years, she has read plenty of police reports generated after a domestic call. Women who are bleeding and broken, physically attacking the officers as they move to arrest the person who inflicted their pain.

God help anyone stupid enough to lay an unwanted hand on her.

MJ begins to think about the fire differently. What drove someone who was willing to risk returning to prison to defend a woman he did not know to commit such a heinous crime?

The Brockton fire articles lack detail, but allude to a conflict-filled relationship with the man killed in the fire. The prior aggravated assault charges and his prison time are prominently discussed, but the positive aspects of the last incident have been omitted. Every article paints Brian as a vindictive, violent man.

No one has looked at the incongruence. Maybe there is an angle there, after all? At a minimum, she can throw Spagnola a bone and spend time with a friend, all while continuing her search for a much more meaningful story.

33

After a lengthy wait, it is finally Brian's turn to use one of the eight ancient pay phones bolted to the concrete wall of a narrow hallway used solely for this purpose. Each inmate gets fifteen minutes to have a discreet conversation, while standing five feet from another inmate whispering on the adjacent phone.

Beyond his sponsor, Walt is the only person Brian can call. His sister refuses to accept collect calls from prison, something he learned last time. He dials Walt's cellphone number and waits for the automated process to ask Walt if he will accept the charges for a call from MCI – Cedar Junction.

"What's up, Brian?"

Brian speaks softly, but urgently. "I forgot to tell you something when you was here before."

"What is that?"

Brian's voice crackles with fear as his head swivels, watching everyone. He cups his hand around the receiver and repeats a phrase that has echoed in this hallway thousands of times before. "Not on the phone."

"Is it about your case?"

"It's important."

"Okay, I can be back there in a couple of hours."

"Good."

With a modicum of relief, Brian moves to hang up the phone when the giant next to him drops his handset and shoves his thickly muscled left forearm under Brian's chin, slamming the back of his head against the concrete wall. Leaning in close with the breath of someone who hasn't brushed his teeth in days, the beast completes the task for which he was hired.

The guards arrive within seconds, pulling the stranger off Brian, who is holding his jaw, and checking for blood coming from the back of his head. The inmates waiting for their turn to use the phone howl with taunts of encouragement.

A prison fight is the only exciting event most of them will see for a long time to come.

34

Brian is taken to the infirmary to address the purple bloom spreading across his chin and throat. He moves his jaw side-to-side with his free hand. It hurts and it's tight, but it doesn't feel broken… and he is alive.

After numbing the pain with an ice pack for ninety minutes, Brian is notified that his attorney is there to see him. A correctional officer whose muscles make his uniform appear to be two sizes too small stands inches from him as he struggles to put the top half of his orange jumpsuit back on using only one hand.

The handcuff attaching him to the hospital bed is switched to his other hand, allowing him to put the previously restrained arm through the corresponding sleeve by repeating the same body contortions. The cuffs are then transitioned to both hands, and his feet are shackled for the trip to the miserable, windowless room of despair.

Once handcuffed to the table, Brian immediately leans forward as far as his restraints will allow. Walt mimics the move, listening to a panicky whisper.

"I am in serious fuckin' trouble, man."

Walt keeps his skepticism to himself. "Why? Did you do something?"

"I got dragged down here to meet with the warden. A CO knocked my tray off the table at lunch, and a member of the Dead Presidents crushed me against the wall between phones after I hung up today. They each told me 'the warden says hello' and warned me to keep my mouth shut."

Puzzlement contorts Walt's face. "Shut for what reason?"

After a cursory look around, Brian sits back in his seat. "Last time I was here, I noticed something. I asked a couple of guys if they saw anything and ended up catching a beating. Six stitches above my right eye, a few cracked ribs, and my body beat to shit. The doc in the infirmary pushed on my ribs when no one was looking and said 'The warden says hello, and to keep your mouth shut.' I was real close to getting out, so I said nothing 'bout nothing to nobody. I was a fuckin' mute."

Brian fights to use his shoulder to wipe away a few beads of sweat traveling down his right temple. "The day I ended up back here, Johansson dragged me into a room like this and told me to fly right. Then I got the other warnings. Each time, I was told, 'The warden says hello.' I am telling you, this is fuckin' bad. I ain't gonna get out of here alive, man."

Walt shakes his head, looking like he is trying to make sense of what he has just heard. He leans forward until he reaches the center of the table and waits for Brian to return to the pose of the day. "Are you telling me you have been threatened? If so, I can take steps to get you transferred into ad seg."

Brian again looks side to side, then at the camera with the small, blinking red light that's enclosed in a steel screen box and attached to the corner of the ceiling. The handcuff chain looped through the metal ring clangs against the table with each of Brian's agitated movements. "They ain't never said that. But it don't fuckin' matter, it's what they mean. They are showing they can get to me anywhere, at any time."

"Brian, anything you tell me is protected. I cannot tell anyone. I will take it to my grave. Okay?" It is Walt's turn to instinctively look left and right. "What do they think you know?"

The confusion on Walt's face exacerbates Brian's worries. "That's the thing. I don't know nothing. I thought

I noticed something. I asked about it, then all hell broke loose. I swear."

Walt leans in close enough to smell Brian's fear. "Okay, what did you notice?"

Brian winces, the pain in his jaw worsening as he clenches his teeth. "I noticed when some inmates get jumped, the guards and doctors are there in a New York fuckin' minute. Others, they take their sweet-ass time. None of the ones who got pulled out fast ever come back."

Walt scratches the side of his head. "None of them?"

"Nope."

"Do you know the names of any of the inmates who did not come back?"

"I heard a couple of names, but I don't know nothing. They just think I do. They're gonna kill me over something I don't even know. I'm fucked!" Brian lunges backward, the chain pulling taut against the scab on his right wrist.

Walt takes control. "Here is what we're going to do. First, you tell me any names you can remember. Second, I helped the father of one of the guards here. I will get word to him to keep an eye out for you. In the meantime, you are going to be the most compliant inmate they have ever seen. Got it?"

On the downward portion of two acknowledging nods, Brian whispers two names, "José LaCampo. Tommy Anderson."

"Okay. Remember, I will work to get you into administrative segregation if that is what you want."

Brian transitions to horizontal head movement, adamant on this point. "No. It will make shit worse."

Walt begrudgingly agrees. "You are the boss, but say the word and I am on it."

35

Traffic inchworm is the name of the game as the vision of a petrified Brian remains at the forefront of Walt's thoughts. He is pondering his unexpected emotional connection with the terrified kid handcuffed to a steel table, accused of murder, and fearing for his life, when the bleat of a car horn startles him. It is his turn to move forward… eight feet.

The welfare of his newest client is being threatened for an undisclosed reason, but in a way that makes intent clear. Walt was stunned to hear the warden had commanded Brian to meet with him within hours of his reintroduction to the prison. Then, to have that discussion followed by two separate attacks, presumably to emphasize the gravity of the initial warning and the capacity to deliver, goes well beyond troublesome. The intensity of the threat level seems extreme for something every prisoner likely knows: inmates were attacked and never returned.

As traffic begins to break up, Walt finds a solution that will allow him to focus on the journey of the mysterious formalin-soaked work glove while also digging into what Brian shared. He asks Siri to place a call.

"Hey there! I think I'm going to call you PPW instead of MJ. What do you think?" Walt loves his own jokes.

No laughter. "You do so at your own peril."

"You find a new story yet?"

"Maybe. I have been evaluating a new angle on the fire you are involved in while drinking cheap cabernet sauvignon from a box and enjoying cold pepperoni pizza. I am confident you hoity-toity, self-taught sommeliers would approve of my pairing."

Walt refuses to contain his vile reaction. "You are fucking killing me! Please let me take you to a nice restaurant and introduce you to Plumpjack, Chimney Rock, or something from Nickel and Nickel. You *must* stay away from the swill you get from a box."

MJ laughs for several seconds, the mirth coming through in her voice. "I like my swill. Besides, they will not let me wear sweatpants in any of those fancy places. Now, are you going to tell me why you called?"

Walt finds MJ's laughter infectious. "Consider it a standing offer." Walt's tone changes to match the topic. "Listen, I have to walk carefully here, but I think I have something I can throw your way without violating privilege. It may be nothing, but I do not have the time to chase it down, and since you have nothing going on…"

MJ jumps on him as he inhales. "That is no way to seek the assistance of a PPW, Attorney Erickson."

"I am much more polite when I have a hearty California cab sitting between me and my date. Since you said no, and I am driving at the moment, you get what you get." More of the Erickson wit.

"Yeah, yeah… let's hear it." The sounds of MJ's fingers tapping on her laptop carry through the receiver.

"Like I said, I have to be careful. But it is my understanding that two inmates, José LaCampo and Tommy Anderson, were both residents at the state-run facility in Walpole. Each was attacked and, within seconds, infirmary personnel removed them from the scene. Neither returned to the facility."

"That is your big story? Seriously? Who is fucking killing who?"

Walt allows the intensity in his tone to deliver an unspoken message. "I am not done. This is where it gets tricky. There are other inmates who were attacked and not so quickly cared for. Majority of those returned to gen pop after a period of convalescence."

There is a curiosity in MJ's voice. "So, you are implying inmates get treated differently?"

"I am not implying anything. I am stating facts as I know them. It is a delicate situation that needs to remain between us for the time being."

Walt desperately wants to spill it all, including the various warnings Brian's received, but cannot. He referenced violating privilege, which signals the source of this information. "That is all I can say. Any interest in looking into those two gentlemen?"

"Way ahead of you, Counselor… as usual."

Walt smiles to himself, knowing the intrigue would trigger an interest. "Of course you are. Remember the standing offer. Talk soon, Fernandez."

Walt is almost back in the office, confident that MJ has already done one of the things she does best: read between the lines.

36

Snoopy climbs onto the sofa and snuggles up to MJ's right thigh. He is asleep within seconds, the familiar clacking of the keyboard his version of white noise. MJ looks down at the only being who has shared her living space for more than a night.

Her work is everything, but the harrowing investigation, which brought her a Pulitzer Prize, coupled with the realization that more than a third of her life is over, has her re-evaluating everything. She smiles at Snoopy and undertakes a methodical review of the articles generated by her initial search.

At the age of thirty-two, José LaCampo was sentenced to twenty years in prison after pleading guilty to manslaughter in connection with the death of a seventy-eight-year-old woman caught in the crossfire of a gang-related shootout. A witness brave enough to come forward relied upon José's distinctive Dead Presidents neck tattoo to confirm his presence at the scene.

MJ did the math in her head. Despite agreeing to the maximum sentence for first-degree manslaughter, the plea would have made it possible for him to get out of prison before turning fifty, but he never got the chance.

José was killed in prison three years into his sentence. Reports indicate LaCampo was shanked by a rival gang member, the grandson of the woman he killed. All was quiet for years, until an ill-fated lunch where the kid delivered on his pledge for vengeance. The obituary was short, but reflective of a mother's unwavering love.

MJ jostles Snoopy as she gets off the couch to stretch and grab an energy drink. Two hours of research have given her nothing. A gang member being killed in prison by a rival gang is far from earth-shattering news, particularly at Walpole.

Upon returning from her lunchtime stroll with Snoopy, MJ asks Spotify to play Miles Davis's *Bitches Brew* and returns to her ergonomically incorrect, crossed-legged position on the couch, which creates the desk upon which her laptop has rested for years.

After striking out with José LaCampo, she enters Tommy Anderson's name into the search bar, hoping the results will provide the few droplets of detail she knows will eventually cascade into a waterfall of consequential information.

Tommy is a twenty-seven-year-old from Newburyport serving ten years for armed robbery. He stuck a handgun into the face of a local jeweler who had taken over the family business after retiring from the Navy. The former SEAL did not hesitate. Tommy was pinned, face down, in less than a second. The surveillance video highlighting the impressive display went viral.

A few more key strokes and she locates an article detailing the tragedy that made Tommy an orphan at age thirteen. A familiar pang twists MJ's gut, empathy only another foster kid possesses.

Articles in *The Daily News* citing Tommy's academic and athletic success while attending Newburyport High School paint a compelling picture. Throughout his four years, Tommy's name appears frequently on the Honor Roll listing, in addition to being the topic of articles that highlight his acumen as the star halfback on the school's soccer team. She also finds a photo of him as a member of the homecoming court in his senior year.

Despite a significant investment of time, she finds nothing for the period between his high school days and his imprisonment for armed robbery. Further, she is unable to find an obituary.

MJ stretches her neck, pondering Tommy Anderson's life cycle. He suffered the tragic loss of his parents, became a foster care success story turned unexplained felon, and has now become a disappearing enigma.

MJ heads to the refrigerator and grabs the familiar box to add a glass of pinot gris to her investigative efforts. Before she can take a sip, she is interrupted by the ringing of the little bell near the bottom of the front door.

She grabs the leash, a few poop bags, and the pepper spray she added to this ritual a few months ago. Snoopy begins his "I gotta go" dance as she finishes putting on a pair of Chucks and contemplating which takeout place to hit on the way home.

The new information tumbles like clothes in a dryer as MJ descends the front steps onto the sidewalk. Snoopy drags her to the left as is his practice.

Fresh air clears her head and often sees the tumbling become insight, but not today.

37

The silence associated with seventy-five inmates eating lukewarm oatmeal and drinking cold coffee is deafening. The scraping of plastic sporks on red pre-formed plastic food trays is the only sound.

Long-established groups sit at the tables they have claimed over the years. The other members of their cadre protect group leaders with the same commitment that the Secret Service demonstrates for the President. No one dares approach another group's "territory" without a previously negotiated agreement. To do so is a declaration of war.

Brian sits at a table that some call the "Land of Misfit Toys." Guys like him are few and far between. If not already affiliated when they enter prison, most seek security from one of the established factions. He does not belong to a gang, nor has he ever sought their protection. Being alone in prison is dangerous, but a couple of the long-timers know he has put more than one man in the hospital with his bare hands. A reputation as a brawler provides his sole measure of protection.

He eats his breakfast in silence, anxiety crippling his thoughts. What does the warden think he knows? What is it about young guys getting jumped and receiving medical attention almost before the first drop of blood hits the floor?

After choking down the tasteless gruel, Brian is one of many being escorted back to their cells when a skirmish breaks out behind him. He immediately spins on the balls of his feet, pressing his back against the scarred cinder block wall, gaining the ability to see any oncoming threat. He silently releases a sigh of relief when he realizes he is not today's target.

The prison grapevine has been carrying the likelihood of an attack because an Irishman from Southie mouthed off to a "made guy" from the North End, while both were lifting weights.

The guards avoid an all-out rumble, but the damage is done. The end of a toothbrush, sharpened against a cell wall in the dark of the night, is stuck deeply into the ribs of the loudmouth. Only the bristles remain visible. The guards jump in quickly and yell for the medical team, who hurriedly haul the bleeding inmate away.

As his heart rate returns to its normal level of anxiety, Brian continues following the yellow line on the floor guiding him toward his cell, his left hand moving subconsciously to rub the area of his healed ribs.

Curiosity gets the best of him once Brian is safely sitting on his bunk. Coupled with a lifelong unwillingness to take direction, another thing upon which he and his sponsor have been working, Brian walks back out of his cell and begins to quietly ask around to identify today's victim.

38

Every sunrise provides a new opportunity to unearth more pieces of a puzzle. After a quick coffee, MJ only finds more disappointment, uncovering a digital desert for Tommy between the ages of seventeen and his unsuccessful attempt to relieve a jeweler of his money and wares ten years later.

After a couple of glasses of wine last night, MJ realized she had discounted José LaCampo too quickly. She took the obituary and news reports at face value and let it drop—a rookie mistake. After hitting the roadblock with Tommy, MJ moves to correct the error.

She re-enters José's name into the search engine. The articles and records she has already saved are reviewed again with a different eye. Digging into José's life reveals his Lawrence, MA, upbringing. In contrast to Tommy's photo-filled Instagram account from his teenage years, José's digital footprint is cluttered with police blotter entries, articles about his various arrests, and his membership in the Dead Presidents. MJ closes her eyes and considers the dichotomy.

We all start out the same way: covered in slime and being slapped on the ass. From there, the individual journey of each person winds its way through time. Opportunity makes a huge difference in the direction some take, but it is not always determinative. Genetics also greatly influences a person's path. When both are combined with the millions of decisions and choices made along the way, an individual's life is as unique as their fingerprints.

With José and Tommy sharing the same final address, the twenty-five miles between the tough neighborhoods of

Lawrence and the ocean view environs of Newburyport have MJ contemplating the "nature vs. nurture" debate.

After a quick trip to the dog park, MJ spends the next few hours adding the foundational information she has collected to Tommy's and José's dossiers while working to identify gaps that will need to be filled in. She has no answers, but the questions multiply exponentially. There is no obvious connection between the two beyond their Walpole residency. The entirety of Jose's story seems to be well-documented, but the end of Tommy's remains elusive.

She climbs off the couch and stretches before heading to the bathroom for a long-overdue shower. The hot water brings with it a simple question: How does someone disappear from a maximum-security prison?

Then it hits her.

39

Walt grapples with the key piece of evidence that holds his client's future in the balance. Brian confirmed that the glove is the one he lost a few days before the fire. But is it? Walt has already confirmed that particular brand and style are the most popular in the country.

Walt looks to the sky for guidance. "It is all about the glove."

Jonathan sits stoically in the uncomfortable chair in front of Walt's desk, watching as his partner verbally solves the problem, something they have done together for years.

Walt drops his head and turns his attention to his favorite sounding board. "Attacking the veracity of the glove is the only chance I have to keep Brian from celebrating all future birthdays in prison."

Jonathan leans forward. "As I see it, there are three angles of attack: scientifically, legally, and appealing to the jury's common sense, although you and I both know common sense is not generally a jury's strength."

"Agreed, so it is the science and the law." Walt shifts in his seat and stares at Jonathan. "There is no DNA analysis of the inside of the glove within the prosecution's materials. If it is not one of the reports that remain outstanding, I will be forced to make a risk-filled decision."

Jonathan nods his head, encouraging his partner to continue exploring his thoughts out loud.

With trepidation, Walt bows his head and lowers his tone. "If I request the analysis and Brian's DNA is inside the glove, I have added another nail to his coffin."

Before continuing, Walt spins his seat to face his desk and jots down his thoughts on a legal pad. He makes a notation aside that dangerous consideration to ensure he has the inside of the glove tested for the presence of nitrile or latex, *if* he decides to go down that path.

Jonathan plays devil's advocate. "Didn't you say the prosecution has already forwarded the results confirming the chemical composition of the formalin found on the exterior of the glove as being identical to what was identified at the scene?"

"Yes, but this is about the *inside* of the glove. If they haven't gone that far, I can spin the missing testing like a top, but if I make a motion to do the testing and the only DNA inside the glove is Brian's, that top becomes an F5 tornado that will demolish his rebuilt life."

Jonathan watches his usually calm and collected friend allow frustration to cloud his thoughts. He shifts in his seat before redirecting the conversation.

"Let's talk about the second angle. If you can successfully challenge the warrants using the Fourth Amendment and get them disqualified, particularly the warrant for Brian's vehicle. Anything flowing from them, including the glove and the warrant for his home, is no longer admissible, toppling the prosecution's case."

Walt nods knowingly as he stands and twists his torso, his vertebrae snapping as he stretches.

"The bottom line: No glove. No worries." Walt writes the phrase on a Post-it and sticks it to the top of his computer screen.

He may tattoo it on his ass if he can pull this off.

40

The call is placed at the designated time, not a second before nor a second after. Punctuality speaks to a person's character and commitment, although years of training have drilled into him that being on time means you are late.

No need for small talk. "Is the operation complete?"

"The transfer has been processed, so yes, absent another snafu." He wants his partner to know he is still pissed about the mess that has been created.

The tweak is ignored. "On to different matters. The new order is a challenge."

He buries his immediate reaction. "Given the resources at your disposal, the statistics say you can deliver."

"Frequency is also a concern. Timeline?"

"We are currently on the clock."

He feels the redness spreading through his closely cropped hair. "I remind you, strategic selection and acquisition have to be cleverly executed."

"I do not need fucking excuses. I need you to do your goddamn job."

His back stiffens. "Understood."

"I await your call… in the *very near* future."

The call takes less than a minute. Neither man will speak of this again, confident the other will do exactly what is required. They have built a very lucrative business, but as with many things in life, time has become their number one enemy.

41

Running for sixty minutes on the treadmill at the gym downstairs is Ginny's way to relax and let her mind contemplate bigger things. The AirPods in her ears vibrate with songs from her "Marathon" playlist. It is filled with high-energy music, which motivated her to maintain her pace as she ran last year's Boston Marathon. She finished in under three and a half hours, a personal best.

Sweat drips from the strands of hair that have found their way from under her sopping wet Celtics cap. She dries the perspiration from her face with a towel and retrieves the cleaning spray and a few paper towels. As she wipes down the treadmill for the next user, a single thought is stuck on repeat.

After a quick shower, Ginny heads back to her office, where she will spend the remainder of the day focused on the one thing that has kept her from sleeping soundly: Reggie Jacobs.

Ginny re-reviews the entire *McMillan* file. She envies Walt's memory skills, though she will never admit it. She is looking for every hole that Walt might use to attack the authorization of the warrants, and focuses on the warrant for the car. The warrant for the home that followed is solid, having been predicated upon the finding of a formalin-soaked glove in the vehicle.

Much to her dismay, Ginny is finding a new angle she would attack every time she reviews the information. At one point, she silently vows to discontinue the exercise, irrationally hoping any issues she has yet to identify will magically vanish. To absolve herself of such a foolish thought, she starts at page one… again.

Her first concern is Brian's arson conviction as a juvenile. She has obtained the sealed records through a court order, which is how Reggie should have. Getting past his skipping this step will be tricky, but not impossible, as the arson conviction is confirmed. However, she quickly notes that Jacobs conveniently omitted the property owner's unyielding demand for retribution. Walt might concede a misdemeanor trespass charge, but he will have a field day with the accidental nature of the fire and the less-than-mediocre effort of Brian's public defender.

On the other hand, the argument and fight with Dylan prior to the fire is pure gold, even if he did not throw a punch. Brian's prior convictions prove he has an anger management problem fueled by a short fuse. She will take great pleasure in putting a bur under his saddle and letting nature take its course, should Walt be unable to keep him from testifying.

She anticipates Walt to play the "good guy" card on the most recent assault, but the counter is simple. He did not have to beat the guy senseless to help the girl. He could have sat in his seat, dialed a 3-digit number, and achieved the desired outcome.

Lastly, the lack of a solid alibi between 10:30 p.m. and 7:30 a.m. is the same as Schrödinger's cat thought experiment. She has dealt with the issue many times, knowing jurors will hold the lack of a confirmed alibi in abeyance, making it the last piece of their deliberation.

She is also fully cognizant of the unspoken expectation for the types of evidence juries see on the police dramas they stream each night. She is confident the lab results will satisfy their investigative appetite. If they embrace the means and motive arguments, they generally use the defendant's lack of an alibi as the final nail in the conviction coffin.

Ginny tosses her pen onto a pile of papers on her desk, agonizing over the corner into which Jacobs' bullshit has thrust her. She renews her private wish for Walt to seek a plea. Unfortunately, history has taught her that the depth of this desire is inversely proportional to the chances of it occurring.

42

MJ ends the shower almost before it begins. She barely dries off before grabbing something to wear and racing back into the living room, where she flops onto the couch and urges her fingers to fly across the keyboard of her laptop.

First, MJ enters José's name into VINELink, a database operated by the Commonwealth of Massachusetts designed to help someone locate a prisoner within the Department of Corrections. The online record reflects that he died in the facility, and his file was closed.

Undeterred she enters Tommy's name, and the shit hits the fan. Tommy's current location is listed as MCI – Cedar Junction.

She leaps up and begins talking to herself while pacing around her small living room in mismatched socks. Her sweats are rolled up to her knees, and her Newport Jazz Festival t-shirt hangs comfortably from her shoulders. Snoopy gives up after watching her mumble for a dozen laps.

She cannot wait another second and dials the phone.

"Holy shit, Erickson, you will not believe it…"

Walt responds cautiously. "Believe what?"

MJ jumps to the punchline. "Tommy Anderson is listed in VINELink as being at Walpole." MJ never pulls punches. She didn't the first time she met Walt, and is not about to start now. "I need to ask your source a few questions myself."

Walt's reaction confirms her belief. "What the hell are you talking about?"

MJ shakes her head. "Keep up! Tommy Anderson was sentenced and sent to Walpole. Your source says he was attacked and never returned, but…"

"The system says he is still there! Holy shit!" Walt's mind sprints to a different conclusion. "It could be a simple data entry error."

MJ's excitement will not be deterred. "We can't discount that possibility. To be sure, I need direct access to your source."

Walt's hesitation is momentary. "I have not mentioned this to anyone but you. To give you what you seek requires the faith of an individual whose trust I do not yet have. I'm not sure he will give it the stamp of approval."

MJ turns the screws. "There is something funky happening, and I need more information. When is the next time you will speak with him?"

"Within the next twenty-four hours."

"Good. Call me after your meeting."

"Okay. So about dinner…"

MJ's cheeks betray her. Thankfully, Walt isn't there to see the reaction. "You are nothing if not persistent. Talk soon, Erickson."

MJ tosses her phone onto the couch as she restarts her tiny laps.

43

Walt pulls his tie loose while sitting in traffic. He is bracing for the heart-to-heart he is about to have with Brian. Often this happens much later in the process, when clients are more receptive to the hard truth. He is not yet there with Brian. Walt has kept the message simple thus far. Things are bad, and he needs every available moment if he is going to identify a solution that keeps Brian from spending the remainder of his life in prison.

As the three lanes of traffic slog forward, Walt silently repeats his new mantra, "No glove. No worries." He breaks today's significant needs into two sizeable but manageable chunks.

For today's visit, Walt is escorted to a different, yet identical, meeting room. The same yearly painted grey concrete, and the same scuffed steel table with a set of handcuffs snaked through a heavy steel ring in the center. The only noticeable variation is the lack of rust on the handcuff ring.

Brian shuffles in looking pale, gaunt, and defeated. The orange jumpsuit hangs more freely, reconfirming everything Walt has heard about the quality of prison food. The circles under Brian's eyes are dark, almost prompting Walt to ask if he was attacked again. After being shackled to the table, Brian flops down, immediately slouching in his chair. His hands are on the tabletop with fingers interlaced, reminding Walt of the pose for which he was scolded every Sunday morning as a child.

"How are you, Brian?"

"How the fuck you think?" There is no anger in the flat response, only resignation.

"Truthfully, you look like you could use a burger." Walt hopes levity will make Brian more open to today's assignment.

"Food sucks. I can barely choke down the shit they give us. Guys call it the 'Walpole Diet.'"

"Prisons are not known for their cuisine." Time to get down to business. "We have a lot of work to do today."

"Whatever."

No time left for niceties. "I am going to give it to you straight. I will never lie, nor sugarcoat anything. Brutal honesty may be the last thing you want, but it is what you need and deserve, so that is what you will get."

"I am fucked."

Walt refuses to openly acknowledge his arrival at the same likely conclusion. "Things do not look good at the moment, but we are a long way from the finish line. I need you to remain positive."

"I wanna fight, but they set me up good. The longer I am in this fuckin' place, the more I know I ain't never getting out."

"We need to take this one step at a time. The first step is for me to capture every detail you can remember about your movements from the day you lost your glove until you noticed the smell in your car. You talk, I write."

"Seriously?"

"Seriously. Details win trials, and I am convinced you know the details that matter. We need to capture them before they fade into the ether."

"The what?"

Walt reminds himself to play to his audience. "Sorry. Fade into the air."

"I already told you about the glove."

Walt takes solace in the stated desire to fight. "Let's start from when you woke up that morning, and go moment by moment until we reach the first time you noticed the odor in your car."

"Okay, but that is a lot of shit." Brian is shifting in his seat.

"Perfect. I like shit."

44

A fter an hour, Walt's sleeves are rolled up, and he has filled half a fresh legal pad. Brian has never been more talkative. He is fully engaged, but Brian was right: most of it is shit.

Walt lets him drop into the first couple of rabbit holes to maintain momentum, but now gently guides him away from any new ones that appear.

"So, me and Kevin were told to put down sheathing and ice shield on the house on Lot 17. It is a huge fuckin' house. Six dormers, crazy twelve over twelve pitch. Anyways, we put down some plywood and wanted to put the ice shield down before we moved to the next section, since we were already tied off. I took off my gloves and threw 'em through a few rafters of the section we was moving to next, like I always do. Then..."

"Brian... sorry. You are doing great! I have a couple of questions. Okay?"

"Sure."

The cross-examination begins. "Did you see the gloves hit the ground?"

"No."

"How long after you threw the gloves did you come off the roof?"

"A couple of hours, maybe. The roof was tricky with the dormers and shit."

"Did you pick up the gloves as soon as you got down?"

"No, I needed to take a leak. Then I went looking for 'em because we were going to do the plywood on the next section."

"What did you do after finding just one?"

"I walked around, figured the wind might have caught it or something."

"Who else was on the site?"

"There is always different trades floating in and out."

"Do you remember who was there?"

"I think the electrician was there in the morning. Plumbers showed up later in the day. I also saw a guy from the gas company."

"Was the electrician there when you dropped your gloves?"

Brian stares at the ceiling. "Uh… No, I dropped 'em after lunch."

"What about the plumbers?"

"Maybe? Can't remember when they showed up."

"Gas company guy?"

"He was there around the same time as the plumbers. They were probably working on the gas line."

"Did you recognize the people on site?"

"Sort of. You see the same faces."

"Do you have any names? Anybody stick out?"

"No. Just know faces. Everybody is bustin' ass to get shit done."

"Last question. Did you ask anybody about the glove?"

"No. I looked around a couple of more times that day. I figured a glove ain't important to nobody but me."

Walt is pleased that Brian has not shied away from the rapid-fire questions. He takes a moment to check his notes before proceeding to the next line of questioning. "Okay. I am going to shift gears. Can you remember everywhere your car was located between that day and the day you noticed the smell? I also need to know if anyone else had access to, or used, your car."

"I don't let nobody use my car. My car's only ever at a few places. I don't go nowhere. There is the street in front of my apartment, different job sites in Union Point, a couple of places where I go to AA, and that is about it."

"Okay, do you remember what day of the week you noticed the smell?"

"A Wednesday, I think."

"How many days passed between losing the glove and the car smelling?"

"I remember being pissed I lost the glove on a Monday. It was the first day of the week, and we had a lot of work to do. That would be…" Brian looks down at the table and silently counts the days on his fingers. "… Nine days."

"And no one drove your car during that time?"

"I already told you, nobody drives my car but me."

"Anybody have access to the keys?"

"I keep 'em in my pocket or the glass dish on the counter near my front door."

"Okay, I will need the locations of the AA meetings you attended during those nine days. And you are saying other than that, it was either parked on the street in front of your apartment, or at a jobsite, right?"

"Yup. I go to meetings at First Evangelical in Brockton. I ain't gone to no other meetings in a while, so that would be the only AA spot."

Walt moves to close out this round of questions. "What can you tell me about the smell?"

Brian scrunches his face. "I thought it was a bunch of old fast food bags I forgot were in the back seat. It was kind of gross. There was a moldy, half-eaten burger and some fuzzy green fries mixed in. I put everything in the trash and left the windows down the whole day, but it didn't help none."

Walt forces a smile. "Okay. That is good for today. I have a lot to digest. You did a great job!"

Brian impulsively looks around, like he's searching for anyone who might be listening. "I got a question."

"Sure."

Brian's voice changes to a whisper as he leans in. "Anything about those two guys?"

Walt matches the conspiratorial posture and tone. "I have an investigator looking into them." Walt swallows hard. "She believes she will find more if she speaks with you directly."

Brian flies back as far as the handcuffs will allow. Whispering be damned. "What the fuck, man! I thought you wasn't going to talk about me."

Walt uses his calmest voice. "I didn't. I asked for her help in finding out about the two guys. I never told her where I got the names."

Brian is still pissed. "Should I?"

"Should you what? Talk with her? She is convinced she would find out more if she had a chance to speak with you, but it is up to you."

The shaky, whispering voice returns. "I'm tryin' to get another name."

Walt is surprised by this statement. He strikes a careful balance. "We talked about this. You need to keep your head down."

"It's okay. I'm being wicked careful."

"Listen, I cannot control what you do, but you have to be *very* cautious in here. Remember the three warnings."

Brian ignores Walt's admonition. "I will talk to her."

Walt nods his head. "Okay, I will see if she is available tomorrow."

Walt jumps up to leave before Brian changes his mind. "Stay positive. You did great today. I will be back tomorrow morning. Your homework is to remember everything you can from the morning you noticed the smell until Jacobs served the warrant. Okay?"

Walt slams the side of his fist on the door twice. He turns back toward his flustered client as the steel door scrapes along the well-established groove in the concrete floor. "I know this sucks, but we will figure it out."

A guard walks in and places the shackles and handcuffs on Brian. Walking behind them, escorted by a guard of his own, Walt watches Brian shuffle down the corridor, likely heading to dinner. He hopes it will be something palatable.

45

After another restless night, MJ rummages around her bedroom, searching for something to match what she has pulled from the closet. Her outfit must send a comforting yet inviting message. She needs to put the source at ease if she is going to identify the critical strings that will unravel this ball of mystery.

She settles on a pair of khakis, a dark blue silk blouse, and the only blazer she owns. A dusty pair of black flats, yanked from the back of her closet, complete the look. They will have to accept her hair as is.

If hitting no traffic on the way to the prison is an omen, today is going to be a magnificent day. MJ goes through the screening protocol and waits for Walt, who walks in a few minutes later.

He hands MJ a blueberry coffee from Dunks with a gleaming smile on his face. "Gooood morning."

MJ is annoyed with her cheeks' betrayal. "Thanks. Surprised you remembered."

Walt smirks. "Even if I didn't have an amazing memory, I remember everything about you."

Their names are called, and a Correctional Officer approaches before MJ can deliver one of her trademark snarky responses.

They are led through the maze of identical-looking hallways. MJ is surprised by the dullness of the atmosphere. She knows prisons are not theme parks, but an eerie feeling of despair belies the colorful, well-manicured grounds outside.

"Morning, Brian. This is MJ Fernandez, the investigator I told you about."

MJ instinctively reaches out to shake his hand. Embarrassed, she quickly drops it back to her side. "Nice to meet you, Brian."

"Yeah." The defeated detainee is back.

Walt tries to revive the talkative Brian. "Did you do your homework?"

"I didn't go nowhere, so…"

"Brian, as an investigator for my office, Ms. Fernandez is bound by the same privilege I am. She cannot say anything about what she hears today."

Brian glances at MJ and shrugs his shoulders. "Whatever."

"MJ will ask a few questions after we finish what we started yesterday. Let's start with where you went after work the day you noticed the smell."

MJ sits in the corner of the room, imagining two detectives playing good cop, bad cop, but is shaken from the vision upon hearing the word "smell." Her chair scrapes against the floor as she readjusts herself and begins consuming every word like it is her last meal.

"I went home, like usual. I didn't go nowhere but work and home. I usually go to AA on Friday nights, but that asshole Jacobs took my car Thursday afternoon. Fucker left me stranded and laughed about it."

Walt needs to keep Brian on task. "Okay, so nowhere but work and home Wednesday and Thursday. Did you park your car on the street Wednesday night?"

"Yes."

"You talked to Detective Jacobs on Wednesday, right?"

"Yeah, he asked me about the fight with Dylan."

"Is that when he noticed the smell?"

"Yeah. He said it was not fast food bags and that he would be back."

"How did he know it was not the trash causing the smell?"

Brian shrugs his shoulders. "I dunno."

"Okay, then he came back on Thursday?"

"Yeah, I was starting to pack up for the day when he showed up with a tow truck. Fucker slammed the warrant in my hand and giggled. The tow truck guy put my car on the flatbed and left. Dickhead videoed it and took some pictures on his phone. I had to use Uber. I was so pissed, I called my sponsor and had the driver drop me off at a meeting."

Walt's eyebrow raises at the mention of the video and photos. "Sounds like Detective Jacobs should have handled the situation differently."

MJ can see the anger oozing from Brian's pores and is impressed with Walt's ability to navigate Brian's emotional rollercoaster.

"He is a fuckin' asshole. I told him I didn't have nothing to do with that fire. He just kept laughing."

"He arrested you that night."

Brian's voice is anything but soft at this point. "I went to grab a slice after the meeting. Three cop cars come flying up as I was walking out of Mario's. Asshole Jacobs pressed his knee into my back, it was hard to breathe as he put the cuffs on. He said I was going where I belonged, then told the other cops the beers were on him."

MJ has never met Jacobs, but if Brian's description is remotely accurate, she has heard enough, quickly agreeing with Brian's assessment of the detective.

"Okay, Brian. I'm going to switch seats so MJ can ask you a few questions."

MJ walks five feet, sliding to her left, and Walt moves to his left to stand in the corner where MJ was sitting. He chooses to lean against the wall.

"Hello, Brian. I am here to ask you questions about Tommy Anderson and José LaCampo."

Brian springs forward with the speed of a cobra. He looks around and clenches his teeth as his whisper erupts. "Don't say their fuckin' names out loud!"

The movement catches MJ by surprise. The back legs of the chair bite into the concrete as she instinctively lurches backward in response. Walt's quick reaction prevents the back of her head from becoming a little flatter. After re-settling herself, she starts again. "Sorry, Brian. What can you tell me about the men you mentioned to Walt?"

"They got shanked and never came back. Saw Tommy get it. Watched his face as the warden pinned him to the ground."

MJ recalls Walt's direction to be gentle. "Please tell me about the warden."

"He is a fuckin' hard ass. Everyone's scared of him." A quick look around and another drop in volume. "He threatened me since I been back."

MJ fights to keep her look neutral. "You said he was there when Tommy was attacked?"

"Yeah, a fight broke out, and someone stuck Tommy. The warden came outta nowhere. He whispered something in Tommy's ear, and Tommy got real scared. I saw it on his face. Then guards rushed Tommy out, while the COs were takin' the rest of us back to our cells."

She has to ask. "Who shanked Tommy?"

Tommy looks at the ceiling. "Don't know."

MJ ignores the obvious lie. "Okay, back to the warden for a second. Why did he threaten you?"

Brian's head's on a swivel, as if the 10'x12' room is filled with people. "He thinks I know something… but I don't."

MJ suspects she's getting close to something. "What does he think you know?"

"I told you, I don't know anything."

Walt gives Brian a gentle nudge. "It is okay, Brian. Tell her what you told me."

The shaking of Brian's hands creates a rhythmic beat as the chain from his handcuffs strikes the metal table. He stares at Walt, who nods with encouragement. A whispering voice breaks the silence.

"When I was here last time, I noticed guys getting attacked and never coming back. Guards moved quicker for those guys. I started asking around, then got jumped in the yard. Fuckin' guards moved slow as shit that day." Brian points to the scar on his right eye. "Got this, a lot of bruises, and a few broken ribs. Then the prison doc delivered a message while pushing on my busted ribs. Told me, 'The warden says hello and to stop asking questions.' I was close to getting out, so I shut the fuck up after that."

MJ leans forward with excitement and a million questions, but her time is limited. "Okay, what about José?"

"Happened a couple of days after I got here. Didn't see it; just heard about it after. Word is it was another gang member. José shot his gramma or something."

"What about the warden?"

"With José? Nothing I know of." Brian looks around, then quickly blurts out a name. "Chicky O'Malley."

MJ pauses and looks over at Walt, uncertain of what she heard. "'Dicky O'Malley'?"

Brian's annoyance is obvious. "Chicky… like chicken."

"Chicky got a first name?"

Brian rolls his eyes. "Chicky."

"What about him?"

Brian's head is on a swivel. "He took a toothbrush to the side the other day. Got carried out quick, like the others."

"Okay, Brian. Anything else?"

Brian leans forward, shaking his head slowly from side to side. "You ain't gonna say nothin' to no one, right? Walt said you can't."

MJ sees and smells his angst. She holds up her right hand. "I swear."

Brian slumps back into the chair. His t-shirt is soaked in nervousness. MJ watches him close his eyes and wonders what is going through his head.

Is it relief for sharing what he has observed? Or dread for what comes next?

• • •

Walt and MJ wordlessly retrace their steps through the drab corridors as they are escorted to the exit. The echo of their footsteps bouncing off the concrete and the clanking of each steel door they pass through is the only sound.

MJ is unsure of what just occurred, but is confident Brian's life will be over if the wrong person finds out he has spoken with her.

Walt walks MJ to her car. "You want to grab a late lunch somewhere to debrief?"

MJ is starving, but passes. "I have to get home and walk Snoopy. I'm hoping I don't find a pile of his frustration on my carpet."

MJ sees Walt working desperately to hide his disappointment. "Got it. No problem. Let's connect later, or in the morning. There is a lot to unpack here, but something is not right. I can feel it."

MJ leans her back against her car door, gazing at Walt. "If the guards do respond differently, the warden must know, right?"

"Probably. On the positive side, Brian is solid on his story about the Tommy Anderson incident and the taking of his car. He told me the exact same things the first time. It does not help the search, but it makes me more convinced his story is legit."

MJ uses the phrase that saved their lives in the past. "Always trust your gut, right?" Now the hard part. "I have a ton of new leads. Give me time to sort through them. I will give you a call when I find something. Okay?" She watches the rejection cut Walt to the bone.

Walt's smile fades. "Sounds good. Happy hunting."

After climbing into her car and waving goodbye to Walt, MJ is subjected to the traffic gods' revenge for their morning failures. She prioritizes things in her mind as she moves a few feet every minute or so. She wants to dig into the warden and Reggie Jacobs, but must find out who the hell Chicky O'Malley is first.

After the brutal two and a half hour trip, MJ finds a beagle who is extremely happy to see her. She grabs the leash and the other usual items. She can barely keep up with the eager dog dragging her toward the elevator.

Standing in the dog park, MJ's mind is flooded by the tidal wave of information dumped into her lap today. The four corners from which to start working on this new puzzle remain elusive. She tugs on the leash to encourage Snoopy to pick a spot. He finishes his business, and then it is his turn to keep up, as her burning desire to find the first corner piece is quickly becoming an inferno.

46

The look of gleeful surprise on Ginny's face twists her mouth into a huge smile when her assistant tells her Walt is on the line. She grounds herself by taking off her heels and sitting at her desk, feet flat on the floor.

"Hey, Walt. What can I do for you today?"

"Morning, Ginny. I am looking for the discovery left out of the three packages we have received on the *McMillan* case."

Ginny's experience tells her to proceed with caution. She senses Walt's restraint. "Left out? I told you there are a handful of lab tests that take a little time. Otherwise, you have everything we have."

"Have you spoken with Detective Jacobs?"

Her initial excitement dives off the cliff. The mention of the reckless detective creates heart-pounding anxiety as the hair on the back of her neck stands up. Ginny closes her eyes and asks herself the same question she has been forced to ask too many times before. *What the fuck did that idiot do now?*

She dips her toe into the uncertain waters. "Yes, he and I have met a few times about this case. Why do you ask?"

"If you have not asked him directly, I believe it prudent for you to inquire whether he has given you everything he has on the *McMillan* case."

Ginny refuses to let her angst bleed through or take her off message. "Like I said, I have spoken with him a few times. I am confident he has provided my office with everything he has."

She has zero confidence when it comes to Jacobs, the subject of many fifty-minute sessions with her therapist, but will not give Walt an opening.

Walt lets out a sigh. "Ginny, you and I have battled before, and will again. I play to win and I play hard, but I play fair. You need to ask him. And you owe me."

The sincerity in Walt's tone strikes a chord. "Thanks, Walt."

The call ends as Ginny takes her fury out on the first thing she can grab.

As it shatters against the wall, she yells to her assistant. "Please get me a new mouse, and get Detective Jacobs in here… NOW!"

47

MJ stands and stretches to reach an abandoned wine glass. After consuming a gulp of warm white wine, she begins her familiar pacing. Round and round, as she works to absorb what she has learned in the past four hours. She knows it happens this way. One question begets ten.

Charles "Chicky" O'Malley is a thirty-four-year-old Irishman from Southie. Through court records and newspaper articles, she learned that Chicky is no one with whom to trifle. He has been in prison more than he has been out. He is currently serving a twenty-year sentence for bribery and attempted murder after being approached by an unfaithful local banker who asked Chicky to ensure his wife never makes it home.

When Chicky found out his new employer had access to hundreds of thousands of dollars every day, greed followed, and Chicky overplayed his hand.

After three $10,000 payments, the banker realized what was happening. He went to the police with a concocted story of extortion, expecting to be hailed as a hero. Despite his valiant efforts, the banker found himself earning a new residence for the next seven to ten years, while his ex-wife enjoyed a quiet life with her new fiancé.

MJ leverages her vast network and learns that Chicky had not been admitted to any hospital in Massachusetts, at least not under his given name. There is a chance he is somewhere under an alias, but the sources she has cultivated over the years are smart enough to know if they have admitted or treated a patient with the head of a toothbrush sticking out of the bloody side of his orange jumpsuit.

She saves the last search request for last. VINELink lists Chicky as being at MCI – Cedar Junction, but that may be because this particular incident is fresh, whereas Tommy's is not. Her sixth sense tells her it does not matter.

Misplacing one inmate is hard to imagine, but the odds of losing track of two, both of whom were shanked at the same prison, would send even the most talented statistician over the edge. The thought brings MJ's twisted sense of excitement roaring to the surface, and despite being asked multiple times, Snoopy refuses to tell her if there are more, and if so, how many.

After updating her Chicky O'Malley dossier, she pulls on the MCI – Cedar Junction string, quickly learning the facility is scheduled to be closed in the next eighteen to twenty-four months as part of the statewide initiative to reduce the inmate population. She ponders whether the prison's high rate of inmate-on-inmate violence, one of the highest in the country, played a role in this decision.

Next is Samuel Johansson.

Articles confirm he was appointed warden five years ago after his predecessor died in an automobile accident. After joining the Marines at eighteen and serving his country honorably for twenty-seven years, he wanted to get into law enforcement. Eventually, he found his way into Corrections, where the skills he developed during his tenure with the Marines could be fully leveraged.

Correctional officers give orders, follow orders, and fight the enemy daily—a perfect fit.

His no-nonsense reputation dominates most articles written about him. But the exposé written after his appointment tells a different story. It details his well-known desire to be elevated to the position of warden, along with a willingness to do whatever it took to get there.

The unnamed sources were plentiful and eager to share all they knew. Each of them confirmed Johansson's preferred method of delivering a message to an inmate: violence. His personnel file reportedly contains numerous complaints from inmates, which stalled his career at the position of assistant warden. That is, until one of the Commonwealth's maximum-security prisons became a war zone.

A source confirmed Johansson leveraged his knowledge of the facility's forthcoming fate to swing for the fences. Johansson pledged to deliver the discipline and control required to deter inmate violence, and most importantly, keep the prison in Walpole off the front page of *The Boston Globe*. In exchange for the appointment, Johansson agreed to step away quietly when the facility was shuttered, approximately two years before he would maximize his retirement benefits.

Once leadership within the Department of Corrections had the Governor publicly breathing down their necks, and with no one else eager to captain a sinking ship, they held their noses and struck the deal.

A follow-up article written a year later confirmed Johansson's initial success. Inmate-on-inmate violence plummeted upon his arrival, but the honeymoon period ended quickly. The months following his appointment eventually saw the attacks begin to climb again, but they plateaued at a level below their historic peak, allowing everyone to declare victory.

MJ stops in her tracks, asking Snoopy a different question. "How does a detail-oriented man who spent his entire life focused on discipline lose two inmates?"

After receiving another disappointing response, she calls the only other person who will appreciate her newfound excitement.

48

Most nights, Walt begins the evening sitting at the bar of one of his favorite restaurants, enjoying an expensive glass of red wine and surveying the crowd in search of someone to join him for dinner and potentially a nightcap at his place. Not tonight. He sat in silence at a table in the back of the restaurant where he enjoyed a medium rare ribeye, paired with a nice Bordeaux, as the conversation with Brian played over and over in his mind.

Now, as he sits at home enjoying a 2013 Duckhorn Merlot before bed, he allows another vision to take control of his thoughts. Walt has been captivated by MJ since their first meeting in his firm's conference room. They were thrust into an untenable situation, which led to a mutually assured destruction-based partnership with the highest-ranking Italian from the North End. That life and death battle left behind an unbreakable bond. A bond Walt would love to explore further.

MJ is extremely smart, beautiful, funny, and tough as nails. She is relentless in her fight for the truth and the underdog. She refuses to shy away from peril even when it puts her life at risk. Some might say she covets dangerous situations. In short, she is remarkable.

They joust with innuendo, but much to his dismay, she has kept him at arm's length, and he fears pushing the boundaries will jeopardize one of the two friendships he holds most dear.

With his last sip of wine, he questions the role his reputation as someone who favors fast cars and faster women plays in MJ's posture. He revisits the benefits of a lifestyle change when a familiar ringtone echoes throughout the room.

His heart skips a beat as a kaleidoscope of butterflies awakens in his stomach. He looks around, as if to ensure everything is perfectly placed. Suddenly, fear takes hold. No one calls at this hour with good news.

He answers the call, working overtime to keep the panic from his voice. "Hey there, everything okay?"

There is a momentary hesitation. "Oh, shit. I lost track of time. Did I wake you? I'm sorry."

The calm from the lack of bad news is quickly replaced by the return of fluttering butterflies. "No, it is all good. I was just having a glass of wine and thinking about our meeting with Brian."

Walt can practically feel her excitement grow with every word. "That is what I wanted to tell you. I found some crazy shit. No idea where it leads, but there is definitely something fucked up going on at the prison."

Walt pours himself another glass of wine and returns to a well-worn leather chair with a matching ottoman. He puts his feet up and listens intently for the next thirty minutes, without interrupting. He finally asks the one question silently bouncing between them.

"So… Johansson?"

MJ takes a breath before answering. "He sounds like a sadistic piece of shit. Takes joy, and probably pride, in their pain."

Walt nods to himself while taking a sip of wine. "I meant beyond him being a grade-A asshole."

"I am not sure, but someone who has a track record for severe treatment of prisoners, has lived a highly disciplined life since his time in the Marines, and is now running a prison where inmates whose current whereabouts do not match state databases makes the hair on the back of my neck stand up."

Walt shakes off the image of MJ's soft, supple neck. "Agreed."

He fights the urge to invite her to his home in the middle of the night, eventually agreeing to sleep on the information and meet for breakfast the next day.

After Walt places the empty wine glass in the sink, he races to his bedroom like a child on Christmas Eve.

49

Walt catches himself staring at MJ. She is wearing a sweatshirt from the 2018 World Series, a pair of black leggings, and her trademark Chuck Taylors. She looks like she just stepped off the Boston University campus, and he is mesmerized.

He stands quickly as she plops into the seat across from him. After the disappointment of learning there is no blueberry flavored coffee, there is only small talk until the speedy delivery of their orders.

With a mouthful of pancake, MJ offers a new thought. "Maybe you have been thinking about this wrong. If you accept the premise that Brian was set up, you should be asking why and by whom. And, why someone wanted Dylan Janssen and his family dead."

A small drop of syrup in the corner of MJ's mouth is Walt's sole focus. "Wait, what?"

"Dude, pay attention. I said, while I am off chasing ghosts, you have a client to worry about. If you think Brian is innocent, spending time figuring out why someone would kill Janssen and his family and frame him makes sense."

"I have been focusing on the glove. The fucking detective is playing games. If I can prove it, Brian has a chance. No glove. No worries." He smiles proudly at his creativity.

MJ's shaking head says it before she speaks. "Cut the shit, you are not representing OJ. What do you know about the victims?"

A chastised Walt refocuses. "Only what is in the papers, and the information from the prosecutor."

"I am gonna find those two guys, and figure out what the hell is going on at the prison, but I can also look into Dylan and his wife if you want."

He mentally flips through the pages he has read. "Lily Whitaker is not Dylan's wife. They were the parents of the two kids, but they were not married."

"Okay, but you did not answer the question. Do you want help looking into why someone wanted one or both of them dead?"

Another page flip, and Walt spills his coffee, almost jumping out of the booth. "Holy shit! Lily Whitaker worked at the prison. She was Johansson's administrative assistant."

If he has heard it once, he has heard it a million times from MJ: *There are no coincidences.*

"Christ, Erickson, where was this yesterday? I thought your memory was better than that. Lily just moved to the top of the research list."

Excitement morphs into protective instincts. "Listen, your 'bull in a china shop' approach almost got us killed last time."

"Yeah, yeah… I know. But, unless Jimmy Rizzo decides he wants to meet your federal friends, I will be fine."

Walt refuses to break eye contact. "I am serious, MJ. No fucking around. I do not need your name added to the list of the missing."

In a rare moment of emotion, MJ grabs her coffee mug to hide her inability to speak. She gulps down the rest of the steaming liquid and slides quickly out of the booth. "Got it. I will let you know what I find. Thanks for breakfast!"

Walt enjoys the view as she leaves. The caring he has kept bottled up for months periodically bleeds through without warning. He grabs his coffee cup and chuckles to himself.

She didn't tell him to shut the fuck up. That's a positive sign, right?

50

Reggie walks into Ginny's office in a crumpled beige colored suit. A dingy yellow tie is hanging around his shoulders, waiting for its eventual end state. He dodged her last evening, but her message made it clear he was to be in her office at 8:30 a.m. sharp. It's 8:42. Ginny is well aware of Reggie's issues with authority, especially women in authority, so his bullshit stunt isn't entirely surprising. She has been behind her desk since 6:30, still chewing on the fury that stole her sleep. "You are late."

"What can I do for you, counselor?"

Ginny keeps her bare feet solidly planted in an effort to control her ire. "I am going to ask you a question… once. If I find out you have lied to me, I will have your badge and your pension. Are we clear?"

Reggie bristles. "I always tell you the truth."

Ginny refuses to blink. "Have you given me everything you have related to the *McMillan* case?"

Reggie pauses to reflect. The words struggle to escape, but when they do, they seem to be dripping with regret. "Shit…" He pulls his phone from his inside jacket pocket. "I have a few pictures and a video I took when we seized the car. Wanted to make sure he could not accuse us of damaging it in the process. I forgot, sorry." He immediately emails them to Ginny.

She cannot decide whether his surprised look is real or an act. "Forget anything else?"

Reggie looks down like a chastised schoolboy. "No."

"You, your actions, and now your shitty memory have put this entire fucking case in jeopardy. I got a call from the defense asking if we had sent everything. I swore we had. Then it was suggested I double-check with you specifically. You made me look fucking stupid!"

"I'm sor—"

Venomous spittle lands on her desk. "Shut the fuck up! Sorry doesn't help. This is unacceptable. Your Captain is my next call."

"What can I…"

"I said shut the fuck up! I have to figure out how to clean up your mess… again!" Ginny stabs her index finger towards her door. "Get out of my office!"

Ginny watches Reggie skulk away as she opens the email, anticipating the worst.

51

After taking Snoopy for his pre-dinner jaunt, MJ grabs her favorite sweats from the Bermuda Triangle on her bedroom floor—the area between the clean pile, the dirty pile, and her bed. She steps into them after giving them a quick sniff and not being completely offended. They are well-worn and have a few obscenely placed holes, which is the reason she only wears them in front of Snoopy. She would refer to them as "lucky sweats" if she believed in such a thing.

MJ settles in for a long night. After starting *Brilliant Corners* by Thelonius Monk as tonight's background music, she follows her gut, looking into Lily Whitaker first.

She learns more about a person stalking their social media accounts than she does with traditional internet searches. She is amazed by people's willingness to expose their entire lives to the world. Her hacker friends only needed to explain the perils of such an approach once.

Lily was a beautiful thirty-five-year-old with scarlet red hair and hazel eyes who graduated from Abington High. No college. She adored her children. Everything MJ finds includes a picture of one or both of her kids. She may not have had a lot of money, but if the number of photos and different locations are any indication, Lily refused to let her children feel it.

Lily's Instagram account includes a photo of her smiling behind the bar at a place called Jazzie's. The date of the picture overlaps with her time as an administrative assistant. Despite the pressures of holding down two jobs while raising two kids, MJ feels the joy radiate from her smile. She imagines what it must have felt like to be in Lily's presence, immediately pledging to have a drink at Jazzie's in her honor.

MJ moves on to Dylan, finding little via social media, but there was plenty to be found. Dylan was thirty-seven years old with a criminal record. He found trouble after graduating from Randolph High. He was convicted of a few petty crimes in his late teens and early twenties but never spent more than a few nights behind bars. After the age of twenty-five, he set himself upon a better path.

According to the stories about the fire, Dylan and Lily had moved into the triple-decker a couple of years prior to that fateful night. Neighbors who were interviewed sang their praises. One woman in particular, Mrs. Agnes Rothschild, talked glowingly of the two as caring human beings and as parents.

MJ is thinking about the horrific way these people lost their lives when she notices tears are sliding down her cheeks.

Her knees are tight after sitting on the couch with her legs under her for almost four hours. She unfolds herself, reminded of the Tin Man in *The Wizard of Oz*... before the oil. For a moment, she wonders what her knees will feel like when she is sixty.

Banishing the thought, MJ retrieves her trusty Post-it notes. She writes a name on each and sticks them to the wall in her apartment, which has seen her through more than one investigation, as the numerous tiny pinpricks can attest.

She adds pushpins to each Post-it and places a piece of neon green string between the names to signify a known relationship. Thirty minutes of effort reflects what she already knew: The one with the most connections is Warden Samuel Johansson, including Lily, Brian, Tommy, José, and Chicky.

Despite her recent efforts, MJ has no idea what happened to the missing inmates. While Lily has been added as a possible target, there is still nothing to explain why Brian was selected as the patsy. It may be time to call in reinforcements.

MJ peers at her phone. It's only 9 p.m., and three energy drinks have done their job. After a couple of laps around the coffee table fail to burn off her frustration, she decides to make good on her pledge.

52

MJ stands at the entrance and allows the atmosphere to wash over her.

Jazzie's is a "shot and a beer" joint. The bar is a gnarled slab of oak that holds deep the thousands of secrets that have passed above it. A lone female bartender, wearing nothing beneath her leather vest, is pacing back and forth behind the bar, occasionally pulling a Bud Light from a cooler and handing it to one of the many patrons enjoying the company of their friends.

MJ squeezes between two small groups, eventually standing at the bar. As the bartender approaches, MJ's pulse quickens.

"What can I get you?"

MJ notices an odd look on the bartender's face. "Patron Anejo neat, please."

The petite brunette returns a minute later, smiling and placing the drink in front of MJ. "One and done, or do you want to start a tab?"

"I'll start a tab." MJ pulls a credit card from the small sleeve on the back of her cellphone and hands it to the bartender, who studies the name on the card intently while walking away.

After clutching her drink, MJ spins and leans her back against the bar, taking in the scene as the tequila's warmth spreads from head to toe. There is a good-natured trash-talking event, complete with flying twenty-dollar bills, at the pool table. There are tables situated throughout. Some are overflowing with people sitting in chairs stolen from an adjacent table. The country music is just loud enough to be heard over the din of the crowd.

MJ remembers Hank Williams, Charlie Pride, Loretta Lynn, and others from her youth, convinced they are rolling in their graves at what some call country music today.

From the corner of her eye, MJ watches the bartender, who is standing at the far end of the bar, scrolling through her phone and occasionally looking back at her. The bartender's stealth is lacking as she strolls back toward MJ, offering refills as she goes. She gets to MJ and stops abruptly. Her head quickly bounces left and right as she leans across the bar. "You're her, right?"

MJ leans over so they can converse below Mitchell Tenpenny's *Truth About You*. "Her who?"

"The famous reporter."

"I do not know about famous, but I am a reporter." She extends a hand across the bar. "MJ Fernandez."

"Wow, I ain't met nobody famous before! I recognized your picture from the paper. I got a thing for faces."

A warm smile appears on MJ's face. "I'm sure that comes in handy in your line of work."

The bartender's shoulders relax as she laughs and offers a hand in return. "Katie."

"Nice to meet you, Katie." MJ hears someone yelling. "Looks like you have a customer."

Katie glances over and scowls. "That's Joey. He is a pain in the ass."

Katie returns to her primary responsibilities. A number of others shouted out her name and their order, suggesting to MJ that Katie had worked behind this bar for a long time.

MJ spins back around, pleased by her stroke of luck in stumbling upon the other woman in the photo she found earlier. She closes her eyes and silently toasts Lily and her family as she throws back the rest of her tequila.

She is lost in thought as a guy wearing an Eversource Gas Company shirt accidentally knocks into her as he squeezes up to the bar to order a Bud Light. He tips his beer in her direction.

"Sorry."

They exchange smiles as MJ returns to her primary objective, formulating a strategy that does not come across like she is looking for something more from Katie than a cup of coffee and a chat.

53

"Ginny Giancomo on line 3, Walt."

Walt has anxiously awaited this call. He knows the photos and videos are there, but he has no idea whether they contain anything of value. "Good morning, Ginny."

Ginny's tone is reflective and appreciative. "Morning, Walt. I double-checked, and it appears some photos and a video were inadvertently omitted from the disclosures. They depict your client's vehicle as we executed the search warrant and took possession. I have certified copies being messengered over as we speak. I apologize for any confusion."

"Thanks, Ginny. I will take a look."

"Walt, I will deny saying this, but we both know he is an asshole. His reaction was either genuine or Academy Award-worthy."

"There is nothing genuine about him. I appreciate you following up. Anything exciting in there?"

"I am positive you will be calling once you have reviewed it all."

As Walt is hanging up the phone, his assistant knocks on the door, holding a package. "This was just messengered over from the D.A.'s office."

Walt chuckles. "When she said 'as we speak,' I guess she meant it. Thanks."

He reaches across his desk and opens the small package. A flash drive sits atop a small pile of photos. The photos show various angles of the vehicle as it was sitting at the construction site. In addition to the views from each corner, there is a photo of the license plate and the VIN number, along with four close-ups of the front and rear seats.

Walt plugs the flash drive into his laptop and plays the ten-minute video. He plays it with the sound off initially. He wants to take in the scene without distraction. He watches the tow truck operator reacting to the smell of the vehicle and handling everything while wearing light blue nitrile gloves. The end of the video shows Brian standing in the driveway with a piece of paper clenched in his right fist. The look in Brian's eyes will send a shiver up any juror's spine.

After watching a couple of times with no sound, Walt does the opposite. The sound of song birds is overtaken by the clanking of the metal hook connected to the car's frame. Next is the slow grinding of the winch as it pulls the car onto the flatbed. Lastly, there is the sound of the tow truck groaning as the driver returns to his seat.

There is very little spoken, but the tone in Jacobs' voice is one of pure joy as he tells Brian he will be back. Once again, Brian was accurate with his description.

After watching the video with full sound a few times, Walt writes a single question on the legal pad in front of him: *Jacobs looked under the car and into every window, but never in the trunk. Why?*

54

It took less than three seconds for MJ to convince Walt to join her for a late breakfast. She told him about Katie and the significant insight she gained from her discussion, but refused to provide details over the phone.

Thanks to Snoopy, she is running late. Another of her top five pet peeves. As she is pulling her ponytail through the back of a Red Sox cap, a disturbing image flashes across the television. The morning news is being shot from a pond near DW Field Park in Brockton, where a morning jogger found the battered body of a young, adult female.

Early in her career, MJ covered stories involving unspeakable acts. She knows well the depravity our world endures. She offers a silent prayer, locks her apartment door, and races to her favorite diner.

Walt is reading the paper and enjoying a cup of coffee when MJ comes flying through the door. Always a gentleman, he stands as she approaches the table.

"Morning… I ordered you a blueberry coffee. Must be why you picked this place."

MJ smiles and throws her jacket across the back of her chair. "Thanks." After ordering an egg-white omelet with spinach, tomato, and onion, MJ leans slightly forward. "I have a lot to tell you."

Walt folds the paper neatly and places it next to a napkin-wrapped fork and knife, and sips his coffee. "Shoot."

"I went to a bar called Jazzie's last night. My goal was to check the place out and see if I could find someone who may have known Lily or Dylan. A woman I noticed from a couple of Lily's posts on Instagram was behind the bar. Her name is

Katie Nichols. She happened to recognize me and we started talking. I convinced her to let me buy her breakfast after the bar closed."

MJ and Walt maintain the habit of vigilance they developed the last time they worked together. Their eyes constantly roam back and forth, watching everything and everyone as their conversation continues.

MJ recoils at the heat of her coffee. "We went to this little dive in Brockton. The pancakes were amazing! Anyway, I told her I was doing a story about the fire and asked her what she could tell me about Lily. She rambled, between bites of eggs, bacon, and pancakes, for nearly thirty minutes. The long and the short of it is this… Lily was worried about something at the prison."

Walt wipes crème cheese from his tie while chewing on a chunk of a bagel. "What?"

"Katie did not know. She said Lily was 'wicked fuckin' nervous,' her words. She pressed for more, but Lily said she did not want to get Katie involved."

Walt rubs his chin. "It could be anything. You said the prison is closing, right? Maybe it was about that?"

"There are no coincidences. This smells as bad as your guy's car."

"Not funny… but let's say you are right. What is next?"

MJ's voice drops a few decibels. "First, I *am* right. Second, I need to go see the warden."

Walt springs backward and holds a hand up, palm facing MJ. "Whoa… hold on a minute. Let's think this through."

MJ craves action and forward momentum. People often make mistakes when pushed, and she loves capitalizing on those mistakes. "I am not going to go in there demanding to know where Tommy Anderson and Chicky O'Malley are. I'm not a moron."

"No one said you were. You like to push people to the edge, and we both know sometimes they push back... hard. We have no idea what Lily was worried about. There is no need to rush to the prison."

MJ's ferocity screams through her glare. "Getting them to push back is the point. We will know we are on the right track if they push back. I will say the same thing to the warden that I said to Katie. I am doing a follow-up story on the family that was killed."

"Walking in blind is premature… and dangerous."

MJ is sipping coffee when her face goes pale, and she loses grip of her coffee cup. As pieces of thick sandstone colored stoneware skitter across the diner floor, she sits speechless, pointing at the small color television hung high in the corner. Across the bottom of the screen scrolls a headline identifying the young woman whose body was found earlier in the day.

MJ slowly stands, oblivious to the coffee spilled on her, the table, and the floor. She grabs her phone as darkness envelops her. She gives Walt a look he has only seen once before and begins mumbling as she stomps toward the exit.

"Someone is going to fucking pay."

55

Warden Johansson personally escorts every inmate injured or killed to the vehicle waiting for them. Today, he is watching a young man's body being loaded into a hearse. A guard once asked why he bothered wasting his time on convicted felons. His answer was simple: Every man deserves respect in death.

It takes Ben Mendoza forty minutes from receipt of the call to back the vehicle into an open space at the prison loading dock. He is opening the rear door when the bay's overhead door is raised from the inside. Four guards surround a black body bag on a rolling stainless steel table.

"Warden Johansson. I am sorry to see you again so soon."

"As am I, Mr. Mendoza. Thank you for coming so quickly."

"Of course." Ben reviews the paperwork and mutters to himself. "Interesting. AB negative is the rarest of blood types."

Johansson shakes his head. "I apologize for the brevity, but as the third death in the past 163 days, the Bureau of Prisons has requested a meeting. I must prepare for the discussion. Is there anything else?"

Ben looks up from the paperwork. "Do you know if this young man has any family I should contact?"

"None. Pursuant to protocol, we reconfirmed by calling the inmate's former attorney. Unfortunately, he will find his way to Potter's Field."

Ben looks ruefully at the warden and the guards who accompany the body. "As always, Mendoza's will show him the utmost respect."

"We expect nothing less. Thank you for what you do." The warden shakes Ben's hand firmly. "I hope to avoid seeing you for a while, Mr. Mendoza."

As the four officers assist Ben with transferring the body into the hearse, Ben hears a muffled clanking which no one else seems to notice. He shakes it off as they complete the task.

Ben bows his head in silent prayer before driving away.

56

MJ meanders around the city for a couple of hours, receiving strange looks as she whispers to herself, mulling over ways to painstakingly torture whoever hurt Katie.

She has been ignoring Walt's calls but finds herself desperate for information that the media does not have, or at a minimum, is not reporting. How was she killed? Who was the last person to see her alive? MJ? And perhaps worst of all, was she sexually assaulted? But the one question on repeat is a simple one: Why?

As one of her favorite mantras cycles through her mind, the belief that she is the reason Katie is dead explodes inside her head.

MJ returns home and engages the multiple deadbolts on her door. On her stroll to the bathroom, her clothes are left lying where she sheds them. She steps into the shower, hoping to wash away the guilt, but not the rage.

Drying off only after the hot water runs out, MJ stands in her bathroom, staring at the blurry naked image in the steam-covered mirror, swallowing the sobs the flowing water masked.

It takes fifteen minutes for the steam on the mirror to dissipate. She then slogs into the bedroom and throws on a sweatshirt and a pair of sweats. Her next stop is the Keurig. Only then does she flop onto the couch and return one of Walt's seventeen messages.

Walt answers the call before the first ring ends. "Are you okay?"

MJ's head droops in despair. "I killed her."

"No, you did not. Where are you? Are you at home? I can be there within the hour."

MJ fights the desire to be held and comforted. Turning to Walt now will convey a message she is uncomfortable sending. "I needed some air." MJ sniffles. "She is dead because of me."

"MJ, this is not on you. I have already reached out to a few contacts. I am being told Katie's injuries are consistent with the injuries seen in a number of other recent assault cases. Something about an identifiable bruise, likely caused by a ring. Although the others survived, the current thinking is she came into contact with the same perp, who took it too far this time."

MJ erupts, screaming to ensure Katie can hear her fighting on her behalf. "Too far? Is that what you fucking call getting beaten to death, and having your naked body tossed aside like a piece of fucking trash? That's the definition of 'too far?'"

She is caught off guard by Walt's gentleness. "I am deeply sorry, MJ. I will meet you wherever you want, whenever you want. I am here for you, no matter what."

MJ takes a few deep breaths before responding. The softness in his tone wraps around her like a warm blanket. "I appreciate it, but right now, I need to find this son-of-a-bitch and make them pay... slowly and painfully." Before she can stop it, vulnerability seeps out. "Seriously, Walt, I am really glad you are concerned. I am, but I am fine."

Walt takes charge. "You have until 7 tonight to wallow, at which time I will be arriving to escort you to dinner, and we will be drinking wine that comes from a bottle, so please wear something more than your 'boxed wine' sweats."

A desperately needed smile slips from MJ's lips as her tone fails to match her attempt at humor. "Don't knock 'boxed wine' sweats. They are very comfortable."

"Call me if you need me. See you at 7 o'clock." He ends the call before she can object.

The phone slips between MJ's fingers as her head drops into her hands. The sobbing returns as Snoopy climbs gingerly onto the couch, this time not stopping until he has nosed his way completely onto her lap.

57

He stares at the screen of his laptop, doing the one thing killers should never do: hesitate. While his most recent activity was not specifically ordered, he has eliminated a risk to his employers, and extra work deserves extra pay.

As a preparatory component of his initial engagement, he tracked his targets to understand their movements and identified Jazzie's as a place where the man and woman were regulars. His social media research also found one photo of the woman and another female, both wearing nothing beneath their leather vests, standing behind the bar.

Contemplating every angle of an assignment is what the experts in his field do. He communicated his findings and corresponding recommendations, only to be severely reprimanded. His sole focus was to be on the specific order and completing it as quickly as possible. Nothing more.

But professionals do not leave loose ends. He does not know the identity of those who placed the order, but from the beginning, it has been obvious that they do not understand how this game is played.

As the last phase of his assignment, he chose to follow the news, attend the funeral, and monitor local activities, including those at the bar. He is on full alert for anything being said or reported about the fire, those killed, or the guy who was arrested.

During his follow-up surveillance, he stopped at Jazzie's every evening, varying his hours to avoid establishing an identifiable pattern. His misspent youth playing pool finally paid dividends, allowing him to pay for his drinks with someone else's money. He choked back the weak-colored water in the twelve-ounce bottles to blend in. Beyond his time at the pool table, he could be found standing at the bar or sitting at a table ordering the bar's famous chicken wings, just like everybody else.

The idiots should have listened.

He discreetly followed the bartender and another woman to a local diner after the bar was locked up for the night. The bartender wept, waving her hands as she spoke. The woman with the pink in her hair did not say much. He thought about going into the diner to see if he could hear something but decided against it since he didn't have a different set of clothes with him. Lesson learned.

After an hour of coffee, crying, and pancakes, the two women stood at the diner's entrance, hugging. He had to make a choice.

He surprised the bartender as she walked home. A quick tap to the back of her head, and she collapsed like a rag doll. He caught her and hooked her right arm around his shoulder, creating the image of a boyfriend helping his girlfriend navigate the sidewalk after having one too many. He dragged her to his car, where he had cable ties and a gag waiting. In less than ninety seconds, she was silent and immobile, no one the wiser.

He slams the palm of his right hand onto the small kitchen table. Like the best killers, he showed initiative by tying off the risky loose end he had identified at the outset. Had they listened to him, the number of loose ends would have stopped at one.

He mumbles to himself and pushes send as a phrase he recently heard crosses his mind.

"Fuck around and find out."

58

Snoopy barks at the buzz of the intercom. MJ glances at the clock: 6:59 p.m.

"Hello?"

"It's me."

MJ tries to be playful, but her heart is not in it. "Me who?"

"Your knight in shining armor."

"Sorry, I am expecting a stuffy, pain-in-the-ass attorney. You will have to come back another time."

MJ hears nerves twist Walt's tongue into a knot of insecurity. "Oh… Um… Wait, I see him parking his car."

She spent the afternoon cleaning. The last man to be in her apartment was almost a year ago, when a former Special Forces guy swept her apartment for hidden listening devices. Snoopy has been lost all day, no longer needing to walk around various pieces of clothing to get to the door, the couch, or his bed.

Once done, she took a long, hot shower, which brought another moment of angst. She struggled with what should have been an easy decision. She is wearing a black pencil skirt with a crème colored blouse. Hairy legs might send the right message, but they will not complement her outfit. Her legs are the least of her worries as MJ now stands at the threshold of her apartment, waiting for the elevator doors to open.

Walt steps out of the elevator wearing crisply pressed chinos, a light blue Tommy Bahama sweater that accents his eyes, and a freshly shined pair of loafers. With a dozen quick strides, he reaches her doorway. "The light from your apartment just created the silhouette of a beautiful siren hypnotically calling me toward the rocks."

MJ blushes and fights the urge to slap Walt and tell him to cut the shit. After a few seconds of strained silence, MJ turns and lifts her right arm, pointing to the inside of her home.

Walt twists his body to the left, creating space for him to squeeze by. The subtle smell of lavender wafts through the doorway. "Nice place." He bends down and scratches Snoopy in his favorite spot. "You must be Snoopy."

MJ's usual rock-solid confidence melts into a puddle of uncertainty. "Thanks. Would you like a glass of wine? I promise it is not from a box."

"Normally, I would say yes, but we have a 7:30 reservation at Prezza. Best wine list in the North End."

"Oh, okay." MJ grabs a sweater from the arm of the couch and directs Snoopy to hold down the fort.

The silence during the elevator ride down to Walt's Porsche is unbearable. Walt opens the passenger door for her and then takes a deep cleansing breath as he walks around the back of the car to reach the driver's side. He climbs in, and MJ saves him from further distress as he buckles his seatbelt.

"What the fuck, Erickson? Why does this feel weird? Getting something to eat should not be this stressful."

Walt's shoulders shed the pressure he has been carrying since he rang her doorbell. "Right? Let's just have some fun. Lord knows you have earned it."

They stick to light-hearted topics on the ride to the North End. The eighteen-year-old valet can barely keep the drool in his mouth when Walt hands him the keys to the $125,000 car.

Walt is welcomed by name as MJ realizes she is in his world, not just a random restaurant. As they are being seated, he chats with the hostess and asks for a bottle of Nickel and Nickel's John C. Sullenger cabernet. It arrives within moments of their seating. MJ watches Walt smell the cork and swirl the wine in his glass, ultimately taking a deep sniff with closed eyes. She is about to tell him what a pretentious ass he is when he takes a small sip.

"Ahhh… perfection."

MJ is determined to keep Walt in the "friend zone" as she deciphers the unfamiliar feelings coursing through her heart and mind.

"How do you really know that bottle of wine is worth what they are charging? I read something about restaurants switching labels on the bottles."

A wide grin is plastered across Walt's face. "Fair point. However, my highly experienced nose and deteriorating liver confirm that is not the case." He raises his wine glass. "To good friends."

They clink their glasses and turn their attention to the menu.

After ordering, Walt takes another sip of wine and clears his throat. "I am worried about you, MJ."

MJ is glad the ambiance does not allow Walt to see any uncontrolled display of her confused thoughts. "Thank you, but I am fine." The steely resolve she is so proud of returns in a nanosecond. "Once I nail this fucker, I will be even better."

Walt notices a well-dressed, older woman scoffing at MJ's fiery comment. He lowers his voice. "Listen, MJ, whoever did this is a bad dude. He has gone from being someone who beats women to someone who kills women. There is no going back once that line is crossed."

Walt stares at MJ as she feels her eyes blazing with fury. She knows he sees them.

With compassion, Walt says, "How can I help?"

Before she can answer, a metal cart with a large wooden bowl atop it stops at their table. They sit quietly, sipping their wine as the server mixes the anchovy paste, garlic, egg yolk, and lemon juice in the bowl. He whisks it smoothly, adding small drops of extra virgin olive oil to the mixture until he is pleased with the result. Lastly, he adds a touch of salt before tossing in the romaine lettuce and a few croutons. After serving equal portions and adding shaved Parmesan, the server smiles and offers fresh ground pepper before heading to his next table.

MJ tips her wine glass toward Walt. "Okay, that was kind of cool."

Walt smiles. "Yeah, it allows them to charge $40 for a $5 salad."

The laughter they share puts their conversation from a few moments ago in the rearview mirror. Tonight, they will enjoy good food, good wine, and good friendship.

59

The unexpected message carries catastrophic potential. The recipients are in different locations, but their reactions are identical. The fury builds within each of them and will not be contained, driving a short text exchange that sets a time and place for lunch.

By the time they meet three hours later, fury has melded with decisiveness, but their customary reactions have been flipped on their heads.

His traditionally muted tone disappears. "He must be neutralized."

There is no emotion today. "While I don't disagree, we must secure additional details before reaching a final decision."

A musing breath is released. "The flaying of flesh will reveal all, and be very satisfying."

A quick look around confirms no eavesdroppers. "Do you have access to the right resources?"

"I will handle this myself... with pleasure."

The unnerving grin he is staring at sends a shiver up his spine. He is well aware of his partner's jungle cat tendencies and the need to periodically feed. Refusing him the ability to satiate his hunger will create exponentially more dangerous conditions for both of them.

"What do you think he wants?"

"Pain will loosen his tongue."

"Slow down. I am not disagreeing, I am trying to get ahead of what he might say as you two... get acquainted."

A quick look around with nothing but his eyes. "I believe he has freelanced and seeks further compensation."

"Freelanced?"

With a crazed smile, he pulls up the headline on his phone and hands it across the table.

His own deeply buried darkness breaches the surface as the clenched teeth of a lion materialize. "Are you fucking kidding me? Stupid son-of-a-bitch! He needs to go away... NOW!"

"Done."

It takes twenty silent seconds for their alter egos to reemerge and attention to shift toward the menu.

"I am thinking about the tuna melt special. You?"

"My cardiologist will not like it, but I am dying for a cheeseburger and fries."

The two friends enjoy their lunch while debating the likelihood of a Tom Brady return to Foxboro. There is no need to discuss the debacle further. Each knows this liability will be eradicated by the next time they meet, and restitution from the party who recommended the assassin will be demanded.

They refuse to pay for ignorance.

60

MJ cannot recall the last time she slept this soundly. Maybe there is more to drinking high-end wine than just being snooty. She rolls over to find Snoopy standing on the bed, glaring at her.

Message received.

She slides out of bed and bounces into the bathroom, full of renewed energy. MJ brushes her teeth and pulls her hair into a ponytail. After grabbing sweats from their new home in her bureau, she throws on a sweatshirt and heads to the kitchen. As the Keurig gurgles and sputters, she grabs the items she needs for the journey and summons Snoopy.

As MJ heads toward the dog park, her imagination paints a vision of a villain, but it is not the monster most would conjure. MJ's menace is an average-looking man who leverages an innate ability to roam the earth unnoticed. The ring he wears contains the DNA of at least one woman and creates the calling card he leaves behind. This devil does not rely upon brute strength. He is charming and unassuming, as evidenced by his ability to catch a bright girl like Katie off guard.

Knowing most of the men in the United States are described as "average-looking," her thoughts keep coming back to distinguishing marks left on his victims by a ring.

MJ bends over and moves through her portion of the well-established routine, bringing this leg of the trip to a successful conclusion. As they begin their return trip home, thoughts of Tommy and Chicky, and how everything is inexplicably connected, replace the pleasant memories of last evening.

As she follows an energetic Snoopy home, she runs through what she knows… again.

There is a fatal fire that kills a family, including a woman who works at a prison with a well-known history of inmate violence. So much so, they bring in a warden with a documented reputation for extreme discipline, who allegedly negotiated a deal to oversee the eventual dismantling of the prison. At least two prisoners have fallen off the planet under his watch.

A friend and co-worker of the dead woman was beaten to death. Her broken body was left alongside a jogging trail, potentially by a man who has done this many times before.

The man arrested for the fire professes innocence despite irrefutable evidence. Walt believes him, and despite meeting him only once, so does she, though she has yet to say that out loud. This presumed innocent man is the one who brings the missing men to her attention. And she is back to where she started—Tommy and Chicky.

She long ago mastered the art of thinking and walking. Out of necessity, she added hypervigilance to her skillset. Her Maui Jims protect her eyes from UV rays and give her the intended benefit of obscurity as she continually scans the horizon in search of danger.

A guy wearing an Eversource Gas shirt and ball cap catches her eye as she and Snoopy are a few blocks from home. He is walking on the sidewalk ahead of her, carrying what looks like a small, brown sack lunch. The logo is all over New England, on everything from trucks to hats, shirts, and jackets, but the hair standing up on her forearms brings forth a memory of a few months ago.

Pursuant to her training, she slows her pace and watches as he crosses the street at the next corner. She takes a mental picture, adding it to the ever-growing list of dangerous people she has created in her mind.

Once safely behind the multiple deadbolts on her apartment door, she throws a pod into the Keurig. As the coffee is brewing, she adds more Post-its to the wall. She adds Katie's name and connects it to Lily's. It is the second new Post-it, labeled "Fucker," that brings an unexpected wave of emotion. Tears escape as her shaking hands add the green string between that Post-it and Katie's.

She wrestles to bury her emotions and resurrect the memories of last evening: a fantastic meal, very expensive wine, and a lot of laughs. For those few hours, the world faded away, but life's unfairness returned with the sunrise and an amplified intensity.

She knows that constantly moving forward is the key. She dials the phone, but after half a dozen rings, she is dumped into voicemail. "I have been thinking about the ring you said left an imprint on Katie's face. If we can identify the ring, we may be able to narrow our search. Have your guys come up with anything? Think I can get a copy of the imprint? Give me a call when you can."

The magnitude of her error smacks her between the eyes. "Oh, and thanks for last night. It was a blast! Talk soon."

For a moment, MJ thinks about calling back and apologizing. She thought she had Walt pegged, but the person with whom she had dinner last night was not the Walt she expected. He is not just banter, bluster, and bullshit. He is a smart, lighthearted, compassionate person who enjoys living life to the fullest and has the financial means to do so. She has never had a $300 bottle of wine before, much less two. MJ knows she will never have that life, and appreciates Walt's willingness to let her look behind the curtain.

She will definitely apologize when he calls back.

Opening her laptop and looking at the "wall of investigation," she becomes overwhelmed. She cannot search for missing people and a killer at the same time. Walt told her last night he would use his influence to keep the police focused on Katie's killer, but they both acknowledged the possibility of ascertaining "Fucker's" identity shrinks with the passing of every hour.

To assist with this massive effort, she reluctantly decided to reach out to "the team," a group to whom a friend from college introduced her. This collection of individuals possesses a very specific set of skills, including superior hacking ability, a deep-seated hatred of all things governmental, and a willingness to cross the lines of legality with impunity. And those she has personally interacted with are lethal specimens. People who would make any Navy SEAL or Green Beret shudder.

Her relationship with "the team" is complicated, to say the least. In the past, their involvement was limited to information exchange, but their last collaboration saw them play a pivotal role in saving her life and the lives of others, including Walt's.

She now waits for their report on Warden Johansson and the current whereabouts of the missing inmates, and she despises waiting.

MJ plugs in an external hard drive and opens Chicky's dossier. What she has found confirms that there are a lot of people who would likely smile at the thought of his permanent disappearance, but her current objective is to do what she could not do with Tommy Anderson: track his departure from Walpole.

Operating from the premise that he survived the attack, logic dictates Chicky was transported from Walpole by ambulance, but which company? Where he was taken is a different question she will answer later.

Getting the Commonwealth to identify its contracted ambulance service will require great effort and too much time. An option springs forth, returning MJ to the internet for answers.

As suspected, the residents of Walpole have voiced concerns over the dangers of the prison and its inmates for years. The content of recent town meeting minutes piggybacked on the articles she found, highlighting the frequency of inmate violence. After half an hour sifting through the complaints of dogs barking and the location of a pickleball court, she finds what she is searching for. Murray Ambulance has a reported practice of speeding through the town without its lights and sirens activated.

She calls Murray's home office in Weymouth and asks to speak to the Operations Manager, who she learns is out of the office for the day. She identifies herself as a reporter investigating a customer complaint, fearing she may never get a return call, or worse, it comes from Murray's attorney.

After getting an energy drink and starting John Coltrane's *Live at the Village Vanguard* on Spotify, she settles back in as another lightbulb appears overhead. Disgruntled employees are almost as valuable as a woman scorned.

Her search for employee complaints leads her to Glassdoor, where she finds quite a few, but they are all written by the same person: "Anonymous."

She refuses to let something so mundane dissuade her. The infusion of caffeine has her mind bubbling with possible avenues to pursue. A few laps around the coffee table do little to calm her racing thoughts, but they do provide an idea.

It is a relatively small industry, one where EMTs and other employees likely move between companies frequently. With a few quick taps on the keyboard, she identifies a couple of geographically appropriate, albeit smaller, possibilities.

MJ loves an unabashed frontal assault, but she knows it is not always the most fruitful approach. Recognizing the power of subtlety, she rummages through her bedroom for the outfit that has brought her the most success over the years.

61

As he awaits a response to his email, it is time to move on to the next loose end.

It was not difficult to identify the bartender's breakfast companion. The word "reporter" rings in his ears, and he would recognize her pink hair anywhere. All it took was a quick Google search and a call to a friend at the Registry of Motor Vehicles to secure what he needed.

From beneath a Bruins cap and a pair of Ray-Bans, he watched her get into the Porsche last night. His RMV friend ran the Porsche's plate this morning, giving him more data and bringing him to an obvious conclusion. Nobody will miss a lawyer who is representing a murderer, but "Pinky" comes first.

He smiles to himself as the thought of a rapidly growing bank balance dances in his head. Future employers will value his preparation, forethought, and follow-up, as the complexity of this assignment winds its way through the underbelly of his chosen profession. His reputation will skyrocket, leading to an ability to pick and choose his assignments… and name his price.

Before heading out for tonight's adventure, he adds a plain black T-shirt from the pile in his top bureau drawer to a tight pair of black jeans. One look at him informs any observer how much time he spends in the gym. He is proud of his physique and loves it when people take notice. Women constantly swoon over him and tell him how good he looks, but he prefers flirting with the men at the gym who look exactly like him.

Shortly after settling in for an expected lengthy surveillance, he is pleasantly surprised by a quick Pinky sighting as she leaves her building's parking garage. He chuckles at the thought of reminding her what a mistake pink hair is.

He follows her to a small bar in Stoughton, a few doors down from Transit Ambulance. He goes around the block and returns to the parking lot, backing his car into a spot abutting a dilapidated stockade fence. He spends thirty minutes counting the patrons who come and go. While locking his car and strutting toward the bar, his situational awareness training has him subconsciously searching for surveillance cameras and potential physical threats.

His cellphone chirps as his right hand lands on the bar's door handle.

He was expecting a call to be scheduled, but a face-to-face discussion with the two bastards who have been busting his balls has reputational advantages. His chat with Pinky will have to wait.

The brilliance of an experienced operator strikes without warning. He returns to his car and grabs something from the glove box. He then strides back toward the bar, stopping to tie his shoe. A quick movement with his right hand gives him what he needs. He stands back up with a distressed look on his face, patting his pockets as if searching for something.

Once back inside his car, he paws through the glove compartment and searches the floor. These movements are for the sole benefit of any cameras he may have missed or any nosy patrons in the parking lot. After a quick check of the transmitter's status via his phone, he enters the address from the text into his Waze app.

Thanks to traffic, he arrives at the warehouse in Southie about forty-five minutes after leaving the bar. The lack of street lights masks the size of the unmarked brick building, but he's glad for the darkness. His choice of clothing gives him the upper hand if they are stupid enough to try anything. He dismantles the interior dome light, slides out of the driver's seat, and closes the door without a sound.

He squeezes his eyes closed for a few seconds, allowing for a quicker adjustment to the absence of light. As he reopens them, he is now able to spot a vehicle parked at the far end of the building. After closing his eyes for a few more seconds, he pulls a Glock from the small of his back, takes the safety off, and begins tiptoeing toward the car. He stops every few steps, straining to listen. There is no sound, but for the occasional crunching of a stone too loud for his rubber soles to absorb.

He cautiously stalks along the side of the building, further reducing the ability to see him or his silhouette. His heart rate has not moved above sixty-two. This is what he does. If anyone should be nervous, it is the two geriatric morons he is about to meet, particularly if they refuse to compensate him for his superior work.

His patience requires fifteen minutes to arrive at the steel door on the back side of the warehouse. A quick check confirms it is unlocked. With his left hand, he silently turns the rusted doorknob. He takes a focusing breath, swings the door open, and steps briskly into the building with his Glock at the end of his fully extended right arm.

He feels it a split second too late. The trip wire causes a series of halogen lights to shine thousands of lumens of light directly into his face. He slams his eyelids shut and repeatedly pulls the trigger, hearing the offending glass scatter across the concrete floor. Rather than stepping backward, he moves to his left with his left hand sliding along the wall. Within seconds, the undamaged lights go dark, plunging his eyesight into further confusion.

After three sidesteps to the left, he recognizes his mistake and quickly retreats toward the door while blindly emptying the handgun's magazine.

The last thing he remembers is the spots dancing behind his eyelids… and the sound of laughter.

62

Heads turn as MJ struts in with swagger and purpose, her heels clicking on the worn hardwood flooring. She gets to the bar, where two men wearing uniforms gladly lean away from each other to create a gap. MJ squeezes between them and their 1950s barstools. She orders a Patron Añejo, neat, to the surprise of the gentlemen on either side of her.

The guy on the right wastes no time. "Let me know if you need any help with that. I am a trained medical professional."

MJ shoots the tequila back and orders another before the bartender can step away. "I should be fine, but thanks." She never turns her head.

The first EMT slinks away as his friends share a belly laugh at his expense. The second slides over, carrying greater confidence and the cheesiest of pick-up lines. "Sorry about my friend. Guessing you are not from around here."

MJ sips the second tequila, looking him in the eye and guessing he will be alone forever, if that is the best he has. "Nope."

Everyone in the place can hear his buddies encouraging him. He cannot walk away now. "Are you waiting for someone?"

Time to start reeling them in. She turns to face him fully. "Actually, yes. I am a reporter doing a story on problems at Murray Ambulance." She raises her voice. "Any of you medical professionals want to help a girl out?"

The second EMT tips his beer towards his friends, who holler in unison: "Murray sucks!" The statement generates a collective cheer and the clinking of pint glasses.

"So I have heard. Care to share? Off the record?" MJ cocks her hips, licks her lips, and gives them her best "come hither" look.

They cannot jump fast enough as a third joins the fray. "Sure, we all got things to say, as long as it is off the record."

"Why don't you guys grab a table, while I get the next round?"

Laughter erupts, and high-fives commence as a smaller group within the mob moves to a table in the corner. MJ asks for another tequila and four draft beers. The bartender is an older gentleman who looks at her with the eyes of a concerned father.

She nods and mouths a quick "Thank you."

The drinks are delivered, and a toast to the fine lady with the pink hair follows. After a moment, MJ lays it out for them. "Look, fellas, I am a reporter, and my story involves Murray, but my interests go beyond any problems they have."

The first EMT wades back in slowly. "Like what?"

"Like how the runs to and from MCI – Cedar Junction work."

The group of EMTs sits back in their rickety wooden chairs and exchanges looks, their mouths agape. Finally, EMT number two steps into the silence as a bucket of ice water is dumped on what could have been a wonderful evening.

"We worked there, but we all signed non-disclosure agreements as part of our new hire paperwork. They are ironclad. They fucked our buddy Jimmy hard when he violated it. Wish we could help you, but we can't." He watches as his friends slowly nod their heads in agreement. "Thanks for the beers, though."

"I am not looking for information on specific inmates, just general information on the response protocol and where injured inmates are taken. Basic stuff."

The group speaks to each other with their eyes. EMT number two, having apparently been promoted to spokesperson, continues. "Everything is covered in the NDAs. Even the basic stuff. Sorry."

MJ switches tactics. "You all worked at Murray at one point, right?"

The collection of bobbleheads nods in silence. She works to keep them talking. "All at the same time? Did you leave together?"

The "spokesman" decides these are reasonable questions. "Our times overlapped. We slowly migrated to Transit over the course of a few months."

"Is the money better?"

The beer has re-fortified EMT number one's confidence. "No fucking way… Oops, sorry. No ma'am."

MJ raises an eyebrow. "Then why leave?"

It is not about procedure or protocols, but their individual rationale for leaving a higher-paying job. EMT number two glances at his co-workers for permission, then breaks the silence.

"The bosses expect some unconventional things. At first, it was funny. Then it wasn't. Sorry, that is all we can say."

The bobbleheads return.

MJ cranks up the heat by leaning against the table, allowing two of her best assets to find additional air.

"I get it, I don't want to get anyone into trouble. I can probably find out which hospital inmates are taken to. There are records about that somewhere, right?"

EMT number one struggles to lift his gaze. "It depends."

MJ holds four fingers above her head. "On what?"

Distracted by the view, the only EMT to remain silent thus far barrels forward. "Not all of them go to the hospital."

Heads swing around wildly, as if the secret recipe for the Colonel's chicken had just been disclosed. The group's spokesman tries to regain control of the conversation.

"Look, things are weird there. Sorry, but that is all we can say."

The beers are quickly delivered as MJ continues the probe. "Where else would they go?"

After the group toasts each other with their newly filled pint glasses, EMT number one winks at her. "Yeah, sorry. We can't say… but you seem like you are as smart as you are beautiful. You can figure it out."

As if on cue, all four take another swig of the freshly delivered beers. Silence ensues, and MJ sits quietly. They are drinking slowly, keeping their eyes aimed at the tabletop, reminding her of a high school classroom where the teacher is looking for a volunteer.

MJ switches gear again, catching them off guard. "Okay, what gives? This seems like basic background information. There are no specifics, no HIPAA violations. Just a group of friends reminiscing about the past." She sips her tequila as the four of them attempt to communicate telepathically.

Three sets of eyes drop back to the table as the spokesman delivers the bad news. "Sorry. We would really like to talk to you about this, but we just can't."

"Okay, I get it. Last question. Did you ever transport dead bodies?"

EMT number three's shoulders relax as he confirms the obvious. "Of course. All ambulances do from time to time."

"And those go to the morgue, right?"

Chairs creak as their occupants shift aimlessly. Another thirty seconds of uncomfortable silence is all the answer MJ needs.

"Thanks, boys, this was fun. Enjoy the beer."

MJ walks back to the bar, orders the EMTs another round, and pays her tab, leaving her elderly protector a healthy tip.

She has an extra lilt in her step as she heads for her car with more evidence that something is going on with the injured and deceased inmates coming out of Walpole.

63

The hood draped over his head is stuck to the dried blood on the right side of his face. He takes mental inventory, confirming all of his limbs are still functional, albeit restrained. The dizziness and nausea indicate a serious concussion.

He adds firsthand knowledge of the discomfort associated with having duct tape wrapped around his head, over his mouth and eyes, to his list of interesting experiences. He wonders how long it will take for his eyebrows to grow back.

For the first time, he feels his pulse quicken with concern as he struggles to breathe through the remnants of a bloody nose and the duct tape; the challenge added to the disorienting darkness and inability to move his arms or legs. His sole comfort comes from knowing these bastards have no idea who they are fucking with. He will make their families pay for their audacity.

The first sound he recognizes is the unmistakable tenor he has heard on the phone.

"Today will be your last on this earth. The choice on how you leave it will be entirely up to you, but make no mistake, this is the end."

He does not react. He has been on that side of the hood many times before and knows that is exactly what they are waiting for. New sounds of movement confirm that more than one person is watching him, but he does not know how many.

"Your answers to the following questions will dictate our next steps… and your final path. Is that clear?"

A simple nod would be sufficient, but he refuses to play their game. He hears the air swoosh before a giant fist connects with the right side of his head.

He is awoken by the violent shaking associated with being doused with water, which he is sure came directly from Antarctica. At this point, he has no idea how long he has been out, nor can he guess the current time or even the day.

The second massive blow increased his disorientation exponentially, and it takes what little energy he has left to maintain control of his stomach as nausea roils.

"I will ask again. Is that clear?"

He remains silent. To speak is to lose.

"My partner is right, you are a fucking idiot. Let's see if a different approach will encourage you to answer a simple question."

Two meaty hands grab his right arm and hand. The violent twisting of his wrist ends with the sounds of ligaments and tendons tearing, and bones exploding. He struggles to control the scream that's fighting to escape from beneath the tape.

"Let's try this again. Is that clear?"

He quickly decides to save his left wrist from a similar fate, as a cold sweat overcomes him. He nods once, sending his world spinning.

"Excellent. Did you kill the bartender?"

He hesitates before quickly concluding that they already know the answer or, at minimum, suspect it, so he is not giving them anything of value. Another slow nod in the affirmative increases the speed of the room's rotation.

"Did you interrogate her beforehand?"

As he was dumping her naked body into the woods, he berated himself for the error of his approach. He intended to knock the bartender out, but underestimated the strength of his blow to the back of her head. He braces for what will come as the painful turning of his head to the left, and then slowly to the right, provides the answer.

He swallows, returning the contents of his stomach to their original location.

"A true professional would have implemented the obvious tactical strategy one takes upon capturing an adversary." A pause. "But, I am not sure I can trust your response."

The sound of small metal objects jangling fights through his hood. A powerful set of hands holds his left arm, adding to the zip tie's restraint. Despite his attempts to prevent it, the index finger is straightened, and the nail is slowly removed. He makes no sound as the pain pulsating from his right wrist overshadows this new injury.

"Tough guy, huh?"

The grip on his left forearm tightens further. He feels a scalpel slowly slicing along the underside of the injured finger. He feels the blood dripping from the wound as a new instrument is inserted just below the surface of the skin of the flayed finger, clamping down tightly. Two quick tugs loosen the skin and represent the first steps in peeling it back to his wrist. This pain makes his dangling right hand seem like a hangnail. His muffled scream is the loudest the tape and hood will allow.

"Did you interrogate her?"

Fear overrides pain, becoming the dominant emotion. Nonetheless, he has only one answer to give. He slowly repeats the prior movement as his mouth fills with vomit.

"You ended her life before obtaining any intelligence. Correct?"

Each heartbeat exacerbates the pulsating pain as he provides the answer once again.

The last thing he hears is someone shouting, "Find his fucking phone," as something is pressed against his forehead.

64

A jumble of possibilities crowds MJ's excitement as she begins the next sixteen miles of tonight's journey. Her phone bounces in the cupholder in the center console.

"Can't wait to see you at breakfast tomorrow! 7 a.m. at Jimbo's Diner, right?"

"Me too, see u there!"

MJ's heart skips a beat. "The team" will deliver their findings in a little more than seven hours from now. MJ's mind is a scrambled mess. Two shots of tequila, on top of the energy drinks, aren't helping.

When she arrives, it is almost midnight, and the limited number of cars in the parking lot doesn't bode well for her objective.

This time, every head turns as she crosses the threshold. She's the only woman in the place. Her heels click against a wooden floor for the second time tonight as she struts toward a well-worn bar whose edges possess the burnt grooves of unattended cigarettes. There are only three taps, and two of them are Bud Light. With bottles of Jack Daniel's and Grey Goose, the only ones she recognizes, sitting on the shelf behind the bar, her choice is limited.

"Bud Light, please." Her eyes dart to the left and right. The only movement has been her entrance, the turned heads with gawking eyes, and the bartender wiping out her future pint glass.

"That is five dollars."

The bartender's unabashed enjoyment of the change in scenery does not faze MJ. The pressure from the Propentus investigation turned an already badass reporter into a diamond.

MJ drops ten bucks on the bar and turns around, quickly locating her target. She arrives at a table with two men who appear to have been stationed there for some time.

"Excuse me. I see you gentlemen work for Aspect Medical Transport."

The two men instinctively look at the patches on their left shoulder. One of them drags his right hand down his beard before speaking. "What of it?"

MJ does not have the patience for more bullshit. She plops into an empty seat, leveraging her assets once again. "I am a reporter doing a story on Murray Ambulance. Did either of you work there at some point?"

The second guy finishes what's left in his glass and clears his throat. "I did. They are fucked up over there."

"How so?"

"I am not supposed to say anything, but it is a fuckin' mess."

She refuses to allow this dance to be a repeat of the earlier one. She waves two fingers toward the bartender, never breaking eye contact. "What kind of mess?"

The bartender retreats after delivering the fresh beers, carefully balancing eight empty glasses on a tray.

After tipping his full pint glass toward MJ in appreciation, "the beard" continues his story. "Murray used to be called to transport dead bodies from the prison. A few went to the coroner's office, but most went straight to a funeral home."

"Isn't that where they are supposed to go?"

"Normally, the coroner or the funeral home picks up the bodies."

"Some guys at Transit told me everyone transports dead bodies."

"Sure. It starts out as an emergency call, and they die on the way, but that is not what this was."

MJ continues probing in the dark, like a blind woman in an unlit closet. "Okay, what was it?"

"Some of us started asking questions…" The silent EMT kicks his partner's chair. "Sorry. I have said too much."

"Let me get this straight. Murray used to get called specifically to transport dead bodies from the prison to the morgue, or to a funeral home, which is highly abnormal?"

These two are fine with silence. They look at each other, sip their beers, and then look at her, before staring at the table. Once again, silence provides the answer.

"Do you know if this is still happening?"

A slight nod from one EMT to the other precedes a solemn statement. "We heard it stopped a couple of years ago… after we left."

"Thanks, guys. I appreciate this."

"The beard" shifts in his chair, suddenly nervous. "Wait, you will keep our names out of the paper, right? We don't want to lose our jobs."

"I don't even know your names." A quick wink returns calm to the table.

MJ receives a cheer from her tiny crowd of admirers as she buys a round for the entire bar before heading for the door.

She presses the dial button on her cellphone and races back to her car, anxious for the next six hours to pass.

65

He navigates the black Range Rover toward home while using a baby wipe to remove the gunshot residue and grey matter from his hands. "It's done."

"And?"

"And, you were right. He was an idiot."

"Concerns?"

"His failures leave open the possibility of additional complications."

"How will we confirm?"

"We will need to…"

His new phone begins bleating. He uses his blood-soaked third thumb to unlock the phone. It opens to a map with a red dot traveling along Route 24 in Stoughton.

"You there?"

"Perhaps he was not entirely useless." The rhythmic beeping continues as the dot continues toward its unknown destination.

"What does that mean?"

"Unsure, but there is a new path to follow."

"And?"

He does a U-turn and mashes on the accelerator. "And, I am moving to follow it, now."

"It is imperative we stop the spread of the disease, but we must be cautious."

"Understood." A diabolical grin appears as the possibilities flood his mind.

"And, *you* must maintain operational control."

Redness blooms at the top of his head. "*You* do not tell me how to do my fucking job."

66

W alt trips as he leaps from the couch, almost splashing red wine onto his antique oriental carpet.

"Christ, MJ… where have you been? I have been calling for hours." The pacing returns.

"Doing my job. I have collected more pieces of the puzzle. I am convinced Brian's observations are the tip of something bigger."

Walt's mind shifts to his client. "Will this 'something bigger' get him out of prison?"

"I do not know."

"What the hell does that mean?"

"It *means* I do not know." Her exasperation catches Walt off guard.

"Where are you?"

"In my car. I visited a couple of bars and bought a bunch of EMTs some drinks."

MJ's fierce independence is one of the things Walt admires, but it also scares the hell out of him. He swallows his concern. "What the hell do EMTs have to do with anything?"

MJ chuckles. "For a smart guy, sometimes I wonder. What happens when an inmate gets injured? The prison has to call an ambulance to take them to the hospital, right? I figured out which company has the contract and then went in search of ex-employees, looking for dirt."

Walt rolls his eyes, once again impressed by her ingenuity. "Did you get any?"

"Murray makes everyone sign NDAs and has apparently made an example of a few who have violated them. That scared the shit out of everyone else."

Walt is starting to understand. "So you bought them drinks to loosen them up?"

He hears the smile in MJ's voice. "Maybe you're not so stupid after all. Yes, but the ROI was limited."

An odd warmth overcomes Walt, and it isn't the wine. "How limited?"

"It appears the prison used Murray to transport an abnormal number of dead bodies, and they were frequently instructed to take them directly to a funeral home, but the practice was discontinued within the past couple of years."

Wine-fueled exhaustion impacts Walt's acuity. "Is that not where dead people go?"

"Yes, but since the deceased are generally murdered by fellow inmates, I would have expected them to go to the coroner for an autopsy. They would need those results to pursue charges, correct?"

Another sip of wine clears the cobwebs. "No autopsy, no confirmed cause of death, no charges." Walt scrunches his face. "Why would they not want to pursue charges?"

"Maybe they do not care about the charges?"

"Or they do not care about the victims. Either way, you are right. There is something bizarre occurring."

MJ laughs. "Have you learned nothing? I am *always* right!"

They share a tender laugh. "Of course. How crass of me."

"I am pulling into my garage. Lots to think about. Oh… thanks again for a wonderful evening. I enjoyed it… a lot. Have a good night, Walt."

"Good—"

MJ disconnects the call before he can finish his sentence.

Walt empties his wine glass and finds himself returning to the rabbit holes that have consumed his evening. His client, the glove, the missing inmates, and the deepest of all… MJ.

67

Brian has not said two words outside the meetings with his attorney, not even during his mandatory AA meetings. Every ear seems poised to pick up any utterance. His biggest fear is talking in his sleep, which a former cellmate told him was a problem. There have been no further "warnings," so he is quasi-confident that nocturnal musings haven't given him away. If true, and his status as a mime has been communicated to those in charge, he might live to see another Christmas.

Brian returns to his now familiar seat with the misfits. Without realizing it, he chooses the same seat at every meal. It is human nature. Familiarity brings comfort, and in prison, it can bring safety, but neither exists for a misfit.

Two "new fish" plop down at his table for breakfast, except they are not new. Brian recognizes the faces, briefly wondering how many recognized him when he returned.

He is surprised by their seat choice, recalling that they had previously been at tables controlled by one of the gangs. He looks straight down, telegraphing his desire for solitude. His two new tablemates look over, then begin to whisper.

"What the fuck happened to Chicky?"

"Went lookin' for him. Was told some asshole shoved the end of a fuckin' toothbrush into his ribs."

"Bad?"

"No one is sayin'."

"Maybe he got the offer?"

Their heads snap toward Brian, who continues to examine the crumbs on his tray.

"Maybe."

"Fuckin' crazy. I hear they get what they want even if you say no."

"You ever talk to anyone who took the fuckin' offer?"

"Nah, I don't think no one has. I ain't never seen no one come back."

"Yeah, me neither."

With a look around and a shrug, the two turn their attention to cold oatmeal and dry toast. They scrape every last oat from the tray. For a moment, Brian thought they might lick their trays clean.

Having heard rumors of "offers" before, Brian peers over, immediately regretting the move.

"Mind your fuckin' business, asshole."

Brian slowly nods his head in understanding, hoping his new friends will rejoin their previously established support system… ideally before lunch.

<h1 align="center">68</h1>

Walt leans backward with his feet on his desk and his fingers laced behind his head, staring at the Post-it on his monitor. He has been in this position for the better part of an hour when Jonathan appears at his door with two Dunkin' coffees: hot for him, iced for Walt.

"Thought you could use one."

Walt sits up and reaches across his desk with the thirst of a camel. "Hell yes! Thanks!"

"How goes it?"

After a long, satisfying pull on the coffee, Walt dives in. "I have two fundamental problems. If I take Brian's innocence as fact, the first question is who picked up the glove? The second is how they got it into his trunk."

Jonathan adopts a familiar posture, silent but encouraging.

"Brian mentioned the electrical contractor, the plumbing contractor, and the gas company as all being on site the day the glove went missing. I have reached out to all three, and despite my charming demeanor, I struck out across the board. The subpoenas have been served, but I project the list of names between the two companies to be as high as twenty-eight. I am praying the gas company's dispatching system is pinpoint accurate, allowing them to easily identify the employee who was on site."

"Okay, what about question number two?"

Walt scrunches his face in turmoil and throws his hands in the air. "I haven't a clue." He re-centers himself and takes another drink. "I have moved on to a question our pink-haired friend has asked. *Why?* Why target these people? Why Brian? Why now?"

"And?"

"If Dylan was the target, successfully setting Brian up would have required knowledge of their fight. Jeremy mentioned it being loud, but he was the only known eyewitness."

"Maybe Jeremy said something to someone?"

"Maybe, or maybe Lily was the target. As the administrative assistant to the warden, Lily would have access to everything. Did she see something or overhear something that made her a liability? According to MJ, Katie said Lily was 'wicked fuckin' nervous' about something at work."

Jonathan stands. "Like what?"

"Again, I have no friggin' clue… and we can't ask her now." Walt adds another Post-it to his monitor. *Did Lily see or hear something? Real target?*

"The more the pieces tumble in my mind, including the fact that the warden found it necessary to personally welcome Brian back to Walpole, the more my gut tells me the prison is the common denominator."

Jonathan leaves their favorite phrase hanging in the air as he turns toward the door. "Always trust your gut."

69

The sun peeks through the crack between the shade and the window casing as the annoying beep of an alarm invades MJ's sleep. She yawns and reaches back with both arms, stretching as her eyes adjust to the light. Snoopy watches as MJ completes her gyrations, patiently waiting.

After a quick wardrobe change, MJ drops a pod in the Keurig and reluctantly turns on the television, prepared to digest the most recent evil in the world. She is not disappointed.

The lead story highlights the finding of a severed arm in Southie, confirmation of the violence found on the other side of her apartment door. She heads out nonetheless.

MJ enjoys the aroma and taste of her coffee as she and Snoopy bask in the sunshine at the dog park. As she bends over to complete the one task she believes to be the sole drawback to owning a dog, she realizes time has gotten away from her.

She all but drags Snoopy home and updates her outfit to something more fitting for a diner, then races to Jimbo's. It is 6:59 a.m. as she enters, out of breath and unsure of who she will be meeting.

A woman with a body most cross-fit champions would kill for, waves to her from the rear of the diner. As MJ approaches, she sees danger lurking deep in the blue eyes of her blonde-haired breakfast companion, who, unsurprisingly, is seated with her back to the wall.

"Hey there! So glad you could make it!"

MJ leans over and briefly embraces her new friend. "Me too. My schedule has been a mess!"

The two lift their menus as a server pours them both a steaming cup of coffee. MJ hopes she does not have to wait until the end of the meal to receive whatever is to be delivered.

A quick glance around is followed by a whisper. "You are swimming in dangerous waters."

MJ scoffs. "What else is new?"

The stern voice of a mother reinforces the message. "He is not one with whom to trifle."

MJ is always amazed at the intelligence level of "the team" members she has met. "Fine. Do you have a gift for me?"

Before she can answer, the bubbly teenager server returns. "Are you ready to order?"

MJ wants to keep this on track. "Only coffee for now. Thanks."

The dejected kid slowly retreats.

MJ is all business now. "The gift?"

"I do." A quick shift of her eyes identifies its location—a spot shielded by a dented aluminum napkin holder.

MJ never saw her move. Was it stashed before she arrived?

MJ tamps down the desire to grab the thumb drive and race home. "Thank you."

"This individual is a former member of the Special Operator community and has a despicable reputation…" Another quick glance, this time without moving her head. "…and he is connected to others across the globe of similar ilk."

The message is concerning; however, it is the tone with which it is delivered that sends a shiver from MJ's tailbone to her head in a split second, only to be replaced by exhilaration even more quickly.

"Got it." MJ reaches over and awkwardly pulls a couple of napkins from the container.

Her new friend jumps up and gives MJ a brief squeeze. "Great to see you! Let's get together again soon!"

The head of every man, and some women, turns as the beautiful blonde glides toward the door. If they only knew the menace hiding behind the pretty face.

MJ asks for a to-go cup for her coffee and throws twenty-five dollars on the table—no need to screw the hard-working kid out of a decent tip.

• • •

MJ is skipping down the sidewalk, her eyes oscillating back and forth behind her sunglasses in search of danger, when her cellphone twitches in her rear pocket.

"Hey…did I wake you?"

"You cannot wake someone who does not sleep." A brief chuckle unleashes her excitement. "I had a special breakfast. Details to follow."

"Excellent!" Walt's tone changes from business-like to caring. "I have some news on Katie's killer."

MJ stops short as the shroud of guilt wraps around her like a python, shattering the joy of a warm, sunny day. She takes a gulp of hot coffee, hoping the physical pain will keep her emotions in check.

"And?"

"A contact of mine says the DPW found a severed left arm in Southie. The index finger and the hand were flayed… but there is a ring."

Coffee splatters all over her feet and legs as the cardboard coffee cup explodes upon impact. "Spit it out, Erickson!"

"It may be the ring that left the imprints noted in Katie's bruising. They are currently comparing the ring to photos and castings taken from all of the victims. They are also looking for DNA within the ring's nooks and crannies."

MJ refuses to react. "So, you are telling me the fucker who killed Katie has lost his arm?"

"Maybe. The fingertips were removed. The next step will be to run the arm's DNA through CODIS, looking for a match. And they are searching Southie for the rest of him."

There is a long silence.

Walt steps delicately. "You okay?"

Like always, MJ's mind crams the multitude of emotions she is experiencing into tiny boxes and places them onto a shelf to be opened at a later date… if at all. "I am fine. If it is him, someone took him out. Why?"

"We will not get far without an identification."

MJ's desire appears. "When will you know?"

"You are my first call as soon as I hear something."

The lid on the "anger" box slides open. "I fucking better be."

70

As he walks into his favorite breakfast spot, anxious to learn the omitted details, he spots his partner sitting comfortably in a booth, enjoying his usual cup of tea and reading the paper. He slides into the opposite seat and waves down the waitress.

After ordering a cup of coffee, two eggs over medium, and dry wheat toast, he dives in. "Good morning."

No sign of emotion… ever. He calmly puts down the paper and slides his reading glasses to the top of his head. "It is not."

After a look around, he plows ahead. "Explain."

"There was a failure to fully explore potential information sharing."

He struggles to keep the angry beast beneath the surface. "Fuck!"

"The road I mentioned terminated at an apartment building housing over one hundred residents. A complete list is being compiled, but there's one of immediate interest. An investigative reporter who won a Pulitzer last year."

He throws his hands up as the beast comes to life. "Fucking great! Connection?"

"Possibly. A poor-quality photograph of two people hugging at night exists, but even the most advanced enhancement attempts have failed to confirm either person's identity. Date stamp reveals it was taken in the early morning hours of the girl's demise."

He has never seen this look on his partner's face. "I trust your expression reflects concern."

He takes a sip of his tea. "We need confirmation."

The breakfast hastily set in front of him by a nervous server is now an afterthought. "How?"

"You have accurately noted the importance of stopping the spread of the disease, but I am concerned with our level of littering around the Commonwealth."

His face scrunches with surprise at his partner's unusual pragmatism. "Options?"

"Acquisition, interrogation, and…" He scans the diner without moving his head. "…Cremation."

He twists his head in disagreement. "We should discontinue operations or place them on pause."

"Such a step will not solve the problem. Do not forget, the clock of opportunity continues to rapidly count down."

He concedes. "We need to understand how extensive the proliferation is."

"The moment my new toy begins to provide information, I will take the necessary steps."

He does not even finish his coffee or touch the uneaten food before throwing a few bills on the table and sliding out of the booth. "Those steps *will* include further collaboration once identification is secured, and *before* final decisions are made."

His partner returns his reading glasses to their prior position. "Whatever." The newspaper crackles as it is reopened.

71

The tormenting traffic on Route 128 gives Walt plenty of time to rearrange the puzzle pieces over and over. Today is not about the glove. His questions will be focused on the "why." Brian may have nothing to offer as to why Dylan and/or Lily were targeted, but Walt is craving answers to a different topic: why Brian?

Brian enters as Walt remains seated, his emotions churning. The profound resignation and sadness in Brian's eyes reflect the devastating impact the weight of his current situation is having on him.

Walt digs deep for optimism. "Hey Brian, how are you?"

"Fine."

Walt ignores the single-word answer and maintains an upbeat posture while looking at the top of Brian's bowed head. "I will start with today's debrief. I have been continuing to look at the issues surrounding the glove, beginning with who had access to the site for the two hours you could not see it. I have subpoenaed the electrical and plumbing contractors, as well as the gas company. I await formal responses."

"I already told you, it ain't gonna fuckin' help."

"It is my job to speak with them." Walt flips to a clean sheet on his legal pad. "Today, we will explore why you were the one selected as the pawn to be sacrificed in this chess match."

Brian refuses to look at Walt as he picks at a bloody hangnail. "Whatever."

"Who might want to punish you?"

Brian tilts his head up, but refuses to look Walt in the eye. "Punish me?"

"Anyone vow to hurt you, or make you pay, or anything along those lines?"

Brian looks around and whispers. "Just the warden."

Walt does not acknowledge the obvious. "Okay, what about a prisoner from your past?"

"Nah, I was good last time. That is why I got out early."

"Do you recall any big arguments or fights you had with someone outside of prison?"

Brian begins picking at his bleeding finger again. "Just the one with Dylan."

His client's documented quick temper makes it difficult for Walt to accept the answers. "Okay. I need to think about this a bit more."

"Whatever. You done?"

Walt is caught off guard by the snarky attitude. "What do you mean 'done'?"

Brian leans forward, motioning with his head for Brian to join him. "I got news."

Walt leans in, unsure if what he smells is fear or excitement. "What?"

"I heard guys talkin' about Chicky. They said something about him getting an offer, and that is why they don't never come back. I heard something about offers last time, too."

Walt sits back in surprise. "What the hell does that mean?"

"When I looked over, they told me to mind my fuckin' business. I stared at my tray after that." Brian looks around the room. "Good, right?"

Walt realizes Brian is trying to be helpful. "Yes, but you have to keep yourself out of trouble, okay? We do not need you getting attacked in the yard again."

Brian purses his lips. "Or anywhere else."

"True enough. I have to run. Remember what I asked you to think about."

Walt watches a defeated Brian waddle away. He cannot decide if it is caring, frustration, or this morning's sausage, egg, and cheese sandwich that is causing his growing heartburn.

72

MJ returns from Jimbo's, upset with herself for not grabbing something to eat, when an unflattering photo of her editor pops onto her phone's screen and Darth Vader's theme music plays. She needs to take control of the conversation.

"I was just going to call you."

"Bullshit. I thought you might be dead."

She has heard this tone plenty of times. "Nope, alive and kicking. Are you going to be around this afternoon? I want to give you an update on a story I am working on."

The screaming forces MJ to pull the phone away from her ear. "A STORY? I have not given you any assignments, nor agreed to any assignments. So how in the hell can you give me an '*UPDATE ON A STORY?*'"

He is pissed and should be. She takes her only shot. "You wanted me to work on the arson, right? I have an angle. And, I have uncovered a couple of things."

The condescension drips into MJ's ear. "I recall you rejecting the arson matter entirely. And don't give me any shit about a miscommunication."

She dredges up a sorrowful tone. "I thought I would look into it after I found out who was representing the accused. You may recall I know him personally, and I thought maybe I could get an exclusive. Figured I would see what I could generate before bringing it to you."

A heavy sigh and a few seconds of silence pass. "You are going to be the death of me, MJ. You got the exclusive, right?"

She smiles, having once again dodged the bullet. "I can swing by around 3."

"No, you can be here at 4 p.m. SHARP!" He ends the call before she can say another word.

MJ enters her apartment and throws her jacket on the floor while hurrying to her favorite seat. She quickly returns to the door to engage the deadbolts.

She only has a few hours to finish putting together her pitch, but she has more pressing work. Before her ass can hit the couch cushion, MJ jams the new thumb drive into the side of her laptop.

He enters the new six-digit code. No one needs a third thumb. The "idiot's" phone comes to life. A new multi-phased operation has been initiated, and confirming the blinking dot's owner will complete phase one.

He went to Logan last evening and rented a Chevy Malibu under one of his many aliases. He has been sitting two blocks away from the building since 4 a.m. in a vehicle that will not draw a single look. Experts know there is no need to sit on the building when there is a transmitter.

Following his gut, he mapped three different paths to the offices of the *Boston Herald*. If the dot heads in that direction, these multiple options allow him to easily intercept his quarry. If not, he will alter his plan and follow wherever it leads.

Eleven hours later, the dot leaves the garage and begins moving toward the *Herald*. Within ten minutes, he is three cars behind his prey, creeping through city traffic like everyone else.

After a torturous round of stop-and-go traffic, he secures the verification he has been seeking. The tracker has been placed on the vehicle of the Pulitzer Prize-winning investigative reporter with pink streaks in her hair.

He drives past the entrance, looking straight ahead, as she enters the fully fenced parking lot. The second phase of this operation, which he has dubbed "Operation Pink," has begun.

He will now return the rental and then head home to plot the transmitter's memory on a map. Determining why she traveled to those locations will take a little more effort.

MJ walks through the glass doors with the engraved *Boston Herald* logo, as she has done many times before, convinced she is onto something but lacks proof of her conviction. She does not stop at her desk. She wants to be at Spagnola's office before 4 p.m. No need to piss him off further.

At 3:57, she knocks on his open door. He looks up, his magnetic CliC Readers separated and hanging around his neck. "Wow… with three minutes to spare. You remember, sucking up does not work with me, right?"

"It is not sucking up; it is respect." It sounds exactly like the horseshit it is.

Spagnola chuckles. "You will never change."

"You would not want me to… Ready?"

"Loaded question. But I am ready to hear what you have. If you cannot sell me within five minutes, I will give you your next assignment. That is a statement, not a proposal." He flips over the small hourglass that MJ has battled many times before.

MJ quickly plops into a chair in front of his desk and opens her laptop. "No problem. Okay, you know about the fire, so I won't bore you with those details. I will skip to the good stuff."

Spagnola taps his fingers impatiently on his desk. "Sands through the hourglass, MJ."

"Right. I called the accused's attorney, with whom I worked on *Propentus*. He initially put me off. A few days later, he called me and asked me to look into two inmates of Walpole. The first was a gang-banger killed in prison by the grandson of the woman he accidentally killed during a shootout. The second is the first one of interest."

"First one?"

MJ works hard to keep her decibel level and pace in check. "I will get there. The second inmate of interest is Tommy Anderson. Tommy robbed the wrong former Navy SEAL turned family jeweler and earned himself a ten-year residency at Walpole. He was shanked a few months ago, and he never returned. However, VINELink says he is there. The attorney's source refutes this. Tommy appears to have fallen off the planet."

She takes a gulp of air. "I pressed the attorney, eventually getting him to persuade his source to meet with me." A little white lie. "The attorney and I went to Walpole, and I met the kid. He walked me through everything, including his belief that he is being set up. Again, something I will get to later." MJ waves her hand dismissively. "He told me during his last period of incarceration that he witnessed Tommy getting shanked and the warden personally rushing into the melee and pinning a bleeding Tommy to the ground. He whispered something into Tommy's ear, and Tommy blanched. He watched the med team take Tommy out, and no one has seen him since."

MJ looks at the tiny hourglass. Half the sand has already fallen into the bottom.

"The kid tells me the warden has threatened him in the past, and again on the first day of his return. He swears he doesn't know what warranted such a welcome. When pressed, he tells me he noticed something during his prior residency. When he poked around and asked questions, he wound up in the infirmary. Took stitches above one eye and sustained a few broken ribs, thanks to some excitement in the yard."

Spagnola leans forward with mild intrigue evident. "What did he notice?"

MJ does not look at the hourglass but smiles at the inquiry. "He says every couple of months or so, a young guy gets jumped or shanked and the med team is there in an instant… as if they knew it was coming. The injured inmate is hauled off and never returns. When others are attacked, including him on the yard, the guards move at a snail's pace."

Spagnola looks at the hourglass as the last grains of sand fall to the bottom half. "All you have is a tale about mistreated inmates?"

"No, inconsistency in performance, as well as two guys with a last known address in Walpole who have disappeared." MJ crosses her fingers.

"Wait. Two missing guys?"

BINGO! "Yes. At the end of my interview, the kid whispered another name, Charles "Chicky" O'Malley. A lifelong felon who reportedly took a sharpened toothbrush handle to the ribs a few days before our meeting."

Spagnola expels an audible sigh, reaches across his desk, and flips over the tiny hourglass to restart the clock.

MJ does not miss a beat. "I leveraged my external network to confirm Chicky wasn't admitted or treated at any hospital in the Commonwealth. Like Tommy, he is still listed as a Walpole resident in VINELink. Another falsehood."

MJ's delivery pace gets away from her. "The believed connection point is Lily Whitaker, the mother of two killed in the fire, who was the administrative assistant for Walpole's warden. Johansson was brought in to bring order to the war zone it had become, until it is shuttered within the next twenty-four months. I am looking more deeply into him."

MJ glances at the depleting sand. "I spoke to a co-worker of Lily's from her second job as a bartender, Katie Nichols, and learned Lily was worried about something at the prison. The night I spoke with Katie was her last on this earth. She was murdered and left naked alongside a running trail near DW Field Pond." MJ gets a little choked up, taking in a slow breath to keep tears from escaping. "Lastly, my sources tell me the severed arm found by the DPW in Southie the other day is likely the man suspected of killing Katie. I do not have time to tell you about the accused and his being set up, but I believe he is telling the truth, as does his attorney." She watches the last grain find its way to the bottom half for the second time. She sits quietly, her bouncing leg reflective of her anxiety.

Spagnola fiddles with the two halves of his glasses as he digests what he's just heard. After a painful period of silence, he looks across his desk. "I said it earlier on the phone. You are going to be the death of me. There are so many angles to what you have just shared, I do not know where to begin."

MJ suppresses a smirk. "It is a lot, and there is more to it, but I focused on the highlights given my limited time."

He ignores the snide comment. "Okay, let's take the time you believe necessary for you to lay it all out for me, or until 5 p.m., whichever comes first. I have to take my son to basketball practice."

75

He pulls a burner phone from one of the many pockets in his army jacket and calls a burner owned by his partner. These phones are only used once.

"Problem confirmed."

A deep, controlled sigh. "Next steps?"

"Already provided. You are the one who stated the disease must be eradicated."

The word "eradicated" causes him to squirm. "I said the spread must be stopped. There is a difference."

"A difference without distinction."

"You are the one who expressed concern with the amount of trash we have left around the Commonwealth."

"Taking out the trash is part of life."

More squirming. "Where do we draw the line?"

"To be determined, but I will concede increased trash will generate greater scrutiny, something neither of us favors."

"I will again suggest we discontinue operations. Loose ends can be tied up, without risk of additional exposure."

"'Operation Million Dollar Men' has been lucrative. We will be at your desired end state soon enough. No need to expedite its arrival."

Irritation seeps through the phone. "Greed is the worst of the seven deadly sins."

"Calculations have been made and agreed upon. We are very close to achieving our goals. We will not allow a few speed bumps to derail us."

He pleads one last time for caution. "Speed bumps can be gently navigated. Not all of them need to be removed."

"We will see."

They have arrived at a rare disagreement on strategy. It has happened a handful of times, but a compromise is always achieved. This feels different, though.

His partner, a lion who has again gotten the taste of blood, seems to be craving more.

76

Dark clouds blanketed the sky during her meeting. With the rain beating down, MJ runs out of the *Herald's* office toward her parked car, holding her "weather-proof" laptop bag above her head in a losing effort. As she pulls the bag from atop her head and begins rummaging through it, her t-shirt is drenched in seconds, leaving little to the imagination. She finally locates the key and takes refuge in the driver's seat. The few napkins she pulls from the center console do very little as she wipes the rain from her face.

She sits in the parking lot for a few moments contemplating her next move. A sudden desire to call Walt catches her by surprise. MJ has been a lone wolf throughout her career. Her first foray into sharing the workload was the Propentus investigation, and while it worked out, the concept of relying on someone else remains undesirable. Working in a pack is still fundamentally a foreign concept, but she hits the speed dial anyway.

"Hey there! Calling to invite me to dinner?"

MJ shakes her head at his doggedness. "We need to talk. I suppose we could chat over a meal, but nothing fancy. I am soaked. Luckily, I have an extra shirt and a Sox cap in my car."

"Where are you?"

"Sitting in the *Herald* parking lot."

A pause. "Okay, Ernesto's is a great pizza joint on Salem Street. Meet me there in twenty minutes."

"I need to park at Dock Square. I will get there as quickly as traffic and my legs will allow."

The joy in his voice is unmistakable. "See you there."

MJ changes her T-shirt as discreetly as one can in a car without tinted windows. She then begins navigating through the evening's mass commuter exodus. Thoughts flood her mind as the inches creep by.

Spagnola asked great questions, which pisses her off, but they always lead to a more robust story. She hopes Walt will have an update on the identification of the arm's owner. If it really is "Fucker," she will take little solace in not being the one who inflicted the pain but immense pleasure in knowing he suffered.

She is lost in thought as a white, nondescript Chevy Malibu becomes the car immediately behind her. As she waits her turn to enter the Dock Square parking structure, the Malibu is forced to inch around her to continue down Clinton Street. She peers over and notices the driver is wearing an army jacket and sunglasses—odd given the weather and the hour of day. In a past life, she would have ignored these peculiarities, but the hair on the back of her neck ignites the fuse of alarm.

A stereotypical Boston driver behind her beeps his horn. She has allowed more than two seconds to elapse before creeping up to fill the void left by the car in front of her, a monumental mistake. She looks at "Mr. Impatient" via her rearview mirror and raises her right hand, letting him know he is number one in her book.

Before heading to Ernesto's, MJ walks around the block twice, looking for an army jacket. This is a challenge given the sea of umbrellas carried by tourists heading to and from Faneuil Hall and Quincy Market.

Finding none, she finally crosses the Surface Road and heads off to meet Walt, her eyes in constant motion.

77

He returns the rental car and hops on the "T." It will take time and a few transfers before he arrives in Braintree to retrieve his own vehicle. The rhythm of the rocking train car, coupled with the clacking of the steel wheels against the track, is a symphony that settles his mind as he contemplates the next phase of Operation Pink.

How will he find out what she knows and whether she's shared the knowledge… without creating a noticeable hole in the universe?

His mind turns over the options as commuters get on and off the train at the various stops. Operationally, the right decision would be to permanently remove all impediments. However, removing this particular obstacle will raise too many eyebrows. Something to avoid as the end of Operation Million Dollar Men is in sight.

He is sitting as if standing at attention. A yardstick placed between him and his seat would be flush against him from the top of his head to the tip of his tailbone. He garners a few looks from thugs who are evaluating his status as a potential target. A bloodthirsty gaze disavows them of their misguided thoughts.

The "idiot" eliminated the original offender, as well as the bartender with whom she *may have* shared what she had learned. Rage boils to the surface at the idiot's failure to confirm this critical fact. The greater the uncertainty, the more his mind demands answers, and his body has been trained to acquire those answers.

He reaches a binary conclusion. The confidence his soul demands can only be restored in one of two ways. Either Pinky volunteers the information, or he coaxes it out of her using his special skill set.

78

As a hot piece of stringy mozzarella is stretched to the full length of MJ's arm, Walt is frozen in a panic. A woman of MJ's independence might get pissed if he reaches across the table and breaks the string. Walt takes the risk and wields his butter knife as if he were D'Artagnan.

MJ smiles as they share a heartfelt moment of laughter.

Walt wipes pizza sauce from his shirt as he asks MJ the key question. "While I am extremely pleased to be here sharing another meal with you, why the urgency?"

MJ finishes devouring her first slice. "'The team' has been helpful, but their delivery came with a DEFCON 1 level warning. We knew Johansson loved his disciplinary tactics, but we did not know his counterintelligence training created an actual monster. He is the guy they brought in when other interrogators were unsuccessful; he has a reputation and a corresponding record for never failing."

Walt is about to speak when MJ lifts her right hand, signaling a continuation. "Let me download, and then you can ask your questions and poke your holes. Okay?"

Walt nods, allowing his concern to be communicated with his eyes.

"The materials provided confirm he has remained in contact with a number of his global contacts who share his taste for blood. He has a very long reach, despite the passage of time. His DOC personnel record is replete with written warnings and suspensions for abusing inmates.

"What I uncovered regarding his escalation to Warden has been confirmed. We also now know he was a key suspect in the mechanical failure determined to be the cause of the accident, which killed his predecessor. Apparently, they had him in the bullseye, but lacked the smoking gun needed to file charges. Bottom line, this guy is a nasty son-of-a-bitch who causes pain, and likely death, for sport." MJ wipes her mouth, as if to remove the distaste of discussing such a horrible individual.

"Onto his finances. Initial findings suggest he is not the saver we posited previously. Exactly how he is supplementing his income and how he is spending it is the next step for 'the team.' As for the missing inmates…"

Walt has been sitting on his hands, his angst over MJ's safety growing with every word she utters. He refuses to remain quiet a second longer. "Goddammit, MJ! How is it you stumble into the craziest shit, and why do you drag me with you?"

"We are just lucky, I guess." MJ flashes a smile that would melt granite. "The inmate discussion is quick. Tommy's and Chicky's prison medical records reflect they were killed in prison, and their bodies were collected by Mendoza's pursuant to a contract with the state. The funeral home's records indicate both men were without family, leading to their cremation and burial in Potter's Field. As you know, this is inconsistent with current VINELink data. 'The team' is exploring the possibility of poor record keeping at the prison level."

MJ takes a sip of water. "Lastly, I spoke to my editor and am officially working to locate two missing inmates and figure out what role the maximum security prison in Walpole played in their disappearance."

Walt's brows come together. "I don't understand. You were already doing those things."

"I now have a valid basis to contact the warden for an interview." MJ shrugs nonchalantly and takes a bite of her pizza.

Like every well-trained attorney, Walt never asks a question without already knowing the answer. "Do you really need to do that?"

MJ cocks her head to the side and gives Walt the "duh" smirk. "You get two stupid questions per meal. That was number one."

Fear wrestles with anger as Walt sits up straight. "Establishing ground rules after the fact is prohibited. Having now been properly instructed, I reclaim my first stupid question, thereby returning me to my full complement."

MJ rubs her temples with one hand to hide her rolling eyes, then grabs another slice from the pizza pan sitting atop a huge can of tomato sauce in the center of their tiny table. "Fine. What questions would you like me to ask him on behalf of your client?"

"On behalf of my client? Simple, why the repeated warnings, and why did he need to personally meet with Brian?"

"I'm serious. Give it some thought. I will be calling the warden in the morning. Tonight is for leaning over my laptop and developing the right phrasing to get me the answers I seek." A broad smirk finally emerges. "Johansson may have a reputation for being a total hard-ass, but he hasn't met me yet."

Walt stops his arm from reflexively reaching across the table to grab MJ's hand. "MJ, last time things got hot, you had a private ninja looking out for you. Right now, all you have is me, and I am whatever the exact opposite of a ninja is."

"Relax. I expect him to demand that the interview take place at the prison, giving him home-field advantage. What is he going to do to me when people know I am meeting with him, inside a prison?"

Walt's response is swift and unyielding. "Ask Tommy Anderson and Chicky O'Malley."

MJ mumbles with a mouthful of pizza. "Touché."

Walt hesitates. "Not to make you salivate more, but Brian shared something with me during my last visit." Walt's eyes take in the whole room. "He said he overheard a couple of inmates talking about some type of offer. Those fortunate enough to get an offer never return."

"What type of offer?"

"He has no idea. Personally, I think it is a jailhouse legend. They make shit up to keep themselves occupied."

Walt watches the wheels spin in MJ's mind and knows she's making a mental note, but then quickly switches topics. "Maybe, but good to know. You have anything more on Katie?"

Walt gags on a large chunk of mozzarella. "Um… DNA takes a while to come back, which you know. The imprints are inconclusive, but cannot be ruled out."

MJ's disappointment sucks the joy from the room. "How long for the DNA?"

"They have put a rush on it, but we are looking at a minimum of a week. Sorry."

"Fine," MJ says with a huff. "My focus needs to be elsewhere anyway. I have a warden to fuck with."

Walt shakes his head from left to right. "Look, we both agree there is something peculiar occurring behind those twenty-foot walls. Whatever it is, either the warden is involved or he is aware. His training would not tolerate any other option." Walt knowingly wastes his words. "Please remember what happened the last time you kicked over a hornet's nest."

"I will let you know when I am meeting with him." MJ closes her eyes when unexpected words spill out. "You can sit outside the prison in the visitors' lot waiting for me, if that will calm your nerves."

Walt jumps at the offer. "Deal."

79

As she enjoys the relaxation properties of steaming water pelting her shoulders, MJ contemplates her motivation for pursuing this story. She has always fought for underdogs. A man wrongfully accused of murder, the deaths of a fun-loving bartender, and a young family of four certainly qualify.

Is it the thrill of uncovering the truth about two missing felons? A desire to find the real killers? The tremendous guilt she is carrying over Katie's death? Or, and this thought she banishes to the end of the list, is it because she is enjoying her time with Walt?

She exits the shower, unable to answer the question, eventually putting on her signature outfit: black leggings, a T-shirt, and her trademark red Chuck Taylors.

With time to kill, MJ grabs the leash. The skies are grey, and while the weather people are not calling for rain, MJ dons the lightweight North Face jacket she has worn to a number of clandestine meetings, just in case. A quick click onto Snoopy's collar and they are off.

They are only a few blocks from home when she senses a set of eyes following her every movement. It is a feeling she has not felt in months, and foolishly hoped she would never experience again. She wants to stop, but the education she has received from former Special Forces members directs her to keep moving, but remain hyper-alert.

MJ's practiced observation skills include sorting "friends" from "foes" beneath a pulled-down Sox cap. She always errs on the side of caution, dubbing many a potential "foe" and following a simple theory: better safe than sorry.

As they arrive at the park, Snoopy drags MJ toward the far corner as she had hoped. MJ positions herself with the corner of the chain-link fence to her back, giving a clear line of sight that covers the expansiveness of the park. There are others going through the same machinations as she, but there are no obvious outliers.

Another eleven people are identified as potential "foes" on her speedy return trip. As MJ barricades herself behind her front door and its multiple deadbolts, she is alarmed by the sudden return of the nerve-wracking fear she thought she had thwarted.

80

Many covet Johansson's controlled ease. He enters the restaurant with a Hugo Boss suit jacket draped over his left arm and sees his dinner companion, advising the hostess accordingly.

He slips her a twenty-dollar bill to express his appreciation for her assistance and heads to the table, as his highly shined Bruno Magli's glide atop the polished hardwood floor. After the perfunctory hellos and the ordering of drinks, they get into the discussion they are here to have.

"She has requested a meeting to secure background information on the woman."

He drops his voice to avoid eavesdroppers. "Perhaps that is true."

Johansson is having none of it. "Bullshit. The 'idiot' was interested in her for a reason."

"And the reason?"

"Exploring previous travel information has proven unproductive."

A different thought occurs to him. "This is a perfect opportunity to redirect her focus."

"I have done my research. She is not easily deterred."

He does not like where this is headed. "Perhaps. Success will be dependent upon the breadcrumbs you leave."

"As previously agreed, I will be limiting my comments on an open investigation."

Redness creeps up his neck, and his ears move as he clenches his teeth. "You have a chance to set her in a different direction, a path of our choosing."

"Expanding the discussion creates unnecessary risk."

"With risk comes reward."

"Our reward has been plentiful and will remain so… if you do as I instruct."

He has no issue laying out the truth, particularly in a busy restaurant where violent reactions will be easily remembered. "Lest we forget why we find ourselves in this position."

A small vein begins throbbing on the side of Johansson's head. Sinister eyes refuse to blink. "A snooping bitch."

His nefarious side rages to the surface. "No. Your failure to compartmentalize information from the Commonwealth is the sole reason for this predicament."

Dangerous eyes send a chilling message. "Enough." Johansson looks around the room, ensuring they have drawn no attention. "You learn from failure. Dwelling on it serves no operational purpose. The past can never be altered, but the future can be modified."

Time to cool things down. "If she is the pitbull you say she is, this is an opportunity we would be foolish to ignore."

Their drinks are delivered, and they use the next few minutes of silence to explore the menu, allowing the tension to dissipate.

It is Johansson who swallows his pride first. "The best strategic decisions arise from the exploration of viable options. I am listening."

They hold up their drinks, nod to signal a truce, and clink their glasses.

A devious smile follows a sip of scotch. "Okay, here's the direction I believe we should send this nosy fucking reporter…"

81

MJ replaces her leggings with a well-worn pair of sweats when her burner cell starts chirping. She slams her right pinky toe into the leg of her bed while sprinting to grab the phone. Adrenaline races throughout her body in conjunction with the pain, but more so in learning that it is a call from a "restricted number." She hops up and down when she touches the green circle.

"Hey, MJ, it's 'Alice.' Everything alright?"

A pain-induced cold sweat strikes MJ. "Yeah, just stubbed my little toe trying to get to the phone. It fucking hurts!"

Alice chuckles. "I am sure it hurts like hell. I was wondering if you wanted to catch a movie tonight."

MJ is relieved that walking will not be involved with this mission. "I can make anything after 8. I have some work to finish up, and I need to take Snoopy for his evening stroll."

"Okay, I will see you at the Showcase Cinema in Randolph. The new Denzel movie just came out. The late showing starts at 8:45."

"Perfect. See you then." The call ends as the fear she has been throttling since returning from the dog park returns with a vengeance. Mixing it with excruciating pain makes it unbearable.

MJ wants nothing more than to curl up on her couch to protect her sanity and her little toe from the dangers lurking on the other side of her door. As she limps toward the bedroom to change into something movie-worthy, she stops and looks at Snoopy, who is peering up from the comfort of his sheepskin-covered bed.

"My toe will not tolerate any shit from you tonight. Got it?"

Snoopy tells her exactly what he thinks of the warning by lumbering to the door and ringing the bell with a smirk.

82

MJ arrives at 8:34 p.m. She buys a ticket and then spends twenty bucks on popcorn and a fountain soda, prompting her to ask the teenage kid behind the candy counter a question with her disapproving eyes: *When did movie theatres decide it was appropriate to mark up their wares by one thousand percent?*

She hobbles into the dimly lit theatre as the previews begin and hears her name being whispered. "MJ... Over here." A petite brunette wearing jeans and an MIT hoodie is waving her right arm in the air.

MJ's toe slows her down as she shuffles her way to the back row on the other side of the theatre. She is not excited to be walking around in the world of hidden toe magnets.

"Hey! Great to see you."

An older woman spins in her seat, shooting lasers at them. They whisper in unison.

"Sorry."

MJ takes a seat. They peacefully enjoy their purchases as the previews conclude and the movie begins with the Dolby Surround Sound vibrating their seats to deliver an immersive experience. MJ steals a look at the older woman, then leans forward in an attempt to use the seat in front of them as a sound barrier. "Do you have a present for me?"

The older woman's head spins like Regan MacNeil's. Alice remains focused on the screen, enjoying her Sno-Caps and letting MJ take the full brunt of the woman's fury.

MJ's toe is throbbing. She struggles to sit still when Alice stands and casually drops a box of Sno-Caps into her lap.

"Excuse me, I have to use the restroom." MJ brings her knees up to her chest, allowing Alice to slide by.

MJ knows she will never see her new friend again. It only takes three minutes of enjoying her popcorn and sipping her soda before her patience is exhausted. As she slinks toward the aisle, MJ screams in pain and launches the remainder of her popcorn onto the few people sitting near her.

"SHIT!"

The entire theatre turns, most realizing what has occurred, having done it themselves at some point in their life. Within seconds, calm returns, and hundreds of eyes refocus their attention to the gigantic silver screen. She uses empty seats to steady herself as she treads gingerly toward the exit.

After enduring the throbbing in her right foot on the ride home, MJ hops into her bedroom, immediately removing the one thing every woman takes off the moment they are home. She shimmies into the sweats she did not believe met the theatre's dress code and sits on the bed to give her toe a break. Within a minute, she is up, hobbling barefoot toward the kitchen.

Before dropping onto the couch cushion, MJ throws ice cubes into a poop bag, creating a cold pack for her swollen appendage. After positioning her pulsating injury on the coffee table with the aid of a pillow, she completes her treatment regimen with a gulp of Sauvignon Blanc.

Time to get to work.

83

Anxiety has crippled Walt's every waking thought. Explaining that he has scheduled a meeting with Brian to overlap MJ's appointment with Johansson as nothing more than an efficiency play is not completely accurate.

In truth, it reflects a heartfelt concern for Brian's physical safety. Walt knows it is foolish to believe that his visiting Brian almost daily will make a difference, but he is convinced his client is innocent. What happens if he cannot figure this out before the warden makes good on his threats?

"Good morning, Brian. How are you doing?"

"I'm in fuckin' prison."

Walt maintains his confident demeanor but realizes it's going to be one of those days. "I will start with an update on the subpoenas. Between the two contractors, I have a total of nineteen people to speak with. Those interviews start the day after tomorrow."

"You ain't gonna get nothing from them."

"Maybe not, but it is my job to try."

"Whatever."

Walt looks closely at Brian as he delivers the next bit of news. "The gas company says they were not at Lot #17, and before I could ask, they stated they did not have anyone within the entire development that day."

Brian contorts his face, perplexed. "Bullshit! I know what I saw."

Walt is shocked at Brian's adamant response. "Why don't you walk me through exactly what you remember seeing relative to the gas company?"

Brian lurches forward, eager to defend his memory. "Like I told you, I saw a guy from the gas company walking around. Guy is huge, hard to miss. He was wearing a fuckin' gas company shirt and hat."

"Do you remember anything else? Was he white? Black? Hispanic? Asian? What color was his hair? Any ink? Anything you can remember will help."

Brian sits back and looks at the ceiling. Walt watches him struggle to dredge up the memory, something with which Walt has never had to contend.

"He was dark, but I don't know if he is black, or Hispanic, or whatever, but I don't think he was white." Brian stops. "He could have had a tan, I guess?"

Walt works to maintain the momentum. "What about hair color or other distinguishing characteristics?"

"Did not see his hair. He was wearing a hat. He is a gym rat, though, probably taking steroids."

Walt tries something different. "Close your eyes, Brian. Go back to the day and tell me what you see."

Brian sits back, closes his eyes, and starts humming, as if rewinding a VCR tape. After a few seconds, he starts. "A truck pulls up. A huge fuckin' guy gets out. He is wearing an Eversource shirt and hat and a pair of shades, like fighter pilots wear. I couldn't see his face. He walks toward the house with a clipboard in his left hand."

"Was it a gas company truck?"

"It was a white pickup…" Brian stops short. "But I don't remember no logo on the side."

"Does he say hello?"

"Nah, just keeps walking toward the house."

"Is that unusual?"

"Not really, most of us just do our shit and leave."

"Did he go into the house?"

"I think. I lost sight of him once he got past the rafters."

"What else do you see?"

Brian squeezes his eyes shut. "Plumbing truck pulls up, and two guys jump out. Two guys I seen before. They said 'Hey!' as they was walking by. I figured they were there with the gas guy, since plumbers handle the gas lines."

"How long is the gas guy there?"

"Don't remember."

"Did you see him leave?"

"No. I noticed his truck was gone after the plumbers left."

"How long were the plumbers there?"

"Maybe half an hour, or so." Brian shrugs.

Walt presses one more time. "Let's go back to the gas guy. What else do you see? Is he wearing jeans? Was it a long-sleeved shirt? What kind of boots was he wearing? Any ink or jewelry?"

"Short-sleeved shirt, jeans, hat, and work boots. The boots looked new. Didn't see no ink, but I remember the sun or something reflecting from his hand, or maybe the clipboard he was swinging as he walked."

Walt captures the information and peers at his watch. "Excellent. I will ask the others if they remember seeing the guy you described. Then I will go back to the gas company and ask them to recheck."

Brian opens his eyes, searching for validation.

"You did great, Brian. Okay, anything you want to talk about today?"

Brian's head droops again. "Nah."

"I wish I could speed up the process. Unfortunately, we have to take it one step at a time. And remember, it is important you keep your head down and mouth shut until we figure this out. Okay?"

Brian looks up again and nods his head. "Yeah..."

Walt's chair scrapes against the concrete floor as he moves to leave. His pounding on the heavy metal door echoes throughout the tiny room.

Instead of following his traditional procedure and waiting for Brian to be escorted out, Walt hustles out the door before the correctional officer can retrieve his handcuff key from his pocket.

His anxiety has taken off like a rocket. He cannot get to the parking lot quickly enough.

84

MJ spots Walt flying through the exit of the prison just as she is pulling into a visitor's spot next to a shiny Mercedes sitting in a spot marked "Reserved – Warden." While trying not to stare, she notes his excitement, but she senses something else behind his cool smile. Possibly a healthy dose of fear? She also notices his labored breathing, which injects a bit of humor into the tense moment.

"Hey…" Walt says while tapping on her window.

MJ dressed professionally for this formal visit, wearing a crème colored blouse and black slacks. The pain she experienced from cramming her toe into black pumps was exacerbated by the stop-and-go traffic she endured to get here. She eases out of the car, standing like a flamingo as she locks the door.

"Jesus, Erickson. You need to let Silverman drag you to the gym once in a while. Either that or give up your fancy wine."

"I would rather die than give up wine." An easy smile forms on Walt's lips.

"You just might."

The smile fades as she watches anxiety cloud his features. "You ready?"

"As I will ever be. I have the information from 'the team' in my back pocket."

Walt continues to catch his breath. "Do *not* poke the fucking bear, MJ."

MJ smiles. "What is the fun in that? Besides, I have my out-of-shape, wine-loving, knight in a shining Porsche sitting out here watching over me."

"I'm serious…"

MJ smirks. "As a heart attack?"

"Not funny. You need to be careful. I do not know what 'the team' has given you, but experience tells me it is probably not easily obtained. Use it wisely."

MJ can feel how much he cares, and in some sense, he's right, but no one keeps the "Pitbull" on a leash. "Relax, Erickson, I am not a fool. I am going to play nice unless…"

"Unless nothing! Get in, and get the fuck out! Then, dinner is on me." Walt storms toward his car to fulfill his promise.

After a kid barely old enough to shave paws through her laptop bag in the name of security, MJ is led to the warden's office, where she finds Warden Johansson waiting in his doorway. His broad shoulders almost touch both door casings simultaneously.

"Samuel Johansson. A pleasure to meet you, Ms. Fernandez." The warden's hand swallows the whole of MJ's. She notices a fresh manicure, making her self-conscious of her habitual fingernail biting.

"Please call me, MJ. Thanks for agreeing to see me, Warden."

MJ walks into a well-appointed corner office the size of her living room. She is surprised by the amount of light coming through the line of windows that runs down two sides of the room. One provides a view of a razor-wire-covered wall, and the other gazes upon the manicured gardens of the compound's entrance. The incongruity is obvious.

"Please have a seat. May I offer you something to drink? Coffee? Tea? Water?"

"I would love a cup of coffee." MJ cannot handle much more of this disingenuous congeniality.

The warden smiles and presses a buzzer to ask his assistant to bring her a cup of coffee and him a cup of tea.

"I am sure you are a busy man, so I will jump right in. As I mentioned to your assistant, I am an investigative reporter doing a story about the horrific fire that claimed the lives of four people, including Lily Whitaker. I want to provide my readers with a well-rounded view of the victims, and I am hoping you are willing to share your thoughts and insight from an employment perspective."

He begins as his assistant walks in, balancing two scalding drinks on a small silver tray. "I am limited in what I am able to share due to the ongoing investigation and prosecution, but I am happy to provide what I can."

"Terrific. What was Lily's official title, and what did her job responsibilities specifically include?"

"Lily was my Administrative Assistant. She answered the phone, managed my calendar, ordered supplies, maintained physical and digital records, and monitored the budget approved by the Commonwealth."

"I spoke to a co-worker from her part-time bartending job who described her as the happiest person she had ever met. How would you—"

"I would echo those sentiments tenfold. She was a shining light in a world of darkness. She was well-liked by her peers and performed her job admirably. We are devastated by this unfortunate situation."

His choice of words strikes MJ, but his lack of emotion screams the loudest. "Would you call her your 'right-hand person'?"

"While an invaluable member of the team, I would not go that far."

MJ tilts her head slightly as one eyebrow rises. "The job responsibilities you outlined might lead others to view her that way?"

The former Marine appears. "Ms. Fernandez, while some may allow their assistants to take control, I am solely responsible for anything and everything to do with this prison. I was appointed to clean up a mess the prior warden allowed to be created and to maintain order until the facility's forthcoming closure."

"Please call me MJ. Certainly, I am not suggesting otherwise. I was merely attempting to put her role into context for my readers. What will happen to your current assistant when the prison closes?"

"She will be offered a position elsewhere within the DOC, just as Lily would have been."

"She must have been a good employee to warrant such a step."

Johansson's eyes laser into MJ's. "I did not say that, Ms. Fernandez. You are again jumping to conclusions. I indicated what step would have been taken without referencing the quality of her performance."

MJ stares back, refusing to sway beneath his burrowing scowl. "Are you saying she was a bad employee?"

"I do not appreciate you attempting to put words into my mouth, Ms. Fernandez. I am stating facts, not opinions. If you continue down this path, I will end this discussion immediately."

MJ notices a slight twitch in the corner of the warden's left eye. "I apologize, that is not my intention." MJ pauses for a moment to check her notes. "Do you have any idea why Mr. McMillan wanted to harm Lily, Dylan Janssen, and their children?"

"I am unable to discuss the investigation or the prosecution." Another eye twitch.

"This is a human interest piece. The logical question is: Why would Mr. McMillan want to hurt these people?"

Johansson's irritation peeks from beneath his collar. "Ms. Fernandez, your question goes to motive, and as I have told you, repeatedly, I might add, I will not speak about the investigation or the prosecution."

"Warden, I am seeking a personal opinion given Mr. McMillan's criminal history and his prior time here at Walpole."

"It is true. Mr. McMillan has been an inmate here before. He has a history of violence, as well as a history of arson. But I am sure you already know that." A sneer appears on Johansson's face. "Just as I know you recently visited Mr. McMillan."

MJ covers her shock in a nanosecond but owns what can't be hidden. "True. He says he is innocent, and his attorney agreed to let me meet with him."

Unblinking eyes bore into MJ's psyche. "Ms. Fernandez, every inmate I speak with professes innocence. I would caution you relative to giving credence to such a claim."

The Pitbull growls back. "I do not give credence to anything I cannot independently validate. But it does seem odd that an individual who seemed to be turning his life around, as evidenced by an early release from this very prison for good behavior, a documented history of attendance at AA meetings, a spotless probationary record, and a positive employment record including a promotion, would suddenly set a home ablaze using unique accelerants and kill four people. Wouldn't you agree?"

Johansson leans forward as his tone changes. "Ms. Fernandez. I am sure your research has made you aware of the recidivism rates for violent offenders."

MJ retakes control. "Did Brian and Lily come into contact with one another when he was previously an inmate? Do you think he was targeting Lily?"

"As you know, the administrative offices are cordoned off, preventing accidental interaction. She may have visited him independently of her employment. I have not reviewed the entire history of his visitor logs."

"Have the homicide detectives sought copies of his visitor logs for all periods of incarceration?"

"Again, that is related to the investigation. Do you have any other questions about Lily, Ms. Fernandez?"

"Just one. Is there anything else you would like to ensure my readers know about Lily?"

"Lily was a well-liked woman who performed her job with deft and grace. Her personal issues were her own. This is a dangerous environment requiring absolute focus. From my first days leading platoons of Marines, I expect those I work with to leave personal issues at the door. Focusing on the job is paramount if a mission is to be successful."

MJ stands. "Thank you again for your time today, Warden. I believe I have all I need at the moment." MJ reaches across the desk, smiling as disdain oozes from her pores.

The Warden's grip is far less welcoming this time. "Of course. Please remember my caution, Ms. Fernandez. This is a dangerous business."

85

Exhilaration overrides the pain in her toe and drives the speed with which MJ hobbles toward her car. She pushed, and he pushed back—harder than she expected, particularly given his background. Better still, she did not need to leverage any of the information that "the team" provided to get a reaction.

Walt jumps from his car the second the door to the Administration Building swings open.

"Are you okay?"

MJ's face lights up with glee. "Not here."

"Fine. We have a table waiting at Ocean Prime."

The drive to the Boston Seaport passes quickly as MJ contemplates the man with whom she spent the past forty minutes, including the details Alice provided.

MJ was stunned by the ease with which she was able to place a bur beneath the saddle of the sixty-two-year-old former special ops leader, who is known in certain circles for his interrogation prowess.

"The team" did one of the things they enjoy most: rummaging undetected around the Pentagon's servers. Johansson's military record shows him as a highly decorated Marine who served for over twenty years, successfully leading covert counterespionage missions in some of the most remote spots on the globe. He employed a skill set many would find abhorrent, in the name of the country, to secure critical information needed by those engaging behind enemy lines.

The most interesting discovery, which helps explain Johansson's ability to dress like a Wall Street banker, is that he continues to maintain several active aliases from his days in the service. They have remained dormant for years, save one.

Mr. Stanley Johnson has had a great deal of activity in a Cayman Islands bank account. It reflects modest deposits in years past, ranging from $5,000 to $10,000. However, the account has ballooned since Johansson became warden, now maintaining an impressive $3.6 million balance. "The team" advised that much of the money has been transferred from different accounts in Switzerland and the Caymans, making their origin difficult but not impossible to ascertain. They await further instruction before pulling on those strings.

There is only one significant financial activity undertaken by Mr. Johnson: the acquisition of a mortgage-free, high-seven-figure luxury penthouse on the water in Naples, Florida.

Walt paces up and down the sidewalk as MJ tosses her keys to the valet. "What took you so long?"

"Relax, Erickson. I got out alive."

Walt holds the door open as MJ totters into the restaurant, wishing she had thought to put a pair of flip-flops in her car. Walt guides her through a crowd of people to the hostess stand, where he is greeted by name.

They are ushered to a table with an amazing view of Boston Harbor. Walt orders a double Oban, and MJ chooses the most expensive Sauvignon Blanc they serve by the glass, following her long-held belief that the higher the price, the better the taste.

Walt's nerves take control as their server delivers their drinks. "I have my drink, now spill."

They clink their glasses, and MJ sips her wine before starting. "Johansson is an asshole, but I was a bigger asshole. I pushed, and he threatened."

Walt almost spits his scotch across the table. "Goddammit, MJ! I told you not to poke the bear!"

"Chill. The guy is a sadistic piece of shit. He has a fully established alias, with a corresponding bank account in the Caymans that holds $3.6 million and a beautiful condo in Naples, Florida, all thanks to an unknown revenue stream that developed since becoming warden. I am convinced it is tied to the prison somehow, and Lily found out." MJ takes another sip.

Walt throws back the remainder of his drink. "Let's take this one piece at a time. I am presuming the military record and financial report came from your team, so I will accept it as credible. But why do you believe Lily is involved?"

Before she can answer, the server returns to take their order. MJ is starving. She orders the wedge salad with red onions, instead of pickled onions, and the sea bass. MJ is not surprised when Walt orders "the usual."

"When I pressed on Lily, Johansson said she 'performed her job admirably,' and they were 'devastated by the unfortunate situation.' Odd word choices. When I mentioned Lily being his 'right-hand person,' his raging narcissism came out swinging."

MJ takes another sip of wine and shares the warden's other responses. "Oh, and by the way, he knew I visited Brian, but this is where he tripped up."

"His looking into you is concerning."

MJ shrugs. "We learned last time that everyone checks up on me. He told me he reviewed Brian's visitor logs and found I had visited him. Then, he said he did not review the logs to see if Lily ever met with Brian, which I found odd. We need those logs. Can you get them?"

"Yes. Why?"

"My guess is we will find Lily's name, maybe more than once, when Brian was in Walpole for the second assault. It smelled like he was trying to lead me in that direction. Why else bring up that he knew I was there but did not check on Lily's activity?"

"Just to fuck with you?"

"Perhaps." MJ picks up her glass of wine and casually offers another option. "I can ask 'the team' to secure them, if you prefer."

Walt bristles. "Your team is going to get you killed. I will have the subpoena served first thing. Now, can we enjoy our meal?"

Walt waves down their server and orders a bottle of the Lail Vineyards Sauvignon Blanc, the one MJ is drinking by the glass.

MJ closes her eyes and moves from sipping her wine to downing what is left, allowing the fermented grapes to work their painkilling magic. When she reopens them, she finds Walt staring adoringly. Instinct forces her to behave like a teenager as she looks down sheepishly.

Their appetizers arrive, creating a diversion and allowing her to ignore the cracks forming in the overloaded shelf she hides in her mind.

The bottle of wine arrives, and Walt religiously follows his routine. Once he nods in approval, the wine is served while they agree to put today's events aside.

They share appetizers and taste each other's meals, and MJ answers Walt's probing questions about her life with an uncomfortable ease.

86

Johansson is seething as the soles of his freshly shined shoes burn a hole in his office carpet. The little bitch pushed his buttons, a capability possessed by less than a handful. Beneath her crazy hair lies a woman who is smart, cunning, and utterly fearless. She never blinked when he less than subtly threatened her. He rips the phone from his suit jacket pocket.

Johansson starts the second the call is picked up, venom in every word. "She is highly intelligent, courageous, and not to be underestimated." He will not make that mistake again.

"Didn't go as planned, huh?"

"Do *not* fuck with me. She knows more than she is letting on."

"Knows, or suspects?"

Johansson hesitates and re-centers himself. "I believe she knows, but I am happy to personally confirm my belief."

"My previous recommendation holds."

Johansson has never allowed anyone or anything to derail a mission. "Our adversaries will expect the route you propose. I suggest the opposite, an escalation in pace."

A scoff precedes the yelling. "You are fucking kidding, right? That approach creates incredible risk."

"We are three to five sales away from achieving our business plan objectives. I will support shutting the business down entirely once they are achieved." Johansson is concerned with his ability to deliver the stated volume in such a truncated timeframe, but achieving the operation's financial goal is paramount.

He tries a different tactic. "Will our partners be able to accommodate your proposed modifications?"

Johansson smiles. The prospect of money initially enticed his partner and has never wavered. "The demand never wanes. They know our back-end has a shelf-life and will understand our rationale."

"Proposed pace?"

"Rather than one every three to five months, I propose one every forty-five to sixty days."

"Goddamn it! You have already made commitments, haven't you?"

A menacing smile appears on Johansson's face. "Yes."

"I am not fucking happy, but I will wait for our next meeting to express that fully. What about your visitor?"

"We will know if she follows the bread crumbs shortly. We will monitor her movements. If something problematic arises, I will notify you."

"I am not convinced I can trust your last statement, but I have little choice."

The call ends as Johansson's pacing slows. He had watched MJ leave the building and meet McMillan's attorney in the parking lot. He failed to mention this tidbit to his partner, knowing that to do so would shift the proposed operational modification from a suggestion to a demand.

Johansson pulls a phone from his desk drawer. He watches the red dot weave its way toward Boston, knowing he has everything under control… like always.

87

Ginny sits in her office after her noontime run. Water droplets create temporary dark stains on the shoulders of her light blue silk blouse. She is tearing through the *McMillan* file when her boss, the District Attorney for Plymouth County, knocks on her door.

Ginny looks up, embarrassment racing toward her cheeks. "Sorry, I was not expecting anyone. I would have dried my hair."

"Relax, Ginny. I wish I were as fit."

Ginny sits up and points toward the chairs in front of her desk. Messages delivered by the boss are never good. "Have a seat."

"Thanks, but I will not be long. I just got off the phone with the Suffolk County D.A. They had an arm turn up in Southie about a week ago. No body, just an arm with a flayed hand wearing a ring. They tested the DNA of the arm and identified the prior owner as a member of the Dead Presidents. More importantly for you, they tested the ring and found the DNA of four different women, including Katie Nichols."

Ginny scrunches her face and mumbles. "Why would a member of the DP's want to kill a bartender?" She scratches a couple of notes onto a legal pad.

"That is yours to figure out. The ring imprints are a close match, but not conclusive. The DNA is definitive."

Ginny looks up, perplexed. "Are you saying the Nichols case is now closed?"

"Your call." He smirks. "Either way, Suffolk County has the privilege of locating the person who expertly removed the arm and flayed the hand."

Ginny looks to the heavens as questions fly about the room. *They removed the entire arm. Why leave the ring? Why dump the arm in Southie? Is Katie Nichols tied to the Dead Presidents? Is the former owner of the arm the one who killed Katie? Are they an accomplice?*

Ginny stops writing and stares across her empty office, as one last question floats to the surface: *Should she keep digging into Katie Nichols' death, or mark her file "CLOSED"?*

The answer seems obvious given her desire to pursue public office... is it?

88

As promised, Walt had his paralegal issue the subpoena for Brian's visitor logs first thing this morning. He now finds himself daydreaming about a luscious head of hair containing bright pink streaks. A wave of guilt runs through him as he admits the visitor logs are more about giving MJ what she wants than giving his client the superior representation he deserves.

Walt returns to his discussion with MJ. He has spent enough time with criminals to know there is only one way the warden could generate the amount of money sitting in the Caymans in such a short period of time: drugs. But how do injured inmates fit into the equation?

He is shaken from his thoughts as "Dun Dun" plays from his cellphone, the theme song to *Law and Order*. It is his ringtone for the Walpole switchboard.

Brian starts screaming in a whisper before Walt can say hello. "It fuckin' happened again!"

"Calm down, Brian. What happened?"

"You know."

"You mean…"

"STOP!"

Even a Phi Beta Kappa with a photographic memory makes mistakes. "Okay. Okay. Got it."

Brian's voice is shaking. "I'm fuckin' nervous, bro."

"I will make the request we discussed ASAP." It is the only arrow Walt has in his quiver to give Brian a modicum of protection.

"I told you nothing special. It won't be no help, anyway."

"Brian, listen to me. If you are in danger, there are steps we can take. You will recall I have offered to move forward with a formal request for protection via administrative segregation a few times. You have rejected those offers." Walt hates needing to cover his ass by preserving the record in the event something horrific happens to Brian. "If you continue to refuse to allow me to pursue those options, there is nothing I can do."

Brian's tone reminds Walt of a whining toddler. "Can you come right now?"

Walt pinches the bridge of his nose and opens his Outlook calendar. "I will be there this afternoon. I have court hearings, but will head there right after."

"This is fuckin' important."

"Understood. Please stay quiet and watch your back."

Walt considers this new piece of information as he places his cellphone on his desk. A second stabbing within a three-week period is significant, even for Walpole.

Walt picks up the phone, bracing himself to be told yet again that she is *always right*.

89

MJ sits with her laptop, as she always does, with Snoopy leaning comfortably against her right thigh. She is listening to *The Miles Davis Quintet*, again poring over the data on Samuel Johansson.

His bullshit does not scare her. He is twice her size, literally, yet she refused to waver when he threatened her. She proudly replays the vision of the top of his head blossoming into a bright red when she refused to bend, much less break. Crazier bastards than him have tried to intimidate her with the same success. His actions strengthen her resolve and prove she is on the right track.

"Fuck him, Snoopy!" Her faithful companion doesn't even lift his head.

She is reviewing Johansson's dossier when her cellphone chirps. "What's up?"

"I just got a call from Brian, and I had a thought. And before you say it, I think you are right."

A fun-loving smugness erases the awkwardness that had overcome her when she answered the call. "Of course I am. What about this time?"

Walt laughs. "I am on my way to see Brian, who is freaking out. Another inmate was attacked."

MJ is poised to enter his next response. "Name?"

"Unknown. Lines are recorded, and Brian is cautious, but like I said, I have a thought."

MJ scoffs. "Okay, Mr. Phi Beta Kappa. What are you thinking?"

"There is only one way the warden can accumulate that much wealth in a relatively short period of time: drugs."

MJ leans her head back and closes her eyes. "I guess I can see the possibility, but what does that have to do with your client or a bunch of inmate attacks?"

Walt's frustration appears. "I haven't figured that piece out yet. Could it be the ambulances are bringing in drugs to be sold in the prison or elsewhere?"

"Or the hearse? I mean those prisoners shanked were pulled out by one or the other, right?"

"Right. But that amount of money as a percentage of the bigger pie means significant weight. Millions of dollars' worth. That is a lot of drugs, no matter what they are."

MJ shakes her head in disagreement. "I did not get a 'drug' vibe from the EMTs. Most of their comments were connected to dead bodies. And again, I ask, why kill Lily and her family? Why set up Brian?"

"I am going to ask Brian that question today."

MJ snickers. "Now who is poking the bear? Get me a name."

"Will do. Dinner tonight to debrief?"

MJ was expecting this. "Sorry. I have to prepare an update for my editor. Call me once you get the name, okay?"

"I know a great sushi place…"

The softness of MJ's tone surprises her. "I would like to… really, but I have a ton to pull together."

"Okay. Like I said before… standing offer. Talk soon."

Guilt smothers MJ as the call ends, but it is the disappointment sitting in the pit of her stomach with which she is most concerned. Not Walt's… hers.

90

Walt is pulled from the prison security line for additional screening. He knows each of the officers working the screening area by first name. He knows their kids' names. Today, they are displaying a silent seriousness that Walt has never experienced.

After being patted down by two different officers, one attempts to look inside Walt's briefcase. "You know I cannot allow that, Dustin. I have protected material in there."

Dustin looks at him with a sorrowful eye. "Mr. Erickson, I need to search you and any materials you are attempting to bring into the prison. It's policy."

Walt realizes this isn't Dustin's idea. "I will remove each folder to ensure its contents remain in place, while allowing you to do your job."

As the two correctional officers look at each other, struggling to find the right answer, Walt begins emptying the case. This gives them plenty of cover if they are questioned about allowing this to occur. Before they can say a word, Walt spins the empty case around on the table, giving them the ability to confirm that the case is empty.

"Um, okay, Mr. Erickson. Thank you for your cooperation. You may proceed back to the line for the regular screening."

Walt's smile hides the full level of his concern. "No problem. Thanks, guys."

He finally moves through the X-ray and metal detector only to find himself sitting in the waiting area for three hours. His aggravation rises to wrath with the passage of each minute.

There can only be one reason for these bullshit games. He looks at his watch. It is approaching dinner time. Although they all swear the food sucks, inmates loathe missing a meal. Steam flows from his ears as he slams his briefcase shut without a word.

Walt's ire erupts as he stabs the vehicle's start button with his index finger. MJ's actions have jeopardized the effectiveness of Brian's defense by creating a situation where retribution is exacted upon his attorney. He envisions the price Brian may be asked to pay as a result of her gamesmanship… if not already collected.

Walt's breath catches as he asks Siri to make the call.

91

MJ is out of breath when she picks up, almost like she ran to answer it. "Get a name?"

Walt's white knuckles grip the steering wheel. "No, and before you give me any shit, you should know that your stunt with Johansson has put Brian at risk. And that I cannot and will not tolerate."

"Whoa, big fella. What the hell are you talking about?"

As Walt is exorcizing his anger verbally, he is unaware of the increased pressure being placed upon the accelerator. "I spent a few hours being all but strip-searched, then waiting to get into a meeting with my client that did not occur because the clock ran out. He would have missed dinner, shitty as it may be. It is Johansson proving who is in control. All because YOU had to push him. Nice fucking job!" Before he knows it, he is doing ninety, weaving in and out of the uncommonly light traffic on Route 128.

The sorrow in MJ's voice is palpable. "Walt, I am sorry. I never thought…"

"You are DAMN right you didn't think. You never do! You just plow forward, others be damned." Walt slams his hands on the steering wheel.

MJ remains silent.

"Now, I have to clear my goddamn calendar to arrive at the prison bright and early tomorrow morning, likely to be stonewalled again. I will sit there as long as it takes, but I *will* meet with Brian. Given the events of today, rest assured I will be packing a fucking bag lunch."

"They cannot prevent you from seeing your client."

"You are not listening! They did not prevent me. I am the one who chose to leave. They slow-played it to the point where it was no longer tenable. I could fucking care less about me, but I cannot let Brian or his defense suffer. I dread a call from the prison saying he got shanked or worse. This is a mess! All because you had to play your fucking mind games."

MJ pushes back. "I am sorry. I truly am. And I know you do not want to hear this, but this response means I struck a nerve. Why else pull this stunt?"

Walt's anger peaks. "Jesus! Fucking listen to yourself! You are hurtling forward blindly, and you are going to get Brian killed."

Walt takes a deep breath, realizing he needs to bring down the temperature. He also lifts his right foot off the accelerator, watching the speedometer quickly drop below eighty miles per hour.

"As to why… because he can, and there is not a goddamn thing I can do about it. This is a warning. Johansson is not fucking around."

MJ refuses to let go of the tiger's tail. "We are onto something, and you know it."

Walt does know it. But he is struggling with what to do with this new information, and how to do it without putting his client's life in jeopardy. "I have to go."

Walt hangs up before MJ can say another word. He needs to decompress and finds himself heading to one of his favorite restaurants for some good wine, a great steak, and an understanding ear.

92

Ben is in his office with the family of a sixteen-year-old boy who died from a fentanyl overdose, another child reportedly experimenting for the first time. Ben is seeing this more frequently as the scourge invades his community, and it breaks his heart.

"I am terribly sorry for your loss."

A distraught mother takes a deep breath. "Thank you. You know we are not a wealthy family, but we want our son to have the very best. We…"

Ben holds his hand up and gently stops them before they say another word. "I will make certain your son receives the respect he deserves, no matter your financial means. He will get the absolute best Mendoza's has to offer. You have my word."

"Thank you, Mr. Mendoza. Everything they say about you is true. You really are a kind and caring person."

Suddenly, Ben's cellphone chirps. He looks at the caller ID. "Excuse me, I must take this call. I will be right back." Ben heads outside.

Johansson doesn't wait for a hello. "The bread crumbs have been followed."

"We have bigger issues."

"Such as?"

"The last tank malfunctioned, making a successful transition impossible."

"Unacceptable."

"I have notified our partners. We have five days to correct the situation."

"That may not be wise."

Ben snaps. "Our current strategy is of *your* design. Make it happen."

Johansson ignores the comment. "As an adversary, she is formidable and will not be dissuaded. She has met with the suspect, colluded with his attorney, and has shifted her sights to me. I have no confidence in our current disinformation campaign."

Mendoza fights to keep Johansson on task. "We must let this play out."

"There is a high probability she will sniff out the ruse."

"We will cross that bridge if and when we get to it. Our sole focus must be the enhanced scheduling *you* have committed us to. I will deliver a new set of supplies at breakfast tomorrow."

Johansson mumbles. "I cannot wait to have another chat with her: a private chat."

Ben has to get his attention. "You are not listening. Our tracks have been covered threefold, according to your very expensive friends. Worrying at this time will only shorten your lifespan, robbing you of the retirement you are on the precipice of enjoying."

The former Marine refuses to be scolded. "*Do not* speak to me that way."

Ben envisions the redness peering through Johansson's brush cut. "She is of no consequence."

"Wrong. She is a problem, and it is my recommendation we solve it, permanently."

"Stay focused. The clock is ticking."

As Ben walks back into the building, he battles to mask his frustration. He refuses to let his ego-driven partner fuck this up now.

Johansson has already pushed him into an impossible corner by shortening the frequency timeline without discussion. Playing unnecessary games with a reporter is a distraction they cannot afford.

93

MJ lowers the phone, cursing the emotional rollercoaster as the exciting high associated with getting the next name to research nosedived into gut-wrenching regret.

Walt kicked her ass. He tore her down like no one ever has, forcing the ramifications of her actions to become front and center. She hates to admit it, but he is absolutely right. She never slows down, nor looks back. Forward momentum rules the day, no matter the impact.

But her self-justification is simple. She operates solely for the greater good in search of the truth. She accepts the risk for her own safety. It is part of the job, but her approach has yet again had a demonstrable adverse impact on someone else. An innocent man may spend the rest of his life in jail or worse because she chose to spar with a vicious son-of-a-bitch.

MJ wipes another tear from her eye and reaches for her phone, about to take an unfamiliar posture. She is not surprised when she is dropped directly into voicemail.

"Walt, I am so sorry. You are right. I never considered his possible reaction, and I own that. You told me to walk lightly, and I did not. I want to make this right. Scratch that, I *WILL* make this right. My sole goal from this moment forward is seeing Brian standing outside the walls of Walpole, a free man… And earning back your trust. I am sorry, Walt. Please call me back."

In truth, she knows she owes the apology to Brian. Yes, Walt wasted a day, but he drove home when it was done. Brian does not have the same ability and may never have it again.

MJ is shaken from her self-flagellation when Snoopy meanders to the door and rings his bell.

She plods around the apartment, grabbing the required paraphernalia. Snoopy was forced to expend a great deal of energy to drag her to the dog park, where she is kicking at pebbles like a chastised child, waiting to complete her part of the process.

MJ trudges home, vowing to leave her self-pity with the little plastic bag she dropped in the trash. With each step, sorrow migrates toward resentment, which morphs into rage by the time she tosses her jacket into its usual spot.

She does not believe it was a mistake to push Johansson, but owns the outcome and will not rest until the person or persons responsible for the murder of a family of four are brought to justice.

Most importantly, she *must* make things right with Walt. Angering him is one thing, but disappointing him is gnawing at her soul.

MJ stumbles into the kitchen and pours a glass of wine. She returns to stand before her investigative wall and asks Siri to play Louis Armstrong's *Basin Street Blues* on Spotify.

She adds a blank Post-it with "TBD" written on it to represent the most recently attacked inmate, and then adds a piece of green string between TBD and Johansson's name. She will update it when she gets the name from Walt… *if* she gets the name from Walt.

MJ tips her head back and closes her eyes. She listens to "Satchmo" play the trumpet like no one before him and very few since, as her focus shifts to the two words trying to find their place in the puzzle: dead bodies.

94

Ginny throws her navy blue suit jacket on the back of a chair in front of her desk and trades her pumps for a pair of running shoes. It was a tough oral argument, but she is confident things will fall her way. As she plops into her leather chair, she notices the results of the outstanding tests on the *McMillan* case in the center of her desk. Below that is a note to call her boss.

In an effort to lock down a truth, which even the talented Walt Erickson cannot elude, Ginny requested that the inside of the glove be tested for DNA. To her chagrin, her sole fear in pursuing such a strategy has become a reality.

The lab identified two different DNA strands inside the glove. One belongs to Brian McMillan, and the other to an unidentified male. The vision of Walt jackhammering on this small crack, eventually turning her rock-solid case into rubble on the courtroom floor, creates a tightness that rises from her shoulders, up her neck, and encircles her head.

Walt cannot dispute the glove being found in Brian's trunk, but she is about to hand Walt the club of reasonable doubt with which he will beat her over and over. As she begins to formulate a response to the anticipated counterattack, her boss appears in her doorway.

He has shown up more in the past week than he has in the past twelve months.

"Did you get my message?"

"I did. I am just returning from oral argument on the *Rankers* case. You were my next call."

"How did it go?"

"I am confident the court will agree with our position."

"Excellent. Now, for the reason I am here."

Ginny sits up straight, waiting to deal with whatever curveball her boss is about to throw.

"It is about the arm found in Southie. They found a foot that they believe matches based on the level of decay of both appendages. DNA will confirm. I have also been told that, in addition to the various DNA strands found on the ring, they have also identified the presence of formalin."

Ginny picks her jaw from the floor and stands. "What? You don't think…"

"I am not thinking anything. The D.A. in Suffolk County thought I should know, given the *McMillan* case. There is nothing in writing notifying me of this finding, yet. I know what I would do, but I will leave the next steps to you." He smirks. "It will help you understand the difficulties of my job."

Ginny is not surprised by the jab, nor his awareness of her aspirations. "Okay. Thanks."

He walks away, leaving Ginny with a handful of shit dribbling between her fingers. What started out as an easy win is now going to be an all-out brawl thanks to a smug detective, disappointing lab results, and the unexpected appearance of a gangbanger's dismembered arm with its fucking ring.

She is confident she can overcome the first two, but she has no clue how to handle the damage the last will inflict. Without anything in writing, she could ignore the last tidbit of information delivered by her boss, a thought that sends her mind reeling.

Ginny embarked on this career with a clear view of justice, but her political aspirations have created a fog that makes her core beliefs more indistinguishable by the day.

95

Walt is in his office, watching the condensation slide down the outside of his cold Dunkin coffee, and contemplating the prior evening.

He was stationed at his favorite spot to hunt, unwinding with a hearty cabernet, when a tall blonde took the barstool next to him and crossed her legs at the knees. The deep slit along the side of her red silk dress gave Walt an eyeful and answered a question that would send a tingle through any man.

A coy smile was followed by her ordering a "dirty martini… extra dirty." Before he could say a word, she leaned toward Walt and breathlessly whispered four little words: "I like everything dirty."

It did not take a Phi Beta Kappa to decipher her message.

A startling vision interrupted him as he opened his mouth to respond. The pink streaks in the invader's hair remained firmly fixed in his mind as he expressed his appreciation for the invitation, then gracefully declined. An unexpected first that he still cannot shake.

Walt takes a sip of his coffee as his law partner, Jonathan, swings by for a visit. "You are in early. Everything okay?"

"Close the door. I need to vent."

Jonathan obeys, then drops into a chair. He doesn't have to wait long.

"It is MJ."

Jonathan sits up. "Oh, shit! Is she okay?"

"She is fine, although I want to ring her fucking neck. I told her not to press the warden at Walpole, and you know her well enough to know what she did. Well, the bastard pushed back. My client called asking me to visit. When I arrived, I was forced to get up close and personal with a couple of COs who checked me more thoroughly than the doctor at my last physical, which included a prostate exam. Then, they left me sitting for hours. Because of their she-nanigans, my client risked missing his shitty dinner, which is unacceptable, so I left."

"He is fucking with you."

"Absolutely, but it is because of MJ's antics. I brought her into this case, and we have stumbled into a shit-show we are still mucking our way through." Walt looks down, his voice reflecting his crushing disappointment. "She pushed my client to the back of the line when he should be front and center. I am not sure I can forgive that."

Jonathan leans forward, putting his elbows on his knees. "I am going to make a statement then leave. I am not looking for a debate, nor a response. Just listen."

Walt looks up.

"You are the brother I never had. I would walk through fire for you... And so would MJ."

Walt opens his mouth as Jonathan wags a finger.

"Let me finish. Whether you admit it or not, I know as sure as the sun will rise tomorrow, you have feelings for her. That is clouding your vision. You know her better than most. You knew she would push the warden. Why else warn her? In my humble, pseudo-psychological assessment, you hoped she would do exactly what she did. One could argue you sowed the seeds with your warning. The consequences were something you never expected, and you are angry with yourself for not anticipating the bullshit stunt and the corre-sponding danger created. Even the brilliant Walter Erickson is fallible. Own it, forgive her, and move on."

As promised, Jonathan stands and walks out, leaving the truth bomb hanging in the air. Walt shakes his head, both hating and loving Jonathan.

• • •

Walt loosens his coffee-stained tie and points his car towards Walpole. Traffic is light today, giving him little time to develop an answer to the question that kept him staring at the ceiling all of last night: *Why didn't you show up yesterday like you promised?* Pointing the finger at MJ is not an option. His failure is his own.

Walt steps cautiously into the security line, prepared to accept whatever the warden dishes out. He fears seeing Brian, not solely because he has no response to the obvious question.

The one short period of sleep he achieved last night ended with a vision of Brian beaten and bloodied. He doubts the warden would go that far, but until yesterday, he did not think he would pull the shit he did.

He is shocked when today's entry runs the smooth course of the past.

96

Exhaustion and monotony are taking their toll. Brian is staring up at rusty springs, which are stretched to their limit. He covers his head with his thin pillow in an attempt to drown out the snoring, while wondering what happened to the guy who said he would always be there for him.

Rather than sleeping, he spent the night berating himself for trusting the smooth-talking attorney who left him hanging, just like everyone else in his life—except for his steadfast sponsor.

As Brian slinks along the chow line, he silently curses the concept of the court-appointed attorney. They are all the same, no matter what they say, nor how well they dress.

Brian places his red plastic tray on the steel picnic table, questioning why his two newest tablemates have not yet found their footing. In addition to considering what they may have done to warrant exile, he considers asking them what they meant by the "offer." A stupid move for sure, but who cares? Certainly not his attorney.

Maybe it is the fatigue, but after another sip of lukewarm coffee, Brian thinks *fuck it*, leaning to his left and whispering out of the side of his mouth, while his eyes stare straight ahead. "I heard Chicky got the offer."

The two guys in the shiny new jumpsuits turn in unison. They put down their plastic sporks and glare at each other, but not Brian, who is now looking down at his tray and the crumbs from dry cereal.

A whisper. "Who you fuckin' hear that from?"

A massive dose of adrenaline floods Brian's system, his face now matching the color of his tray. "Can't say."

More silence as the two other guys communicate with each other with their eyes. A different whispering voice follows. "What the fuck you know about the 'offer'?"

Brian recognizes that the pace of the conversation aligns with the movement of the guards. Smart. "Not much. You?" Brian is convinced the entire room can hear the pounding of his heart. A genuine Edgar Allan Poe moment.

"They offer to shave time, but you gotta get fuckin' hurt first."

Brian counts the guard's steps in his head… 38, 39, 40… "Then?"

"Dunno. Your turn."

Information is the most valuable commodity in prison. The problem… Brian does not have any currency. He says the first thing that comes to mind. "Heard you get paroled. That is why they never come back."

Brian's two new friends look at each other, evaluate the veracity of his statement, and scoff louder than they intended. "Bullshit!"

Brian plays out his hand. "What I heard." He shrugs, returning to his Frosted Flakes.

Within seconds, the silence is destroyed by the striking of a baton on the edge of the misfit's table. "Let's go, McMillan. You got a visitor. Stand up and turn around."

Brian thinks he knows who it is. He contemplates sending his visitor a message, explaining in detail how he feels using only two words, the first of which is one of his favorite four-letter words that start with "F," but a thought stops him.

What if it is the pretty investigator with the pink hair, not that lying bastard who pretends to care about him?

97

Walt closes his eyes, takes a deep breath, and prays he won't see last night's dream become a reality as the heavy steel door scrapes along the groove worn into the concrete floor.

Brian loses one of his slides as he shuffles toward his seat. There are no obvious injuries. A thankful Walt grabs the shoe and positions it beneath the table, allowing Brian to put it back on his foot.

Walt starts the moment the latch on the door clicks. "Brian, I apologize. I have no excuse. I failed to live up to my commitment, and for that, I am sorry. All I can say is I am here now, and I remain committed to seeing you a free man."

Walt then sits back, bracing for a barrage of well-deserved expletives. After thirty seconds of eerie silence, Walt realizes his acceptance of accountability is not what Brian expected. Brian spends another moment, still wrestling with how to respond, before breaking the silence with an excited whisper.

"I got another name, plus I learned other stuff this morning."

"Okay. Before that, let me walk you through what I have been working on. I have spoken with a handful of electricians and plumbers so far. All say they were not on site the day in question, and none recall seeing or speaking with anyone from the gas company."

Brian leans forward, the handcuff chains jingling along the top of the table. "I ain't lying… I saw a guy from the gas company, some plumbers, and some electricians."

"Brian, as we have discussed in the past, I am reporting what I have learned since the last time we met, not what I believe. I still have people to speak with, and I am also waiting on a couple of reports from the prosecution."

Walt makes a note to follow up with Ginny Giancomo. He should have received the outstanding lab results by now.

"Okay, I want to hear the news you called me about."

"I saw another guy get shanked and rushed out. I think his name is Rutherford. Not sure about his first name." Brian lowers his voice. "And I got some other information."

Walt remains silent, poised with his pen and legal pad, encouraging Brian to continue with nothing more than a reassuring look.

"I was talking to two guys this morning. They was saying some guys get some kind of offer. They gotta get hurt, but if they agree, their time gets shaved. That's why none of them ever come back."

Walt is flabbergasted. "Wait. Are you saying inmates are offered reductions in their sentence if they agree to get shanked?"

Brian demands acknowledgment with his eyes. "I did good, right?"

Walt is mystified by the concept. The drugs must be coming in via the ambulances, but what happens to the inmates after they are released?

"You did great. But you cannot talk to anyone but me about this. Do not ask questions or try to figure this out. Remember that scar above your right eye?"

"You gonna ask your assistant to check on the guy?"

"Yes, I will have my team work to locate inmate Rutherford." Walt hopes his attempt at a stern parental look drives home the message. "I am serious, Brian. You have to keep your head down. Understood?"

"Got it."

Walt feels compelled to ask again. "Are you sure you don't want me to apply for ad seg?"

Brian shakes his head violently from left to right. "Yes."

Walt packs his briefcase, his voice full of regret. "Brian, I have to run to court, but I want to say again I am sorry for yesterday. I am here for you, and we will figure this out. I promise."

As he exits the confines of the prison, Walt's attention shifts to his next problem.

His refusal of companionship last night forced him to lie motionless on his king-sized bed as solitude and darkness deprived him of sleep, yearning for a different life. He is smart, moderately attractive, and successful from a career standpoint, but his personal life has been nothing more than a lengthy string of non-committal, self-centered pleasure-seeking. He had relegated himself to such a lifestyle long ago, but the woman with the pink streaks in her hair, who dropped into his life under the craziest of circumstances, had created strong doubts about that eventuality.

He fights back a shiver of fear and makes the call. It is answered before the first ring ends.

"I am sorry, Walt. Tell me what to do to make this right?"

Walt double-checks the number he dialed. "I'm sorry. I must have dialed the wrong number. I am trying to reach a headstrong, independent, take no bullshit, nothing is going to stop me woman." He hopes the return of banter telegraphs his feelings.

"From whom do you seek an apology?"

"A relentless, pain in the ass with pink streaks in her hair. Do you know her?"

"Fuck you."

"Ah… there she is." A relaxed smile appears.

"I really am sorry."

Walt drops the act. "Me too. Truce?"

"Truce, but only if you delete the voicemail I left. All evidence of my transgression and corresponding sorrow must be erased."

A hearty laugh. "Not going to happen."

"I have been thinking…"

Walt takes a shot before she finishes. "Me too. Listen, I am leaving the prison. Brian offered some additional information. Lunch?"

No hesitation. "Tell me where and when."

Walt cannot keep the joy from his voice. "LaGrassa's on Province Street. Say 12:30?"

"See you then."

Walt unlocks the Porsche and tosses his phone on the front passenger's seat. As he slides into the soft leather, a calm cascades over him. He presses the start button and bursts into laughter.

Jonathan knows him better than he knows himself.

98

MJ and Snoopy are basking in the sunshine, traveling at an easy pace. She is amazed by the relief generated by shedding the crushing weight of disappointing Walt. It is freeing, yet disturbing. As many can attest, she has never cared about stepping on toes, pissing people off, or forcing them into difficult positions in her quest for the truth.

Watching her ceiling fan rotate hour after hour last night drove a reordering of her priorities, with getting Brian out of prison as the new number one. There is no better demonstration of her regret. Words are nice, but actions are better.

She is eager to learn what Walt uncovered this morning, but even more so, to share her own recent conclusion.

If the plan is to smuggle drugs into the prison using ambulances, what happens to the inmates who are attacked? Are they part of it? If so, even the most hardcore criminals have trouble keeping their mouths shut, making it impossible for MJ to believe this secret would not find daylight. Preventing leaks is paramount for such a scheme to be successful.

What did Benjamin Franklin say about three people keeping a secret?

This supposition led to the next step in last evening's research, as she repeatedly checked her phone like a teenage girl wishing for a text from that special boy in math class. She pored over public records for hours, eventually learning Mendoza's Funeral Home in Brockton had secured the state contract to handle the deceased from various prison facilities, including MCI – Cedar Junction. She spent the next few sleepless hours trying to jam these new puzzle pieces into their rightful spots, but the combination of unexplained emotions and lack of sleep prevented success.

MJ looks at her watch and tugs on Snoopy's leash. "Come on, Snoop! I have work to do!"

Her sense of urgency is interrupted when she almost face plants, thanks to Snoopy's abrupt stop. He peers at a maroon Honda Accord waiting for the stoplight to change. MJ follows his gaze, seeing an elderly man with a Bruins cap and sunglasses sitting behind the wheel. He looks familiar, but before she could get any closer, the light changes. A familiar angst sends a shiver up her spine as she recalls the white Malibu at Dock Square.

She jerks the leash as panic fights for control. "Let's go!"

In addition to concerns about the Malibu and now the Accord, she is battling the clock. She needs to get home, shower, and paw through her limited clothing options to identify something that reaffirms her apologetic posture.

99

Walt watches MJ approach the deli, continually amazed by the ease and confidence with which she moves. His impressions of MJ have long been focused on her intelligence, self-assuredness, and badass approach in her pursuit of the truth, no matter where it leads. However, those thoughts have been dwarfed by a deeper sentiment that is foreign to him. He buries the unfamiliar feelings, vowing to cross whatever emotional bridge exists once Brian is a free man, and not a second before.

"Hey… you find it okay?"

"I am here, so…"

A shared laugh eases the tension. "Excellent point."

People are cramped, bumping into one another as they navigate the small space, made tinier by the addition of a handful of tables. They find a table the size of a checker-board near the front windows, where everyone walking by can pass judgment on their lunch choices.

After ordering for both of them at the counter, Walt returns to the table with a plastic number in a small steel stand.

He makes a quick visual security sweep before jumping in. "I met with Brian this morning. He thinks the new guy we should look into is named Rutherford. He does not know the first name. It is not much, but…"

MJ is writing on a napkin. "It is plenty. I will have some-thing for you later tonight."

"Great. He also mentioned talking to a couple of guys this morning at breakfast."

The server slides a pastrami on rye with chips in front of Walt and a ham and Swiss on wheat, no pickle or chips, in front of MJ.

She grabs half of the sandwich, checks to make sure it doesn't have any dressing or oil, and starts munching. "And?"

"And he said they told him inmates are made some type of offer. They must agree to get shanked or injured severely enough to warrant an ambulance as a sign of acceptance. The belief is that their sentences are reduced to time served, in exchange for their agreement. That is how they explain no one returning."

MJ takes another bite, watching Walt trying to eat the pastrami without any of the excessive mustard he added, ending up in his lap.

It is her turn to complete the security sweep. "Their failure to return is not because of a deal… it is because they are dead."

The casualness with which the statement is made sees Walt stop mid-bite. "What?"

"It makes perfect sense."

Walt's puzzled expression looks like it surprises her. She smiles. "Benjamin Franklin is right: 'Three people may keep a secret if two of them are dead.' Whatever the offer, whatever the arrangement, the only way to ensure there are no leaks is to ensure the injured inmates end up dead."

Walt discontinues his sandwich wrangling, focusing on the potato chips. "Jesus, you really do have a fucking dark side."

"Not dark, brilliantly logical." MJ takes another bite. "Think about it, if they are using the attacks to smuggle drugs into the prison, which I am not conceding is the objective, why is no one talking about it on the inside or the outside? Keeping that quiet is impossible."

Walt considers her line of thinking. "So, you are saying inmates are offered something if they agree to be killed?"

"I am saying one of the keys to making this work is the inmates being permanently silenced. Whether or not they know what is on the horizon when they accept the offer is a different question. For the record, I refuse to believe it is a suicide pact."

"Then what is it?"

MJ scans the room again. "Let's walk through what we know. There is an arson that kills four people, including a woman who works as the warden's administrative assistant. Your client is framed for the crime. The warden has it in for your client for previously stumbling upon a larger conspiracy, which is connected to multiple inmates disappearing from Walpole."

MJ continues after Walt leans over to pick up the small paper napkin that has fallen from his lap. "We know the warden's alias is sitting on a ton of money in the Caymans. Our hypothesis is that it is tied to drugs, given the amount."

"What else could it be?"

"Someone gets attacked, leaves, and never comes back. The reported understanding of the inmates is that their sentences will be commuted for playing along. The reality is they never come back because they are dead."

Walt feels MJ's anxiety as he watches her scan the crowd for a third time.

"If they die at the prison, there is only one funeral home contracted to remove bodies, Mendoza's in Brockton. If they die in the ambulance, they are often taken directly to a funeral home, according to the EMTs, or at least that is the way it worked a couple of years ago. I am presuming that, too, is Mendoza's."

Walt raises one eyebrow. "Okay, following your logic, other than the people in prison who may have questions, why are the families of these deceased deal-makers not asking questions?"

"I know Tommy and Chicky had no known family. Mendoza's contract with the state encompasses all deaths, but it gives him great latitude with indigent deaths. Perhaps this group is the target, so as to avoid a problem outside the prison?"

"Some of these guys are gangbangers. Even if they had no family, their brothers-in-arms would want to know what happened."

"The only gangbanger we know of is José, and there is a clear, documented trail of his demise."

Walt sits back and stretches, hitting the woman standing behind him. "Oh, I am sorry. Are you okay?"

The woman tells him to fuck off and keeps moving.

Walt looks at MJ and shrugs. "Presuming you're right…"

MJ cannot help herself. "Presuming?"

Walt's smile beams as he concedes the point. "Okay, you are right *as usual*. Better?"

MJ's smirk becomes a relaxed grin. "Much."

Walt continues. "So, they are killing inmates with no families to have the hearse smuggle drugs into the prison. The warden gets a cut and has been adding his profits to his friend 'Stanley's' retirement account in the Caymans. The warden thinks Brian is on to him, so he sets him up for arson and murder, with the added bonus of personally keeping an eye on him. Is that what you are saying?"

"Again, I am not convinced it is drugs, but essentially, yes."

"Let's go back to the question you asked a couple of weeks ago. Why kill Lily Whitaker? And let us not forget the coincidental death of her friend Katie."

Remorse seems to battle with enthusiasm as MJ responds. "There are no coincidences." MJ bows her head for a second and then continues. "Based upon what Katie told me, Lily was worried about something at work. Maybe she saw or heard something. It would give Johansson a chance to kill two birds with one stone, no pun intended."

Walt continues to devour the sandwich, mustard be damned.

MJ moves on. "He can take out the person who saw or heard too much by using Brian's past crime as a means to eliminate the risk. All that is left is sitting back and allowing the natural investigative approach to proceed."

Walt scowls. "You forgot stealing a glove without being caught, using it when the fire is set, and then planting it in Brian's trunk."

MJ concedes those points with a nod. "The key is ensuring it is pinned to the guy who was an inquisitive thorn in Johansson's side in the past. Final result: Threat removed, and Brian's eventual return to an environment over which Johansson maintains absolute control."

Walt holds up his hands. "If they are killing people and using the hearse to deliver the drugs to the prison, what do we know about the funeral home?"

"Tonight's homework, along with identifying 'Rutherford'."

"What am I supposed to do in the meantime?"

"Defend your client and tell me if you need *anything* from me. We were not able to protect Lily and her family, nor Katie. We cannot let anything happen to Brian."

On that they both agree.

100

Walt returns to the office, his mind dancing with disparate thoughts. Brian's safety. Johansson. Dead inmates. Drugs. The glove. And… her. He drops his laptop into its docking station and stares at the monitor as the computer goes through its sign-in and security protocols.

The Post-its stare back: "*No glove. No worries.*" "*Did Lily see or hear something? Real target?*" He adds a third. "*Drugs and dead inmates?*"

He considers MJ's most recent theory. The thought of voluntarily agreeing to be stabbed with a filthy, germ-ridden, make-shift knife is unimaginable. If, in fact, inmates are agreeing to this step, MJ is right; they must be unaware of their journey's true end.

Walt closes his eyes and shakes the thoughts from his mind, returning to his primary duties. He has a handful of electrical and plumbing employees left to interview, but his hope of identifying something useful diminishes with each discussion.

Walt needs to identify the gas company employee. Brian is adamant and provided a decent description. He is contemplating calling the gas company's attorney again when his secretary buzzes the intercom.

"Attorney Giancomo on line two."

Walt clears his mind and his desk. He grabs a fresh legal pad and answers the phone. "Good afternoon, Ginny. What can I do for you?"

"Walt, it is what I can do for you, actually. I have received the remaining lab results and wanted to give you a call before I sent them over."

Ginny's tone is weird. He gives her his full attention. "Okay. What's up?"

A deep breath is followed by a quick statement. "The DNA tests for the interior of the glove retrieved from your client's car confirm the presence of two different strands, with the predominant strand being that of your client."

Walt sits up straight and begins scribbling on the legal pad. "*Two* strands of DNA?"

"Yes, both male."

"So you are calling to tell me you are dropping the charges against my client because you have identified the other strand?"

A chuckle. "No. It might be a different story if your guy's DNA was not on the inside. But it is, and lest we forget, the glove was found in the trunk of his car. The presence of a second strand is a red herring, and you know it. Anyone could have worn it for any reason."

"Including framing my client."

"I will give you points for persistence. The results are on their way to you."

"Thanks. While I have you, may I ask a question?"

"Sure."

"When you reviewed Jacobs' video of the car's retrieval, did you notice anything suspicious?"

There is hesitancy in Ginny's voice. "No. Nothing out of the ordinary."

Walt refuses to tip his hand. He loves surprises at trial, but even better, Ginny will go bonkers trying to figure out the purpose of his question. Walt takes great pride in finding ways to make the prosecutor's life miserable.

"Okay. Thanks. I will review the test results with my client. Then we can talk about dismissal."

Walt checks one question off his list. Ginny has done the work for him, and it bit her in the ass. She is right: the presence of a second DNA strand is not going to do much on its own, but it is the first meaningful arrow to be added to Brian's defense quiver.

He and MJ need to find a few more.

101

Ginny hangs up, scratching her head. She has watched the video at least a dozen times, and for once in his life, Jacobs did not make a complete ass of himself. Sure, he made a couple of bullshit comments, but she can get around those. What did she miss? She puts on her running shoes and heads downstairs to think.

She slowly increases her speed for the first three miles, reaching her eventual pace by mile four. This timing also coincides with the endorphin boost she gets from running. Some refer to it as a runner's high or getting into the zone. It is here that her mind is always the clearest.

After a few more miles and replaying the video in her mind for the millionth time, Ginny concludes Walt is screwing with her. She blows a piece of hair out of her face as she moves onto the next difficult decision. What to do about the body parts found in Suffolk County?

She is under no obligation to do anything. The limbs have been tied to the *Nichols* case, but there is no paper trail connecting them to the *McMillan* case. Should Walt somehow stumble upon the information, the situation is easily explained away as a miss because of geography.

As she reaches mile seven, Ginny begins exploring things from every angle, eventually flipping the initial question. It is no longer about the downside potential of comparing the data. If the tests confirm the DNA in the glove matches the DNA of the severed arm, she can position herself as a champion of truth, creating a media event announcing the dismissal of charges against McMillan, and a campaign slogan rolls off her tongue: "Ginny Giancomo: a champion for justice."

Or she could name McMillan a co-conspirator. She can leverage the fight with Janssen and the location where the glove was found to secure a plea agreement, thereby bringing *both* killers to justice. If they do not match, no harm, no foul. She was given a piece of information, and she pursued it with vigor. The end.

After completing mile nine, Ginny dramatically reduces her speed, using the last mile as a cool-down. Ten minutes later, she heads for the shower, where the steaming water mixes with the relief of making a difficult decision.

102

MJ pulls her feet beneath her on the couch and asks Spotify to play Coltrane's *Blue Train* as she begins her search for Rutherford. As the music guides the clicking on the keyboard, MJ identifies twelve possibilities, of which she quickly eliminates nine.

After an hour of sifting, she zeroes in on Nicholas "The Knick" Rutherford, age twenty-nine, from Fall River, a young man with a reputation for using a knife to solve his problems. He was convicted of attempted murder two years ago. To her surprise, she locates a brief obituary reflecting that he passed away a few days ago "from injuries sustained in an accident."

After looking at Snoopy and declaring bullshit, MJ mocks the vision of a prisoner "accidentally" falling onto a shiv multiple times. The obituary, which makes no mention of family, is attached to the Mendoza Funeral Home website. It is five poorly written, soulless sentences. She jostles Snoopy as she scooches off the couch.

Sixty-five minutes later, MJ is standing at the door of Mendoza's Funeral Home, dancing back and forth on the balls of her feet, ignoring the pain in her little toe and manifesting an approach. She has no plan for this conversation beyond meeting a self-imposed commitment to not poke the bear… again.

The front door opens before her index finger reaches the doorbell.

"Good afternoon. I am Ben Mendoza. How may I help you today?" Ben holds the door open and encourages MJ to enter the foyer with a wave of his arm.

"Hello, Mr. Mendoza. My name is MJ Fernandez. I am an investigative reporter doing a story on the recent tragedy, which took the lives of Dylan Janssen, Lily Whitaker, and their two children. My online research indicates you handled their arrangements."

"Yes, that is correct. I gifted my services to the family at the suggestion of another member of the community." He smiles modestly. "It was the right thing to do."

"That is very generous. What a great angle for my article." MJ captures this information in her tiny notebook. "I am hoping you can provide some insight about the family."

"I am sorry, Ms. Fernandez, but I do not believe I can offer much. I knew them from the neighborhood well enough to say hello, but nothing more. In truth, this tragedy has spurred me to invest in getting to know all of my neighbors at a deeper level."

"Please call me MJ. Another wonderful angle. Learning from a tragedy and investing personal time and effort to become a better neighbor." MJ smiles as Ben frowns. MJ's grin fades to embarrassment. "Sorry, I will find a better way to say that."

Ben looks at his watch. "Ms. Fernandez, I am terribly sorry, but I need to prepare for an appointment."

"May I ask one last question?" MJ can't help herself. "My research also revealed the Commonwealth has contracted you to handle the deceased coming from Walpole and other prisons, including indigent deaths."

"All people deserve respect in death. I am pleased to provide services to those who would otherwise be cast on the trash heap. It aligns with my core values."

MJ makes a couple more notes. "Thank you for your time, Mr. Mendoza. And thank you for all that you do to make your community a better place."

"Happy to help, and I hope you contact me in the unfortunate event you have a need for the services we offer. I would be happy to help. Have a good afternoon, Ms. Fernandez."

MJ leaves carrying an eerie feeling mixed with excitement and confusion. She is heading toward her car when she encounters an elderly woman shuffling up the sidewalk, dragging a small metal cart carrying two bags of groceries.

"Excuse me, do you need any help?"

The woman raises her head and looks at MJ with the confidence of a Green Beret. "No."

MJ smiles, quietly admiring the spitfire standing before her, when a lightbulb appears above her head.

"My name is MJ Fernandez. I am an investigative reporter doing a story about the tragic fire that occurred recently. May I ask you a few questions?"

The woman's shoulders slump. "I will tell you the same thing I told the other reporter. This was a senseless loss of life. They were terrific people. Two loving and caring human beings raising two strong children."

The phrase strikes a chord. "By any chance, are you Agnes Rothschild?"

Agnes' penetrating eyes confirm the answer. "How did…"

"I read your comments about Dylan, Lily, and their children. They must have meant a lot to you."

Fortitude is replaced by anger. "Their lives were ruthlessly snuffed out for no apparent reason, and the police don't seem to be doing a damn thing to find their killer."

"I am looking into the fire and would love to get your perspective or anything you might want to share."

Agnes winces as she shifts her weight from one foot to the other. "I have said everything except for this…" Grief and anger shoot from Agnes' eyes. "Their killer best hope that our paths never cross." Agnes re-grips her cart and steps forward. "I have to get these groceries home before they spoil. Good day, Ms. Fernandez."

MJ watches in awe and mumbles to herself as Agnes restarts her journey.

"Always nice to meet a fellow bad-ass."

103

Ben's cellphone begins ringing before he finishes closing the door.

"I was just about to…"

Johansson is all business. "She is there."

Ben is nodding. "Ah, right. Your recently acquired capability. She is gone, but we should talk further. I reluctantly admit the accuracy of your assessment."

"This hurdle needs to be removed, not avoided."

Ben can picture the smug look on Johansson's face. "Agreed, but in due course. First, we must meet our current obligation."

"We are under a microscope."

Ben is confused. "You are prepared to dispatch an external problem, but are slow-playing our internal need? Pick a fucking lane."

"My view is consistent, but I am duty-bound to ensure all strategic obstacles are acknowledged and understood."

Ben rolls his eyes. "These are not new obstacles, and we have thirty-six hours to complete our pressing objective."

"Fine. The resident in cell 218B has the…"

Ben's anger clouds his normally thoughtful choice of words. "Are you out of your fucking mind? Do you really…"

Johansson's diabolical laughter is unnerving. "Fine. I recommend slowing our adversary's advancement with a message."

Ben hesitates. "We could use what we know works. That should create the space we need to fulfill the outstanding contracts."

"Agreed."

Ben ends the call and drops his head in disgust. The depravity of his feral partner is becoming all-consuming. His only escape is pushing through the last few deliveries before Johansson's thirst for blood becomes uncontrollable.

104

Facing the likelihood of spending the rest of his life in prison, Brian took the "offer" and agreed to take the shiv. A deep sense of calm, like he has not felt in years, followed. He could finally say good-fucking-bye to the hellhole once and for all.

A creaking sound awakens Brian to the sight of a hairy beer belly as his cellmate climbs down from the top bunk. The wave of disappointment upon realizing it was only a dream hits Brian like a tsunami.

After two small boxes of Frosted Flakes, Brian chooses to follow Walt's direction as he keeps to himself and wanders the yard silently searching for Rutherford.

As the inmates are being shuffled back to the cellblock, Brian is pondering the gas company's inability or unwillingness to identify their huge employee. He asks himself over and over: *How can the gas company deny his presence when…*

The yelling and screaming catch Brian by surprise. A skirmish between Brian's cellmate and the inmate immediately behind him breaks out. They are swinging and kicking wildly, most of their blows connecting with nothing but air. The others move quickly to create a circular barrier, giving themselves a ringside seat while preventing the guards from doing their job.

Brian is too slow today. Unidentified hands propel him forward prior to his back reaching the security of the concrete wall. He crashes into the two combatants, who turn their intentions toward their new common foe. Rather than fight back, Brian turns to escape the circle as their punches and kicks begin to land.

He catches a glint in his peripheral vision, giving him the split second needed to prevent the shiv from being driven deep into his stomach. The thrust deeply slashes his arm, but his quick-thinking reaction prevents any real damage.

Dropping to his knees, Brian grabs his bleeding arm as the two original fighters return to their own battle. He is sweating profusely as he looks up to see the guards wrangling their way through the circular rows of inmates. The gash to his arm continues to leak, but it is nothing compared to the blood pouring from his cellmate, who is groaning in agony on the floor.

A guard hollers for the medical extraction team, who arrive within seconds. One of the nurses notices the blood soaking into Brian's jumpsuit. She rushes to him, quickly declaring the injury serious but not life-threatening. The laceration is wrapped in a towel, and Brian is escorted to the infirmary by the nurse and four large guards.

Upon arrival, he is handcuffed to a bed as the entire medical team rushes toward his cellmate. He watches in awe as the medical team scrambles to save the shanked inmate's life. Orders are being yelled, an IV is started, and an oxygen mask is added after someone screams the word "pneumothorax." Brian has no idea what that is, but it does not sound good. Watching the medical team create another hole in the side of his cellmate's chest confirms his assessment.

After twenty minutes, the medical team steps back from the blood-soaked surgical table as the doctor looks at the clock on the wall and announces the time of death.

Brian has seen dead bodies at funerals before, but has never watched a man die. The light-headedness caused by his own injuries adds to his shock, but he cannot pry his eyes from the lifeless body. He watches as nurses remove the IV lines, drop blood-soaked bandages into red biohazard bags, and bring in mops to begin cleaning the floor.

Brian is dumbstruck by the lack of emotion displayed by those who roll the body onto its side and slide the heavy black bag beneath it. They bend each knee, one at a time, so the legs can be slipped into the bag, and then they place the arms at the sides of the body, before gently positioning the head inside. Lastly, he watches the doctor place a small green tank into the top corner of the bag.

The low, staccato sound of the heavy zipper being closed returns Brian to his own reality. He was shoved into the circle, where someone attempted to stick him. Was it for shits and giggles, or was he also a target? Did his new tablemates rat him out? Is the warden sending another message?

The local anesthetic and pain medication finally kick in, forcing Brian's eyes to close as a nurse lays the suture kit on the table next to him. He has one last thought as the small stainless steel hook punctures the skin on his arm.

Accepting the "offer" will not bring the relief his dream promised.

105

With her Yeti filled with steaming blueberry coffee, MJ and her best friend head out for their morning stroll. A chilly mist hits her in the face as she leaves her building. She shivers and flips up the hood on her jacket.

MJ's mind is in full cyclone mode. Information and theories spin, crashing into one another, but never interlocking. Her gut delivered a message the moment Mendoza closed the door. Following the mantra she, Walt, and Jonathan relied upon in the past prompted her to ask "the team" to take a look into the friendly mortician.

She is struggling to disprove Walt's drug theory. While it makes sense given the dollars involved, there are too many variables and too many people needing to be controlled… or silenced.

Her thoughts flip to Johansson. She fantasizes about him swapping places with Brian. Orange jumpsuits are a long way from Armani. As a smile crosses her face, she notices a man with no four-legged companion on the opposite side of the dog park.

MJ's pulse quickens as the hair on her arms and the back of her neck react. She watches him from the corner of her eye. If he is there for her, his covert skills suck.

After picking up the warm pile Snoopy left behind, she takes two purpose-driven steps in the stranger's direction, when he suddenly whistles—a German shepherd, running around in violation of the park's leash requirement, returns and heels. The man reconnects a leash and heads out, without so much as another glance in MJ's direction.

Her heartbeat returns to normal as her eyes sweep back and forth, peering through the rain dripping from the lip of her hood. "The team" would be proud of her development in this area. Practice makes perfect. Well, closer to perfect anyway.

MJ shoves her memorized picture of today's stranger into the "foe" folder as her mind returns to its swirling, eventually landing in the place where she should have started: money. She is angry with herself for violating her number one rule.

The drug trade is lucrative, and using an ambulance or hearse to get the drugs into the prison is creative. But that is where the logic stops for MJ.

Retrieving the drugs from the vehicle is easy, but getting them distributed throughout the prison is a daunting task, requiring a lot of players. This is in addition to the secrecy concerns, which grow exponentially with the addition of each step or participant. More people mean more payoffs. More payoffs mean less profit, pushing the volume of drugs required to mathematically generate the bank account upon which Johansson is sitting to prodigious levels.

It cannot be drugs.

She shakes her head to reshuffle the puzzle pieces and begins anew. They start falling into place one after another, but again, she stalls, unable to paint the entire picture.

As she and Snoopy are heading up to her apartment, it hits her like a piano falling from the sky. When she exits the elevator and regains service, MJ dials the phone and leaves a brief voicemail.

"Hey… I think it would be nice if you took me to dinner tonight. Something relaxed. Beers and wings?"

106

"**S**he took a special interest, Colonel."

Johansson shakes his head. "You were trained better, Sergeant."

"Yes, sir. She is on high alert. I am not sure if it is a transitory state or a permanent one."

"Observations?"

"Predominantly static location-wise. No visitors. Beyond trips to the location where she was observed today, and the occasional trip with the attorney, no consequential movement."

"Tactical assessment?"

"Opportunities for accidental removal will be limited."

"Recommendations?"

"Her evening stroll occurs consistently within the same two-hour period and provides the best opportunity for a remote engagement."

Johansson pauses briefly. "Develop multiple operational strategies that will achieve the desired outcome and hold."

"You will have them before end of day."

Johansson is relentless in his pursuit of preparedness, a critical element in the success of any mission. Infusing this behavior into his side business, along with a ruthlessness both he and Mendoza keep hidden, has brought them the wealth they both so richly deserve..

They are close to reaching their established financial target of five million dollars each. His calculations confirm the need for a handful of deliveries to see his retirement account surpass that threshold. Had the last delivery not failed, they would be even closer, but shit happens.

He plugs a tiny thumb drive, which he keeps on the same chain as his dog tags, into his laptop and enters a twelve-digit password. After completing the two-factor authentication process, he checks the status of his Cayman account, shuts down the laptop, and returns the chain to its place of absolute safety.

He has a hearse to meet at the loading dock.

107

Walt's heart flutters as he listens to the voicemail. He knows exactly where they should go.

"Hey… got your message."

There is a playfulness in MJ's voice. "A bit presumptuous, perhaps, but you did say standing invitation."

"That I did. Given your proposed choice of cuisine, what do you think about The Jury Room? I can pick you up in thirty minutes."

"That is the place you and Jonathan always talk about, right? No need for you to come across town, I will hop the 'T' and meet you there. But, it has to be in an hour, I have to finish something first."

Walt's excitement cannot be contained. "See you soon!"

The call ends, and Walt looks down at his shirt, which has a dollop of mayo from today's lunch. He keeps clean shirts hanging in his office closet for occasions like this. He yanks wildly at desk drawers, searching for the toothbrush and toothpaste hidden within.

After a quick trip to the bathroom, he returns to his office to change his shirt for the second time in five minutes—spitting toothpaste into the sink can be tricky— and heads out to ensure they get a great table.

Arriving first, Walt grabs a table and orders a scotch to calm his nerves before MJ arrives. His eyes continue to flick to the door, anticipating her arrival.

About fifty minutes after their call ended, MJ strolls in with her hair in a ponytail pulled through a white Red Sox cap. She is wearing a pair of tight-fitting black Levi's, a maroon Harvard quarter-zip with the sleeves pushed up to the elbows, and her signature Chucks. Walt isn't the only one whose eyes refuse to blink.

MJ slides into her side of the booth and spies the empty rocks glass. "Started without me?

Embarrassment turns Walt's cheeks the same color as the streaks in MJ's hair. "Oh… yeah. Got here early to make sure we would get a good table."

MJ looks around like she's taking in the scenery, but Walt knows she is actually doing a security sweep. "Cool place. I like the décor. Very Perry Mason retro."

"You are not old enough to know who Perry Mason is."

They share a laugh as their server arrives with a couple of beers and takes their order: two dozen wings, mild for him and extra hot for her. They clink their frosted mugs of Sam Adams, take a swig, and get down to business.

MJ wastes no time. "The drug angle is all wrong. It's not about what they are trying to get into the prison, but what they are working to get out."

Walt raises an eyebrow. "And that is?"

"Dead bodies."

Walt scoffs. "That makes no sense. Why the secrecy around removing dead bodies from a prison? And that does not account for the cash 'Stan' is sitting on."

The last time Walt saw this smile was when MJ told him she would handle contacting the mobsters threatening to kill them.

MJ looks left and then right. "It's been sitting in front of us the whole time. How do you make money from dead bodies?"

Walt shrugs. "Selling them to Harvard Medical School as cadavers?"

MJ smiles like the cat that ate the canary. "Close, but that is a lot of cadavers to generate millions of dollars. You get another guess."

Walt hates this game. "No idea. How?"

"They are doing the same thing car thieves do: chopping them up and selling the parts."

Walt leans back into the seat. "Christ, MJ! I stick by my prior assertion. You have a nasty, fucking dark side." He stifles his nervous laugh as he lifts the beer mug to his lips.

"Think about it. Black market organ donation is a multi-billion-dollar international business. Young, healthy inmates with no families make great resources."

Walt sits forward, elbows on the table. "Organ viability is short once a body dies."

"That is not an issue."

Walt shakes his head side-to-side. "You don't call a hearse for someone who is alive."

MJ leans in. "Here is what we know or believe we know. Young inmates are reportedly made some type of offer. They get shanked, or beaten, and are hurried off to the infirmary. If they die, they are put into a body bag, and Mendoza's is called. I think they have figured out a way to make the bodies only appear dead. Mendoza then rushes them to wherever the organs are harvested. My guess is the funeral home. The desired parts are taken, and everything else is cremated." MJ sits back, beaming. "*That* is why they never return."

MJ asks for a side of hot sauce when the wings are delivered. Walt's nose starts to run as the heat from MJ's wings wafts across the booth. He dunks one of his wings into blue cheese, transforming it from a mildly spicy wing into a tolerable wing.

"That is a lot of supposition. And the only way any of this works, drugs or whatever, is if Johansson has a lot of help within the prison."

MJ dips a flat into the hot sauce and deftly removes the meat in a few quick movements. Walt is amazed at her tolerance for pain as she licks the sauce from her fingers.

A sip of beer and MJ continues. "I figure the prison doc is in on it at a minimum. There is probably a nurse or two and a couple of guards involved, too, but the doc is key. He would declare the inmate dead and control the movement of the body. He is the inside man they would need."

Walt finishes his second wing after using his beer to douse what little heat is left after its blue cheese bath. He waves to the server to order another round of Sam's and jumps back in.

"Okay, since we *know* you are always right, let's tear your premise apart. The first and most obvious question is, how do you make a live body look like a dead body?"

MJ smiles. "I have some thoughts."

Walt rolls his eyes and smiles. "Of course you do."

"There is a very rare medical condition called catalepsy. A person goes into a trance or has a seizure, which results in a loss of consciousness and sensation. The body also becomes rigid, which can be confused with rigor mortis. All of which give the appearance of death, but the individual is very much alive. The odds of having a large number of inmates with the disease are astronomical, making that avenue improbable."

The server delivers the next round as MJ finishes her first beer, swapping the empty mug for a new ice-cold draft.

"I have found a few articles relative to the use of a modified version of tetrodotoxin as a paralytic. It is the neurotoxin in pufferfish, which makes them wicked dangerous to eat if not prepared properly. Many say it is voodoo, but while a complicated mixture would be needed to avoid instant death, in the right dosage it reportedly slows breathing to almost nothing."

MJ takes a long pull from the fresh beer. "Also, there are other drugs, like sevoflurane, that are inhaled. They are a class of drugs used to relax muscles before and during surgery. I am presuming a physician has the necessary training. Any combination of these possibilities makes the infirmary doctor a critical component of the strategy."

Walt is not surprised by her thoroughness. "Sounds overly complicated, but let's keep going. They would need access to these paralytics or other neuromuscular blocking agents. You cannot buy those with your Amazon Prime account. Second, it still does not address the skill set required to harvest organs. It is not like gutting a fish. It has to be done with expertise and precision. Does Mendoza strike you as someone with those abilities?"

"Mendoza is a fucking chameleon with the perfect cover. As a beloved community member, he is the last person anyone would consider for something this twisted. Maybe the infirmary doctor races to the funeral home?"

Walt's acid reflux is triggered as he watches MJ dunk another wing into her side of hot sauce. He douses his own wing with blue cheese—twice—to counteract MJ's approach.

"What do we know about Mendoza?"

"I have asked 'the team' to look into him. We should have something shortly."

Walt's caring tone creeps out. "Listen, MJ. You have once again waded into unbelievably dangerous waters. Maybe I should rethink hanging out with you?"

MJ tilts her head to the left and shrugs her shoulders as a broad, wing-sauce-covered smile spreads across her face. "Your call."

Walt looks around. "Seriously, you have already poked Johansson. And now you have gone to see Mendoza. If they're smart enough to put something like this together, they have the mental capacity to worry about what you know, or think you know. As a healthy young female, you are worth a lot of money. We have to make sure you keep all of your organs intact."

MJ blushes. "Thanks, but it is Brian's organs we should be worried about."

Walt nods in agreement when his cellphone rings in a familiar tone: "Dun. Dun."

108

Walt spends five minutes in the back of The Jury Room to prevent other patrons from overhearing the unexpected conversation. Walt slides back into his seat and waves down their server. They order another round of drinks.

This time, it's a double Oban neat for Walt and a Sauvignon Blanc for MJ.

Without noticing Walt's glare, MJ digs a pen out of her laptop bag, ignoring the wing sauce on her fingers. "Okay, what did he say?"

Walt remains silent until the drinks are served. As the server walks away, rage comes through clenched teeth. "You get one chance. Tell me exactly what you said to Mendoza."

"Why? What the hell happened?"

Walt is seething. "Brian is in the infirmary. His arm was slashed when he dodged an attempted stabbing."

MJ lurches backward, shaken, her voice cracking with concern. "What?"

"He says there was a fight behind him. He was shoved into the middle of it and attacked. But he didn't get the worst of it. He watched them place his cellmate into a body bag."

"Holy shit! How badly was he injured?"

Walt is squeezing every ounce of blood from his fists. "He took twenty-eight sutures, but says he will be fine. I will make my own assessment when I see him first thing in the morning. Now, back to my question."

MJ never breaks eye contact. "Do you trust me or not?"

"You were told not to push Johansson, and you shoved him to the edge of the cliff. I am having difficulty reconciling the timing here."

MJ pushes her wine to the side, signaling her preparation for battle. "Have you considered that it is a diversion? If they wanted him dead, he would be the one in the goddamn body bag, and you know it."

Walt sits back, his mind spiraling. "You still haven't answered the question. This is serious shit, MJ."

No one questions MJ's integrity. "Fuck you, Erickson! I am working to help your client. I am convinced the two assholes we have been talking about are the culprits. If you want to get your client out of prison permanently, we need to continue to push this forward."

"I do not want the permanency to come with a funeral." Walt is tempted to pay the bill and leave without another word. "This is not just a bunch of words on the page or another Pulitzer Prize. This is a man's life!"

Their heads are swinging back and forth in search of danger as they battle to keep their voices down, but emotions continue to drive the heated exchange.

"You're goddamn right it is, and once again I have provided information you did not have, nor could have obtained. And, let's not forget… *You* called me!"

Walt closes his eyes, tilts his head downward, and takes a huge breath. He looks back up, staring at the rage behind MJ's eyes as he throws back what is left of his drink. She is right. He knows what she does and how she does it. Jonathan is also right; that is why he called her. Walt waves down the server and asks for another drink. MJ's wine glass remains untouched.

Civility returns to Walt's voice. "Okay. Let's take a breath." He follows his own suggestion before plowing ahead. "First, I do trust you… implicitly. If I didn't, you would not be here. Second, you are right, I did call you because I prefer to work with the best when given the option. Lastly, we need to protect Brian and nail these bastards!"

MJ downs her entire glass of wine in two gulps and allows the empty glass to hover over the table.

Walt knows that is the best apology he is going to get. He takes the glass and points it toward their server before starting again. "Where were we?"

MJ refuses to give an inch. She never does. "I was being right. You were being an asshole."

Walt ignores the bait, proceeding to replay the entirety of his conversation with Brian in excruciating detail, without interruption until…

"Wait, what did Brian say he saw the doctor putting into the body bag?"

109

Johansson and Mendoza meet for breakfast at a diner built from an old train car that screams the fifties. The servers are wearing poodle skirts, saddle shoes, and a smile. The authenticity of the décor would return them to their youth were it not for the eighteen-dollar omelets.

A steaming mug of coffee and one hot tea are delivered to their red leatherette booth, as Elvis' "Hound Dog" begins playing on the juke box. Menus sit untouched. Eating is not today's objective.

Mendoza sips the hot coffee and initiates the whispering. "You ruined a lung."

Johansson glowers back. "A lot less than you ruined last time."

"Impact breathing, and you do more than piss away $100,000."

"Did the buyers take everything else?"

"All but the corneas. I also needed to give a discount on the liver, which was nicked."

Johansson rolls his eyes. "Whatever. Now, about our problem."

"She has nothing."

"Surveillance reflects…"

Mendoza's eyes bulge. "Surveillance? Who the hell authorized surveillance?"

"Once an enemy is located, surveillance until a tactical decision is made is a logical step."

Mendoza closes his eyes and takes a slow cleansing breath. "Reflects what?"

"Limited opportunity for undetected removal."

"No."

"No, what?"

"I have said this before. Our sole focus is on achieving the financial target. Then and only then do we consider tying up loose ends."

"My nosy resident in cell 218B shared an observation."

Mendoza scrunches his face in confusion. "Observation?"

"His mind was clouded by painkillers, and he forgot calls were recorded. He mentioned a small green oxygen tank."

Mendoza slams himself back into his bench seat and throws his hands into the air. "What in the goddamn fuck?"

Johansson fills their booth with smugness as he sips his tea. "This is why you would have never made it as a soldier, much less a special operator. Shit happens. Success is dependent upon one's resiliency, willingness to adapt on the fly, and most importantly, the ability to remain calm in the face of adversity."

Mendoza's clenched fists are resting on the table. "Increased risk has again appeared because of *you*. This time, a witness observed the most secretive step in the process. A step relayed to others, including..."

Johansson scoffs. "It is time for a thorough house-cleaning. Slow our delivery rate for ninety days, then re-engage at Mach 1 until we reach the finish line."

Mendoza digs in. "We have enough to live on comfortably for the rest of our lives. We should discontinue operations immediately and take our leave."

"Surveillance will continue with periodic updates. We will re-evaluate clean-up protocols in ninety days." Johansson stares, demanding consensus.

Mendoza eventually nods in resignation, wondering how long his partner can look through him without blinking.

110

The analysis Ginny has been waiting for arrives. She sits at her desk; a half-eaten energy bar rests in the corner next to her lime-green reusable water bottle. She turns the envelope over and over in her hands, evaluating the pros and cons with each flip as her closed eyes face the ceiling. She is startled by a knock on the door.

"Oh… sorry, Ginny. Just wanted to make sure you saw the lab results you requested."

Ginny settles herself and smiles. "I did, thank you."

She has no choice. Ginny cannot discard them, nor ignore them. Too many people know about the request, the test, and her receipt of the results.

She opens the envelope pensively.

Ginny gasps as reality slams into her chest, stealing her breath. She had played this out in her head on the treadmill, but the actuality of these findings is far worse. She knows from first-hand experience that Walt Erickson fights like a cornered honey badger, and she is about to sharpen his claws.

Erickson will immediately demand that all charges be dropped. He will bluster about prosecutorial misconduct, send motion after motion demanding his client's release, and not hesitate to create a media shit storm. Negotiating the impact of this information will require the political deftness of a future District Attorney.

For as long as she can remember, Ginny has viewed the world through the black and white lenses of right and wrong. In the darkest moments of her career, she concedes, only to herself and her therapist, that there is too much grey in the law. She has accepted the realities of the criminal justice system, but refuses to let it erode her core values. People who commit a crime should pay. Period. It is the level of payment, driven by that non-committal color, which has caused many a sleepless night.

Securing a conviction in a case where the detective put the warrants in question is tough enough. Tying the dismembered arm of a man who has beaten a number of women and killed his most recent victim to DNA found inside the accused's glove forces her to wrap her unwilling arms around the color she loathes.

Still, McMillan *must* pay.

If he pleads guilty to the conspiracy charges, she will drop the murder and arson charges and recommend a sentence of twelve to fifteen years, but is willing to go as low as eight to ten years to bring this matter to a close without the need for a trial… a trial she is all but certain she will lose.

She reviews her notes one last time, places her feet firmly on the floor, and asks her assistant to make a call.

111

MJ sits on the Green Line, returning from an update with her editor. Her left leg dangles over her right knee, and her foot bounces like a jackhammer in a futile attempt to burn off her anger and frustration.

Spagnola is not buying her organ theory, agreeing with Walt that, given the amount of money involved, drugs are far more likely. She explained, with exceptional detail and her usual level of aggressiveness, why her theory was the right one.

She wanted to slap him when he peered over his reading glasses, simply said, "No," and flipped over the tiny hourglass. Over the course of the next five minutes, she re-summarized the facts.

There was a devastating fire that killed four people. The fire was ruled arson, and the investigating detective zeroed in on Brian McMillan very quickly, eventually arresting him within seventy-two hours of the fire. The arrest was predicated upon McMillan's past arson conviction, his physical altercation with Dylan, two prior convictions for aggravated assault, and a work glove found in the trunk of his car that was covered with the same formalin identified as an accelerant used in the fire.

During an initial meeting with his attorney, McMillan mentioned an observation he made during his last period of incarceration and provided a couple of names, which triggered the investigation that MJ is now aggressively pursuing.

Her research has led her to conclude that the warden, Samuel Johansson, and Benjamin Mendoza, the respected owner of a local funeral home, are preying on healthy inmates without any familial ties. The inmates are pronounced deceased after being attacked and then transported from the prison by Mendoza, the sole funeral home contracted with the Commonwealth to cover Walpole. This gives them easy cover to smuggle the inmates who are actually injured, not dead, out of the prison in a hearse. She believes the funeral home is the location where the organs are harvested, but that has yet to be confirmed. By whom and where they go once removed also remains a mystery.

Spagnola hammered her with two questions: "*What evidence do you have to support this?*" and "*What is the connection between the fatal fire and your body-snatching theory?*"

After repeating the results of her searches for Tommy Anderson and the others, MJ struggled on the hard evidence front. She has not been able to confirm the information she received from "the team" independently, thus needing to keep that damning evidence to herself.

Ultimately, she conceded a lack of a verifiable connection but closed her presentation by highlighting the working theory that Lily Whitaker saw or heard something that would have shed a bright light on the devious and disgusting plot.

He shrugged and hit her with one of his favorite lines. "*We do not write about presumptions or assumptions; we write about facts and truths.*" With a red face and spiked determination, MJ leapt from her seat and left his office without another word.

Now, she paces the length of the train car as it travels through the tunnels below Boston. She pushes aside the doubts of her editor and returns to the issue that robbed her of the little sleep she enjoys most evenings... her conversation with Walt.

Sure, he tried to bring the temperature down at the end of the meal, but the mind-numbing tension with which she walked away dominated her thoughts.

She is fighting for Brian and the others killed because Johansson and Mendoza are despicable fucking creatures, exploiting young men with no families for the sake of money.

As proof of her commitment, she tapped into "the team," a brilliant group of hackers with a profoundly ingrained sense of right and wrong who eagerly secure the most deeply buried information, regardless of the lines they need to cross.

The train jolts, forcing MJ to grasp a steel pole to regain her balance. At that moment, as MJ attempts to decipher the garbled conductor's announcement, it hits her between the eyes.

Johansson and Mendoza are running out of time.

She is three stops from her destination when a burner phone in her laptop bag buzzes. It is a restricted number.

"Hey, MJ. It's 'Missy'!"

"Hey, Miss. How are you? It's been a minute."

"You up for a quick lunch?"

"Sure. The Usual Place?"

"Sounds great, say noon?"

"See you then!"

112

As one of the newest bars opened near her office, The Usual Place has become a favorite haunt. MJ arrives a few minutes early, finding the lunch crowd filling every seat at the bar, as well as most of the tables. She is waved in ahead of others standing in line, and given a table for two in the back—the benefits of being a regular.

At noon sharp, Missy walks in, a specimen of supreme athleticism, with short brown hair and eyes that absorb every detail and face in the room, just like the handful of other members of "the team" MJ has met over the years. She often imagines the talent pool from which "the team" recruits, given the diversity of skill sets they require.

MJ stands and waves her arm. Missy glides to the back and sits in one smooth motion. "So great to see you, Missy."

"Good to see you, too."

A server drops a couple of menus and darts to the next table before asking if they would like a drink. A teenage boy in desperate need of a dermatology appointment smiles unabashedly, fills their water glasses, and then leaves as quickly as he appeared.

MJ leaves the menu on the table. "The burgers are to die for. I highly recommend."

Missy's eyes continue to sweep the room without moving as MJ realizes her mistake. She sat with her back to the wall, another habit she picked up from some of Missy's coworkers. MJ should have yielded the seat to Missy.

"I am more of a salad girl."

Of that, MJ has no doubt.

Missy's phone chirps, and she answers it without reservation. She motions an inability to hear and walks toward the door. MJ does not move. Ten minutes later, MJ pockets the thumb drive left next to Missy's water glass and orders a burger and fries to go.

Thirty-seven minutes later, MJ is met at the door by her four-legged roommate, who is doing his special dance. She is eager to look at the new information she has received, but is well aware of the steps Snoopy will take to make her regret forgoing his request.

They are walking toward the dog park as a familiar feeling overcomes MJ. She has felt it before but hopes this time is different. She stops and spins around without warning. Her pursuer was not prepared for the maneuver.

She sees a middle-aged man stopping and starting again. He recovers quickly by dropping his phone, but it is too late. MJ nailed him. Snoopy tugs on the leash, letting her know he is not pleased with the delay. MJ restarts the journey with adrenaline-fed urgency.

Fortunately, Snoopy heads to the back corner of the park where MJ has the best view. She zeroes in on her follower as he kneels and pets a Labradoodle that is not his. He is flirting with the dog's attractive owner as MJ saunters past them on her way out of the park. MJ never looks in his direction.

MJ alternates her pace between something quicker than usual and a snail's pace to make her unwanted friend's life miserable, another tactic she learned from the pros. She also never looks back, maintaining the perception of ignorance and calm as she returns to her apartment building. However, the swiftness with which she engages the deadbolts on her door reveals the truth.

She unhooks Snoopy as her back slides down the rear of the door. Her ass hits the floor in the same spot she has sat a few times before. She calls it her "holy shit seat," the only one in the apartment she hates.

MJ loves jazz, but right now she channels Alan Jackson and Jimmy Buffett as she fills a wine glass to the rim and heads to her preferred seat. After a few deep breaths and a healthy sip, she plugs in her newest gift.

The financial section held a few surprises. Mendoza has not created an alter ego like Johansson. His escape plan includes traveling to his new home in the Maldives, which he acquired fourteen months ago. As a country without an extradition treaty with the United States, he would be safe once his feet hit the sands of those beautiful islands in the Indian Ocean.

He, too, is the proud owner of a healthy bank account in the Cayman Islands, although there has been more activity than the withdrawal associated with the purchase of his safe haven. "The team" highlighted the transfer of a $125,000 payment to another account in the Caymans, one owned by an Angel Jiménez, the day after the fire. Another of the same amount followed the day after the glove was discovered. It did not take many keystrokes to identify Mr. Jiménez as a member of the Dead Presidents who spent a significant portion of his adult life behind bars in Walpole.

There are no coincidences.

MJ looks at the names on her "wall of investigation" and identifies two obvious gaps in the current design. First, she adds Mendoza's name, connecting it to Johansson's. Then, she creates one for "Arsonist/Angel Jiménez?" and uses a green string to connect his Post-It to Lily's, Dylan's, and Mendoza's.

She returns to her seat on the couch and moves on to the chronology of Mendoza's life as another puzzle piece snaps into place. Prior to becoming a funeral director, Benjamin

Mendoza was enrolled in medical school in the city she called home while obtaining her undergraduate degree. He attended SUNY Upstate Medical University in Syracuse, NY, where his exceptional academic talent and surgical skill only went so far. He was apparently invited to leave after he smashed a female professor's head onto a desk in response to a poor grade. MJ is surprised to find no reference to criminal charges and wonders if they were exchanged for a voluntary withdrawal in an effort to avoid bad publicity for the school.

MJ looks at Snoopy, attempting to reconcile the new information. This is not the Ben Mendoza she met the other day. His outward appearance, tone, and compassionate words reflect a committed, caring member of the community whose life's purpose is helping others deal with their grief. The cover of Robert Louis Stevenson's *Strange Case of Dr. Jekyll and Mr. Hyde* flashes through her mind.

A rumbling in her stomach interrupts her thoughts, prompting MJ to look for her phone to determine the time. She moves to retrieve it from the counter where she had placed it as the wine was poured. As she approaches the counter, she bursts into laughter.

It is not the passing of three hours that explains her hunger. It is the unopened takeout bag from The Usual Place. After a few cold fries, and with a smile on her face, she heads for the shower with a decision to make.

To call or not to call?

Walt is wrapping up his review of a deposition transcript from the last of the various contractor employees when his assistant buzzes his line.

"Attorney Giancomo on line two, Walt."

Walt twists in his chair to stretch his stiff back and picks up the call. "Hey, Ginny. Calling to tell me you noticed something new on the video from Jacobs?"

The hesitation in Ginny's voice is unmistakable. "Afternoon, Walt. I am calling because something was brought to my attention. I pursued it, and have confirmed it has bearing on the *McMillan* case."

Walt sits up, dumbfounded. "Okay... What is it, and what is its relevance?"

"I was contacted by the Suffolk County D.A.'s office. You may have heard about a dismembered arm found in Southie that possessed a flayed hand. It also had a ring on one of the fingers. They tested the DNA of the arm and also tested the ring." A brief pause. "The ring possessed DNA that matched a number of women who were attacked in the past few months, including the woman who was recently found murdered near DW Field Pond, which is why it crossed my desk."

Walt gasps. She is talking about Katie Nichols. "What is the connection to Brian McMillan?"

"The testing of the ring also revealed the presence of formalin. On a hunch, I had the arm's DNA matched against the unknown DNA found inside your client's glove." Ginny clears her throat. "The second strand is a match."

"Holy shit! That's great news, Ginny! My client has been saying from the beginning it was not him, and now you have proven it. I presume all charges will be dropped, and my client will be breathing the air of the innocent before the end of the day."

"It's not that simple. As I mentioned the last time we spoke, the glove also possesses your client's DNA and was found in the trunk of your client's car. Let us also not forget about the altercation between your client and Dylan Janssen." Another pause. "I will be adding charges for conspiracy to commit murder, and I wanted to give you a heads up."

"Before I tell you how ridiculous that is, I want to know if you ran the DNA through CODIS?"

A heavy sigh precedes the answer. "Yes. The arm belongs to a gangbanger named Angel Jiménez who did time for domestic abuse, weapons possession, and aggravated assault. He has been out for a couple of years."

"Doesn't sound like much of an Angel? Did he do time in Walpole?"

"Why does that matter?"

"It may not. Now, onto why that sounds ridiculous. You just handed me reasonable doubt on a silver platter. This will be the easiest case I have ever tried."

"I have always admired your confidence, Walt, but even if Jiménez wore the glove and/or was involved in the arson, you cannot get around ownership of the glove, the matching formalin, and where it was found. There is not a single shred of evidence that it was planted, if that is where you are headed. Furthermore, your client had motive. The testimony of Jeremy Carter is clear about that."

Walt smiles broadly. "There are millions of those gloves manufactured and sold in the United States, and don't forget, Jeremy Carter will testify that Dylan Janssen beat the snot out of my guy. Brian never lifted his hands, and he will confirm this fact with a nifty visual since the Commonwealth refuses to replace his tooth. As to your statement relative to where the glove was found, I would suggest you spend a meaningful period of time with the video that Jacobs took. Give me a call once you have. Talk soon, Ginny."

He hangs up without allowing her to say another word. He needs to tell Brian what has been found and break the news that he will be arraigned on additional charges. He grabs his suit jacket and sprints for the door.

Now, he has a reason to make the call he has desperately wanted to make.

114

MJ slips as she runs across the tile floor of her bathroom to get to the cellphone ringing on her bedside table. She sees the caller ID and blushes. Her birthday suit is soaking wet, and her towel is still hanging on the hook next to the shower.

She takes a deep breath and answers the call. "Hey there…"

"Hey… sounds like you could use some time at the gym, too."

Laughing doesn't help her catch her breath. "True enough. What's up?"

"Got some crazy news. I am headed to Walpole now, hoping to catch Brian before dinner."

MJ heads for the living room, grabs her laptop from the coffee table, and drops onto the couch to take notes. Snoopy looks disapprovingly at her choice of attire. "I heard from 'the team.'" She walks back to the bedroom, pinching the phone between her shoulder and her head as she rummages through the piles on the floor, settling on an oversized t-shirt. She returns to the living room, smirks at Snoopy, and whispers. "Happy now?"

Walt's excitement is obvious. "Good. I am ten minutes from the prison parking lot, but here are the highlights. The severed arm found in Southie matches the second strand of DNA found inside Brian's glove. It is also tied to Katie's murder. But the D.A. is going to add conspiracy to commit murder."

MJ shudders. She will never stop blaming herself for Katie's death. She looks to the sky and mouths the words "I am so sorry" as a tear slides down her cheek. She decides at that moment to withhold information about her new "friend" from the dog park—no need to create more drama.

"My turn. Our second guy has a similar retirement fund. Instead of a new ID, he has purchased property in the Maldives, a country with no extradition treaty. But more importantly, time is running out."

"What do you mean, time is running out?"

"They cannot play this game for much longer. Tommy and Chicky create a huge problem."

"You have lost me… and before you mock my intelligence, which is likely warranted yet again, remember my mind is elsewhere. I have to tell Brian he is going to have additional charges brought."

MJ slows down. "It is warranted, but you need to focus on Brian. That is your first priority."

"It is. I know this is all intertwined, but I cannot abandon my role. I am his lifeline… literally. I cannot let go of my end."

"Understood. Hey…" The next question escapes before she can stop it.

Walt cannot answer fast enough. "Of course. I told you… Standing invitation. Text me an address, and I will meet you there around 7. I have to run."

Snoopy turns his head with a judgmental glare.

MJ shrugs her shoulders. "Don't look at me like that. A girl has to eat."

115

"**A**re you 110 percent positive the target did not see you, Sergeant?"

"Yes, sir. They used a novice's technique in attempting to detect surveillance. It was anticipated and easily avoided."

"Observations?"

"As noted before, the subject's movements are predictable in scope and timing. There has been no deviation beyond the increased sensitivity to her surroundings I reported previously."

Johansson is disappointed in his overconfident subordinate. A few years ago, he met Michael O'Leary, a twelve-year veteran of the Brockton Police Department, at a joint convention between the International Brotherhood of Police Officers and its sister organization, the International Brotherhood of Correctional Officers. They sat next to each other on the flight out of Logan, hitting it off despite the age difference. They spent the next four hours drinking lousy airplane coffee and chatting.

After too many beers at the final evening's gala, the two law enforcement professionals created a private mantra: *One arrests them; the other detests them.*

They have remained in frequent contact, with Johansson taking advantage of their friendship over the years. He pays handsomely, ensuring his one-time protégé will do what he wants, when he wants it.

"I am shutting down this aspect of the operation, Sergeant. Payment will be transferred within twenty-four hours."

"Yes, sir. Drinks soon. First round is on me."

"Absolutely." Johansson knows that will never happen.

Operation Pink will continue, but with different talent. Johansson closes his eyes, hoping he will not be forced to add another name to the clean-up list. He grabs a burner phone from the inside pocket of his Hugo Boss suit jacket. His call goes directly to voicemail.

"Breakfast tomorrow. I have reconsidered the strategy. The schedule, which I continue to support, is appropriate. It is the objective that will be the topic of discussion."

He does not want to leave money on the table, but Mendoza may be right. Perhaps a slight reduction in the financial goal will achieve what they both seek.

Besides, "Stan" is anxious about his coming-out party.

Brian is led to the concrete box with the flickering light bulb. It is annoying, and he is convinced the guards have not fixed it for that very reason.

Today's escort is not aggressive when he handcuffs Brian to the table in the center of the room; for that, Brian is thankful. His laceration throbs, and the prison aspirin is useless.

Walt ignores the bandage Brian is wearing. "Hey, Brian. I know it is almost dinner time, so I will not be long. I have some news to share with you. Some good, some not so good."

Brian slides into his usual "whatever" posture. "What is not so good?"

Walt takes a deep breath. "I am going to start with the good, which leads into the news that may be of concern. First, they have identified two different strands of DNA inside your glove: yours and another's. The second DNA has been identified as belonging to an Angel Jiménez, a former member of the Dead Presidents. Angel's arm and I believe a foot were found in Southie. They tested the DNA to identify the arm, and the information cascaded from there."

Brian strains against the handcuffs, as belligerence screams forth. "I fuckin' told you I didn't have nothin' to do with this."

"This new information allows us to create a significant level of reasonable doubt on the arson and murder charges. However, the glove was still found in your car, its match was found in the back of your closet, and you did have an argument and fight with Dylan a few days prior to the fire. And…"

Resentment is burning deep in Brian's eyes. "Someone put that fucking glove there. I do not know who, how, or when, but that is what happened, cuz I didn't do it. And, I never took no swing. Jeremy better fuckin' admit that!"

"Brian, please let me finish so you have all the current information, and we can go from there, okay?"

Brian leans back slowly, struggling to remain silent.

"First, I am still working on how the glove got into the trunk. Yes, Jeremy will testify that you never swung at Dylan, but we have discussed how the prosecution will spin that. Now, the not-so-good news." Walt pauses for a second. "I have spoken to the nineteen employees of the various contractors, and none of them admit to being on site the day in question, and the gas company reiterated their position." A longer pause this time. "As a result of the new DNA findings, the prosecution is going to add conspiracy to commit murder to the current charges."

Brian almost dislocates his shoulders as he leaps to his feet. "What the fuck?"

Walt lurches backward but remains calm. "You have to sit before the guard comes in." He waits for Brian to return to his seat before continuing. "In short, they will argue that you started the fire and killed four people to get revenge for Dylan beating you. They will use your prior convictions to highlight your penchant for fire and a willingness to inflict harm, but the presence of the additional DNA gives us hope there."

Walt pauses to let Brian absorb the information. "The Angel Jiménez identification drove them to revisit and expand their position. Their next angle will be that you and Angel conspired to commit the crime, you both wore the glove at some point, your car held the evidence, and you had the motive. If they cannot convict on the arson or murder charges, they believe they have enough to convict on conspiracy to commit murder."

Anger is oozing from every pore. "I got no idea who the fuck Angel Jiménez is."

"Brian, remember what I have said. My job is to tell you what they are going to say and do. It does not mean I agree with them. We have a lot to work with, as long as you keep your temper in check."

Brian glares at Walt. "You gotta get me out of here. I keep getting attacked. They're gonna kill me."

"I am working to get all of the charges voluntarily dismissed. I may be able to convince them to drop the murder charges, which are the most serious, but they are not likely to give up on the arson or conspiracy charges, which are arguably the easiest to prove. Getting them to drop everything is not a realistic expectation." Walt drops the next bomb. "But, they might now be open to a plea deal, and…"

Brian shakes his head violently from left to right, and back again. "I told you… I didn't do nothing, so I ain't gonna plead to nothing. You gotta get me out. Watching that guy die in the infirmary freaked me the fuck out."

"I am sure it did. Why don't you walk me through what happened? Every detail you can remember."

Brian repositions himself. "I told you already. My cellie and another guy started fighting right behind me, and some asshole pushed me into the middle of it. Someone tried to stick me, I dodged it, but they sliced my arm. They took me and my cellie to the infirmary, where I watched them work on him. They stopped after a while and said he was dead. Then they put him in a body bag, right in front of me. They didn't pull no curtain or nothing."

"How is the arm?"

"I ain't worried about my goddamn arm. Ain't you listening? They keep coming after me. You gotta get me out."

"You said something about an air tank?"

Brian sighs as his frustration takes hold. "I saw the doc put a real small tank, like an oxygen tank, in the body bag. That's it."

"Why would they do that?"

Brian can't keep his temper under wraps. "How the hell do I know? I ain't no fuckin' doctor."

"Okay." Walt looks at his watch. "I don't want you to miss dinner. I have a lot of work to do, and yes, I am focused on getting you out of here. In the interim, I can petition the court to put you in administrative segregation given the latest attack."

Brian has been thinking about this. He has kept his mouth shut for the most part, but they are still not leaving him alone. He needs to protect himself. "It's gonna piss people off, but fuck it. Maybe it will slow them down long enough for you to get me out."

"I will start the paperwork tonight. Listen, these new charges are a hassle, but they show they know their case has gotten weaker—a lot weaker. I know it does not sound like it, but this is a good thing."

117

Since their last meal was a memorable event for all the wrong reasons, MJ picks a restaurant whose online menu appears to possess a decent wine list, if their prices are any indication. She takes a shower, breaks out her razor again, and dresses in her only other blouse and pair of slacks in the hopes Walt accepts the unspoken olive branch.

MJ heads for the restaurant early. The extra time is used to restart an old habit. She noticed the valet's puzzlement as she moved forward with her reconnaissance efforts after handing him her keys. After two uneventful circuits, she is satisfied no one is on her tail and enters the restaurant. She is led to the table where the maitre d' pulls out her seat.

Walt will love this place.

Upon his arrival, Walt is directed to the table without fanfare. He decides against a more intimate hello and takes his seat, quickly resolving an initial moment of embarrassing confusion. "You look nice."

MJ is frustrated by her accelerated heartbeat and the blood rushing to her cheeks. "Thanks. You have something on your tie."

Ice broken.

Without looking, Walt chuckles and shrugs at the obvious. Before he can make himself comfortable, their server arrives with two menus and a wine list, promising details on tonight's specials on his next visit. Walt opens the wine list first. "Red or white?"

"I picked the restaurant, you pick the wine."

The server returns, mumbling something about sea bass and a double pork chop as specials. Walt orders a 2018 Far

Niente Cabernet Sauvignon. The server heads off, and his assistant for the evening offers a choice between sparkling and still water.

"I picked the wine, you pick the water."

"Are we going to do this all night?"

"I hope so." Walt is grinning from ear to ear.

MJ cannot suppress her own smile. She looks at the patient assistant. "We will have the sparkling, please."

After the San Pelligrino is poured, they settle in with the menus.

"I have wanted to try this place. Nice choice."

MJ tilts her head and smirks. "So, you're saying I am…"

"Less wrong than you usually are."

A comfortable laugh turns into a discussion about the available entrées as the server returns with the bottle of wine. Walt never skips the bottle opening routine, having it decanted so it can breathe.

MJ is not adventurous when it comes to food, which she spins to mean she knows what she likes and sticks to it. She orders the sea bass with saffron rice. Walt smiles, orders the tableside Caesar, and then chooses the pork chop special in lieu of his traditional choice.

MJ needs to regain control of the situation and her feelings. "Okay, are you ready for business?"

Walt waits as their water glasses are refilled, and the assistant scampers to the next table. "Ladies first."

MJ shifts around in her seat and takes in the entirety of her surroundings. "Mendoza is a medical school dropout. He had a gift but also an anger management issue, which eventually reached a boiling point. He was offered the chance to leave, presumably in exchange for no criminal charges being brought. Oddly, he chose a career that requires empathy and caring, which seemed to be missing during medical school. After completing a degree in mortuary science, he opened a moderately successful funeral home business. And by all accounts, he is revered in Brockton and the surrounding area."

MJ halts her presentation as the waiter returns to pour the wine. They clink the crystal wine glasses, and each takes a satisfying sip before MJ jumps back in.

"Like our other friend, he too has an account in the Caymans. But, no new identity. He has chosen to take his ill-gotten gains and retire in the Maldives, a country without an extradition treaty with the US. There are two transactions which I believe represent payment to the bastard who started the fire… and killed Katie."

Walt moves quickly to disperse the sadness that's attempting to shroud the table. "It is not your fault. Lily brought Katie to their attention accidentally. Your speaking to her had nothing to do with her death. They were tying up what they believed to be a loose end."

"Maybe, but we need to nail these fuckers… and soon."

"You mentioned time was running out?"

MJ takes a sip of wine, then leans forward and speaks softly. "Tommy Anderson, Chicky O'Malley, and Nick Rutherford all have one thing in common: no family, which means no one will be looking for them… until the prison closes. They will need to reconcile inmate lists to determine transfer locations and timing. Eventually, these three, and likely others, will come up missing, which means questions will be asked."

Walt nods his head, acknowledging the logic in her comments. "Makes sense. How much time do we have?"

"Rutherford had a shitty obituary, written like a form letter. It is also something they did not do with Tommy and Chicky. I believe it to be a half-assed attempt to redirect any suspicion until they decide to bail, but I have no idea how long we have." MJ grabs her wine glass, takes a sip, and then tilts in Walt's direction. "Your turn."

Walt puts down his wine glass and makes sure no one is listening. "I got a call from the D.A. They matched the DNA, which you already know. They are going to add conspiracy charges because they can no longer definitively say Brian was the arsonist. They have motive and opportunity, as well as the glove being found in his trunk, but Angel Jiménez's DNA being found inside the glove creates doubt. I am hoping to get them to drop the murder charges because they cannot put the match in Brian's hand. And..."

"Wait... Did you say Angel Jiménez?"

A confused Walt cocks an eyebrow. "Yeah, why?"

She can barely contain her excitement. "He is the son of a bitch Mendoza paid! Holy shit, Walt, we got the bastards!"

Before another word can be spoken, a young woman dressed in a chef's jacket pushes a stainless steel cart to their table.

MJ blushes as the fond memory sprints through her mind. She finishes her first glass of wine to recenter her thinking. Her focus is on a lot of people right now, and Walt cannot be one of them.

118

Walt has been watching MJ scan the room throughout their meal, a habit he re-adopted more easily than he anticipated. His eyes make a quick sweep while finishing his crème brûlée.

MJ went with the mango sorbet. "Okay, so now what?"

The server delivers another Tawny Port. "Now, we figure out how to take these guys down and get Brian out of prison."

MJ smirks. "Thanks, 'Captain Obvious.' How?"

Walt chuckles. "I have a pretty good relationship with the D.A.'s office. Maybe we should bring them into the loop."

"How do you explain getting your hands on their financials?"

"I never said it was a perfect plan."

MJ pauses, sipping her cappuccino. "I am okay with turning this over to the right people, at the right time, but I will not lose this story."

Walt smiles and lifts his hand slightly. "I get it." A sip of port helps him think. "What is the one piece of this puzzle they cannot walk away from?"

"Harvesting the organs. The authorities bust in while whoever, likely Mendoza, has their hands deep in the body cavity of an inmate, or finding organs sitting in coolers full of ice."

"To do that, we would need advance notice of an attack, right?"

"Maybe. But, if they have any sense that the walls are closing in, they will scatter like cockroaches."

"There are not many flights to the Maldives, and we know of 'Stan's' existence, so it will not be the quick escape they anticipate."

MJ gets quiet. "And, it does not tie them to Lily, her family… or Katie."

Walt reaches across the table, surprised as MJ lets him take her hand. "We will get them justice, I promise."

MJ wipes away a rogue tear. "We need to go back to the beginning and answer a question we have skipped over. Why did they want Lily Whitaker dead? We know Jiménez lit the match, killed Katie to close the loop, and we know who he was working for… but why Lily? That is how this whole thing started. And that is how we save Brian."

"It *has* to be something she saw or heard at the prison."

MJ's eyes open wide as she sits up straight. "I need to go see Johansson ASAP."

Walt almost spits his port across the table. "No fucking way. You cannot return to that prison."

Her back stiffens, fearless defiance in her voice. "I'm a big girl. I can, and will, go anywhere I want."

"All I am saying is you should not do this alone." Walt swallows hard, like he's grappling with something other than the prison predicament, and looks MJ in the eye. "What do you need from me?"

119

Mendoza has been working the math. With the most recent delivery, their respective coffers are slightly more than four million dollars each, presuming Johansson has not made any significant withdrawals. If they can get full price, or very close, it will only take two more deliveries for them to achieve the operation's financial objective, which should silence his sadistic partner.

Mendoza steps into the bar and finds Johansson, who has secured the two seats at the end next to a wall. The location creates a strategic vantage point and reduces the possibility of unwanted ears.

"You're late." Johansson swings his long legs around to allow Mendoza to sit. "I ordered you a Woodford Manhattan."

Mendoza takes the empty seat that's in line with Johansson's view of a young woman with blonde hair, plenty of make-up, and a skirt that leaves little to the imagination, who appears to be captivated by the handsome young man to her left.

"Thank you." Mendoza takes a sizeable drink and lets the brown liquid warm him before continuing. "Any problems?"

Johansson responds with a disapproving look. "Beyond an aggravating reporter and her attorney boyfriend?"

Mendoza cuts to the chase as the vision of his beautiful bungalow on the beach, with blue water lapping the sand, hypnotizes him. "I have done the math. As long as we secure the maximum amount on each, only two additional campaigns are required to reach the goal."

Johansson takes a sip of his trademark single malt scotch, staring at Mendoza with the blackest, most piercing eyes

Mendoza has ever encountered. "Our adversary is advancing. We either engage or retreat. Those are the only options."

Mendoza was expecting Johansson to jump on this proposal. A bloodthirst has put their operation at risk in the past, and it rears its ugly head again. He must remain calm.

"Engaging is a mistake, and we do not need to retreat… not yet. As I said, we only need two."

"We are not initiating the engagement. We are responding."

Mendoza spins slightly, enough to confirm the blonde's attention is firmly on her date. "What does that mean?"

Another sip of scotch precedes a logic that catches Mendoza off guard. "I told you before. She is smart, tenacious, and unafraid. We know she is digging. We have covered our tracks professionally, so that is of no concern. The sole issue is unwanted attention during the last phase of our retirement plan."

"Future attention is not a concern. Yes, there will be a flurry of activity at the outset, but as you rightly point out, no one will unearth our secrets or location, thanks to your friends and their exorbitant fee."

Johansson is all business. "You get what you pay for." He waves down the bartender and points to his empty rocks glass.

Mendoza uses this break in the discussion to reevaluate his approach. He needs to refocus Johansson without pissing him off. "I propose a new strategy that expedites our sprint to the finish. We attempt our first and only double. Departures out of Logan bought and paid for in advance. Deliver and depart."

Johansson inhales the aroma of the scotch, mulling over the proposed strategy. Mendoza can read his thoughts, hoping that the realization that he can jump on a plane as soon as the hearse leaves the prison will solidify his agreement to the plan.

"Identification and coordination make a double exponentially more difficult. And the DOC will be breathing down my neck before you can pull out of the cargo area." He sips his scotch before proceeding. "The safest approach will be for me to leave within moments of your departure from the facility, leaving you alone to complete the balance of the campaign."

Got him! "As it is today. It will be awkward explaining why we are putting two in the vehicle at the same time, but we can come up with something reasonable enough to buy us the time needed."

"What about her, the attorney, and the resident in cell 218B?"

Mendoza shudders at the pleasure Johansson will enjoy as the pain is inflicted. "I will leave that in your capable hands, with complete autonomy to do what you deem best once we have reached the end state, and I am enjoying champagne in first class."

Mendoza watches as Johansson throws back the rest of his drink, signaling they have reached consensus.

"Ready to grab a steak?"

120

MJ's leg bounces uncontrollably as she sits in front of the mountain of paper on Spagnola's desk. She jokes about him being a dinosaur, unwilling to adapt to the digital age. He just smiles and points to the "I'm the boss" name-plate on his desk.

Spagnola closes the door, disconnects his reading glasses at the bridge, allowing them to hang loosely around his neck, and all but disappears behind the piles as he sits behind his desk. "What have you got, MJ?"

MJ struggles to keep her excitement in check. "The President Street fire was an arson, which you know. I have learned that the inside of the primary suspect's glove, the one found in the trunk of his car, possesses two different DNA strands. The suspect's and that of a former gangbanger named Angel Jiménez. I say former because they have found his arm and a foot, but nothing else. Jiménez is also tied to the murder of Katie Nichols, a friend and co-worker of Lily Whitaker."

Spagnola peers around the piles, surprised. "Wait, someone else started the fire?"

"That has been Brian McMillan's claim from day one. Now, there is hard evidence to support that assertion. However, the glove was still found in his car. He alleges he lost it shortly before the fire. How it ended up in his trunk remains undetermined." MJ shifts in her seat, preparing for the hard part of this discussion. "I am convinced Brian McMillan was set up." It is now or never. "I suspect the warden of MCI – Cedar Junction of running a black market organ donation scheme which takes advantage of inmates without families or any genuine connection outside the prison walls. They are attacked and shuffled off to the state-contracted funeral home, Mendoza's in Brockton, where I believe the organs are harvested. Whatever is left is then cremated."

Spagnola leans forward and snatches the tiny hourglass. "You still have not answered the questions I have asked."

"I believe Lily Whitaker, the warden's administrative assistant, saw or heard something relative to the forthcoming inmate reconciliation, which would expose their reprehensible scheme. They hired Jiménez to kill Lily and frame McMillan. Her family was collateral damage. He then killed Katie Nichols, a friend and co-worker of Lily Whitaker, in an attempt to stop the spread of the information because he and/or those who hired him presumed Lily shared whatever she had learned." MJ pauses and watches this land.

He sets the hourglass down without turning it over, pondering this information dump. "Okay, there are a million questions yet to be answered. Why McMillan?"

"Brian McMillan noticed strange happenings at Walpole during his last period of incarceration. Specifically, that younger men, and only younger men, were attacked and never heard from again. When he started making inquiries, he was attacked in the yard and then threatened by Johansson, who reinforced the threat personally when McMillan returned to Walpole to await trial for the President Street arson and murders."

"How are they keeping the organs viable long enough to be harvested?"

"Brian McMillan was in the infirmary being treated for an arm laceration when he observed a shanked inmate being declared dead and placed into a body bag along with a small green air tank."

The puzzled look on Spagnola's face matches the look she wore the first time she heard this. "Why put oxygen in with a dead body?"

"Because it is not oxygen. There are different drugs that can impair one's breathing to the point of being presumed dead. Tetrodotoxin can be diluted in a way to achieve that goal. Others, such as sevoflurane, are inhaled and serve as muscle relaxants. The presumption is that the prison doctor administers the paralytic—and no, I do not know how they get their hands on it—and declares the inmate deceased, which triggers the call to the funeral home. Mendoza rushes to the prison, retrieves the body bag containing the inmate, who is still alive, thus maintaining the viability of the organs."

"You are talking about the poison in pufferfish, right?"

MJ is constantly surprised by his knowledge base. "Yes."

"Then what? The funeral director harvests the organs?"

"That is my working hypothesis. Mendoza is a former medical student who, by all accounts, was very talented but possessed an anger management problem that permanently derailed his career path. He chose mortuary science as a backup."

Spagnola shakes his head in disbelief. "Christ, MJ. Do you have any hard evidence? You have heard me say this before. We do not trade in theories or presumptions; we report facts."

MJ knew it would come down to this. "The evidence relative to the DNA and Jiménez is solid. It is coming from the D.A.'s office. After that, it gets shaky. I have three inmates who were residents at Walpole who have vanished, although VINELink reflects no change in their location. Two are more recent and arguably could be discounted as entry errors, but one is almost a year old. Lastly, I have a warden who is living well beyond his means, based on his clothing and vehicle choice alone."

"And after that?"

"The rest is dubious. I have to identify why Lily Whitaker was targeted. As I mentioned, I believe Lily saw or heard something that put her in harm's way. That is the first domino that has to fall, and it has to fall soon."

A perplexed expression crosses his face. "Soon? Why?"

She smiles. "They are going to close Walpole. Eventually, the Commonwealth is going to take a headcount and compare it against their records. For their scheme to work, Johansson and Mendoza have to skip town before that occurs. The closure is slated to occur within the next eighteen to twenty-four months, but I presume the inmate reconciliation process will begin long before so they can determine who is going where."

MJ watches her editor with angst as he digests the last forty minutes, but it does not matter what Spagnola says.

Brian's life depends upon her toppling this first domino… and she owes him.

121

MJ walks out of the newspaper building and takes a moment to observe her surroundings before beginning her trek toward the "T." While scanning the crowds and silently replaying Spagnola's comments, she notices a white Chevy Malibu traveling slowly behind her.

She cannot see the driver, but her anxiety tells her to pick up the pace for the three seconds it takes her to make a choice she is not used to making. Today, it will be "flight," not "fight."

MJ battles the adrenaline rush to remain calm until she reaches the entrance to the "T," where she races down the steps and through the turnstile before jumping onto the first train to arrive at the platform. It is not the right train, but it provides the needed distance between her and the danger the familiar white vehicle may represent.

She cannot see Mendoza following her, but then again, she did not see him killing young men and relieving them of their body parts, either. It has to be Johansson. For a moment, she wonders how he would stack up against the special "teammates" who had her back the last time things got hot.

MJ contemplates the past few months of her life as the train bounces along the track. She has become reasonably good at observing her surroundings, evaluating the dangers, and memorizing key elements, including faces and available exits. She has also worked tirelessly to bolster her self-defense proficiency, which has enhanced her ability to control her fear, not overcome it.

While most look to avoid confrontation, MJ thrives in that realm, generally preferring fight over flight. Sure, she will jump on the couch and scream at the sight of a spider, but she will have no problem getting into Johansson's face and calling him a cold-blooded killer.

The train's wheels creak and scrape to a halt. She jumps from the train and completes her transfer from the Red Line to the Green Line as she revisits her discussion with Walt.

In addition to offering to take a bullet for her, he advised that his petition to have Brian moved to administrative segregation had been granted, and Brian's relocation was completed earlier in the day. She was quick to point out that if Johansson wants it badly enough, Brian being alone in a special wing of the prison will not make a difference. In fact, it may make it easier.

They spent the last thirty minutes of their meal debating strategy on *how* she would accuse the bastard of his treachery. Whether or not she would do so was never the question.

They finished their planning over dessert, and after a short period of pleading, MJ reluctantly agreed to proceed with caution. Walt would accept nothing less than her full-throated agreement to immediately race back to the parking lot, where Walt would be waiting if there was even a whiff of danger.

Despite her acceptance of his terms, she is confident Walt knows her definition of "whiff" is far different than his.

122

Johansson is impressed with Pinky's ferocity and is not surprised she seeks another meeting. It drives him insane to admit that she would have made a tremendous special operator… once he shaved her head. She has demonstrated tenacity, intelligence, adaptability, calmness under pressure, and a willingness to walk into the lion's den.

It's time to see what she's really made of. "Ms. Fernandez, I'm sorry I missed your call. How may I help you?"

"Thank you for returning my call, Warden. I was hoping to get some time on your calendar. I have a few more questions about Lily Whitaker."

He smirks, knowing the answer to this question. "Is this something we can handle on this call?"

"I am afraid I have a few, and I know you are a busy man. Scheduling a short meeting would probably work best for both of us."

"I can be available tomorrow afternoon. Say, 2:30?"

"Perfect. Thank you, Warden. I will see you tomorrow."

Johansson ends the call and, within seconds, initiates another. "I am meeting with her tomorrow afternoon."

Mendoza's voice cracks and goes up an octave. "What the fuck are you doing? We are inches away from an amazing life. You have the orders in hand for the double. Now is not the time."

"Now is exactly the time. Have you read *The Art of War* by Sun Tzu? 'Knowing the enemy enables you to take the offensive, knowing yourself enables you to stand on the defensive.'"

"Have you considered this? 'The greatest victory is that which requires no battle.'"

Johansson leans back, surprised. "I'm impressed. Good for you! Now, back to the business at hand."

Mendoza will not rollover on this one. "Pulling off the double requires absolute precision. This is an unnecessary distraction."

"You worry about your end, and I will worry about mine."

Johansson disconnects the call before Mendoza can challenge him further. He has lost his patience with the man's drivel. He has served his purpose, but that ends once "Operation Doppelgänger" is initiated.

He looks at "Stanley Johnson's" reflection in his computer monitor. They share a rare smile and laugh as he utters his next thought aloud.

"Besides, it is not often the gazelle finds its way into the lion's jaws voluntarily."

123

MJ sits at the well-worn end of the couch, nursing her third cup of coffee with Snoopy snoring gently beside her. Her fingers are dancing across the keyboard at a feverish pace as she works on her article. She has a well-crafted beginning, a mediocre middle, and no ending.

She saves the latest version of the story on the external hard drive dedicated to this endeavor and moves on to tomorrow. In addition to finding justice for the deaths of at least eight people, the life of a man she barely knows but has come to care about hangs in the balance. She does not give a shit about Jiménez, hoping he was wide awake and forced to watch as each of his limbs was severed.

She and Walt have a straw plan drawn up for her visit with Johansson, but he is unlikely to follow the script as they have played it out in their heads. She takes comfort in knowing she possesses information Johansson believes to be buried, unable to be unearthed.

Information is power, and she is a firm believer in the six P's of life: Proper Preparation Prevents Piss Poor Performance. What she cannot control is Johansson's reaction.

As they negotiated her approach, Walt made her swear to one thing: on the life of the being she cares about most. MJ will make an excuse and reschedule the meeting if Johansson's assistant is not around, if he moves to close the shades on the window, or if he moves to close the door that separates him from his assistant. Being alone with him is not an option.

She knows this is a dangerous play, but MJ is going to explain to Johansson that a recent discovery during her investigation has suggested Lily was the target of the arsonist, not

Dylan. She is exploring possible motives emanating from both her personal and professional life and hopes to garner any insight Johansson may possess.

She is counting on Johansson's narcissism to dictate his responses.

MJ is staring at Brian's mugshot, feeling the full weight of tomorrow's activity press her deep into the couch cushion, when her cellphone pings. The text brings a warm smile to her face.

"U got this! See u at 2:15."

124

As part of their agreed-upon strategy, Walt will press the D.A.'s office to drop the charges pending against Johansson's handpicked patsy. Not only is this appropriate, but they are hoping Johansson learns of the effort, or better still, that the D.A. has agreed, and this unexpected distraction will cause a misstep when he meets with MJ.

Walt has been sitting at his desk since 7 a.m. Sleep is not his friend at the moment. He is putting together his pitch, which will eventually become a Motion to Dismiss if Ginny declines to do what is right. He takes one last read through his notes before asking his assistant to make the call.

"Attorney Giancomo on line three."

"Gooooood morning, Ginny. How are we today?"

"We? I don't know about you, but I'm great. Calling to tell me your client wants to plead guilty to all counts before I add more?"

"I am, in fact, calling to discuss the charges against my client. I would like to start at the top and work my way down." He continues before she can respond. "You are going nowhere on the murder charges with the match and identification of Jiménez's DNA inside the glove. We both know that to be true."

Ginny is a fighter. "What I know is that I have a glove, whose match was found in the back of your client's closet, soaked in formalin with a chemical match for the accelerant used at the crime scene. It contains your client's DNA on the inside and was discovered in the trunk of your client's car. I am happy to ride that all the way to conviction."

Walt allows his grin to invade his tone. "You still haven't seen it, have you?"

"What the hell are you talking about now, Erickson?"

"Did you go back and look at the video Jacobs took, as I suggested?"

There is an obvious hesitation in the response. "No need. He videotaped the vehicle being confiscated pursuant to the terms and provisions of the warrant."

"Ginny, I respect you as a person, and you are a hell of an attorney. And I know you have to back Jacobs, but the guy is a cancer in the department…"

"Wait just a min—"

Walt cuts her off before the conversation is sidetracked. "Ginny, please let me finish, and it will become clear. He drinks more than most cops, is lazy, and cuts corners. I am not sure what chit he cashed to get the judge to sign the initial warrant, which is complete bullshit and easily challenged, by the way, but that is a separate issue. I told you before that I play hard, but I play fair."

"Get to the point, Erickson."

"Your star detective, who cracked a quadruple murder in less than seventy-two hours without any evidence of looking at other suspects. He videotaped the exterior of the car, making certain to take advantage of the open windows by videotaping the nooks and crannies of the car's interior, but was still unable to locate the source of the odor. Where is the one place he didn't look, Ginny?"

Walt swears he can hear the movie replaying in her head.

In a whisper to herself, she answers. "The trunk."

"That's right, Ginny—the trunk. And when I ask him if he did not look in the trunk because he already knew the glove was there, you will object, and the judge will likely sustain your objection. But the damage is done, particularly after I spend time extolling the stupidity that is Detective Jacobs. Reasonable doubt out the whazzoo. You are going nowhere on the murder charges, Ginny." Walt pauses and lets her digest his opening salvo.

"Are you telling me you want to plead him out if I drop the murder charges?"

Forgetting she can't see him, Walt shakes his head to emphasize his point. "No, I am not saying that. I told you I was starting at the top. Once you do the right thing there, I will point out the arson charges will suffer the same fate, thanks to the fine work of the DPW in Southie."

"You are expecting me to drop all of the charges against your guy? Are you out of your damn mind, Erickson?"

Walt remains calm. "I am expecting you to do the right thing, Ginny. I have always played square with you. It's your turn. My client is no angel, but he did not torch that triple-decker. Jiménez did."

Ginny stops herself upon realizing she's saying her thoughts aloud. "And why would Jiménez…"

"I have some thoughts on that, and while they are irrelevant for the purposes of this discussion, they will grab a jury's attention. Look, Ginny, the finding of Jiménez's arm was a shitty break for you, but the Holy Grail for my client." He pauses for effect. "But you still have the ability to put the 'CLOSED' stamp on a quadruple murder." Walt decides to take his final swing. "And, if the rumors are true, spinning this as someone who fights for the truth covers you across the board."

Walt hears Ginny shuffling papers on her desk and the squeak of her chair as she shifts in her seat. He has hit a nerve.

Ginny clears her throat and regains her footing. "First, you know better than to listen to rumors. Second, I presume your next move is to tell me not to bother with the conspiracy charges?"

"Ginny, I respect you too much to tell you what to do or not do. I am giving you my thoughts. Thoughts which are outlined in great detail in the Motion to Dismiss I have sitting on my desk. A motion that will remain in its current spot for the next twenty-four hours. After that, I have to do what is best for my client."

"I have always loved the Erickson bluster. A strong suit of yours, for sure, but your guy killed four people, including two children. He needs to pay for his crimes."

"Call me before tomorrow at this time; otherwise, I have to file. And remember what I said about playing fair, Ginny."

"Do not hold your breath, Erickson." Ginny disconnects the call.

Walt knows she needs time to evaluate everything he just said. She is smart, but he puts the chances she will drop the charges at no better than sixty/forty. He would feel better if she were not planning a political run—looking through the lens of power clouds one's judgment.

As he grabs his phone to text an update to MJ, a solution begins to take shape in his mind.

125

MJ's head is on a swivel as she enjoys the warmth of the day while she and Snoopy take their morning stroll. She has circled her block twice before proceeding to the park, varying her pace and route as she walks. No one matched her speed or changed direction.

This afternoon's meeting is weighing heavily on her mind, but anger is what robbed her of last night's sleep. Her personal vow to make Katie's killer pay cannot be kept. Yes, Jiménez got everything he deserved, but those who originally set him on the path of death are on the brink of escape. That cannot happen. It will not happen. Her rage has reached the firestorm stage, but she must prevent the wildfire from burning her or Brian this afternoon.

MJ enjoys her coffee as Snoopy drags her along when her cellphone buzzes. She slides the loop at the end of the leash around her left wrist and reaches into the pocket of her sweatshirt, retrieving the phone. She reads a text, and a look of uncertainty appears on her face. She looks around, as if others can read her mind. She stops to respond.

"can u trust her"

"I trust her, and it works for everyone, except…"

"what did u tell her"

"Nothing, yet. But she knows her case has collapsed. We can hand her the key to the castle, AND rescue the prince."

"what do i need to do"

"Get the first domino to fall. Poke the bear… GENTLY!"

A smile emerges as the exhaustion from a lack of sleep is erased by a blast of excitement. Her pace quickens, and Snoopy struggles to keep up.

"with pleasure"
"I said… GENTLY!"
"i have a plan"
"Please stick to the plan we agreed to."
"u know me"
"That's what worries me.☺ See you at 2:15"

MJ felt the concern ooze from Walt's fingertips as he typed each word, but now is not the time to be squeamish.

Snoopy's meandering around the dog park in search of this morning's special spot provides terrific cover as MJ scouts the area in search of danger. She completes a thorough analysis of every person in the park while Snoopy takes care of business. She releases a small sigh of relief as she recognizes each of the dogs and most of the faces they brought with them.

Today is going to be a good day!

126

What feels like months has only been forty-three hours, and Brian is already rethinking his decision. He did not realize the true meaning of "segregation" when he agreed to have Walt request the move. Before all of this bullshit, he lived a quiet life, engaging with people at work and the group at AA, but no one else. That was a solitary existence in his mind.

His only conversations occur three times a day, and only for a few seconds. Last night, the guard who did rounds at lights out would not respond when Brian requested to call his attorney.

While the answer he received was silence, the officer apparently did listen.

Brian is amazed by his level of excitement as the shackles are placed so he can be escorted to the phone bank. He never imagined he would be this happy to speak to an attorney.

"I will accept." Walt waits for the call to finish connecting. "Hey, Brian. How are you holding up?"

Brian shuffles his feet back and forth as he monitors the area for others. His voice is desperate. "We need to meet."

"Is everything alright? You have been moved, right?"

"Yeah, but…" This time, Brian remembers the lines are recorded. "I will tell you more when you get here."

"Is it an emergency?"

Brian ponders the question. Most would not consider the circumstances an emergency, but being alone at home for eight to ten hours a day, where he has a TV, a radio, and a PS3, is very different. And he could leave the house whenever he wanted. The past few days have been increasingly intolerable. Maybe the dangers of the general population are worth it?

"Never mind. I will figure it out."

"Brian. I didn't say it was impossible. I will need to rearrange everything, but I'm happy to do so if that's what you need. I am here for you."

After a few seconds, Brian remembers who the boss is in this relationship. "Can you come this afternoon?"

There's a pause before Walt answers. "I will be there around 2:30."

Brian sighs, the tension in his shoulders peeling away. "Thanks."

As the sound of his shuffling feet echoes the length of the empty concrete hallway, Brian silently decides that he will not live this way for the rest of his life, no matter what it takes.

127

I t is not quite 2 p.m., and MJ sits in the prison parking lot reviewing her notes, which is a waste of time. She has them memorized, but she also knows that going in with a script is of no value. The real purpose of her preparation is to create the agility needed to take the conversation wherever Johansson wants it to go.

MJ squirms in her seat. She promised to wait for Walt before she went inside, but the Pitbull's leash is on the verge of snapping.

She checks herself in the rearview mirror, gets out, locks the door, and stands there. She looks at her phone; it is 2:01. Maybe Walt hit traffic or got called to court unexpectedly?

She paces around the car three times. The small circles eat up another forty seconds. Her gaze repeatedly flips between her phone and the driveway entrance to the prison. Suddenly, a Porsche comes screeching around the corner and skids into a parking space.

Walt jumps from his car and slams the door, breathing like he just ran the hundred and ten-meter hurdles at the Olympics. "Whew… I was trying to… get here early. I wasn't sure… you would wait."

MJ laughs out loud. "You had another sixty seconds. But I would have sent a text."

"I have a problem. Brian called this morning and asked to see me."

Laughter turns to concern. "Is everything okay?"

His breath is less ragged. "I'm not sure. He might just be lonely. This happens right after someone goes into isolation, even when it is for their own safety. After being surrounded by others, they are not used to being alone twenty-four hours a day. Their attorney is the only contact they have."

MJ paces along the side of her car. "Or something has happened? Maybe that asshole Johansson is fucking with him because I asked to meet again?"

"Take a breath, MJ. I did not get that vibe, and now is not the time to get paranoid. You need to stay on task."

Without realizing it, MJ does as instructed. "What are you going to do?"

"I am going in to see what Brian needs… while you are in with Johansson."

A tinge of anger seeps out. "Now, who is not following the plan?"

"I am on the premises. A different wing, but still on-site. I will be back in this exact spot no later than 3. Okay?"

"We will both be within Johansson's kingdom. What if he chooses to lock both of us in the dungeon?"

"Relax. I brought Jonathan up to speed. He knows where we are, and if I don't text or call by 4 p.m., he will send the cavalry."

MJ paces around the car one more time. She looks at her phone. It is 2:10. "Fuck it! By the time they finish with the screening process, it will be 2:30."

"You got this!"

She takes one last deep breath and heads for the door. Walt follows, albeit a few steps behind. They get inside, and he gives MJ one last reassuring smile and walks toward the line for inmate visitors.

The intensity in MJ's eyes says it all. In less than an hour, she will have Johansson and Mendoza dead to rights. No pun intended.

128

After rifling her laptop bag and two trips through the metal detector, MJ is escorted to her destination. She takes a seat outside the office after Johansson's assistant advises her that he is meeting with correctional officers in one of the inmate wings and should be returning shortly.

MJ is flipping through her notebook, focusing on her most recent grocery list, when a lightbulb goes off. "Excuse me. You are new here, right?"

"You already know that."

MJ is stunned by the clipped answer. She expected the matronly assistant to be congenial. "I do. It was a poor attempt at small talk, sorry."

Silence.

At 2:30 p.m. sharp, Johansson walks in. Today, he has accessorized his five-thousand-dollar suit with a shit-eating grin. The air of pomposity that trails behind him churns MJ's stomach.

"Hello, Ms. Fernandez. Please come in." He walks into his office, not waiting for her to enter first.

MJ smiles. Let the games begin.

Johansson waves to the seat in front of the desk and moves to sit in the large leather chair, which reminds MJ of a throne. This time, there is no handshake, nor an offer of something to drink.

MJ sits in the same chair as before, pleased that he does not move to close the shades or his door.

"Thank you for seeing me again, Warden. I know you are busy, so I will get to it."

"Please."

The Pitbull sits up straight, notebook open on her lap, and pen poised to capture whatever bullshit spews from Johansson's mouth. "I meant to say this at the outset, please call me MJ."

She clears her throat and dives in headfirst, with her arms tied behind her back. "As you know, I'm looking into the fire that killed Lily Whitaker and her family. Since our last meeting, I have learned a few things that I am hoping you may be able to help me understand."

Johansson leans back with a smugness that drips from his smile. "What might that be?"

Without it being obvious, she bites the inside of her lip—a trick to keep her focused that she learned years ago. "It has been suggested that the fire was not a random arson, nor an act with Dylan Janssen as the target. Some believe that killing Lily was the goal. I am attempting to identify possible motives that drove someone to murder a young mother of two, and I am exploring both her personal and professional life."

Johansson's cold, steely eyes emphasize his fiery response. "I have told you before, Ms. Fernandez, I will not discuss any aspects of the pending criminal charges."

He is a fool to think she will accept his response. "Please call me MJ. Did Lily have any enemies here at work?"

He smirks. "I will say this again. Lily was a shining light in a world of darkness. She was well-liked by her peers and performed her job admirably."

The Pitbull becomes a gnat. "She never argued with anyone?"

"Ms. Fernandez, how many times must I say no? If there is nothing else I have…"

"Please call me MJ. Is it possible she saw something about an inmate that placed her in harm's way?"

Johansson shifts in his seat. "As my assistant, she had access to inmate information. But again, Ms. Fernandez, you know this. I have—"

Time to poke the bear. "Do you remember an Angel Jiménez? He was an inmate here at one time." MJ catches a micro-twitch in Johansson's left eye.

"I do not recall the name. I would have to check the records."

"His arm and foot were found in Southie recently. My sources tell me his DNA is connected to Lily's murder."

Another micro-twitch.

"As is Mr. McMillan's, if *my* sources are accurate."

Keeping him talking remains the goal. "True. But Mr. McMillan denies knowing Mr. Jiménez. The sole connection I can find is that they both served time here at Walpole."

Johansson sits up a little straighter and clears his throat. "Ms. Fernandez, a connection of that nature could apply to thousands of individuals. And I fail to see the relationship of this line of questioning to your stated purpose."

"I am wondering if Lily came across something about McMillan or Jiménez during her work here that would have driven them to murder her, her partner, and their two young children."

"As with most inmates, I have no idea what drove them to take the actions which brought them here, nor do I care. My job is to ensure this facility is running effectively and efficiently."

No segue, another arrow in a reporter's quiver. "The last time I was here, we discussed the closing of this facility. Is that still on track?"

"Yes. But again, how is this connected to the reason you asked for this meeting?"

"Where will the inmates go?"

A third twitch. Johansson sits up fully. "They will be transferred to the facility aligned with their crime and sentence."

"Will they—"

Without warning, klaxons begin to bleat throughout the building. MJ's hands reflexively fly up to cover her ears as Johansson's assistant sprints into his office without knocking.

"Warden, we have a situation in C-block! The Lieutenant has declared a lockdown, and the others are following suit. Do you want to implement the lockdown procedures for the administrative building as well?"

"Yes, until we know more." Johansson leaps to his feet. "I am heading to C-block."

A sinister sneer comes across his face as he looks at MJ. "This discussion is over. I have real work to do. And you are required to sit here until *I* choose to discontinue the lockdown."

Confusion dominates MJ's thoughts as Johansson walks out. She is effectively his prisoner. Perhaps she and Walt should have given more thought to her joke about being thrown into the dungeon? As her hands fail to minimize the klaxon's impact, another thought pushes her confusion to panic.

Walt is in C-Block.

129

Brian instinctively drops to the floor, face down. His head is turned to one side, and his arms are uncomfortably handcuffed in front of him. The officer has his foot on Brian's back, forcing his hands to slowly dig into his stomach and pelvis and preventing him from turning his head.

Walt pulls open the heavy steel door, desperate to know what is happening. He looks down the hall and finds Brian being pinned face down by the guard. He uses the palms of his hands to protect his hearing as he approaches the officer and yells over the alarm. "Get your fucking foot off his back! He cannot breathe! He has cuffs on his hands and feet. Where the hell is he going?"

The guard raises his PR-24. "Back away and shut the fuck up. Get down. Face first and stay there. This is your only warning." Walt sees anger mixed with fear and uncertainty in the guard's eyes.

Walt steps back. They are in the middle of a hallway that is at least seventy-five feet long. The klaxons echo off the government grey concrete like pinballs, amplifying their assault on his hearing. He refuses to lie face down, deciding to take two steps back and sit with his back against the wall. The officer silently accepts the proposed compromise but keeps his boot firmly planted between Brian's shoulder blades.

Walt's ass hits the worn tile floor as his anxiety skyrockets. MJ is alone with Johansson, and the bastard is using the alert to demonstrate the magnitude of his power and control. In this moment, only one thing matters: MJ. Brian drops into second place. A very close second, but second nonetheless.

Where is she? Is she safe? Does she know what is going on? Fear controls his thoughts.

It feels like hours have passed before the klaxons stop as quickly as they began. But the damage is done. Walt's ears are ringing, as if he were leaving a rock concert after standing next to a stack of speakers. He reaches back and places the palms of his hands on the wall to help him stand back up when the guard screams.

"Sit the fuck down. We go nowhere until I get the all clear."

Walt watches as the guard repositions his earpiece and nods in response to the various orders being barked through the small piece of plastic. Walt's hearing is fighting to restore itself when, without warning, the guard takes his foot off of Brian's back, reaches down, and yanks him to his feet. The guard's menacing tone leaves little doubt about his expectations. "We are cleared to go to the meeting room, where you will remain until further notice."

Walt gives Brian an apologetic look before declaring his intention to the guard. "I need to leave immediately. You cannot legally keep me here."

The guard bears his teeth and growls. "Wrong. Didn't they teach you in law school to read everything thoroughly before signing it… Like a prison waiver? Now let's fucking go."

Walt relents and follows directions by walking two steps ahead of the guard, who is now pushing Brian forward. After they reach the concrete conference room and the required handcuff transition is complete, the guard takes a different key from his pocket.

"You are in our world, counselor. The lockdown alarm grants the warden complete autonomy over the premises. I hope you don't have dinner reservations." His laughter bounces around the room as he locks the door from the outside.

130

Johansson is alone, walking briskly toward the melee in C-block when he steps into the infirmary, finds a quiet corner, and hits the only number in his speed dial.

"It has begun."

Mendoza clears his throat. "Complications?"

Johansson does not miss a beat. "Nothing that cannot be handled."

"So, something?"

"I have operational control of our adversaries."

Mendoza's ire explodes in Johansson's ear. "What the fuck does that mean?"

"It means I am taking care of my end. Now get your ass in the car and take care of yours." Johansson disconnects the call and resumes his trip toward the chaos.

Within minutes, he is standing in the recreational area of C-Block with twenty-five correctional officers who are decked out in full riot gear and awaiting orders. There are a handful of inmates hiding behind a makeshift barricade made from two tables that were pried from their floor bolts and flipped over. The other inmates are face down, arms and legs sprawled. And between these two groups lay two individuals bleeding heavily from stab wounds.

Johansson adopts the posture he has used so many times in the past as an experienced battle commander. In a show of fearlessness, he walks ahead of three riot-ready guards hiding behind full-length, polycarbonate SWAT protection shields. He stops within eight feet of the overturned tables and crosses his arms in front of him. He stands there for a moment before ordering the klaxons to be turned off.

Once the silence returns, he points at the overturned tables. "I am ordering the medical extraction team to enter this area and remove the two injured inmates behind me. You will allow this to happen." He turns toward the doors and nods.

Within seconds, the bleeding men are strapped to backboards and rushed out with the infirmary physician and two nurses trailing closely behind.

Johansson's focus returns to the overturned tables. "Next, those on the floor are going to be returned to their cells." He nods again, this time not taking his eyes from the small group of instigators.

A dozen officers methodically collect those who dropped to the floor and move them back into their cells, which are then locked for everyone's safety. After ten minutes, the only people who remain are the four inmates behind the tables, Johansson, and a small group of adrenaline-filled guards, anxious to find a release for their fear and frustration.

Johansson watches as the trouble-makers behind the tables jump at the sound of his booming voice. "NOW, we deal with you four. You have a choice: the easy way or the hard way. The gentlemen behind me are praying you choose the hard way. While I am more than comfortable with such an approach, my preference is the easy way, but the choice is yours. You have ten seconds to decide."

With that, Johansson loudly counts down from ten and steps behind the semi-circle of correctional officers. He gets to two, and after a lot of head nodding to communicate with each other silently, the men behind the tables stand with their arms raised.

The Lieutenant of C-Block takes immediate control, screaming for the inmates to hit the floor face first, which they do without hesitation. As the men are being searched and handcuffed by the group of angry guards, Johansson places his hands behind his back and begins to meander, examining the entire cell block.

Johansson moves deliberately, responding to the inquiring eyes staring at him from behind small wire-embedded glass windows with a simple look. He stops at the cell of a known gang shot-caller. He peers through the window to find a smiling man sitting on the lower bunk.

The look Johansson gives him is different... and includes an imperceptible nod and a wink.

131

The klaxons in the administrative building stopped within minutes of starting, but it doesn't matter as MJ battles to overcome the sound of the bells now reverberating inside her head. She is stunned as Johansson's assistant returns to her work, as if today's event is a common occurrence.

The alarm interrupted MJ's momentum, but the stillness of the air now creates the tension that has stiffened her body and mind. She sits in Johansson's office, paralyzed by fear as Walt's safety obscures her thoughts.

As the ringing in her ears begins to subside, she contemplates another attempt at engaging the woman sitting in the other room, but quickly dismisses the idea. Unfazed by the alarm, she has no reason to believe the brusque assistant will be any more congenial this time.

As MJ twists, attempting to release the knotted muscles in her back, she notices a number of folders on Johansson's desk. Standing will allow her a better sight line, but she must do so without her personal prison guard catching her in the act. Maybe having the door closed wouldn't have been such a bad thing after all.

MJ realizes that her small window of opportunity is quickly closing. "Excuse me."

Silence.

Louder. "Um… Excuse me."

The assistant pushes her chair back and turns towards the open door that MJ is yelling through. Her tone is telling. "What?"

"I have a bad back. I need to stand and stretch it, and I wanted to let you know what I was doing before getting up."

MJ leans over the arm of the chair to look out the door. She hopes the thought bubble she envisions over her captor's head is not what comes from her mouth.

"Make it quick." The woman spins back around and resumes typing.

Phew!

MJ stands and slowly moves behind the chair. She grabs the back and uses it to support the torque she is applying to her back and shoulders. The maneuver partially blocks the open doorway while concurrently allowing MJ to scan the top of Johansson's desk. She takes inventory, quickly recognizing the code that has been employed. The red folders are inmate files. The green folders refer to financial matters, like the prison budget. It is the one blue folder on the edge of the desk she now covets, as two words come into focus. "Inmate Reconciliation."

Despite the folder screaming her name, MJ finds the resolve to stay put. She slowly twists left to right, right to left… repeat. She needs to get a look at what is inside the blue folder, but how?

Her mind is scrambling for an answer when she hears the phone ring in the outer office. The words that follow are music to her ears. *"Warden Johansson's office, how may I help you?"*

It is now or never.

MJ crouches below the window ledge and waddles like a duck to the side of Johansson's desk. With her eyes fixed on the door, she uses her right arm to reach over her head and snags the blue folder from the top of the stack. It takes less than ten seconds to find what she is looking for.

She smiles, returns the folder to the exact spot from which it came, and begins waddling back to the chair. She is almost…

"What the hell are you doing?"

MJ stands up slowly. "Stretching my back. You said it was okay. I have a set of different twisting exercises, but squatting like this, while pointing my chin at my chest, stretches it as well."

MJ watches as the assistant's chin drops slightly, presumably visualizing her own spine if she were to complete the maneuver. MJ is blown away when she concludes it is feasible.

The irritation remains. "Whatever. Let's go. I need to walk you out."

MJ doesn't blink. She wants to sprint to the exit before someone changes their mind, but keeps her cool and walks side-by-side with her escort.

Within seconds of arriving at her car, she bends over and places her hands on her knees, and the excitement from her discovery is replaced by a single, heartfelt question.

132

Walt finds himself imitating the one creature he believes all successful attorneys hold dear: the duck. On top of the water, they are calm, cool, and collected. Below the surface is another story altogether. He smiles at Brian as fear swirls beneath him.

Did MJ make it to Johansson's office? Is she still meeting with him? Has Johansson done anything to MJ? Is she being held in the administrative building, or somewhere else? Walt makes a silent vow of excruciating retribution if Johansson has harmed a single pink strand of hair.

Walt is pacing around the perimeter of the small room when he notices Brian's head bobbing upward as he catches himself that split second before falling asleep. In his haste, Walt remembers that he came to speak to Brian for a reason.

"Brian, I forgot to mention that I have spoken with the prosecutor's office. I demanded they drop all charges. I have drafted a motion which outlines the basis for the request in great detail."

Brian shakes away his lethargy. "What did she say?"

Walt has to walk gingerly. "She told me she would take it under advisement. They know they have problems with their case. They have put all of their eggs into the wrong basket. But that may not stop them from proceeding."

Brian becomes animated. "I fuckin' told you… I didn't do nothing!"

"Try to relax. This is a process, a much longer process than you and I prefer, but we have to let the wheels of justice turn."

Brian slumps again. "Yeah, but your wheels is gonna take you to your big fuckin' house when the lockdown is over. Mine just keep spinning in the mud."

Walt looks at his watch and smiles. It is 4:28. If Jonathan kept his word, there should be at least a couple of police cruisers sitting at the entrance of the prison right now. As quickly as the smile appears, the reality of his current situation slaps him across the face.

Jonathan's actions are irrelevant. The alarm has thrown the entire facility into lockdown. No one gets in or out. As part of the formal response to the alarm, multiple police cruisers from the state and surrounding towns are probably sitting in the parking circle.

In less than sixty seconds after the rusted hinges of the room's steel door begin to complain, Walt has said goodbye to Brian and is jogging down the poorly lit hallway toward freedom… and MJ.

Despite being reprimanded by the guard assigned to escort him for running, he has gone from prisoner to free man in less than five minutes. Sunshine has never felt better. Like every miner returning to the surface, Walt sucks in as much fresh air as his lungs will hold the moment he breaches the last door.

His mind grips a single fear like a python.

Walt sprints toward the administrative building at the front of the prison, being reminded yet again that less time with a wine glass and more time on a treadmill might be a good idea. He clears the admin building quickly, again subjecting his eyes to a drastic change in lighting.

He is disoriented. Walt's ears are still ringing, and his photographic memory fails to recall where he parked, so he reaches into his suit coat pocket, raises his right arm, and presses the alarm button on the key fob.

133

MJ's adrenal glands are thrown into chaos. The adrenaline is dissipating slowly as a new round of alarms begins blaring behind her, spiking her heart rate yet again. But it does not matter what is happening inside the prison now; she is outside.

It is not until she blocks the sun with her outstretched hand and spots Walt wobbling toward her like a newborn calf that she realizes the noise is coming from his car.

Walt stops the alarm as he approaches. He walks the last few steps, breathing like an asthmatic in a field of flowers.

MJ allows a caring smile to escape. "Do I need to call 911?"

Walt drops his briefcase onto the blacktop and rips off his tie. "Are… you… okay?"

"I am better than okay. Can I buy you a glass of wine?"

Walt is bent over, staring at the parking lot, hands on his knees. "Hell yes. But… I get… to choose… the wine. Pick… a decent spot… I will follow you." Walt retrieves his briefcase and slinks around to the driver's side of his car.

• • •

It took them almost an hour to get to Del Frisco's in the Seaport. Walt was following so closely that he almost rear-ended MJ three times as they navigated the stop-and-go rush hour traffic.

After handing their keys to the valet, Walt jogs the few steps it takes to get in front of MJ so he can hold the door, but MJ has other ideas. She refuses to forgo her situational awareness and scans the area for danger before entering.

With one last glance, MJ walks in. "Thank you."

"Any time."

Walt presses a hundred-dollar bill into the palm of the hostess, who welcomes him by name. They are led to a table ahead of the angry crowd standing around the hostess stand.

Walt offers MJ the wine list. "I was too pushy before. You're paying, so maybe you should choose?"

MJ smirks. "Do they have anything in a box?"

Walt pulls the list back hastily, knocking over his empty water glass. "Never mind. I was right the first time."

They share a laugh. Something they both desperately need after today's experience. Walt orders a bottle of Pio Cesare Barolo and leans forward the moment the server walks away. "Seriously, are you okay?"

MJ sighs. "It was messed up, but I'm fine. You?"

"I was scared to death… for you."

MJ sees the genuine caring and concern in Walt's eyes. She silently embraces the warmth of someone worrying about her. "They held me in Johansson's office, being guarded by the most 'no-bullshit' administrative assistant I have ever met." Then she smiles. "And that was their mistake."

The sommelier returns with the wine. MJ's desire for a drink is delayed by Walt's step-by-step, thorough analysis. She taps her foot beneath the table, waiting for "the nod."

"Must you do that *every fucking time*? I need a glass of wine, and you are preventing that from occurring with your tiresome routine!" MJ gives him a smile to relay her intention.

There is affection in the return smile. "Yes. Get used to it."

They clink their glasses as MJ makes a toast. "To getting out alive."

"Not funny." Walt swirls the wine to aerate it a bit more. "So, what is this big news of yours?"

MJ surveys the room and the tables on either side of them. They are closer than she would prefer, so she leans in. "While detained in Johansson's office, I noticed folders on his desk, including one labeled 'Inmate Reconciliation.'"

Walt uses his practice with Brian and mimics MJ's posture, his voice optimistic. "And?"

"Thanks to a few stretching exercises, I was able to glance inside. It holds two documents. The first was a notification from the Commonwealth, dated two weeks before Lily was killed, outlining the intention to begin the transfer planning later this month. The second was a list of inmates. Some had small stars next to their names with two words scribbled in the margin: 'death certificate?' Any guesses?"

"Tommy Anderson."

"BINGO! And others."

Walt can barely stay seated. "Lily must have opened the reconciliation notification and began working through the names. She brings a noticeable discrepancy to Johansson's attention and..."

MJ gives Walt her best "I told you so" look. "Exactly!"

Walt lurches forward. "Wait... you said later this month?"

It hits MJ like a sledgehammer. She jumps up, almost spilling her wine. "We have to go. NOW!" She is heading for the door before Walt can wave down their server.

He doesn't wait. Walt drops four one-hundred-dollar bills on the table and trips over the chair leg as he struggles to catch up. Everyone in the place turns at the commotion and watches as he fights to regain his balance.

MJ gets into her car just as he reaches the sidewalk and hands his ticket to the valet. She yells over the top, "Call me as soon as you get in the car, and I will explain."

"Where are we going?"

"Mendoza's."

134

The basis for MJ's quick retreat becomes clear to Walt as he waits for his car. He asks Siri to make a call as the tires of the Porsche squeal, leaving the smell of burnt rubber on Northern Avenue.

"Erickson?"

"Ginny, sorry for the after-hours call, but we need to talk. Are you still in the office?"

"I've had a long day. The last thing I need is more Erickson bluster."

Walt beeps his horn as a car cuts him off. "Ginny, listen. I'm not fucking around. I am about to hand you a case that will put you on the front page of every newspaper in the country."

"What the hell are you talking about? Are you drunk?"

"No. Are you at your office?"

"Yes, but…"

"Stay there. We will be there in forty-five minutes." Walt hangs up before Ginny can say another word. He dials the next number.

"What took you so long?"

Walt is breathing heavily, and his heart is slamming against the inside of his breastplate. "Listen, I know why you want to head to Mendoza's, but there has been a change in plans."

"What the hell are you talking about?"

He knows MJ is going to be pissed, but Walt needs this to go down the right way. "We need to meet Ginny Giancomo in her office in forty-five minutes."

"What the fuck did you do, Erickson?"

"Nothing. This needs to go by the book. Remember what you said about the ideal way to put this to bed? I think we have an opportunity to do just that. The clock is ticking, so I called Ginny before I called you."

Her exasperation escapes. "Goddamn it. What did you tell her?"

"That I have a case that would make her famous, and to meet us in her office. I know you are pissed. We will protect your story, I promise, but this is huge, and today you confirmed your suspicions of running out of time."

"Pissed doesn't even come close. We have information that was gained in a manner that makes it impossible to be shared publicly. You have really fucked me on this!"

"I have a solution. Just meet me at the D.A.'s office… and look to your left."

MJ peers to her left and sees Walt looking to his right.

Driving a Porsche has its advantages.

135

For the first time in his career, Mendoza has two bodies in the back of the hearse. No matter his transgressions, he has always prided himself on treating each deceased person with the respect the dead deserve. He has treated the undead the same way until today.

He bounces between two thoughts: money and escape. Period. He has ten to twelve hours of delicate work ahead of him, and then it is over. Today, he takes the back roads for his return trip to Brockton. He is dreaming of the sand in the Maldives when his cellphone rings.

"We have a problem."

Frustration dominates his tone. "No, we don't. In twenty minutes, I'm initiating the first procedure."

"I warned you about our adversaries. I have been watching since they left the prison. A quick stop in the Seaport, followed by what initially appeared to be a race to you. It wasn't. She is currently parked on Main Street in Brockton, and I presume he is with her."

"So what?"

"If I am correct, it is 166 Main Street."

Mendoza's breath catches as he recognizes the address. "Are you sure?"

"The equipment is limited in its accuracy."

"Now what?"

Johansson sighs. "Now, I head to the conference room to meet with the Department of Corrections. They have expressed dire concerns about today's events. Five minutes after they leave, I initiate Operation Doppelgänger."

"And me?"

"Stay focused. We are a few hours away from enjoying the fruits of our labors."

"Final delivery is scheduled for 3 a.m. Funds should be transferred by 6 a.m."

Johansson hesitates. "Excellent. I would propose one final debrief at breakfast. 7 a.m. at the usual spot."

"Until then."

Mendoza disconnects the call, knowing he will never see Johansson again, and that is just fine with him. Before he can pull down the driveway of the funeral home, he has to wait for Mrs. Rothschild to shuffle along the sidewalk. His fake smile causes her to bend her head to one side and adopt an inquisitive stare. For a split second, he wonders if she knows the truth.

After a quick exchange of waves, his patience is tested by the speed of her waddle. He can finally cross the sidewalk and must use every ounce of restraint he can muster to navigate slowly to the rear of the funeral home.

As he is backing into the unloading area, a previously unconsidered reality causes him to slam his hand against the steering wheel.

He only has one ventilator.

136

After a forty-three-minute drive and a brief strategy discussion, Walt holds the door for MJ as they enter the Plymouth County D.A.'s office. Ginny Giancomo is standing in the lobby, wearing running shoes with her business suit.

Her hip is cocked, and her arms are crossed, eliminating the need to guess how she feels about Walt's stunt. "This better be good, Erickson. I am missing my kid's soccer game for this."

"Ginny, this is MJ Fernandez. And trust me, this will be worth it."

Ginny ushers them toward her office, past a couple of paralegals wearing AirPods and pounding on keyboards, and closes her door.

"If you cannot convince me within the next five minutes, this meeting is over. Are we clear?"

Walt clears his throat. "Crystal." He looks at MJ, who nods as an indication that he should take the lead.

"Okay, so this is all tied to the *McMillan* matter."

"Christ, Erickson. I told you not to waste my time with this shit."

"You said I have five minutes."

"Four minutes and forty seconds."

"McMillan was set up. He noticed something during his last bit in Walpole. Records will confirm he was attacked in the yard shortly before his release. He will testify to receiving a warning from the warden to keep his mouth shut about what he was seeing. A warning the warden delivered again in person the day you sent him back pending trial."

Walt looks at MJ and nods. It is her turn.

"As the administrative assistant to the warden, Lily Whitaker came across a request from the state to initiate plans for the inmate reassignment, which will occur at the time of the prison's closing. This was two weeks prior to her death. She started the work and found a handful of inmates who were reportedly killed in prison, but she could not locate a death certificate, nor anything from the Office of the Chief Medical Examiner. She brings the discrepancy to the warden's attention and is dead shortly thereafter, along with her partner and two children."

Ginny grabs her reading glasses and begins scribbling furiously on a legal pad.

Being very familiar with the five-minute rule, MJ doesn't skip a beat. "There is nothing for Tommy Anderson or Charles 'Chicky' O'Malley, and I believe Nicholas 'The Knick' Rutherford is also missing. VINELink still reflects that all three remain current residents at MCI – Cedar Junction." MJ takes a breath to control her pace. "These gentlemen were young, in good health, and none of them had family that would look for them."

Walt encourages MJ to continue. "Go on, we can trust her."

MJ shrugs and begins telling the story she has been drafting. "In my line of business, you follow the money to get to the truth. And that is the case here. Samuel Johansson is living far beyond his means, and he flaunts it. His extravagances include a multi-million-dollar beachside condo in Naples, Florida, purchased under the alias 'Stanley Johnson.' Benjamin Mendoza runs a funeral home that barely breaks even each year, but he recently purchased a very nice bungalow on the water in the Maldives. Records demonstrate that both homes were bought with cash. So, where do they get their money?"

Ginny is writing furiously and moves onto the next page of her legal pad.

MJ continues. "Mendoza was awarded the state contract to handle the deceased from Walpole and other jails and prisons a couple of years ago, with particular leeway given to him in his handling of indigent deaths. We all know Walpole was a war zone before Johansson showed up. Closer scrutiny shows an immediate decline in inmate-on-inmate attacks, but there has been a steady climb since then. The number of deaths at the facility far exceeds both state and national averages. That means a lot of business for Mendoza." MJ clears her throat again. "Do you have any water?"

Ginny reaches backward and grabs a bottle of Poland Spring from the small refrigerator next to her credenza.

MJ downs half of it before continuing. "Brian McMillan was thrust into one of the most recent attacks, receiving a number of bruises and a laceration that required sutures. While in the infirmary, the primary target of the attack was declared deceased and loaded into a body bag, along with a small green oxygen tank."

Ginny's eyebrows shoot up in surprise. "Why does a deceased person need oxygen?"

"The very question I was stuck on for a minute. Then the pieces of the puzzle converged." MJ fights to keep the smile from her face. "They aren't dead. They are kept alive long enough for Mendoza to remove them from the premises and harvest their organs."

Ginny bolts back in her seat. "Wait… WHAT? Where the hell did that come from?"

"Follow the money. I have been informed that Johansson and Mendoza both possess accounts in the Caymans with significant seven-figure balances. And both accounts receive six-figure deposits within twenty-four hours of each inmate on inmate attack."

"How the hell do you know that? Securing that information is all but impossible."

"Not a question you want answered, Counselor, I assure you. I only have a minute or so left." MJ shifts slightly in her seat. "I believe Lily noticed the discrepancies in the records, and Brian was selected to be the fall guy because he, too, noticed something fishy and got caught poking around."

Walt jumps in. "He was the perfect patsy. Prior arson conviction and two prior assault convictions helped. The fight with Dylan Janssen was an unexpected bonus. However, you know through independent witnesses that Brian never lifted his hands. He was putting his life back together, so he took the punches."

MJ tags back in. "Lily identifies irregularities, and they decide to shut her up. They hire Angel Jiménez, a former resident of Walpole, who grabs one of Brian's gloves from a jobsite while disguised as an Eversource employee. He wears it when he sets the home on fire using kerosene and formalin as accelerants. We don't know if he secured the latter from Mendoza."

MJ sees Ginny wrestling to put the puzzle pieces in their proper spot.

The words flow freely from MJ now. "He sets the fire and moves on. But he witnesses Lily talking to Katie Nichols and moves to shut Katie up too, believing Lily may have shared what she had found."

Walt takes over as MJ takes a slug of water. "We believe that today's event at the prison, which we were both on the premises for, was a planned attack designed to produce another donor. And it follows that Mendoza is harvesting the organs while we are sitting here."

Ginny sits back, stunned. "Jesus, this is right out of a Michael Connelly novel. You are an amazing storyteller, Ms. Fernandez. We all know that. But what irrefutable evidence do you have supporting this theory of yours?"

"Please call me MJ. You yourself confirmed Jiménez's involvement in the fire and Katie's death. The Commonwealth can produce copies of the documentation relative to the reconciliation. You will find those names and likely others without a corresponding inmate or a confirmable death. Our working theory is that the warden altered or hired some of his former special operations friends to alter the prison records in a manner that wouldn't raise eyebrows at the state or local level. In the unlikely event someone questioned the discrepancy with VINELink, it could be easily blamed on poor documentation update protocols for the database."

MJ takes another sip of water. "You will have to engage your best investigators, but you will be able to get your hands on the real estate records. You will also learn that Mendoza started medical school but was kicked out for anger management issues. He was on a surgical track, meaning he has the basic training and fundamental skills to do the harvesting himself. As to the Caymans, well, that might present a problem for you." MJ shifts in her seat. "They knew from the beginning they would have a limited time to exploit this group of inmates. But if you follow us to Mendoza's right now, I would bet everything I have that we will find Benjamin Mendoza with his hands deep in an inmate's chest and abdomen."

Ginny holds up her palm. "Slow down. There are a lot of steps before we get there."

Walt stands up. "Ginny, I have told you this before. I play hard, but I play fair. We are now going to leave and head to Mendoza's. We hope you will come with us."

MJ stands and joins Walt as they head toward the door.

Ginny stops them. "Okay, okay… sit back down. The pieces fit, but you are talking about an organized effort to exploit young inmates without anyone to look into their reported deaths. Those inmates are reduced to organs that are sold on the black market. No one else the wiser… until the reconciliation."

MJ's tone softens. "This is a lot to digest, I know. But time is of the essence. The Commonwealth is going to officially start relocation planning within the next couple of weeks. The clock is ticking, and I believe Johansson and Mendoza both plan to be long gone before that first meeting. If today's event is their farewell act, they could be in the wind by tomorrow morning."

"It goes well beyond it being 'a lot to digest.' Give me five minutes to think."

MJ stands again. "Can you please point me toward the ladies' room? It's the water."

Ginny points. "Turn left and go down the hall. It is close to the end, right-hand side."

MJ smiles oddly, leaving the two attorneys to talk and heads for the restroom… with her laptop bag slung over her shoulder.

137

Bach is playing on the Bose speakers positioned in the four corners of the room. Classical music is one of the few things that brings Mendoza true peace. Another item on that very short list is about to begin.

After checking on the canister being administered to the second inmate, Mendoza positions the first donor on an embalming table and intubates him. He moves over to the sink area and begins the exhaustive disinfecting protocol all surgeons follow. After fifteen minutes of scrubbing every inch of his arms from his elbows to his fingertips, twice, he puts on two pairs of surgical gloves, a gown, and a face shield. Normally, a scrub nurse would hold the gloves open for him, but he does not have that luxury. Beyond that, everything else is by the book.

This section of the basement resembles the surgical suites he once coveted. It took convincing, but eventually, Johansson agreed to split the significant cost to ensure they would maximize the income generated by each donor.

Before making the first incision, Mendoza says a prayer, as he always does. He places his left hand on the body and brings the scalpel over the abdomen with his right hand when his thoughts unexpectedly shift to Johansson.

He steps back from the table as rage overrides the impact of the soothing music. He has a lot to do before 3 a.m., including removing the organs of two men with the precision every transplant surgeon wishes they possessed, preparing their remains for cremation, and delivering a number of ice-filled coolers.

Mendoza's hands begin to tremble with fury as he thinks about all he has to do, while Johansson merely grabs his already packed bags and heads to wherever. The more he thinks about it, the angrier he gets.

The scalpel creates a pinging sound as it bounces off the suite's steel wall and skitters back toward his feet. The guttural sound of a wounded animal echoes around the suite as he yells to release the tension that is creeping into his arms, neck, and shoulders.

Tension creates tremors. Tremors cause mistakes.

He shakes out his arms and rotates his head around his neck while taking three cleansing breaths. Finally calm again, he steps back over the donor, grabs another scalpel, repeats the prayer, and makes the first cut. As the blood runs toward the table's drain, he looks at the liter of blood hanging from the adjacent IV pole to ensure the proper replacement flow.

And so it begins… for the final time.

138

Ten minutes pass before Walt deciphers the meaning of MJ's weird grin. He looks up at Ginny, who is alternating between typing and scribbling on a legal pad.

"I believe MJ may have left the building."

Ginny looks up. "What? Why? Wait, she isn't going to Mendoza's, is she?"

"That would be my best guess."

"Shit!" Ginny plows ahead. "I just checked the three names MJ provided. The local prison system says they died while incarcerated, and VINELink says they are still in Walpole. I can't get into the Medical Examiner's records directly, and their office is closed for the day. Let me make some other calls."

"They are likely ashes in Potter's Field."

"So says the woman who tells stories for a living." Before Walt can say anything, Ginny holds up her hand to stop him. "You have to give me some time to sort this out. I want to believe you, Walt, truly I do. The pieces appear to fit, but as I said, Fernandez is a talented storyteller. Even if I wanted to move forward, no judge is going to give me a warrant based upon a reporter's story and the questionable testimony of a felon with murder charges hanging over his head who, coincidentally, benefits from all of this."

"Ginny, this is no bullshit, and we are at zero hour. You have to move on this before Johansson and Mendoza fade into obscurity. My gut tells me this is our last chance to catch them with their hand in the cookie jar, so to speak."

The clock ticking on the wall is all that can be heard. Ginny is torn. This is either the case that will catapult her into the Plymouth County D.A.'s seat and possibly beyond, or it is the greatest scam anyone has ever tried to run on her. As slippery as Walt can be, he has never lied to her. He will stretch the law to the point of breaking, but he never goes beyond that.

And if she tells her boss about this, he will scoop her… and she cannot allow that to happen.

"If this is true, she cannot go to Mendoza's. She will be putting herself in danger and will tip our hands. Run me through it again, but this time let's highlight what we have that might get us a warrant."

Walt makes a call but hangs up without speaking. Ginny's guess is that it was to MJ and was sent to voicemail. Then, his fingers frantically move across his phone screen as he sends a text. She is within range to read it before Walt tucks his phone away: *"She's on board. PLEASE come back."*

He scoots his chair closer to Ginny's desk, where he proceeds to take Ginny through it again, twice. Each time Ginny asks better questions. It does not take long for her to agree that it points to something highly illegal. But what?

They allow silence to return as two talented legal minds mentally sort through cases and experience, searching for something… anything.

Walt sits on the edge of his seat and gives Ginny a puzzled look. "Maybe we are starting too high in the food chain. This cannot be accomplished without the help of others, right? At a bare minimum, the prison doctor has to be in on it along with a handful of nurses and guards."

A knowing smile brightens Ginny's face. "Time to find us some bait fish."

She picks up her desk phone and punches in a set of numbers. As the call is answered, she holds up her other hand with her fingers crossed and smiles at Walt. Sixty seconds later, she scribbles down the information they need and hangs up the phone.

"It pays to have 'District Attorney's Office' show up on caller ID." She jumps from behind the desk and looks at Walt as she sprints toward the door. "You coming or what?"

139

MJ parks across the street from Mendoza's Funeral Home, her jaw aching from clenched teeth. She is convinced that in the basement of the white clapboard building, a body is being dismantled as she sits there… doing nothing. If she rushes in, she may save the life of whoever is on the table. Or is she too late? How does she stop the madness and keep herself from ending up on Mendoza's table?

She lowers her window for some air.

The birds are singing, and people are walking by, laughing and enjoying the warm weather. She is struck by the contrast created by a couple giggling as they pass within 100 feet of Mendoza's front door. On one side of the street, there is love, joy, and happiness. On the other, a butcher is turning a young man into a collection of body parts to be sold to the highest bidder.

MJ looks at her phone: multiple missed calls from Walt and a couple of texts. There is also a voicemail from her editor, who is looking for an update on her story. If he only knew.

After four different starts, she finally arrives at a response to Walt's most recent text.

'i have to stop them'

Perhaps obvious, but the meaning is clear to those who know her. Her primary objective is no longer writing a blockbuster story. This is about fighting for the underdog and taking down those who take advantage of the weak. She pushes send.

MJ refuses to take her eyes off the front door of the building. As she ponders her next step, there is a slight movement in the white lace covering one of the front windows. She blinks her eyes and quickly narrows her focus, willing it to move again.

It does.

MJ spins her head and stares straight ahead, weighing her options. Her knuckles turn white from the pressure she is applying to the steering wheel, and her thoughts land on a decision which she announces to the windshield.

She slowly returns her head to its prior position and looks at the faded green awning covering a portion of the sidewalk leading to the primary entrance. Everyone views this building as a refuge that brings comfort to those who have lost a loved one. It isn't.

She must destroy this house of horrors and bring its hidden darkness into the light for all to see.

140

After tossing his bloody gloves into the hazardous materials bucket, Mendoza heads upstairs, still wearing a surgical gown covered in blood, and his phone pressed against his head.

Johansson is all business. "Surveillance places her outside your door."

The combination of the stress and sprinting up the stairs is wreaking havoc with Mendoza's breathing. "What the fuck! I thought you said she was at the D.A.'s office?"

Johansson snickers. "She moved. And you would be oblivious to this fact had I not called."

"Not the point."

Mendoza carefully walks perpendicular to the front wall, carefully placing himself between the two windows to ensure there is no change in lighting. He gently leans over, with nothing but the top third of his head getting past the window molding, which wears multiple layers of high-gloss white paint.

He reaches up and gently moves the drape, which grabs the sheer lace curtain below it. Too late now. He peers out to see a car with a sole occupant sitting across the street. Her hair confirms his suspicions.

He slowly returns the drape to its normal position and steps back. "She is across the street."

"Just her?"

Mendoza takes another peek. "I believe so."

"What is your contingency plan?"

Mendoza is sick of the military jargon. "My only plan is to finish the fucking job and catch my flight."

"Every operation faces a number of risks. This is a known possibility for which a contingency should have been developed."

"Suggestions?"

"Abort, evade, and escape."

Years of frustration boil over. "Easy for you to fucking say. I hear the airline announcements in the background. You are already at Logan or some other airport, and I am here with two former inmates. One of whom has half his organs sitting on ice."

"We have long agreed, you take care of your end, and I will take care of mine. My work is complete." Johansson disconnects the call.

Mendoza begins retracing his steps back to the basement when his inability to control his anger takes over. He hurls the cellphone across the viewing room. The impact makes an odd sound as the pieces of the phone find different places on the carpeted floor. He stops cold when he realizes the true genesis of the odd, rhythmic thuds.

141

Ginny's marathon preparation allows her to maintain a pace Walt has no chance of matching. He has run, jogged, and walked more during this case than he has in years. He vows to work with Jonathan to establish a workout routine to improve his stamina, if he does not have a heart attack first.

The only break Walt catches is that they are going down the stairs instead of up. Ginny drops a couple of steps at a time as Walt slides his hand along the rail, hitting each step along the way.

"You okay back there, Erickson?"

"I'm… fine."

Ginny reaches the second floor and opens the door that leads directly into the detective's bullpen. She waits, holding the door open and tapping her foot. Walt hits the landing and stops to catch his breath.

"Next time… we take… the elevator."

Ginny smiles. "Let's find a detective to take us for a ride."

They walk into the windowless corner, searching for someone to assist them. What they find is disappointment.

Ginny pulls up short, putting her right arm out to stop Walt. They look at each other and shake their heads. Ginny whispers. "Shit."

They step back as Walt closes his eyes in thought. "I don't trust him. We have to find someone else."

"You said that time is of the essence."

"For the record, it was MJ who said that. You have to work with him… I don't." Walt turns to walk away.

"Wait. I will deny ever saying this, but I hate this guy with every fiber of my being. He is a disgrace to the badge, as well as the human race. On that we agree. But we should have someone with a badge *and* a gun with us."

Walt turns around. "Don't you have a badge as an A.D.A.? And if we need a gunslinger, I can make a few calls and have someone here ASAP."

"I am not going to get big-footed by the Staties or the Feds." Ginny needs this for her campaign materials. "I can control him."

Walt relents. "The slightest hint of bullshit from him, and I call my guys. That is the deal. Take it or leave it."

Ginny does not flinch. "Take it."

They turn and head back toward Jacobs, who is oblivious to their presence. Ginny clears her throat. "Detective, we need your help."

A startled Reggie does not bother to clear the solitaire game on his computer screen. He stands and points at Walt. "I don't help the enemy."

Walt takes a step toward Jacobs when Ginny steps between them.

"He is not the enemy. In fact, he has brought us critical information that needs to be looked into quickly. If it pans out, this is the case of a lifetime. We need you on this."

Ginny can taste the bile these words produce.

Jacobs steps back. "What kind of case?"

Ginny refuses to break eye contact. "We need you to drive us to this address and be present when we question the homeowner. He may not be welcoming, so you need to be prepared to respond to any attempts at hostility or escape. And we need to go now."

Jacobs looks around the empty bullpen and shrugs his shoulders. "What the hell. Meet me out front."

<h1 style="text-align:center">142</h1>

Mendoza remains motionless as the pounding continues. She's got balls; he will give her that. Unbeknownst to him, as he stands frozen in place, one droplet of blood makes its way down his gown and drips onto the worn beige carpet beneath his feet.

He is rubbing his hands together, and the talc from inside the surgical gloves is making them slippery. *Should he answer the door? Should he let her in and subdue her? Should he let her in and add her organs to those he will be delivering later?* He is pulled from his thoughts as the doorbell rings, followed by more pounding.

The darkness that took his surgical career from him years ago controls his movements as he chooses option one. He finds his way to the office and removes the bloody gown and booties. He tosses them into a trash can to be taken care of later. He peers in a mirror, runs his hands over his thinning hair, and heads back toward the front door.

Mendoza takes a deep breath, pastes a smile on his face, and twists the doorknob. "Ms. Fernandez. I'm sorry, I was downstairs. How may I help you?" By the look on her face, Mendoza's strategy has caught her off guard.

"Mr. Mendoza… I wanted to speak with you about the Lily Whitaker case."

"I am sorry, but I'm extremely busy at the moment. Can we meet tomorrow morning? Say around 10?"

MJ steps forward. Mendoza is now looking down on her thanks to the slight elevation provided by the door's threshold. He holds his ground, but his anger is bursting through the façade. She has invaded his personal space, something he detests.

"This cannot wait, and will only take a few moments."

"Ms. Fernandez. To put this delicately, I am in the middle of a… procedure, and must return immediately. I am sorry. Tomorrow morning is my first availability. Thank you for understanding."

He moves to close the door as MJ slides a Chuck Taylor between the door and the casing.

MJ moans in pain, even though he didn't slam the door closed like he wanted to do. "Do you know Angel Jiménez? Tommy Anderson? What about Charles O'Malley? Or Nicholas Rutherford?"

Mendoza reopens the door and steps quickly back to the threshold, preventing MJ from entering fully.

"Ms. Fernandez, this has gone too far. I have told you I have time-sensitive work to do, and I am happy to speak with you first thing tomorrow morning. Good day." He kicks her foot from the door's path and slams it shut. It stops millimeters from MJ's nose.

Mendoza retreats, sweat pouring down his back. He sprints toward the basement, cursing himself for failing to choose option two or three.

<h1 align="center">143</h1>

Despite no interior door handles and a screen between the front and back seats, Walt agreed to sit in the back of Jacobs' unmarked patrol car. Jacobs' laughter forced Walt to bite his tongue until it bled. He will deal with the asshole later. He has different priorities at the moment.

They arrive at the address on Cypress Drive in Brockton to find a "For Sale" sign planted firmly in the front lawn. Ginny looks through the screen at Walt, who shrugs and tilts his head to the left. More proof that their window is closing quickly.

Jacobs looks at Ginny. "Now what?"

Walt speaks. "Now, you let me out of the back of this car, and we knock on the front door."

Ginny nods in agreement.

She and Walt discussed various approaches and landed on a strategy as Jacobs played chauffeur. They climb two granite steps as Ginny removes the badge she rarely uses from her handbag. She takes a deep breath and knocks on the door. Walt is on her right, and Jacobs remains behind them, down on the sidewalk, with his hand on the butt of his department-issued firearm.

A middle-aged gentleman in a Bruins t-shirt and blue jeans answers the door. The blood drains from his face. "May I help you?"

"Dr. Henderson, I'm A.D.A. Ginny Giancomo, and this is attorney Walter Erickson. We would like to speak with you. May we come in?"

Jacobs steps up onto the lower step.

Walt can see the doctor running through his options. It takes less than ten seconds, when a heavy sigh signals his acceptance of what is about to happen. "I only have folding chairs. Everything else has been taken away by the movers." He steps back and holds his right arm out, inviting them into his home.

Before they sit down, and Ginny can begin, Walt jumps into the fray. "Do you know why we are here, Doctor?"

"Yes, I believe I do."

Ginny and Walt exchanged stunned looks.

Ginny goes for broke. "Dr. Henderson, Brian McMillan has shared some disturbing information, and we are hoping you might be willing to address its accuracy."

"I would like to call my attorney before we proceed." He presses a speed dial number on his cellphone and steps away from them. After a ten-minute, hushed conversation, he holds the phone away from his ear and makes a simple statement. "I am happy to cooperate fully in exchange for full and complete immunity and witness protection."

Within fifteen minutes of their arrival, Ginny recites the Miranda warning to Dr. Henderson, Jacobs cuffs him, and Walt ends up with a seatmate for the trip back to the D.A.'s office, where Dr. Henderson's attorney is waiting.

Jacobs beams as he perp walks the doctor into the building. After electronically securing his fingerprints and taking a couple of mugshots, he escorts Dr. Henderson to one of the interrogation rooms.

It pisses Walt off to know Jacobs will share in the credit for the arrest and the breaking of this monumental case, but he swallows his rage, understanding this needs to occur so his client can be a free man.

Now... where the hell is MJ?

144

MJ returns to her vehicle, limping and seething. The door closing on her injured toe caused pain to course through her body like she had just stubbed it. The car shifts from the force of her slamming the door shut. She is tempted to set the funeral home on fire, an act that will serve two purposes. First, the funeral home will be swarming with first responders within minutes. More importantly, it will exact justice in a method that Mendoza and Johansson clearly understand.

The faces of Lily Whitaker, Dylan Janssen, and their children join Katie Nichols', Tommy Anderson's, Charles O'Malley's, and Nicholas Rutherford's as adrenaline is released through MJ's freely flowing tears. The escaping emotions are interrupted by the chirp of her cellphone.

"Where are you? The doctor is spilling RIGHT NOW! Please call me. I am worried!"

A wave of joy overcomes her. She shifts in her seat, and her thumbs begin flying across the tiny keypad.

"u know where i am."

"Thank god you are safe! Please come to the D.A.'s office."

"im not leaving until i see him in cuffs"

"Then I am coming to you. Leaving this second."

Just then, a hearse lurches across the sidewalk as it races from behind the funeral home, almost colliding with an oncoming car as it makes a wide swing out of the narrow driveway.

MJ's smile evaporates. *"he is escaping"*

"DO NOT FOLLOW!!"

The desperation in the plea strikes MJ deep in her chest.

"2 late"

MJ starts the car and pulls away from the curb. There are half a dozen cars between her and the hearse. On the positive side, a hearse is easy to keep track of. Within moments, the chase turns onto President Street, where Mendoza suddenly screeches to a halt, as do all of the cars behind him. MJ hears a bleating car horn.

MJ uses the stop to fire off a quick text. *"heading 2 logan i think"*

She peers around the cars ahead of her to see Mrs. Rothschild holding steadfast in the crosswalk, inches from the front of the hearse and blocking Mendoza's escape.

MJ watches the brake lights on the rear of the hearse go out as Mendoza tries to move forward. The elderly bad-ass MJ met a few days ago proves yet again that she will not be pushed around by anyone.

Without warning, Mendoza throws the hearse into reverse and slams into the front end of the vehicle immediately behind him. He then swerves and guns it around Mrs. Rothschild, who raises her cane in defiance and then swings it, striking the windshield of the speeding car, creating a spider-web of glass that likely obscures Mendoza's vision.

The sound of the cane slamming against the glass is replaced by the wailing of tires as Mendoza fails to maintain control of the heavy vehicle.

145

It's been a long day.

MJ sits in her editor's office at 11 p.m. with one leg slung over the arm of the chair in front of his desk, watching the look on his face as he rereads her story for the second time. He takes off his reading glasses, stretches his neck, and then lets them hang in their usual spot.

"You do have a death wish, don't you?"

MJ blushes. "No, but I concede chasing Mendoza was ill-advised."

She opens her notebook and begins. "The prison doctor is singing like a canary. He is an avid diver with an infatuation with pufferfish, the whole, 'How can you eat something that is so poisonous' thing. It took a few tries to get it right, but he professed pride in being able to leverage his medical background to create the delicate paralytic."

MJ swings her leg back around as she sits squarely facing Spagnola's desk. "He has given up one of the nurses and three correctional officers. Those arrests were made this afternoon. A Red Notice was issued for both Samuel Johansson and his alter ego, 'Stanley Johnson.' His escape was short-lived, however. He, or should I say what was left of him, was located within twenty-four hours of landing in Paris."

Spagnola looks over the reading glasses sitting on the tip of his nose. "Is it true?"

"Yes. It is our understanding that most of him was found in a hotel bathtub. His eyes and internal organs had all been removed, and a printed copy of a price sheet was nailed—not stapled, nailed—to his forehead. I convinced them to fax me a copy."

MJ hands Spagnola a sheet of paper:

Heart	$200,000	4-6 hours
Lungs – 2 @ $100,000 each	$200,000	6-8 hours
Liver – 2 lobes @ $100,000 each	$200,000	8-12 hours
Pancreas	$200,000	12-18 hours
Kidneys – 2 @ $75,000 each	$150,000	24-36 hours
Corneas – 2 @ $25,000 each	$50,000	11 days
	$1,000,000	

"Jesus Christ!"

"There are two current theories. First, he did not hear from Mendoza, so he decided to reach out to their contact to secure his last payment, thereby tipping his hand relative to location. The second is that whoever established the 'Stanley Johnson' identity has been waiting for it to become active. Either way, it is clear their buyers were prepared to clear the decks the moment the well dried up."

MJ flips to the next page of her notes. "They also obtained a cellphone believed to have been used by Angel Jiménez, whom they presume Johansson dismembered. There is a Vyncs GPS tracking app on the phone. It took me all of two minutes to find the device, once I knew to look for one. I have no idea how it got there, or how long I drove around with it affixed to the frame of my car. Truthfully, I am surprised a spec ops guy would have held onto the phone."

Spagnola shakes his head. "You and I both know why."

MJ shudders. "Probably. I have a call scheduled with the Director-General at 4 a.m. our time, to get confirmation and a quote."

"How many?"

"I saw a half dozen asterisks on the one page I saw in Johansson's office, but a full reconciliation is currently underway."

"Buyers?"

"The doctor doesn't know, and Mendoza isn't talking. After the fire department used the 'jaws of life' to extract him from the crashed hearse, he was transported to an undisclosed location where he was treated for his injuries. He is now heavily sedated, and they have him on suicide watch."

"What is happening with McMillan?"

"Plymouth County D.A. is dropping all charges and has pressed for an expedited release. He should be out in time to enjoy something more than powdered eggs and cold oatmeal tomorrow morning. I have a commitment from his attorney for an exclusive."

"Okay, I just sent this down to be formatted. I am going to let it run as is, under the headline 'Million Dollar Men.' I will put a stronger eye on your follow-up, but we will have this out within the hour."

MJ smiles, excited by his support for her headline recommendation—a first. "I'm heading home to start working on the next chapter of this story. My plan is to join Brian and his attorney for a celebratory breakfast. I'll have something for you later in the afternoon."

"Jesus, MJ. This is unbelievable." He stands and offers a handshake. "Really great work."

146

Snoopy stares up at MJ from the white shag bathmat in her bathroom. She is grumbling while attempting to put on make-up in a way that does not end with her looking like the featured clown in Barnum and Bailey's Big Top Extravaganza. She gazes downward. Snoopy looks away.

"That bad, huh?"

After another fifteen minutes of applying foundation, blush, eyeliner, and crimping her eyelashes, MJ surrenders and heads to her bedroom to dress for the evening. Spread across the duvet cover are the most expensive matching bra and panties she has ever purchased, compliments of Victoria's Secret. After removing the price tags and putting them on, she opens her closet and stares at the new beige blouse, dark blue pencil skirt, and shoes she purchased just for this occasion, hoping that all of this isn't a monumental mistake.

At precisely 7 p.m., the buzzer indicating she has a visitor waiting outside drowns out the soft jazz she is playing. "Yes?"

"Hey, it's me!"

MJ's giddy response is something new. "Me who?"

Walt chuckles. "Your knight in shining armor."

"I will be the judge of that." She presses the small black button on the bottom of the aluminum speaker, unlocking the building's front entrance.

Within minutes, there is a gentle knock on her door. Snoopy looks up from his bed, unfazed. MJ unlocks the multitude of deadbolts while peering through the peephole.

Walt is standing there in a freshly pressed suit, holding a beautiful bouquet of fresh-cut flowers… and there is nothing on his tie. She takes a deep breath and opens the door. They exchange a hug that sends a tingle through MJ's heart.

After entering the apartment, Walt turns back toward MJ, his face flushed. " These are for you." He holds out the flowers.

MJ notices his hand is trembling. "Thank you."

After placing the flowers in a vase with some water, they exit the apartment without MJ giving Walt a tour. She locks the door behind them as Walt heads to catch the elevator. After a quiet ride to the lobby, he opens the passenger's door on the Porsche, and after MJ slides in gingerly, he shuts the door gently and sprints to his side of the car.

Walt starts the car and looks over at MJ. "You made the plans for this evening, so where to?"

The warmth MJ feels radiating from Walt's smile brings a sense of calm and relief that she did not expect, but she promised herself that she would lean into whatever emotions surfaced tonight.

"Del Frisco's has a table waiting for us."

Walt pulls away from the curb as if his car is filled with Waterford crystal. MJ doesn't recall him being so discerning the last time he drove them to dinner.

MJ goes for broke. "It was amazing to watch the relief wash over Brian as he walked out of Walpole, a free man. You should be proud."

"It is certainly rare when I have the ability to help a truly innocent man. But *we* should be proud. I couldn't have done this without you." Walt reaches over and takes MJ's hand. They don't look at one another, but she doesn't pull it back.

The remainder of the trip to the restaurant is filled with light-hearted conversation, which MJ finds fitting given the intensity of the past few weeks.

After swapping the keys to Porsche for a small yellow ticket, the two enter the restaurant and MJ takes charge the moment they arrive at the hostess stand. "Two for Fernandez at 7:30."

The hostess hands two menus and a wine list to a woman dressed in black slacks, a white tuxedo dress shirt, and a black bowtie, who then leads them to a table with an amazing view.

Walt seems impressed. "Wow! Great table."

Nerves get the best of her as MJ reaches for the wine list before it can be handed to Walt. "We won't be needing this. We would like a bottle of the 2018 Chimney Rock Cabernet, please."

The smile on Walt's face warms MJ's heart.

The sommelier arrives with the bottle and mistakenly stands beside Walt, who corrects the error quickly. "The lady ordered the wine."

"My apologies, ma'am."

MJ smirks. "It's fine as long as you don't call me 'ma'am' again."

The three of them laugh as MJ examines the bottle carefully and acknowledges that it is correct. She struggles to control her breathing at this point, desperate to get it right.

The sommelier opens the bottle and hands the cork to MJ, who lifts it to her nose. After another almost imperceptible nod, a small amount of the wine is poured into MJ's glass. She swirls it gently before raising the glass to her nose and breathing in the dark cherry and black currant aroma of the wine. Next, she takes a small sip, amazed at how wonderful it tastes this evening.

One last nod, and MJ turns her gaze toward Walt. "Did I do it right?"

A tear forms in the corner of Walt's eye. "Perfect… absolutely, perfect."

About the Author

Joe is a Canastota, NY, native and an award-winning author who lives in Rhode Island with his wife of thirty-five years. They have two talented daughters and relish any opportunity to spoil their two amazing grandsons.

When not behind the keyboard working to bring stories and characters to life, Joe can be found at any number of golf courses searching the woods for an errant shot, sitting at the bridge table sharpening his burgeoning skills, or at an airport waiting to board a flight to whatever locale his wife has identified as their next destination.

Having witnessed the staggering impact of dementia firsthand, Joe has become a passionate and engaged advocate of the innovative work done every day by the Alzheimer's Association. He's an active Board member of the MA/NH chapter, and firmly believes the first survivor of Alzheimer's is out there.

* A portion of the proceeds will be donated to the Alzheimer's Association *

**Keep reading for a preview of book 3
in the MJ Fernandez series:**

The Truth

1

Pam Atkins stands ramrod straight, naked on a fluffy white bath mat, water dripping from her curly blonde hair as her right hand creates streaks in the steam on the bathroom mirror. She stares at the dark circles under her eyes and recites the three affirmations posted on the top left corner aloud, just as she has every day for the past twelve years. *"I am strong. I am worth it. I am enough."*

As the Vice President of Public Relations for Central New York Metals, the premier supplier of steel in the northeast, today is the day every public relations expert dreads.

After yesterday's collapse of a twenty-story building under construction in Chicago's financial district, CNY Metals is in full crisis management mode. As the supplier of the steel girders and rivets used on the project, questions have already begun to arise. Metallurgical experts will soon be evaluating the integrity of their steel, determining if it played a role in the deaths of three ironworkers.

Pam slept for less than two hours, spending most of the past twenty-one hours digesting everything she could about the project and speaking with the on-site construction manager, the company's new CEO, and everyone in between. Corporate attorneys in Illinois and New York have also swooped in, adding another level of complexity to the challenge that lay ahead.

But today, October seventeenth, holds another meaning for Pam. Twelve years ago, at precisely 2:18 p.m., she learned Ed and Rosie Atkins had been fraudulently professing to be her biological parents for nineteen years. She was staring at the clock on the wall of her hospital room when the word "adopted" began ricocheting inside her heavily medicated mind.

That life-altering day started spectacularly. The weather was perfect for field hockey. She arrived early, holding the sun at bay with a pair of Maui Jim's she borrowed from her roommate. She closed her eyes and sniffed the air, enjoying the smell of a wood fire that had been lit by a nearby home to address the morning chill.

She was going to start for the Syracuse University women's team in their conference game against Wake Forest... as a freshman. Something rare, to say the least. Her parents had driven in from her hometown of Canastota, New York, to watch her play. She proudly chuckled to herself as she caught a glimpse of them sitting in the stands, wearing the brightest orange sweatshirts she had ever seen.

The game had barely begun when a player from the other team attempted a flat stick tackle. The player's stick ended up between Pam's sprinting legs, leading to the fracture of her left tibia, near the kneecap, which required plates and screws to stabilize. She still feels it when it rains.

Now, she stares at the smudged mirror, vividly recounting the exchange that became the underlying source of severe self-doubt and anger, and years of weekly therapy sessions with Dr. Robertson.

Her mother walked to the bed and gently held her hand. "How do you feel, honey?"

Pam's tongue was thick, fuzzy, and not working the way she wanted. "I'm groggy."

"The nurse said you might be for a while. It is the anesthesia."

Her mom looked at her dad, who moved to the other side of the bed and gently took Pam's right hand, mindful to avoid hitting the I.V. taped to its top. He smiled and looked every bit the loving father.

"Hey, kiddo, doc said everything went well. The break was a little worse than what the X-ray showed, but they were able to put Humpty Dumpty back together again."

Pam smiled sluggishly at the "dad joke." "How long until I can play?" The look her parents shared told Pam everything she needed to know. "Out for the season?"

Her mother did what moms do. "Let's get you up and around again, then we can worry about field hockey. Okay?"

Despite the mental fog, Pam understood what was at stake. The monitor next to her bed beeped in sync with her increasing heartbeat. "I gotta play! If I don't, I lose my scholarship. We cannot afford SU."

Pam and her father had a special bond. He was always able to help Pam maintain a positive perspective. "We will figure all this out when the time comes. Right now, let's focus on your health."

Pam closed her eyes and acknowledged his comment by gently shaking a head that felt three times its normal size, her mind clouded with the remnants of anesthesia, and the morphine she delivered to herself via the small button in her left hand.

She was desperately willing the fog to dissipate. "I had the weirdest dream on my way to surgery. You guys told me I was adopted."

Hearing no response, Pam reopened her eyes and slowly turned her head from left to right, watching the blood drain from the two caring faces staring back at her. A tear fell, leaving a salty trail on her mother's right cheek as she and Pam's father looked at each other, unable to speak.

Pam's voice crackled with trepidation. "Stupid, right?"

Her father squeezed Pam's hand tenderly. "We are your parents. You have been our child since you were two days old. Biology does not dictate parentage."

With that declaration, her well-planned life spiraled into a pit of despair, uncertainty, abandonment, and failure. Nothing was as it seemed, nor would it ever be again.

Pam stuffs the painful memory back into the little box in her mind where she fights daily to keep it hidden. She reads the affirmations again, hoping they will bring a modicum of relief and generate the clarity of thought she needs to successfully face the onslaught that today will bring.

It doesn't work.

Without warning, exhaustion and stress unleash a surge of deeply buried anger. "ENOUGH!"

Pam squeezes her eyes shut, allowing her ire to burn brightly. She breathes in deeply through her nose and slowly releases the air through her mouth before a guttural voice screams out a desperately needed decision.

Pam wraps a towel around her body and stomps back into her bedroom, where she snatches her phone from the bedside table. Her fingers scramble with urgency across the tiny screen.

Hey there! I'm sure you have a lot going on, but I need your help. Please call when you have a second.

Pam tosses the phone atop her unmade bed as she takes another cleansing breath, her mind flip-flopping between hoping her phone rings before she loses her nerve... and praying it doesn't.

2

He is wearing a hole in the antique Persian carpet, which covers only a fraction of their enormous bedroom floor. "This is going to be a problem."

She remains focused on counting each brush stroke as his reflection appears behind hers.

"There is no reason to overreact."

He stops, anger seeping through his clenched jaw. "I haven't begun to overreact."

His bluster is of no concern. "What do you want to do?"

He finishes the remnants in a Simon Pearce rocks glass, placing it atop a large black maple bureau. "We have spent the past fifty years focused on one objective. I will not be denied."

She decides now is not the time to remind him that his glass will leave a watermark. The brush strokes continue rhythmically. "And?"

"There are options. This loose end has been flapping in the breeze for far too long. An unequivocal elimination of the perilous connection is the only answer."

She puts down her hairbrush and spins slowly on the antique stool that accompanies her great-grandmother's massive cherry vanity. "We have discussed this before, and I have been very clear. Have I not?"

His unblinking, steely eyes plead with the only person who understands him. "Our failure to take swift action initially was a mistake; one that has finally created a ripple of catastrophic concern and now needs to be corrected."

"We took the action commensurate with our beliefs, and have paid handsomely for absolute confidentiality. There is zero evidence that it has been breached, or ever will be." She uses the one look she knows scares the shit out of him… and it should. "You will not open Pandora's Box. Are we clear?"

Rebuked yet again, he turns his back on her and shuffles to his side of the bed while attempting to get the last word. "I have long thought that instead of following our beliefs, we should have heeded the words of Benjamin Franklin."

She spins slowly back toward the mirror and resumes her counting. His musing is meaningless. The one person who actually crafted, guided, and controlled their family's ascension over the past fifty years is smiling back at her.

If something is to be done, *she* will decide what, when, and how it will occur.

3

MJ Fernandez, an award-winning, Boston-based investigative reporter, is scanning the news online in search of a story that might be worthy of her talents when she notices an article detailing the collapse of a building under construction in Chicago. It is not the death of three iron-workers that catches her eye. It is the name of the company that provided the steel for the twenty-story project: Central New York Metals.

MJ reads the quotes of her best friend from college, Pam Atkins, whose employer is in the center of the maelstrom. The two teenage women were thrust into each other's lives by a computer model that analyzed their answers to fifty questions, declared them compatible, and spit out their freshman room assignment.

After meeting Pam, MJ did something she has rarely done since: she kept her skepticism to herself. How could the university's geniuses designate two women, who were opposite in almost every way, to cohabitate in the same small 130 square foot cinder block room for the next ten months?

Pam Atkins grew up in a small upstate New York town situated between Syracuse and Utica—a town whose claim to fame is producing onions, potatoes, and two Undisputed Welterweight boxing champions, the latter being the impetus for the location of the International Boxing Hall of Fame. She was the salutatorian of her graduating class, the President of the National Honor Society, a member of various school clubs, and an active member of St. Agatha's church. To top it off, Pam was attending SU on a full-ride to play field hockey.

After a rough start in life, MJ found her forever family and a permanent home in Belmont, MA, an affluent suburb of Boston. She was as much "city" as Pam was "small town." She is comfortable riding the "T" alone at night, and enjoys strolling down the street with a Starbucks coffee, long-rebelling against the Dunkin Donuts dynasty, and the norm in general. She fights for the underdog and refuses to lose any such battle.

MJ fell in love with the concept of searching for the truth the first time she read *All the President's Men*—the only non-required book she read in high school. She did not play sports or think much of those who did. She wrote for the school newspaper. Her first exposé included the photos she personally secured of a cafeteria worker selling the school's food out of the trunk of a car.

Despite the overwhelming differences, the confident, take-no-shit city girl with pink streaks in her hair and the studious, blond-haired, blue-eyed girl, always weighed down by a full backpack, became inseparable.

After a particularly difficult mid-term exam in their freshman year, the two wandered toward Marshall Street to burn off stress. Pam had recently undergone surgery after an ugly field hockey injury and was hobbling on crutches. After a couple of Appletinis purchased with the customary fake ID of every college freshman, the tears and words flowed from Pam uncontrollably. She uttered a secret that caught MJ completely off guard, having expected her friend's dismay to be caused by her career-ending injury.

It wasn't.

MJ was dumbstruck when she learned of the bewildering news Pam's parents dumped on her immediately before she was wheeled into the surgical suite. MJ's mantra remains as simple today as it was all those years ago: *"Truth above all else."* This core belief led to her recent win of a Pulitzer Prize, just like those of her idols, Woodward and Bernstein.

Pam's parents' reckless disregard for Pam's sense of self, until they had no other choice, fueled by a fair amount of vodka, infuriated MJ. She leapt from the high-top chair and demanded they race to Pam's childhood home to confront the impostors.

Pam sobbed harder.

After raising her fist and pontificating on the concept of accountability, MJ swallowed hard and pledged to keep her best friend's secret. She went to the bar and returned with another round of Appletinis. Vows and intertwined pinkies followed, and they have never spoken of it again.

MJ leans forward and rifles through the discarded papers and shoves aside a half-empty pizza box sitting atop her coffee table to locate her phone. As her right hand grips the device, it bleats out a notification of an incoming text.

"Hey there! I'm sure you have a lot going on, but I need your help. Please call when you have a second."

MJ can't press the dial button fast enough.